To Ruth,

Lots of lo

Richard, Susan, Isabel, Simon

Helen Ruth.

XXXXXX

Happy Christmas 1988.

BEST STORIES
of
HENRY LAWSON

Best Stories
of
HENRY LAWSON

CHOSEN BY CECIL MANN

ANGUS & ROBERTSON PUBLISHERS

Unit 4, Eden Park, 31 Waterloo Road,
North Ryde, NSW, Australia 2113, and
16 Golden Square, London W1R 4BN,
United Kingdom

This collection first published in Australia
by Angus & Robertson Publishers in 1966
Australian Literary Heritage Series edition 1981
Reprinted 1983, 1984, 1986

National Library of Australia
Cataloguing-in-publication data.

Lawson, Henry, 1867-1922.
Best stories of Henry Lawson.

This ed. first published: Sydney:
Angus & Robertson, 1966.
ISBN 0 207 14456 7.

I. Mann, Cecil, 1896-1967. II. Title
(Series: Australian literary heritage series)

A823'.2

Printed in Singapore

PREFACE

HENRY LAWSON'S varied prose writings—mainly short stories and character or narrative sketches—have been published over the years in several "collected" editions, including at this date the latest, three-volume edition, considerably enlarged to embrace all of his prose work which, in my privileged task of editing and making the final siftings, I had felt that Lawson himself could have endorsed as worthy of thus preserving under his name. From that task this present selected edition of what has seemed to me the best of his prose work can be said to have emerged. In the title, *Henry Lawson's Best Stories*, the last word may need emphasis —"stories"; not in all instances strictly "short stories". All but one or two are, however, clearly classifiable as short stories, meeting the essential requirements of a narrative beginning, a middle body of development of theme or plot, and an end that is final—for perfection, nothing may be added, nor anything taken away without loss; an achievement towards which Henry Lawson, in his finest work, would seem to approach as closely as may be humanly possible. That quality of near-perfection, of completeness, will be found at its richest in such outstanding examples as "The Drover's Wife", "Bill, the Ventriloquial Rooster", "The Loaded Dog", "The Union Buries Its Dead", "Send Round the Hat", "A Double Buggy at Lahey's Creek", "The Bush Undertaker", "The Geological Spieler" and "A Wild Irishman", and it is freely present, too, in most other inclusions. In this context it is worth noting that Henry Lawson's beginnings especially, and often his endings also, are of a kind almost peculiar to himself; his evident aim in both being to convey an effect of simple, and spoken, naturalness. (To quote one striking example, the beginning of "A Vision of Sandy-blight", which apparently has only a very slim connection with the actual yarn that Mitchell goes on to tell, and which yet has the effect of making that yarn—almost certainly a recollection from Henry Lawson's own boyhood—completely convincing.) Henry Lawson emphatically rejected the notion that anything can be called a short story; but, in a characteristic twist, he labelled as "sketches" some pieces which seem to fulfil all the needed short story requirements, among them notably "A Daughter of Maoriland", to which he added the subtitle "A Sketch of Poor-class Maoris": in the same category there is the just about word-perfect brevity titled "Mitchell: A Character Sketch". Of the few inclusions which merit classification as "stories" for their narrative content, but which could not by any stretch be called "short stories", the most obvious one is "The Darling River", the masterpiece of Henry Lawson's many purely prose sketches. In general, however, nearly all the inclusions have been selected almost primarily for their short story values; above that, they have been chosen to comply with the book's title as closely as, after numerous readings, personal choosing could attain, whilst keeping within a limit of about 100,000 words. Even with that impressive total, no doubt some omissions may be regretted—a few familiar titles, perhaps more honoured in that familiarity than in critical reading. One such omission which seems to demand explanation is that of the widely name-familiar "Water Them Geraniums"; omitted because (*a*) while it is an integral chapter in the *Joe Wilson* book, it is, like the other two similarly omitted chapters ("Joe Wilson's Courtship" and "Brighten's Sister-in-law"), far better in its episodes than as a whole; (*b*) also like those two chapters, it would have to be either very heavily sub-edited or elaborately explained; (*c*) it disastrously, and artificially, repeats one of the neatest and most natural strokes in "The Drover's Wife" story. What is felt to be true of this present book is that it does include all of Henry Lawson's very best complete stories; and, for the rest, that they, too, are in his best writing vein, his most truly characteristic, unforced, and altogether most engaging story-telling style. A thought for variety, to ensure sustained and continuous reading interest and enjoyment, has chiefly influenced the sequence arrangement of contents; departing from chronology, for instance, as of no real value in any such compiled and patterned book as this, if ever of value at all in any Henry Lawson context. In this respect, though, whatever purpose chronological sequence might be thought to serve is felt to be sufficiently covered by listing in the table of contents the relevant books of the current collected edition from which these stories have been selected as representing Australia's most noted short story writer at his excellent best.

C. M.

CONTENTS

The Drover's Wife

THE two-roomed house is built of round timber, slabs, and stringybark, and floored with split slabs. A big bark kitchen standing at one end is larger than the house itself, veranda included.

Bush all round—bush with no horizon, for the country is flat. No ranges in the distance. The bush consists of stunted, rotten native apple-trees. No undergrowth. Nothing to relieve the eye save the darker green of a few she-oaks which are sighing above the narrow, almost waterless creek. Nineteen miles to the nearest sign of civilization—a shanty on the main road.

The drover, an ex-squatter, is away with sheep. His wife and children are left here alone.

Four ragged, dried-up-looking children are playing about the house. Suddenly one of them yells: "Snake! Mother, here's a snake!"

The gaunt, sun-browned bushwoman dashes from the kitchen, snatches her baby from the ground, holds it on her left hip, and reaches for a stick.

"Where is it?"

"Here! gone into the woodheap!" yells the eldest boy—a sharp-faced urchin of eleven. "Stop there, mother! I'll have him. Stand back! I'll have the beggar!"

"Tommy, come here, or you'll be bit. Come here at once when I tell you, you little wretch!"

The youngster comes reluctantly, carrying a stick bigger than himself. Then he yells, triumphantly:

"There it goes—under the house!" and darts away with club uplifted. At the same time the big, black, yellow-eyed dog-of-all-breeds, who has shown the wildest interest in the proceedings, breaks his chain and rushes after that snake. He is a moment late, however, and his nose reaches the crack in the slabs just as the end of its tail disappears. Almost at the same moment the boy's club comes down and skins the aforesaid nose. Alligator takes small notice of this, and proceeds to undermine the building; but he is subdued after a struggle and chained up. They cannot afford to lose him.

The drover's wife makes the children stand together near the dog-house while she watches for the snake. She gets two small dishes of milk and sets them down near the wall to tempt it to come out; but an hour goes by and it does not show itself.

It is near sunset, and a thunderstorm is coming. The children must be brought inside. She will not take them into the house, for she knows the snake is there, and may at any moment come up through a crack in the rough slab floor: so she carries several armfuls of firewood into the kitchen, and then takes the children there. The kitchen has no floor—or, rather, an earthen one—called a "ground floor" in this part of the bush. There is a large, roughly-made table in the centre of the place. She brings the children in, and makes them get on this table. They are two boys and two girls—mere babies. She gives them some supper, and then, before it gets dark, she goes into the house, and snatches up some pillows and bedclothes—expecting to see or lay her hand on the snake any minute. She makes a bed on the kitchen table for the children, and sits down beside it to watch all night.

She has an eye on the corner, and a green sapling club laid in readiness on the dresser by her side; also her sewing basket and a copy of the *Young Ladies' Journal*. She has brought the dog into the room.

Tommy turns in, under protest, but says he'll lie awake all night and smash that blinded snake.

His mother asks him how many times she has told him not to swear.

He has his club with him under the bedclothes, and Jacky protests:

"Mummy! Tommy's skinnin' me alive wif his club. Make him take it out."

Tommy: "Shet up, you little ——! D'yer want to be bit with the snake?"

Jacky shuts up.

"If yer bit," says Tommy, after a pause, "you'll swell up, an' smell, an' turn red an' green an' blue all over till yer bust. Won't he, mother?"

"Now then, don't frighten the child. Go to sleep," she says.

The two younger children go to sleep, and now and then Jacky complains of being "skeezed". More room is made for him. Presently Tommy says:

"Mother! listen to them (adjective) little possums. I'd like to screw their blanky necks."

And Jacky protests drowsily.

"But they don't hurt us, the little blanks!"

Mother: "There, I told you you'd teach Jacky to swear." But the remark makes her smile. Jacky goes to sleep.

Presently Tommy asks:

"Mother! Do you think they'll ever extricate the (adjective) kangaroo?"

"Lord! How am I to know, child? Go to sleep."

"Will you wake me if the snake comes out?"

"Yes. Go to sleep."

Near midnight. The children are all asleep and she sits there still, sewing and reading by turns. From time to time she glances round the floor and wall-plate, and whenever she hears a noise she reaches for the stick. The thunderstorm comes on, and the wind, rushing through the cracks in the slab wall, threatens to blow out her candle. She places it on a sheltered part of the dresser and fixes up a newspaper to protect it. At every flash of lightning the cracks between the slabs gleam like polished silver. The thunder rolls, and the rain comes down in torrents.

Alligator lies at full length on the floor, with his eyes turned towards the partition. She knows by this that the snake is there. There are large cracks in that wall opening under the floor of the dwelling-house.

She is not a coward, but recent events have shaken her nerves. A little son of her brother-in-law was lately bitten by a snake, and died. Besides, she has not heard from her husband for six months, and is anxious about him.

He was a drover, and started squatting here when they were married. The drought of 18— ruined him. He had to sacrifice the remnant of his flock and go droving again. He intends to move his family into the nearest town when he comes back, and, in the meantime, his brother, who keeps a shanty on the main road, comes over about once a month with provisions. The wife has still a couple of cows, one horse, and a few sheep. The brother-in-law kills one of the latter occasionally, gives her what she needs of it, and takes the rest in return for other provisions.

She is used to being left alone. She once lived like this for eighteen months. As a girl she built the usual castles in the air; but all her girlish hopes and aspirations have long been dead. She finds all the excitement and recreation she needs in the *Young Ladies' Journal*, and—Heaven help her!—takes a pleasure in the fashion-plates.

Her husband is an Australian, and so is she. He is careless, but a good enough husband. If he had the means he would take her to the city and keep her there like a princess. They are used to being apart, or at least she is. "No use fretting," she says. He may forget sometimes that he is married; but if he has a good cheque when he comes back he will give most of it to her. When he had money he took her to the city several times—hired a railway sleeping compartment, and put up at the best hotels. He also bought her a buggy, but they had to sacrifice that along with the rest.

The last two children were born in the bush—one while her husband was bringing a drunken doctor, by force, to attend to her. She was alone on this occasion, and very weak. She had been ill with a fever. She prayed to God to send her assistance. God sent Black Mary—the "whitest" gin in all the land. Or, at least, God sent King Jimmy first, and he sent Black Mary. He put his black face round the door-post, took in the situation at a glance, and said cheerfully: "All right, missus—I bring my old woman, she down alonga creek."

One of the children died while she was here alone. She rode nineteen miles for assistance, carrying the dead child.

It must be near one or two o'clock. The fire is burning low. Alligator lies with his head resting on his paws, and watches the wall. He is not a very beautiful dog, and the light shows numerous old wounds where the hair will not grow. He is afraid of nothing on the face of the earth or under it. He will tackle a bullock as readily as he will tackle a flea. He hates all other dogs—except kangaroo-dogs—and has a marked dislike to friends or relations of the family. They seldom call, however. He sometimes makes friends with strangers. He hates snakes and has killed many, but he will be bitten some day and die; most snake-dogs end that way.

Now and then the bushwoman lays down her work and watches, and listens, and thinks. She thinks of things in her own life, for there is little else to think about.

The rain will make the grass grow, and this reminds her how she fought a bushfire once while her husband was away. The grass was long, and very dry, and the fire threatened to burn her out. She put on an old pair of her husband's trousers and beat out the flames with a green bough, till great drops of sooty perspiration stood out on her forehead and ran in streaks down her blackened arms. The sight of his mother in trousers greatly amused Tommy, who worked like a little hero by her side, but the terrified baby howled lustily for his "mummy". The fire would have mastered her but for four excited bushmen who arrived in the nick of time. It was a mixed-up affair all round; when she went to take up the baby he screamed and struggled convulsively, thinking it was a "blackman"; and Alligator, trusting more to the child's sense than his own instinct, charged furiously, and (being old and slightly deaf) did not in his excitement at first recognize his mistress's voice, but continued to hang on to the moleskins until choked off by Tommy with a saddle-strap. The dog's sorrow for his blunder, and his anxiety to let it be known that it was all a mistake, was as evident as his ragged tail and twelve-inch grin could make it. It was a glorious time for the boys; a day to look back to, and talk about, and laugh over for many years.

She thinks how she fought a flood during her husband's absence. She stood for hours in the drenching downpour, and dug an overflow gutter to save the dam across the creek. But she could not save it. There are things that a bushwoman cannot do. Next morning the dam was broken, and her heart was nearly broken too, for she thought how her husband would feel when he came home and saw the result of years of labour swept away. She cried then.

She also fought the pleuro-pneumonia—dosed and bled the few remaining cattle, and wept again when her two best cows died.

Again, she fought a mad bullock that besieged the house for a day. She made bullets and fired at him through the cracks in the slabs with an old shot-gun. He was dead in the morning. She skinned him and got seventeen-and-sixpence for the hide.

She also fights the crows and eagles that have designs on her chickens. Her plan of campaign is very original. The children cry "Crows, mother!" and she rushes out and aims a broomstick at the birds as though it were a gun, and says "Bung!" The crows leave in a hurry; they are cunning, but a woman's cunning is greater.

Occasionally a bushman in the horrors, or a villainous-looking sundowner, comes and nearly scares the life out of her. She generally tells the suspicious-looking stranger that her husband and two sons are at work below the dam, or over at the yard, for he always cunningly inquires for the boss.

Only last week a gallows-faced swagman—having satisfied himself that there were no men on the place—threw his swag down on the veranda, and demanded tucker. She gave him something to eat; then he expressed his intention of staying for the night. It was sundown then. She got a batten from the sofa, loosened the dog, and confronted the stranger, holding the batten in one hand and the dog's collar with the other. "Now you go!" she said. He looked at her and at the dog, said "All right, mum," in a cringing tone, and left. She was a determined-looking woman, and Alligator's yellow eyes glared unpleasantly—besides, the dog's chawing-up apparatus greatly resembled that of the reptile he was named after.

She has few pleasures to think of as she sits here alone by the fire, on guard against a snake. All days are much the same to her; but on Sunday afternoon she dresses herself, tidies the children, smartens up baby, and goes for a lonely walk along the bush-track, pushing an old perambulator in front of her. She does this every Sunday. She takes as much care to make herself and the children look smart as she would if she were going to do the block in the city. There is nothing to see, however, and not a soul to meet. You might walk twenty miles along this track without being able to fix a point in your mind, unless you are a bushman. This is because of the everlasting, maddening sameness of the stunted trees—that monotony which makes a man long to break away and travel as far as trains can go, and sail as far as ship can sail—and further.

But this bushwoman is used to the loneliness of it. As a girl-wife she hated it, and now she would feel strange away from it.

She is glad when her husband returns, but she does not gush or make a fuss about it. She gets him something good to eat, and tidies up the children.

She seems contented with her lot. She loves her children, but has no time to show it. She seems harsh to them. Her surroundings are not favourable to the development of the "womanly" or sentimental side of nature.

It must be near morning now; but the clock is in the dwelling-house. Her candle is nearly done; she forgot that she was out of candles. Some more wood must be got to keep the fire up, and so she shuts the dog inside and hurries round to the woodheap. The rain has cleared off. She seizes a stick, pulls it out, and—crash! the whole pile collapses.

Yesterday she bargained with a stray blackfellow to bring her some wood, and while he was at work she went in search of a missing cow. She was absent an hour or so, and the native black made good use of his time. On her return she was so astonished to see a good heap of wood by the chimney that she gave him an extra fig of tobacco, and praised him for not being lazy. He thanked her, and left with head erect and chest well out. He was the last of his tribe and a King; but he had built that woodheap hollow.

She is hurt now, and tears spring to her eyes as she sits down again by the table. She takes up a handkerchief to wipe the tears away, but pokes her eyes with her bare fingers instead. The handkerchief is full of holes, and she finds that she has put her thumb through one, and her forefinger through another.

This makes her laugh, to the surprise of the dog. She has a keen, very keen, sense of the ridiculous; and some time or other she will amuse bushmen with the story.

She had been amused before like that. One day she sat down "to have a good cry", as she said—and the old cat rubbed against her dress and "cried too". Then she had to laugh.

It must be near daylight now. The room is very close and hot because of the fire. Alligator still watches the wall from time to time. Suddenly he becomes greatly interested; he draws himself a few inches nearer the partition, and a thrill runs through his body. The hair on the back of his neck begins to bristle, and the battle-light is in his yellow eyes. She knows what this means, and lays her hand on the stick. The lower end of one of the partition slabs has a large crack on both sides. An evil pair of small bright bead-like eyes glisten at one of these holes. The snake—a black one—comes slowly out, about a foot, and moves its head up and down. The dog lies still, and the woman sits as one fascinated. The snake comes out a foot further. She lifts her stick, and the reptile, as though suddenly aware of danger, sticks his head in through the crack on the other side of the slab, and hurries to get his tail round after him. Alligator springs, and his jaws come together with a snap. He misses, for his nose is large, and the snake's body close down in the angle formed by the slabs and the floor. He snaps again as the tail comes round. He has the snake now, and tugs it out eighteen inches. Thud, thud, comes the woman's club on the ground. Alligator pulls again. Thud, thud. Alligator gives another pull and he has the snake out—a black brute, five feet long. The head rises to dart about, but the dog has the enemy close to the neck. He is a big, heavy dog, but quick as a terrier. He shakes the snake as though he felt the original curse in common with mankind. The eldest boy wakes up, seizes his stick, and tries to get out of bed, but his mother forces him back with a grip of iron. Thud, thud—the snake's back is broken in several places. Thud, thud—its head is crushed, and Alligator's nose skinned again.

She lifts the mangled reptile on the point of her stick, carries it to the fire, and throws it in; then piles on the wood and watches the snake burn. The boy and dog watch too. She lays her hand on the dog's head, and all the fierce, angry light dies out of his yellow eyes. The younger children are quieted, and presently go to sleep. The dirty-legged boy stands for a moment in his shirt, watching the fire. Presently he looks up at her, sees the tears in her eyes, and, throwing his arms round her neck, exclaims:

"Mother, I won't never go drovin'; blast me if I do!"

And she hugs him to her worn-out breast and kisses him; and they sit thus together while the sickly daylight breaks over the bush.

The Loaded Dog

Dave Regan, Jim Bently, and Andy Page were sinking a shaft at Stony Creek in search of a rich gold quartz reef which was supposed to exist in the vicinity. There is always a rich reef supposed to exist in the vicinity; the only questions are whether it is ten feet or hundreds beneath the surface, and in which direction. They had struck some pretty solid rock, also water which kept them bailing. They used the old-fashioned blasting-powder and time-fuse. They'd make a sausage or cartridge of blasting-powder in a skin of strong calico or canvas, the mouth sewn and bound round the end of the fuse; they'd dip the cartridge in melted tallow to make it watertight, get the drill-hole as dry as possible, drop in the cartridge with some dry dust, and wad and ram with stiff clay and broken brick. Then they'd light the fuse and get out of the hole and wait. The result was usually an ugly pot-hole in the bottom of the shaft and a half a barrow-load of broken rock.

There was plenty of fish in the creek, fresh-water bream, cod, cat-fish, and tailers. The party were fond of fish, and Andy and Dave of fishing. Andy would fish for three hours at a stretch if encouraged by a nibble or a bite now and then—say once in twenty minutes. The butcher was always willing to give meat in exchange for fish when they caught more than they could eat; but now it was winter, and these fish wouldn't bite. However, the creek was low, just a chain of muddy waterholes, from the hole with a few bucketfuls in it to the sizeable pool with an average depth of six or seven feet, and they could get fish by bailing out the smaller holes or muddying up the water in the larger ones till the fish rose to the surface. There was the cat-fish, with spikes growing out of the sides of its head, and if you got pricked you'd know it, as Dave said. Andy took off his boots, tucked up his trousers, and went into a hole one day to stir up the mud with his feet, and he knew it. Dave scooped one out with his hand and got pricked, and he knew it too; his arm swelled, and the pain throbbed up into his shoulder, and down into his stomach, too, he said, like a toothache he had once, and kept him awake for two nights—only the toothache pain had a "burred edge", Dave said.

Dave got an idea.

"Why not blow the fish up in the big waterhole with a cartridge?" he said. "I'll try it."

He thought the thing out and Andy Page worked it out. Andy usually put Dave's theories into practice if they were practicable, or bore the blame for the failure and the chaffing of his mates if they weren't.

He made a cartridge about three times the size of those they used in the rock. Jim Bently said it was big enough to blow the bottom out of the river. The inner skin was of stout calico; Andy stuck the end of a six-foot piece of fuse well down in the powder and bound the mouth of the bag firmly to it with whipcord. The idea was to sink the cartridge in the water with the open end of the fuse attached to a float on the surface, ready for lighting. Andy dipped the cartridge in melted bees-wax to make it watertight. "We'll have to leave it some time before we light it," said Dave, "to give the fish time to get over their scare when we put it in, and come nosing round again; so we'll want it well watertight."

Round the cartridge Andy, at Dave's suggestion, bound a strip of sail canvas—that they used for making water-bags—to increase the force of the explosion, and round that he pasted layers of stiff brown paper—on the plan of the sort of fireworks we called "gun-crackers". He let the paper dry in the sun, then he sewed a covering of two thicknesses of canvas over it, and bound the thing from end to end with stout fishing-line. Dave's schemes were elaborate, and he often worked his inventions out to nothing. The cartridge was rigid and solid enough now—a formidable bomb; but Andy and Dave wanted to be sure. Andy sewed on another layer of canvas, dipped the cartridge in melted tallow, twisted a length of fencing-wire round it as an afterthought, dipped it in tallow again, and stood it carefully against a tent-peg, where he'd know where to find it, and wound the fuse loosely round it. Then he went to the camp-fire to try some potatoes which were boiling in their jackets in a billy, and to see about frying some chops for dinner. Dave and Jim were at work in the claim that morning.

They had a big black young retriever dog—or rather an over-grown pup, a big, foolish, four-footed mate, who was always slobbering round them and lashing their legs with his heavy tail that swung round like a stockwhip. Most of his head was usually a red, idiotic slobbering grin of appreciation of his own silliness. He seemed to take life, the world, his two-legged mates, and his own instinct as a huge joke. He'd retrieve anything; he carted back most of the camp rubbish that Andy threw away. They had a cat that died in hot weather, and Andy threw it a good distance away in the scrub; and early one morning the dog found the cat, after it had been dead a week or so, and carried it back to camp, and laid it just inside the tent-flaps, where it could best make its presence known when the mates should rise and begin to sniff suspiciously in the sickly smothering atmosphere of the summer sunrise. He used to retrieve them when they went in swimming; he'd jump in after them, and take their hands in his mouth, and try to swim out with them, and scratch their naked bodies with his paws. They loved him for his good-heartedness and his foolishness, but when they wished to enjoy a swim they had to tie him up in camp.

He watched Andy with great interest all the morning making the cartridge, and hindered him considerably, trying to help; but about noon he went off to the claim to see how Dave and Jim were getting on, and to come home to dinner with them. Andy saw them coming, and put a panful of mutton-chops on the fire. Andy was cook today; Dave and Jim stood with their backs to the fire, as bushmen do in all weathers, waiting till dinner should be ready. The retriever went nosing round after something he seemed to have missed.

Andy's brain still worked on the cartridge; his eye was caught by the glare of an empty kerosene-tin lying in the bushes, and it struck him that it wouldn't be a bad idea to sink the cartridge packed with clay, sand, or stones in the tin, to increase the force of the explosion. He may have been all out, from a scientific point of view, but the notion looked all right to him. Jim Bently, by the way, wasn't interested in their "damned silliness". Andy noticed an empty treacle-tin—the sort with the little tin neck or spout soldered on to the top for the convenience of pouring out the treacle—and it struck him that this would have made the best kind of cartridge-case: he would only have had to pour in the powder, stick the fuse in through the neck, and cork and seal it with bees-wax. He was turning to suggest this to Dave, when Dave glanced over his shoulder to see how the chops were doing—and bolted. He explained afterwards that he thought he heard the pan spluttering extra, and looked to see if the chops were burning. Jim Bently looked behind and bolted after Dave. Andy stood stock-still, staring after them.

"Run, Andy! Run!" they shouted back at him. "Run! Look behind you, you fool!" Andy turned slowly and looked, and there, close behind him, was the retriever with the cartridge in his mouth—wedged into his broadest and silliest grin. And that wasn't all. The dog had come round the fire to Andy, and the loose end of the fuse had trailed and waggled over the burning sticks into the blaze; Andy had slit and nicked the firing end of the fuse well, and now it was hissing and spitting properly.

Andy's legs started with a jolt; his legs started before his brain did, and he made after Dave and Jim. And the dog followed Andy.

Dave and Jim were good runners—Jim the best—for a short distance; Andy was slow and heavy, but he had the strength and the wind and could last. The dog capered round him, delighted as a dog could be to find his mates, as he thought, on for a frolic. Dave and Jim kept shouting back, "Don't foller us! Don't foller us, you coloured fool!" But Andy kept on, no matter how they dodged. They could never explain, any more than the dog, why they followed each other, but so they ran, Dave keeping in Jim's track in all its turnings, Andy after Dave, and the dog circling round Andy—the live fuse swishing in all directions and hissing and spluttering and stinking. Jim yelling to Dave not to follow him, Dave shouting to Andy to go in another direction—to "spread out", and Andy roaring at the dog to go home. Then Andy's brain began to work, stimulated by the crisis: he tried to get a running kick at the dog, but the dog dodged; he snatched up sticks and stones and threw them at the dog and ran on again. The retriever saw that he'd made a mistake about Andy, and left him and bounded after Dave. Dave, who had the presence of mind to think that the fuse's time wasn't up yet, made a dive and a grab for the dog, caught him by the tail, and as he swung round snatched the cartridge out of his mouth and flung it as far as he could; the dog immediately bounded after it and retrieved it. Dave roared and cursed at the dog, who, seeing that Dave was offended, left him and went after Jim, who was well ahead. Jim swung to a sapling and went up it like a native bear; it was a young sapling, and Jim couldn't safely get more than ten or twelve feet from the ground. The dog laid the cartridge, as carefully as if it were a kitten, at the foot of the sapling, and capered and leaped and whooped joyously round under Jim. The big pup reckoned that this was part of the lark—he was all right now—it was Jim who was out for a spree. The fuse sounded as if it were going a mile a minute. Jim tried to climb higher and the sapling bent and cracked. Jim fell on his feet and ran. The dog swooped on the cartridge and followed. It all took but a very few moments. Jim ran to a digger's hole, about ten feet deep, and dropped down into it—landing on soft mud—and was safe. The dog grinned sardonically down on him, over the edge, for a moment, as if he thought it would be a good lark to drop the cartridge down on Jim.

"Go away, Tommy," said Jim feebly, "go away."

The dog bounded off after Dave, who was the only one in sight now; Andy had dropped behind a log, where he lay flat on his face, having suddenly remembered a picture of the Russo-Turkish war with a circle of Turks lying flat on their faces (as if they were ashamed) round a newly-arrived shell.

There was a small hotel or shanty on the creek, on the main road, not far from the claim. Dave was desperate, the time flew much faster in his stimulated imagination than it did in reality, so he made for the shanty. There were several casual bushmen on the veranda and in the bar; Dave rushed into the bar, banging the door to behind him. "My dog!" he gasped, in reply to the astonished stare of the publican, "the blanky retriever—he's got a live cartridge in his mouth——"

The retriever, finding the front door shut against him, had bounded round and in by the back way, and now stood smiling in the doorway leading from the passage, the cartridge still in his mouth and the fuse spluttering. They burst out of that bar; Tommy bounded first after one and then after another, for, being a young dog, he tried to make friends with everybody.

The bushmen ran round corners, and some shut themselves in the stable. There was a new weatherboard and corrugated-iron kitchen and wash-house on piles in the backyard, with some women washing clothes inside. Dave and the publican bundled in there and shut the door—the publican cursing Dave and calling him a crimson fool, in hurried tones, and wanting to know what the hell he came here for.

The retriever went in under the kitchen, amongst the piles, but, luckily for those inside, there was a vicious yellow mongrel cattle-dog sulking and nursing his nastiness under there—a sneaking, fighting, thieving canine, whom neighbours had tried for years to shoot or poison. Tommy saw his danger—he'd had experience from this dog—and started out and across the yard, still sticking to the cartridge. Half-way across the yellow dog caught him and nipped him. Tommy dropped the cartridge, gave one terrified yell, and took to the bush. The yellow dog followed him to the fence and then ran back to see what he had dropped. Nearly a dozen other dogs came from round all the corners and under the buildings—spidery, thievish, cold-blooded kangaroo-dogs, mongrel sheep- and cattle-dogs, vicious black and yellow dogs—that slip after you in the dark, nip your heels, and vanish without explaining—and yapping, yelping small fry. They kept at a respectable distance round the nasty yellow dog, for it was dangerous to go near him when he thought he had found something which might be good for a dog or cat. He sniffed at the cartridge twice, and was just taking a third cautious sniff when——

It was very good blasting-powder—a new brand that Dave had recently got up from Sydney; and the cartridge had been excellently well made. Andy was very patient and painstaking in all he did, and nearly as handy as the average sailor with needles, twine, canvas and rope.

Bushmen say that that kitchen jumped off its piles and on again. When the smoke and dust cleared away, the remains of the nasty yellow dog were lying against the paling fence of the yard looking as if he had been kicked into a fire by a horse and afterwards rolled in the dust under a barrow, and finally thrown against the fence from a distance. Several saddle-horses, which had been "hanging-up" round the veranda, were galloping wildly down the road in clouds of dust, with broken bridle-reins flying; and from a circle round the outskirts, from every point of the compass in the scrub, came the yelping of dogs. Two of them went home, to the place where they were born, thirty miles away, and reached it the same night and stayed there; it was not till towards evening that the rest came back cautiously to make inquiries. One was trying to walk on two legs, and most of 'em looked more or less singed; and a little, singed, stumpy-tailed dog, who had been in the habit of hopping the back half of him along on one leg, had reason to be glad that he'd saved up the other leg all those years, for he needed it now. There was one old one-eyed cattle-dog round that shanty for years afterwards, who couldn't stand the smell of a gun being cleaned. He it was who had taken an interest, only second to that of the yellow dog, in the cartridge. Bushmen said that it was amusing to slip up on his blind side and stick a dirty ramrod under his nose: he wouldn't wait to bring his solitary eye to bear—he'd take to the bush and stay out all night.

For half an hour or so after the explosion there were several bushmen round behind the stable who crouched, doubled up, against the wall, or rolled gently on the dust, trying to laugh without shrieking. There were two white women in hysterics at the house, and a half-caste rushing aimlessly round with a dipper of cold water. The publican was holding his wife tight and begging her between her squawks, to "Hold up for my sake, Mary, or I'll lam the life out of ye!"

Dave decided to apologize later on, "when things had settled a bit", and went back to camp. And the dog that had done it all, Tommy, the great, idiotic mongrel retriever, came slobbering round Dave and lashing his legs with his tail, and trotted home after him, smiling his broadest, longest, and reddest smile of amiability, and apparently satisfied for one afternoon with the fun he'd had.

Andy chained the dog up securely, and cooked some more chops, while Dave went to help Jim out of the hole.

And most of this is why, for years afterwards, lanky, easygoing bushmen, riding lazily past Dave's camp, would cry, in a lazy drawl and with just a hint of the nasal twang:

" 'Ello, Da-a-ve! How's the fishin' getting on, Da-a-ve?"

The Union Buries Its Dead

WHILE out boating one Sunday afternoon on a billabong across the river, we saw a young man on horseback driving some horses along the bank. He said it was a fine day, and asked if the water was deep there. The joker of our party said it was deep enough to drown him, and he laughed and rode further up. We didn't take much notice of him.

Next day a funeral gathered at a corner pub and asked each other in to have a drink while waiting for the hearse. They passed away some of the time dancing jigs to a piano in the bar parlour. They passed away the rest of the time skylarking and fighting.

The defunct was a young union labourer, about twenty-five, who had been drowned the previous day while trying to swim some horses across a billabong of the Darling.

He was almost a stranger in town, and the fact of his having been a union man accounted for the funeral. The police found some union papers in his swag, and called at the General Labourers' Union office for information about him. That's how we knew. The secretary had very little information to give. The departed was a "Roman", and the majority of the town were otherwise—but unionism is stronger than creed. Liquor, however, is stronger than unionism; and, when the hearse presently arrived, more than two-thirds of the funeral were unable to follow.

The procession numbered fifteen; fourteen souls following the broken shell of a soul. Perhaps not one of the fourteen possessed a soul any more than the corpse did—but that doesn't matter.

Four or five of the funeral, who were boarders at the pub, borrowed a trap which the landlord used to carry passengers to and from the railway-station. They were strangers to us who were on foot, and we to them. We were all strangers to the corpse.

A horseman, who looked like a drover just returned from a big trip, dropped into our dusty wake and followed us a few hundred yards, dragging his pack-horse behind him, but a friend made wild and demonstrative signals from an hotel veranda—hooking at the air in front with his right hand and jobbing his left thumb over his shoulder in the direction of the bar—so the drover hauled off and didn't catch up to us any more. He was a stranger to the entire show.

We walked in twos. There were three twos. It was very hot and dusty; the heat rushed in fierce dazzling rays across every iron roof and light-coloured wall that was turned to the sun. One or two pubs closed respectfully until we got past. They closed their bar doors and the patrons went in and out through some side or back entrance for a few minutes. Bushmen seldom grumble at an inconvenience of this sort, when it is caused by a funeral. They have too much respect for the dead.

On the way to the cemetery we passed three shearers sitting on the shady side of a fence. One was drunk—very drunk. The other two covered their right ears with their hats, out of respect for the departed—whoever he might have been—and one of them kicked the drunk and muttered something to him.

He straightened himself up, stared, and reached helplessly for his hat, which he shoved half off and then on again. Then he made a great effort to pull himself together—and succeeded. He stood up, braced his back against the fence, knocked off his hat, and remorsefully placed his foot on it—to keep it off his head till the funeral passed.

A tall, sentimental drover, who walked by my side, cynically quoted Byronic verses suitable to the occasion—to death—and asked with pathetic humour whether we thought the dead man's ticket would be recognized "over yonder". It was a G.L.U. ticket, and the general opinion was that it would be recognized.

Presently my friend said:

"You remember when we were in the boat yesterday, we saw a man driving some horses along the bank?"

"Yes."

He nodded at the hearse and said:

"Well, that's him."

I thought a while.

"I didn't take any particular notice of him," I said. "He said something, didn't he?"

"Yes; said it was a fine day. You'd have taken more notice if you'd known that he was doomed to die in the hour, and that those were the last words he would say to any man in this world."

"To be sure," said a full voice from the rear. "If ye'd known that, ye'd have prolonged the conversation."

We plodded on across the railway-line and along the hot, dusty road which ran to the cemetery, some of us talking about the accident, and lying about the narrow escapes we had had ourselves. Presently someone said:

"There's the Devil."

I looked up and saw a priest standing in the shade of the tree by the cemetery gate.

The hearse was drawn up and the tail-boards were opened. The funeral extinguished its right ear with its hat as four men lifted the coffin out and laid it over the grave. The priest—a pale, quiet young fellow—stood under the shade of a sapling which grew at the head of the grave. He took off his hat, dropped it carelessly on the ground, and proceeded to business. I noticed that one or two heathens winced slightly when the holy water was sprinkled on the coffin. The drops quickly evaporated, and the little round black spots they left were soon dusted over; but the spots showed, by contrast, the cheapness and shabbiness of the cloth with which the coffin was covered. It seemed black before; now it looked a dusky grey.

Just here man's ignorance and vanity made a farce of the funeral. A big, bull-necked publican, with heavy, blotchy features, and a supremely ignorant expression, picked up the priest's straw hat and held it about two inches over the head of his reverence during the whole of the service. The Father, be it remembered, was standing in the shade. A few shoved their hats on and off uneasily, struggling between their disgust for the living and their respect for the dead. The hat had a conical crown and a brim sloping down all round like a sunshade, and the publican held it with his great red claw spread over the crown. To do the priest justice, perhaps he didn't notice the incident. A stage priest or parson in the same position might have said, "Put the hat down, my friend; is not the memory of our departed brother worth more than my complexion?" A wattle-bark layman might have expressed himself in stronger language, none the less to the point. But my priest seemed unconscious of what was going on. Besides, the publican was a great and important pillar of the Church. He couldn't, as an ignorant and conceited ass, lose such a good opportunity of asserting his faithfulness and importance to his Church.

The grave looked very narrow under the coffin, and I drew a

breath of relief when the box slid easily down. I saw a coffin get stuck once, at Rookwood, and it had to be yanked out with difficulty, and laid on the sods at the feet of the heart-broken relations, who howled dismally while the grave-diggers widened the hole. But they don't cut contracts so fine in the West. Our grave-digger was not altogether bowelless, and, out of respect for that human quality described as "feelin's", he scraped up some light and dusty soil and threw it down to deaden the fall of the clay lumps on the coffin. He also tried to steer the first few shovelfuls gently down against the end of the grave with the back of the shovel turned outwards, but the hard dry Darling River clods rebounded and knocked all the same. It didn't matter much—nothing does. The fall of lumps of clay on a stranger's coffin doesn't sound any different from the fall of the same things on an ordinary wooden box—at least I didn't notice anything awesome or unusual in the sound; but, perhaps, one of us—the most sensitive—might have been impressed by being reminded of a burial long ago, when the thump of every sod jolted his heart.

I have left out the wattle—because it wasn't there. I have also neglected to mention the heart-broken old mate, with his grizzled head bowed and great drops streaming down his rugged cheeks. He was absent—he was probably "outback". For similar reasons I have omitted reference to the suspicious moisture in the eyes of a bearded bush ruffian named Bill. Bill failed to turn up, and the only moisture was that which was induced by the heat. I have left out the "sad Australian sunset", because the sun was not going down at the time. The burial took place exactly at midday.

The dead bushman's name was Jim, apparently; but they found no portraits, nor locks of hair, nor any love-letters, nor anything of that kind in his swag—not even a reference to his mother; only some papers relating to union matters. Most of us didn't know the name till we saw it on the coffin; we knew him as "that poor chap that got drowned yesterday".

"So his name's James Tyson," said my drover acquaintance, looking at the plate.

"Why! Didn't you know that before?" I asked.

"No; but I knew he was a union man."

It turned out, afterwards, that J. T. wasn't his real name—only "the name he went by".

Anyhow he was buried by it, and most of the "Great Australian Dailies" have mentioned in their brevity columns that a young man named James John Tyson was drowned in a billabong of the Darling last Sunday.

We did hear, later on, what his real name was; but if we ever chance to read it in the "Missing Friends Column" we shall not be able to give any information to heart-broken mother or sister or wife, nor to anyone who could let him hear something to his advantage—for we have already forgotten the name.

An Old Mate of Your Father's

You remember when we hurried home from the old bush school how we were sometimes startled by a bearded apparition, who smiled kindly down on us, and whom our mother introduced, as we raked off our hats, as "An old mate of your father's on the diggings, Johnny." And he would pat our heads and say we were fine boys, or girls—as the case may have been—and that we had our father's nose but our mother's eyes, or the other way about; and say that the baby was the dead spit of its mother, and then added, for father's benefit: "But yet he's like you, Tom." It did seem strange to the children to hear him address the old man by his christian name—considering that the mother always referred to him as "Father". She called the old mate Mr So-and-so, and father called him Bill, or something to that effect.

Occasionally the old mate would come dressed in the latest city fashion, and at other times in a new suit of reach-me-downs, and yet again he would turn up in clean white moleskins, washed tweed coat, Crimean shirt, blucher boots, soft felt hat, with a fresh-looking speckled handkerchief round his neck. But his face was mostly round and brown and jolly, his hands were always horny, and his beard grey. Sometimes he might have seemed strange and uncouth to us at first, but the old man never appeared the least surprised at anything he said or did—they understood each other so well—and we would soon take to this relic of our father's past, who would have fruit or lollies for us—strange that he always remembered them—and would surreptitiously slip "shilluns" into our dirty little hands, and tell us stories about the old days, "when me an' yer father was on the diggin's, an' you wasn't thought of, my boy".

Sometimes the old mate would stay over Sunday, and in the forenoon or after dinner he and father would take a walk amongst the deserted shafts of Sapling Gully or along Quartz Ridge, and criticize old ground, and talk of past diggers' mistakes, and second bottoms, and feelers, and dips, and leads—also outcrops—and absently pick up pieces of quartz and slate, rub them on their sleeves, look at them in an abstracted manner, and drop them again; and they would talk of some old lead they had worked on: "Hogan's party was here on one side of us, Macintosh was here on the other, Mac was getting good gold and so was Hogan, and now, why the blanky blank weren't we on gold?" And the mate would always agree that there was "gold in them ridges and gullies yet, if a man only had the money behind him to git at it". And then perhaps the guv'nor would show him a spot where he intended to put down a shaft some day—the old man was always thinking of putting down a shaft. And these two old fifty-niners would mooch round and sit on their heels on the sunny mullock-heaps and break clay lumps between their hands, and lay plans for the putting down of shafts, and smoke, till an urchin was sent to "look for your father and Mr So-and-so, and tell 'em to come to their dinner".

And again—mostly in the fresh of the morning—they would hang about the fences on the selection and review the livestock: five dusty skeletons of cows, a hollow-sided calf or two, and one shocking piece of equine scenery—which, by the way, the old mate always praised. But the selector's heart was not in farming nor on selections —it was far away with the last new rush in Western Australia or Queensland, or perhaps buried in the worked-out ground of Tambaroora, Married Man's Creek, or Araluen; and by and by the memory of some half-forgotten reef or lead or Last Chance, Nil Desperandum, or Brown Snake claim would take their thoughts far back and away from the dusty patch of sods and struggling sprouts called the crop, or the few discouraged, half-dead slips which comprised the orchard. Then their conversation would be pointed with many Golden Points, Bakery Hills, Deep Creeks, Maitland Bars, Specimen Flats, and Chinamen's Gullies. And so they'd yarn, till the youngster came to tell them that "Mother sez the breakfus is gettin' cold," and then the old mate would rouse himself and stretch and say, "Well, we mustn't keep the missus waitin', Tom!"

And, after tea, they would sit on a log of the woodheap, or the edge of the veranda—that is, in warm weather—and yarn about Ballarat and Bendigo—of the days when we spoke of being on a place oftener than at it: *on* Ballarat, *on* Gulgong, *on* Lambing Flat, *on* Creswick—and they would use the definite article before the names, as: on The Turon; The Lachlan; The Home Rule; The Canadian Lead. Then again they'd yarn of old mates, such as Tom Brook, Jack Henright, and poor Martin Ratcliff—who was killed in his golden hole—and of other men whom they didn't seem to have known much about, and who went by the names of "Adelaide Adolphus", "Corney George", and other names which might have been more or less applicable.

And sometimes they'd get talking, low and mysterious like, about "Th' Eureka Stockade"; and if we didn't understand and asked questions, "What was the Eureka Stockade?" or "What did they do it for?" father'd say: "Now, run away, sonny, and don't bother; me and Mr So-and-so want to talk." Father had the mark of a hole on his leg, which he said he got through a gun accident when a boy, and a scar on his side, that we saw when he was in swimming with us; he said he got that in an accident in a quartz-crushing machine. Mr So-and-so had a big scar on the side of his forehead that was caused by a pick accidentally slipping out of a loop in the rope, and falling down a shaft where he was working. But how was it they talked low, and their eyes brightened up, and they didn't look at each other, but away over the sunset, and had to get up and walk about, and take a stroll in the cool of the evening when they talked about Eureka?

And, again they'd talk lower and more mysterious like, and perhaps mother would be passing the woodheap and catch a word, and ask:

"Who was she, Tom?"

And Tom—father—would say:

"Oh, you didn't know her, Mary; she belonged to a family Bill knew at home."

And Bill would look solemn till mother had gone, and then they would smile a quiet smile, and stretch and say, "Ah, well!" and start something else.

They had yarns for the fireside, too, some of those old mates of father's and one of them would often tell how a girl—a queen of the diggings—was married, and had her wedding-ring made out of the gold of that field; and how the diggers weighed their gold with the new wedding-ring—for luck—by hanging the ring on the hook of the scales and attaching their chamois-leather gold-bags to it (whereupon she boasted that four hundred ounces of the precious metal passed through her wedding-ring); and how they lowered the young bride, blindfolded, down a golden hole in a big bucket, and got her to point out the drive from which the gold came that her ring was made out of. The point of this story seems to have been lost—or else we forget it—but it was characteristic. Had the girl been lowered down a duffer, and asked to point out the way to the gold, and had she done so successfully, there would have been some sense in it.

And they would talk of King, and Maggie Oliver, and G. V. Brooke, and others, and remember how the diggers went five miles out to meet the coach that brought the girl actress, and took the horses out and brought her in in triumph, and worshipped her, and sent her off in glory, and threw nuggets into her lap. And how she stood upon the box-seat and tore her sailor hat to pieces, and threw the fragments amongst the crowd; and how the diggers fought for the bits and thrust them inside their shirt bosoms; and how she broke down and cried, and could in her turn have worshipped those men—loved them, every one. They were boys all, and gentlemen all. There were college men, artists, poets, musicians, journalists—Bohemians all. Men from all the lands and one. They understood art—and poverty was dead.

And perhaps the old mate would say slyly, but with a sad, quiet smile:

"Have you got that bit of straw yet, Tom?"

Those old mates had each three pasts behind them. The two they told each other when they became mates, and the one they had shared.

And when the visitor had gone by the coach we noticed that the old man would smoke a lot, and think as much, and take great interest in the fire, and be a trifle irritable perhaps.

Those old mates of our father's are getting few and far between, and only happen along once in a way to keep the old man's memory fresh, as it were. We met one today, and had a yarn with him, and afterwards we got thinking, and somehow began to wonder whether those ancient friends of ours were, or were not, better and kinder to their mates than we of the rising generation are to our fathers; and the doubt is painfully on the wrong side.

The Bush Undertaker

"FIVE BOB!"

The old man shaded his eyes and peered through the dazzling glow of that broiling Christmas Day. He stood within the door of a slab-and-bark hut situated upon the bank of a barren creek; sheep-yards lay to the right, and a low line of bare brown ridges formed a suitable background to the scene.

"Five Bob!" shouted he again; and a dusty sheep-dog rose wearily from the shaded side of the hut and looked inquiringly at his master, who pointed towards some sheep which were straggling from the flock.

"Fetch 'em back," he said confidently.

The dog went off, and his master returned to the interior of the hut.

"We'll yard 'em early," he said to himself; "the super won't know. We'll yard 'em early, and have the arternoon to ourselves.

"We'll get dinner," he added, glancing at some pots on the fire. "I cud do a bit of doughboy, an' that theer boggabri'll eat like tater-marrer along of the salt meat." He moved one of the black buckets from the blaze. "I likes to keep it jist on the sizzle," he said in explanation to himself; "hard bilin' makes it tough—I'll keep it jist a-simmerin'."

Here his soliloquy was interrupted by the return of the dog.

"All right, Five Bob," said the hatter, "dinner'll be ready dreckly. Jist keep yer eye on the sheep till I call yer; keep 'em well rounded up, an' we'll yard 'em afterwards and have a holiday."

This speech was accompanied by a gesture evidently intelligible, for the dog retired as though he understood English, and the cooking proceeded.

"I'll take a pick an' shovel with me an' root up that old black-fellow," mused the shepherd, evidently following up a recent train of thought. "I reckon it'll do now; I'll put in the spuds."

The last sentence referred to the cooking, the first to a black-fellow's grave about which he was curious.

"The sheep's a-campin'," said the soliloquizer, glancing through the door. "So me an' Five Bob'll be able to get our dinner in peace. I wish I had just enough fat to make the pan siss; I'd treat myself to a leather-jacket; but it took three weeks' skimmin' to get enough for them theer doughboys."

In due time the dinner was dished up; and the old man seated himself on a block, with the lid of a gin-case across his knees for a table. Five Bob squatted opposite with the liveliest interest and appreciation depicted on his intelligent countenance.

Dinner proceeded very quietly, except when the carver paused to ask the dog how some tasty morsel went with him, and Five Bob's tail declared that it went very well indeed.

"Here y'are, try this," cried the old man, tossing him a large piece of doughboy. A click of Five Bob's jaws and the dough was gone.

"Clean into his liver!" said the old man with a faint smile.

He washed up the tinware in the water the duff had been boiled in, and then, with the assistance of the dog, yarded the sheep.

This accomplished, he took a pick and shovel and an old sack, and started out over the ridge, followed, of course, by his four-legged mate. After tramping some three miles he reached a spur, running out from the main ridge. At the extreme end of this, under some gum-trees, was a little mound of earth, barely defined in the grass, and indented in the centre as all blackfellows' graves were.

He set to work to dig it up, and sure enough, in about half an hour he bottomed on payable dirt.

When he had raked up all the bones, he amused himself by putting them together on the grass and by speculating as to whether they had belonged to black or white, male or female. Failing, however, to arrive at any satisfactory conclusion, he dusted them with great care, put them in the bag, and started for home.

He took a short cut this time over the ridge and down a gully which was full of ringbarked trees and long white grass. He had nearly reached its mouth when a great greasy black goanna clambered up a sapling from under his feet and looked fightable.

"Dang the jumpt-up thing!" cried the old man. "It gin me a start!"

At the foot of the sapling he espied an object which he at first thought was the blackened carcass of a sheep, but on closer examination discovered to be the body of a man; it lay with its forehead resting on its hands, dried to a mummy by the intense heat of the western summer.

"Me luck's in for the day and no mistake!" said the shepherd, scratching the back of his head, while he took stock of the remains. He picked up a stick and tapped the body on the shoulder; the flesh sounded like leather. He turned it over on its side; it fell flat on its back like a board, and the shrivelled eyes seemed to peer up at him from under the blackened wrists.

He stepped back involuntarily, but, recovering himself, leant on his stick and took in all the ghastly details.

There was nothing in the blackened features to tell aught of name or face, but the dress proclaimed the remains to be those of a European. The old man caught sight of a black bottle in the grass, close beside the corpse. This set him thinking. Presently he knelt down and examined the soles of the dead man's blucher boots, and then, rising with an air of conviction, exclaimed: "Brummy! by gosh!—busted up at last!

"I tole yer so, Brummy," he said impressively, addressing the corpse. "I allers told yer as how it 'ud be—an' here y'are, you thundering jumpt-up cus-o'-God fool. Yer cud earn more'n any man in the colony, but yer'd lush it all away. I allers sed as how it 'ud end, an' now yer kin see fur y'self.

"I spect yer was a-comin' t' me t' get fixt up an' set straight agin; then yer was a-goin' to swear off, same as yer allers did; an' here y'are, an' now I expect I'll have t' fix yer up for the last time an' make yer decent, for 'twon't do t' leave yer a-lyin' out here like a dead sheep."

He picked up the corked bottle and examined it. To his great surprise it was nearly full of rum.

"Well, this gits me," exclaimed the old man; "me luck's in, this Christmas, an' no mistake. He must 'a' got the jams early in his spree, or he wouldn't be a-making for me with near a bottleful left. Howsomenever, here goes."

Looking around, his eyes lit up with satisfaction as he saw some bits of bark which had been left by a party of strippers who had been getting bark there for the stations. He picked up two pieces, one about four and the other six feet long, and each about two feet wide, and brought them over to the body. He laid the longest strip by the side of the corpse, which he proceeded to lift on to it.

"Come on, Brummy," he said, in a softer tone than usual, "ye ain't as bad as yer might be, considerin' as it must be three good months since yer slipped yer wind. I s'pect it was the rum as preserved yer. It was the death of yer when yer was alive, an' now yer dead, it preserves yer like—like a mummy."

Then he placed the other strip on top, with the hollow side downwards—thus sandwiching the defunct between the two pieces—removed the saddle-strap which he wore for a belt, and buckled it round one end, while he tried to think of something with which to tie up the other.

"I can't take any more strips off my shirt," he said, critically examining the skirts of the old blue overshirt he wore. "I might get a strip or two more off, but it's short enough already. Let's see; how long have I been a-wearin' of that shirt; oh, I remember, I bought it jist two days afore Five Bob was pupped. I can't afford a new shirt jist yet; howsomenever, seein' it's Brummy, I'll jist borrow a couple more strips and sew 'em on agen when I git home."

He up-ended Brummy, and placing his shoulder against the middle of the lower sheet of bark, lifted the corpse to a horizontal position; then, taking the bag of bones in his hand, he started for home.

"I ain't a-spendin' sech a dull Christmas arter all," he reflected, as he plodded on; but he had not walked above a hundred yards when he saw a black goanna sidling into the grass.

"That's another of them theer dang things!" he exclaimed. "That's two I've seed this mornin'."

Presently he remarked: "Yer don't smell none too sweet, Brummy. It must 'a' been jist about the middle of shearin' when yer pegged out. I wonder who got yer last cheque. Shoo! theer's another black goanner—there must be a flock of 'em."

He rested Brummy on the ground while he had another pull at the bottle, and, before going on, packed the bag of bones on his shoulder under the body, but he soon stopped again.

"The thunderin' jumpt-up bones is all skew-whift," he said. " 'Ole on, Brummy, an' I'll fix 'em"—and he leaned the dead man against a tree while he settled the bones on his shoulder, and took another pull at the bottle.

About a mile further on he heard a rustling in the grass to the right, and, looking round, saw another goanna gliding off sideways, with its long snaky neck turned towards him.

This puzzled the shepherd considerably, the strangest part of it being that Five Bob wouldn't touch the reptile, but slunk off with his tail down when ordered to "sick 'em!"

"Theer's sothin' comic about them theer goanners," said the old man at last. "I've seed swarms of grasshoppers an' big mobs of kangaroos, but dang me if I ever seed a flock of black goanners afore!"

On reaching the hut the old man dumped the corpse against the wall, wrong end up, and stood scratching his head while he endeavoured to collect his muddled thoughts; but he had not placed Brummy at the correct angle, and, consequently, that individual fell forward and struck him a violent blow on the shoulder with the iron toes of his blucher boots.

The shock sobered him. He sprang a good yard, instinctively hitching up his moleskins in preparation for flight; but a backward glance revealed to him the true cause of this supposed attack from the rear. Then he lifted the body, stood it on its feet against the chimney, and ruminated as to where he should lodge his mate for the night, not noticing that the shorter sheet of bark had slipped down on the boots and left the face exposed.

"I s'pect I'll have ter put yer into the chimney-trough for the night, Brummy," said he, turning round to confront the corpse. "Yer can't expect me to take yer into the hut, though I did it when yer was in a worse state than—*Lord!*"

The shepherd was not prepared for the awful scrutiny that gleamed on him from those empty sockets; his nerves received a shock, and it was some time before he recovered himself sufficiently to speak.

"Now, look a-here, Brummy," said he, shaking his finger severely at the delinquent, "I don't want to pick a row with yer; I'd do as much for yer an' more than any other man, an' well yer knows it; but if yer starts playin' any of yer jumpt-up pranktical jokes on me, and a-scarin' of me after a-humpin' of yer 'ome, by the 'oly frost I'll kick yer to jim-rags, so I will."

This admonition delivered, he hoisted Brummy into the chimney-trough, and, with a last glance towards the sheep-yards, he retired to his bunk to have, as he said, a snooze.

He had more than a snooze, however, for when he woke, it was dark, and the bushman's instinct told him it must be nearly nine o'clock.

He lit a slush-lamp and poured the remainder of the rum into a pannikin; but, just as he was about to lift the draught to his lips, he heard a peculiar rustling sound overhead, and put the pot down on the table with a slam that spilled some of the precious liquor.

Five Bob whimpered, and the old shepherd, though used to the weird and dismal, as one living alone in the bush must necessarily be, felt the icy breath of fear in his heart.

He reached hastily for his old shot-gun, and went out to investigate. He walked round the hut several times and examined the roof on all sides, but saw nothing. Brummy appeared to be in the same position.

At last, persuading himself that the noise was caused by possums or the wind, the old man went inside, boiled his billy, and, after composing his nerves somewhat with a light supper and a meditative smoke, retired for the night. He was aroused several times before midnight by the same mysterious sound overhead, but, though he rose and examined the roof on each occasion by the light of the rising moon, he discovered nothing.

At last he determined to sit up and watch until daybreak, and for this purpose took up a position on a log a short distance from the hut, with his gun laid in readiness across his knee.

After watching for about an hour, he saw a black object coming over the ridge-pole. He grabbed his gun and fired. The thing disappeared. He ran round to the other side of the hut, and there was a great black goanna in violent convulsions on the ground.

Then the old man saw it all. "The thunderin' jumpt-up thing has been a-havin' o' me," he exclaimed. "The same cus-o'-God wretch has a-follered me 'ome, an' has been a-havin' its Christmas dinner off of Brummy, an' a-hauntin' o' me into the bargain, the jumpt-up tinker!"

As there was no one by whom he could send a message to the station, and the old man dared not leave the sheep and go himself, he determined to bury the body the next afternoon, reflecting that the authorities could disinter it for inquest if they pleased.

So he brought the sheep home early and made arrangements for the burial by measuring the outer casing of Brummy and digging a hole according to those dimensions.

"That 'minds me," he said. "I never rightly knowed Brummy's religion, blest if I ever did. Howsomenever, there's one thing sartin —none o' them theer pianer-fingered parsons is a-goin' ter take the trouble ter travel out inter this God-forgotten part to hold service over him, seein' as how his last cheque's blued. But, as I've got the fun'ral arrangements all in me own hands, I'll do jestice to it, and see that Brummy has a good comfortable buryin'—and more's unpossible."

"It's time yer turned in, Brum," he said, lifting the body down.

He carried it to the grave and dropped it into one corner like a post. He arranged the bark so as to cover the face, and, by means of a piece of clothes-line, lowered the body to a horizontal position. Then he threw in an armful of gum-leaves, and then, very reluctantly, took the shovel and dropped in a few shovelfuls of earth.

"An' this is the last of Brummy," he said, leaning on his spade and looking away over the tops of the ragged gums on the distant range.

This reflection seemed to engender a flood of memories, in which the old man became absorbed. He leaned heavily upon his spade and thought.

"Arter all," he murmured sadly, "arter all—it were Brummy."

"Brummy," he said at last. "It's all over now; nothin' matters now —nothin' didn't ever matter, nor—nor don't. You uster say as how it 'ud be all right termorrer" (pause); "termorrer's come, Brummy —come fur you—it ain't come fur me yet, but—it's a-comin'."

He threw in some more earth.

"Yer don't remember, Brummy, an' mebbe yer don't want to remember—I don't want to remember—but—well, but, yer see that's where yer got the pull on me."

He shovelled in some more earth and paused again.

The dog arose, with ears erect, and looked anxiously first at his master and then into the grave.

"Theer oughter be somethin' sed," muttered the old man; " 'tain't right to put 'im under like a dog. Theer oughter be some sort o' sarmin." He sighed heavily in the listening silence that followed this remark and proceeded with his work. He filled the grave to the brim this time, and fashioned the mound carefully with his spade. Once or twice he muttered the words, "I am the rassaraction." As he laid the tools quietly aside, and stood at the head of the grave, he was evidently trying to remember the something that ought to be said. He removed his hat, placed it carefully on the grass, held his hands out from his sides and a little to the front, drew a long deep breath, and said with a solemnity that greatly disturbed Five Bob:

"Hashes ter hashes, dus ter dus, Brummy—an'—an' in hopes of a great an' gerlorious rassaraction!"

He sat down on a log near by, rested his elbows on his knees and passed his hand wearily over his forehead—but only as one who was tired and felt the heat; and presently he rose, took up the tools, and walked back to the hut.

And the sun sank again on the grand Australian bush—the nurse and tutor of eccentric minds, the home of the weird.

That There Dog of Mine

Macquarie the shearer had met with an accident. To tell the truth, he had been in a drunken row at a wayside shanty, from which he had escaped with three fractured ribs, a cracked head, and various minor abrasions. His dog, Tally, had been a sober but savage participator in the drunken row, and had escaped with a broken leg. Macquarie afterwards shouldered his swag and staggered and struggled along the track ten miles to the Union Town hospital. Lord knows how he did it. He didn't exactly know himself. Tally limped behind all the way, on three legs.

The doctors examined the man's injuries and were surprised at his endurance. Even doctors are surprised sometimes—though they don't always show it. Of course they would take him in, but they objected to Tally. Dogs were not allowed on the premises.

"You will have to turn that dog out," they said to the shearer, as he sat on the edge of a bed.

Macquarie said nothing.

"We cannot allow dogs about the place, my man," said the doctor in a louder tone, thinking the man was deaf.

"Tie him up in the yard then."

"No. He must go out. Dogs are not permitted on the grounds."

Macquarie rose slowly to his feet, shut his agony behind his set teeth, painfully buttoned his shirt over his hairy chest, took up his waistcoat, and staggered to the corner where the swag lay.

"What are you going to do?" they asked.

"You ain't going to let my dog stop?"

"No. It's against the rules. There are no dogs allowed on the premises."

He stooped and lifted his swag, but the pain was too great, and he leaned back against the wall.

"Come, come now! man alive!" exclaimed the doctor, impatiently. "You must be mad. You know you are not in a fit state to go out. Let the wardsman help you to undress."

"No!" said Macquarie. "No. If you won't take my dog in you don't take me. He's got a broken leg and wants fixing up just—

just as much as—as I do. If I'm good enough to come in, he's good enough—and—and better."

He paused a while, breathing painfully, and then went on.

"That—that there old dog of mine has follered me faithful and true, these twelve long hard and hungry years. He's about—about the only thing that ever cared whether I lived or fell and rotted on the cursed track."

He rested again; then he continued: "That—that there dog was pupped on the track," he said, with a sad sort of a smile. "I carried him for months in a billy, and afterwards on my swag when he knocked up. . . . And the old slut—his mother—she'd foller along quite contented—and sniff the billy now and again—just to see if he was all right. . . . She follered me for God knows how many years. She follered me till she was blind—and for a year after. She follered me till she could crawl along through the dust no longer, and—and then I killed her, because I couldn't leave her behind alive!"

He rested again.

"And this here old dog," he continued, touching Tally's upturned nose with his knotted fingers, "this here old dog has follered me for —for ten years; through floods and droughts, through fair times and—and hard—mostly hard; and kept me from going mad when I had no mate nor money on the lonely track; and watched over me for weeks when I was drunk—drugged and poisoned at the cursed shanties; and saved my life more'n once, and got kicks and curses very often for thanks; and forgave me for it all; and—and fought for me. He was the only living thing that stood up for me against that crawling push of curs when they set onter me at the shanty back yonder—and he left his mark on some of 'em too; and—and so did I."

He took another spell.

Then he drew in his breath, shut his teeth hard, shouldered his swag, stepped into the doorway, and faced round again.

The dog limped out of the corner and looked up anxiously.

"That there dog," said Macquarie to the hospital staff in general, "is a better dog than I'm a man—or you too, it seems—and a better Christian. He's been a better mate to me than I ever was to any man—or any man to me. He's watched over me; kep' me from getting robbed many a time; fought for me; saved my life and took drunken kicks and curses for thanks—and forgave me. He's been a true, straight, honest, and faithful mate to me—and I ain't going to desert him now. I ain't going to kick him out in the road with a broken leg. I—Oh, my God! my back!"

He groaned and lurched forward, but they caught him, slipped off the swag and laid him on the bed.

Half an hour later the shearer was comfortably fixed up. "Where's my dog?" he asked, when he came to himself.

"Oh, the dog's all right," said the nurse, rather impatiently. "Don't bother. The doctor's setting his leg out in the yard."

The Geological Spieler

THERE'S nothing so interesting as Geology, even to common and ignorant people, especially when you have a bank or the side of a cutting, studded with fossil fish and things and oysters that were stale when Adam was fresh, to illustrate by.
(*Remark made by Steelman, professional wanderer, to his pal and pupil, Smith.*)

THE first man that Steelman and Smith came up to on the last embankment, where they struck the new railway-line, was a heavy, gloomy, labouring man with bowyangs on and straps round his wrists. Steelman bade him the time of day and had a few words with him over the weather. The man of mullock gave it as his opinion that the fine weather wouldn't last, and seemed to take a gloomy kind of pleasure in that reflection; he said there was more rain down yonder, pointing to the south-east, than the moon could swallow up—the moon was in its first quarter, during which time it is popularly believed in some parts of Maoriland that the south-easter is most likely to be out on the wallaby and the weather bad. Steelman regarded that quarter of the sky with an expression of gentle remonstrance mingled, as it were, with a sort of fatherly indulgence, agreed mildly with the labouring man, and seemed lost for a moment in a reverie from which he roused himself to inquire cautiously after the boss. There was no boss, it was a co-operative party. That chap standing over there by the dray in the end of the cutting was their spokesman—their representative: they called him boss, but that was only his nickname in camp. Steelman expressed his thanks and moved on towards the cutting, followed respectfully by Smith.

Steelman wore a snuff-coloured sac suit, a wide-awake hat, a pair of professional-looking spectacles, and a scientific expression; there was a clerical atmosphere about him, strengthened, however, by an air as of unconscious dignity and superiority, born of intellect and knowledge. He carried a black bag, which was an indispensable article in his profession in more senses than one. Smith was decently dressed in sober tweed and looked like a man of no account who was mechanically devoted to his employer's interests, pleasures, or whims.

The boss was a decent-looking young fellow, with a good face—rather solemn—and a quiet manner.

"Good day, sir," said Steelman.

"Good day, sir," said the boss.

"Nice weather this."

"Yes, it is, but I'm afraid it won't last."

"I am afraid it will not by the look of the sky down there," ventured Steelman.

"No, I go mostly by the look of our weather prophet," said the boss with a quiet smile, indicating the gloomy man.

"I suppose bad weather would put you back in your work?"

"Yes, it will; we didn't want any bad weather just now."

Steelman got the weather question satisfactorily settled; then he said:

"You seem to be getting on with the railway."

"Oh yes, we are about over the worst of it."

"The worst of it?" echoed Steelman, with mild surprise. "I should have thought you were just coming into it," and he pointed to the ridge ahead.

"Oh, our section doesn't go any further than the pole you see sticking up yonder. We had the worst of it back there across the swamps—working up to our waists in water most of the time, in mid-winter too—and at eighteen-pence a yard."

"That was bad."

"Yes, rather rough. Did you come from the terminus?"

"Yes, I sent my baggage on in the brake."

"Commercial traveller, I suppose?" asked the boss, glancing at Smith, who stood a little to the rear of Steelman, seeming interested in the work.

"Oh no," said Steelman, smiling—"I am—well—I'm a geologist; this is my man here," indicating Smith. "You may put down the bag, James, and have a smoke. . . . My name is Stoneleigh—you might have heard it."

The boss said, "Oh," and then presently he added "Indeed," in an undecided tone.

There was a pause—embarrassed on the part of the boss—he was silent not knowing what to say. Meanwhile Steelman studied his man and concluded that he would do.

"Having a look at the country, I suppose?" asked the boss presently.

"Yes," said Steelman; then after a moment's reflection: "I am travelling for my own amusement and improvement, and also in the interests of science, which amounts to the same thing. I am a member of the Royal Geological Society—vice-president in fact of a leading Australian branch;" and then, as if conscious that he had appeared guilty of egotism, he shifted the subject a bit. "Yes. Very interesting country this—very interesting indeed. I should like to make a stay here for a day or so. Your work opens right into my hands. I cannot remember seeing a geological formation which interested me so much. Look at the face of that cutting, for instance. Why! you can almost read the history of the geological world from yesterday—this morning as it were—beginning with the super-surface and going right down through the different layers and stratas—through the vanished ages—right down and back to the pre-historical—to the very primeval or fundamental geological formations!" And Steelman studied the face of the cutting as if he could read it like a book, with every layer or stratum a chapter, and every streak a note of explanation. The boss seemed to be getting interested, and Steelman gained confidence and proceeded to identify and classify the different "stratas and layers", and fix their ages, and describe the conditions and politics of man in their different times, for the boss's benefit.

"Now," continued Steelman, turning slowly from the cutting, removing his glasses, and letting his thoughtful eyes wander casually over the general scenery—"now the first impression that this country would leave on an ordinary intelligent mind—though maybe unconsciously, would be as of a new country—new in a geological sense; with patches of an older geological and vegetable formation cropping out here and there; as for instance that clump of dead trees on that clear alluvial slope there, that outcrop of limestone, or that timber yonder," and he indicated a dead forest which seemed alive and green because of the parasites. "But the country is old—old; perhaps the oldest geological formation in the world is to be seen here, the oldest vegetable formation in Australasia. I am not using the words old and new in an ordinary sense, you understand, but in a geological sense."

The boss said, "I understand," and that geology must be a very interesting study.

Steelman ran his eye meditatively over the cutting again, and turning to Smith said:

"Go up there, James, and fetch me a specimen of that slaty outcrop you see there—just above the coeval strata."

It was a stiff climb and slippery, but Smith had to do it, and he did it.

"This," said Steelman, breaking the rotten piece between his fingers, "belongs probably to an older geological period than its position would indicate—a primitive sandstone level perhaps. Its position on that layer is no doubt due to volcanic upheavals—such disturbances, or rather the results of such disturbances, have been and are the cause of the greatest trouble to geologists—endless errors and controversy. You see, we must study the country, not as it appears now, but as it would appear had the natural geological growth been left to mature undisturbed; we must restore and reconstruct such disorganized portions of the mineral kingdom, if you understand me."

The boss said he understood.

Steelman found an opportunity to wink sharply and severely at Smith, who had been careless enough to allow his features to relapse into a vacant grin.

"It is generally known even amongst the ignorant that rock grows—grows from the outside—but the rock here, a specimen of which I hold in my hand, is now in the process of decomposition; to be plain, it is rotting—in an advanced stage of decomposition—so much so that you are not able to identify it with any geological period or formation, even as you may not be able to identify any other extremely decomposed body."

The boss blinked and knitted his brow, but had the presence of mind to say: "Just so."

"Had the rock on that cutting been healthy—been alive, as it were—you would have had your work cut out; but it is dead and has been for ages perhaps. You find less trouble in working it than you would ordinary clay or sand, or even gravel, which formations together are really rock in embryo—before birth as it were."

The boss's brow cleared.

"The country round here is simply rotting down—simply rotting down."

He removed his spectacles, wiped them, and wiped his face; then his attention seemed to be attracted by some stones at his feet. He picked one up and examined it.

"I shouldn't wonder," he mused, absently, "I shouldn't wonder if there is alluvial gold in some of these creeks and gullies, perhaps tin or even silver, quite probably antimony."

The boss seemed interested.

"Can you tell me if there is any place in this neighbourhood where I could get accommodation for myself and my servant for a day or two?" asked Steelman presently. "I should very much like to break my journey here."

"Well, no," said the boss. "I can't say I do—I don't know of any place nearer than Pahiatua, and that's seven miles from here."

"I know that," said Steelman reflectively, "but I fully expected to have found a house or accommodation of some sort on the way, else I would have gone on in the van."

"Well," said the boss, "if you like to camp with us for tonight, at least, and don't mind roughing it, you'll be welcome, I'm sure."

"If I was sure that I would not be putting you to any trouble, or interfering in any way with your domestic economy——"

"No trouble at all," interrupted the boss. "The boys will be only too glad, and there's an empty whare where you can sleep. Better stay. It's going to be a rough night."

After tea Steelman entertained the boss and a few of the more thoughtful members of the party with short chatty lectures on geology and other subjects.

In the meantime Smith, in another part of the camp, gave selections on a tin whistle, sang a song or two, contributed, in his turn, to the sailor yarns, and ensured his popularity for several nights at least. After several draughts of something that was poured out of a demijohn into a pint-pot, his tongue became loosened, and he expressed an opinion that geology was all bosh, and said if he had half his employer's money he'd be dashed if he would go rooting round in the mud liked a blessed old ant-eater; he also irreverently referred to his learned boss as "Old Rocks over there." He had a pretty easy billet of it though, he said, taking it all round, when the weather was fine; he got a couple of notes a week and all expenses paid, and the money was sure; he was only required to look after the luggage and arrange for accommodation, grub out a chunk of rock now and then, and (what perhaps was the most irksome of his duties) he had to appear interested in old rocks and clay.

Towards midnight Steelman and Smith retired to the unoccupied whare which had been shown them, Smith carrying a bundle of bags, blankets, and rugs, which had been placed at their disposal by their good-natured hosts. Smith lit a candle and proceeded to make the beds. Steelman sat down, removed his specs and scientific expression, placed the glasses carefully on a ledge close at hand, took a book from his bag, and commenced to read. The volume was a cheap copy of Jules Verne's *Journey to the Centre of the Earth.* A little later there was a knock at the door. Steelman hastily resumed the spectacles, together with the scientific expression, took a note-book from his pocket, opened it on the table, and said, "Come in." One of the chaps appeared with a billy of hot coffee, two pint-pots, and some cake. He said he thought you chaps might like a drop of coffee before you turned in, and the boys forgot to ask you to wait for it down in the camp. He also wanted to know whether Mr Stoneleigh and his man would be all right and quite comfortable for the night, and whether they had blankets enough. There was some wood at the back of the whare and they could light a fire if they liked.

Mr Stoneleigh expressed his thanks and his appreciation of the kindness shown him and his servant. He was extremely sorry to give them any trouble.

The navvy, a serious man, who respected genius or intellect in any shape or form, said that it was no trouble at all, the camp was very dull and the boys were always glad to have someone come round. Then, after a brief comparison of opinions concerning the probable duration of the weather which had arrived, they bade each other good night, and the darkness swallowed the serious man.

Steelman turned into the top bunk on one side and Smith took the lower on the other. Steelman had the candle by his bunk, as usual; he lit his pipe for a final puff before going to sleep, and held the light up for a moment so as to give Smith the full benefit of a solemn, uncompromising wink. The wink was silently applauded and dutifully returned by Smith. Then Steelman blew out the light, lay back, and puffed at his pipe for a while. Presently he chuckled, and the chuckle was echoed by Smith; by and by Steelman chuckled once more, and then Smith chuckled again. There was silence in the darkness, and after a bit Smith chuckled twice. Then Steelman said:

"For God's sake give her a rest, Smith, and give a man a show to get some sleep."

Then the silence in the darkness remained unbroken.

The invitation was extended next day, and Steelman sent Smith on to see that his baggage was safe. Smith stayed out of sight for two or three hours, and then returned and reported all well.

They stayed on for several days. After breakfast and when the men were going to work Steelman and Smith would go out along the line with the black bag and poke round amongst the "layers and stratas" in sight of the works for a while, as an evidence of good faith; then they'd drift off casually into the bush, camp in a retired and sheltered spot, and light a fire when the weather was cold, and Steelman would lie on the grass and read and smoke and lay plans for the future and improve Smith's mind until they reckoned it was about dinner-time. And in the evening they would come home with the black bag full of stones and bits of rock, and Steelman would lecture on those minerals after tea.

On about the fourth morning Steelman had a yarn with one of the men going to work. He was a lanky young fellow with a sandy complexion, and seemingly harmless grin. In Australia he might have been regarded as a "cove" rather than a "chap", but there was nothing of the "bloke" about him. Presently the cove said:

"What do you think of the boss, Mr Stoneleigh? He seems to have taken a great fancy for you, and he's fair gone on geology."

"I think he is a very decent fellow indeed, a very intelligent young man. He seems very well read and well informed."

"You wouldn't think he was a University man," said the cove.

"No, indeed! Is he?"

"Yes. I thought you knew!"

Steelman knitted his brows. He seemed slightly disturbed for the moment. He walked on a few paces in silence and thought hard.

"What might have been his special line?" he asked the cove.

"Why, something the same as yours. I thought you knew. He was reckoned the best—what do you call it?—the best minrologist in the country. He had a first-class billet in the Mines Department, but he lost it—you know—the booze."

"I think we will be making a move, Smith," said Steelman, later on, when they were private. "There's a little too much intellect in this camp to suit me. But we haven't done so bad, anyway. We've had three days' good board and lodging with entertainments and refreshments thrown in." Then he said to himself: "We'll stay for another day anyway. If those beggars are having a lark with us, we're getting the worth of it anyway, and I'm not thin-skinned.

They're the mugs and not us, anyhow it goes, and I can take them down before I leave."

But on the way home he had a talk with another man whom we might set down as a "chap".

"I wouldn't have thought the boss was a college man," said Steelman to the chap.

"A what?"

"A University man—University education."

"Why! Who's been telling you that?"

"One of your mates."

"Oh, he's been getting at you. Why, it's all the boss can do to write his own name. Now that lanky sandy cove with the birth-mark grin—it's him that's had the college education."

"I think we'll make a start tomorrow," said Steelman to Smith in the privacy of their whare. "There's too much humour and levity in this camp to suit a serious scientific gentleman like myself."

His Country—After All

THE Blenheim coach was descending into the valley of the Avetere River—pronounced Aveterry—from the saddle of Taylor's Pass. Across the river to the right, the grey slopes and flats stretched away to the distant sea from a range of tussock hills. There was no native bush there; but there were several groves of imported timber standing wide apart—sentinel-like—seeming lonely and striking in their isolation.

"Grand country, New Zealand, eh?" said a stout man with a brown face, grey beard, and grey eyes, who sat between the driver and another passenger on the box.

"You don't call this grand country!" exclaimed the other passenger, who claimed to be, and looked like, a commercial traveller, and might have been a professional spieler—quite possibly both. "Why it's about the poorest country in New Zealand! You ought to see some of the country in the North Island—Wairarapa and Napier districts, round about Pahiatua. I call this damn poor country."

"Well, I reckon you wouldn't if you'd ever been in Australia—back in New South Wales. The people here don't seem to know what a grand country they've got. You say this is the worst, eh? Well, this would make an Australian cockatoo's mouth water—the worst of New Zealand would."

"I always thought Australia was all good country," mused the driver—a flax-stick. "I always thought——"

"Good country!" exclaimed the man with the grey beard, in a tone of disgust. "Why, it's only a mongrel desert, except some bits round the coast. The worst dried-up and God-forsaken country I was ever in."

There was a silence, thoughtful on the driver's part, and aggressive on that of the stranger.

"I always thought," said the driver, reflectively, after the pause—"I always thought Australia was a good country," and he placed his foot on the brake.

They let him think. The coach descended the natural terraces above the river bank, and pulled up at the pub.

"So you're a native of Australia?" said the bagman to the grey-beard, as the coach went on again.

"Well, I suppose I am. Anyway, I was born there. That's the main thing I've got against the darned country."

"How long did you stay there?"

"Till I got away," said the stranger. Then, after a think, he added, "I went away first when I was thirty-five—went to the islands. I swore I'd never go back to Australia again; but I did. I thought I had a kind of affection for old Sydney. I knocked about the blasted country for five or six years, and then I cleared out to Frisco. I swore I'd never go back again, and I never will."

"But surely you'll take a run over and have a look at old Sydney and those places, before you go back to America, after getting so near?"

"What the blazes do I want to have a look at the blamed country for?" snapped the stranger, who had refreshed considerably. "I've got nothing to thank Australia for—except getting out of it. It's the best country to get out of that I was ever in."

"Oh, well, I only thought you might have had some friends over there," interposed the traveller in an injured tone.

"Friends! That's another reason. I wouldn't go back there for all the friends and relations since Adam. I had more than quite enough of it while I was there. The worst and hardest years of my life were spent in Australia. I might have starved there, and did do it half my time. I worked harder and got less in my own country in five years than I ever did in any other in fifteen"—he was getting mixed—"and I've been in a few since then. No, Australia is the worst country that ever the Lord had the sense to forget. I mean to stick to the country that stuck to me, when I was starved out of my own dear native land—and that country is the United States of America. What's Australia? A big, thirsty, hungry wilderness, with one or two cities for the convenience of foreign speculators, and a few collections of humpies, called towns—also for the convenience of foreign speculators; and populated mostly by mongrel sheep, and partly by fools, who live like European slaves in the town, and like dingoes in the bush—who drivel about 'democracy', and yet haven't any more spunk than to graft for a few Cockney dudes that razzle-dazzle most of the time in Paris. Why, the Australians haven't even got the grit to claim enough of their own money to throw a few dams across their watercourses, and so make some of the interior fit to live in. America's bad enough, but it was never so small as that. . . . Bah! The curse of Australia is sheep, and the Australian war-cry is Baa!"

"Well, you're the first man I ever heard talk as you've been doing about his own country," said the bagman, getting tired and impatient of being sat on all the time. " 'Lives there a man with a soul so dead, who never said—to—to himself' . . . I forget the darned thing."

He tried to remember it. The man whose soul was dead cleared his throat for action, and the driver—for whom the bagman had shouted twice as against the stranger's once—took the opportunity to observe that he always thought a man ought to stick up for his own country.

The stranger ignored him and opened fire on the bagman. He proceeded to prove that that was all rot—that patriotism was the greatest curse on earth; that it had been the cause of all war; that it was the false, ignorant sentiment which moved men to slave, starve, and fight for the comfort of their sluggish masters; that it was the enemy of universal brotherhood, the mother of hatred, murder, and slavery, and that the world would never be any better until the deadly poison, called the sentiment of patriotism, had been "educated" out of the stomachs of the people. "Patriotism!" he exclaimed scornfully. "My country! The darned fools; the country never belonged to them, but to the speculators, the absentees, land-boomers, swindlers, gangs of thieves—the men the patriotic fools starve and fight for—their masters. Ba-a!"

The opposition collapsed.

The coach had climbed the terraces on the south side of the river, and was bowling along on a level stretch of road across the elevated flat.

"What trees are those?" asked the stranger, breaking the aggressive silence which followed his unpatriotic argument, and pointing to a grove ahead by the roadside. "They look as if they've been planted there. There ain't been a forest here surely?"

"Oh, they're some trees the Government imported," said the bagman, whose knowledge on the subject was limited. "Our own bush won't grow in this soil."

"But it looks as if anything else would——"

Here the stranger sniffed once by accident, and then several times with interest. It was a warm morning after rain. He fixed his eyes on those trees.

They didn't look like Australian gums; they tapered to the tops, the branches were pretty regular, and the boughs hung in shipshape fashion. There was not the Australian heat to twist the branches and turn the leaves.

"Why!" exclaimed the stranger, still staring and sniffing hard. "Why, dang me if they ain't (sniff) Australian gums!"

"Yes," said the driver, flicking his horses, "they are."

"Blanky (sniff) blanky old Australian gums!" exclaimed the ex-Australian, with strange enthusiasm.

"They're not old," said the driver; "they're only young trees. But they say they don't grow like that in Australia—'count of the difference in the climate. I always thought——"

But the other did not appear to hear him; he kept staring hard at the trees they were passing. They had been planted in rows and cross-rows, and were coming on grandly.

There was a rabbit-trapper's camp amongst those trees; he had made a fire to boil his billy with gum-leaves and twigs, and it was the scent of that fire which interested the exile's nose, and brought a wave of memories with it.

"Good day, mate!" he shouted suddenly to the rabbit-trapper, and to the astonishment of his fellow-passengers.

"Good day, mate!" The answer came back like an echo—it seemed to him—from the past.

Presently he caught sight of a few trees which had evidently been planted before the others—as an experiment, perhaps—and, somehow, one of them had grown after its own erratic native fashion—gnarled and twisted and ragged, and could not be mistaken for anything else but an Australian gum.

"A thunderin' old blue-gum!" ejaculated the traveller, regarding the tree with great interest.

He screwed his neck to get a last glimpse, and then sat silently smoking and gazing straight ahead, as if the past lay before him—and it *was* before him.

"Ah, well!" he said, in explanation of a long meditative silence on his part; "ah, well—them saplings—the smell of them gum-leaves set me thinking." And he thought some more.

"Well, for my part," said a tourist in the coach, presently, in a condescending tone, "I can't see much in Australia. The bally colonies are——"

"Oh, that be damned!" snarled the Australian-born—they had finished the second flask of whisky. "What do you Britishers know about Australia? She's as good as England, anyway."

"Well, I suppose you'll go straight back to the States as soon as you've done your business in Christchurch," said the bagman, when near their journey's end they had become confidential.

"Well, I dunno. I reckon I'll just take a run over to Australia first. There's an old mate of mine in business in Sydney, and I'd like to have a yarn with him."

Bill, the Ventriloquial Rooster

"WHEN we were up-country on the selection we had a rooster at our place named Bill," said Mitchell; "a big mongrel of no particular breed, though the old lady said he was a 'brammer'—and many an argument she had with the old man about it too; she was just as stubborn and obstinate in her opinion as the governor was in his. But, anyway, we called him Bill, and didn't take any particular notice of him till a cousin of some of us came from Sydney on a visit to the country, and stayed at our place because it was cheaper than stopping at a pub. Well, somehow this chap got interested in Bill, and studied him for two or three days, and at last he says:

" 'Why, that rooster's a ventriloquist!'

" 'A what?'

" 'A ventriloquist!'

" 'Go along with yer!

" 'But he is. I've heard of cases like this before; but this is the first I've come across. Bill's a ventriloquist right enough.'

"Then we remembered that there wasn't another rooster within five miles—our only neighbour, an Irishman named Page, didn't have one at the time—and we'd often heard another cock crow, but didn't think to take any notice of it. We watched Bill, and sure enough he *was* a ventriloquist. The 'ka-cocka' would come all right, but the 'co-ka-koo-oi-oo' seemed to come from a distance. And sometimes the whole crow would go wrong, and come back like an echo that had been lost for a year. Bill would stand on tiptoe, and hold his elbows out, and curve his neck, and go two or three times as if he was swallowing nest-eggs, and nearly break his neck and burst his gizzard; and then there'd be no sound at all where he was—only a cock crowing in the distance.

"And pretty soon we could see that Bill was in great trouble about it himself. You see, he didn't know it was himself—thought it was another rooster challenging him, and he wanted badly to find that other bird. He would get up on the woodheap, and crow and listen—crow and listen again—crow and listen, and then he'd go up to the top of the paddock, and get up on the stack, and crow and listen there. Then down to the other end of the paddock, and get up on the mullock-heap, and crow and listen there. Then across to the other side and up on a log among the saplings, and crow 'n' listen some more. He searched all over the place for that other rooster, but of course couldn't find him. Sometimes he'd be out all day crowing and listening all over the country, and then come home dead tired, and rest and cool off in a hole that the hens had scratched for him in a damp place under the water-cask sledge.

"Well, one day Page brought home a big white rooster, and when he let it go it climbed up on Page's stack and crowed, to see if there was any more roosters round there. Bill had come home tired; it was a hot day, and he'd rooted out the hens, and was having a spell-oh under the cask when the white rooster crowed. Bill didn't lose any time getting out and on to the woodheap, and then he waited till he heard the crow again; then he crowed, and the other rooster crowed again, and they crowed at each other for three days, and called each other all the wretches they could lay their tongues to, and after that they implored each other to come out and be made into chicken soup and feather pillows. But neither'd come. You see, there were *three* crows—there was Bill's crow, and the ventriloquist crow, and the white rooster's crow—and each rooster thought that there was *two* roosters in the opposition camp, and that he mightn't get fair play, and, consequently, both were afraid to put up their hands.

"But at last Bill couldn't stand it any longer. He made up his mind to go and have it out, even if there was a whole agricultural show of prize and honourable-mention fighting-cocks in Page's yard. He got down from the woodheap and started off across the ploughed field, his head down, his elbows out, and his thick awkward legs prodding away at the furrows behind for all they were worth.

"I wanted to go down badly and see the fight, and barrack for Bill. But I daren't, because I'd been coming up the road late the night before with my brother Joe, and there was about three panels of turkeys roosting along on the top rail of Page's front fence; and we brushed 'em with a bough, and they got up such a blessed gobbling fuss about it that Page came out in his shirt and saw us running away; and I knew he was laying for us with a bullock-whip. Besides, there was friction between the two families on account of a thoroughbred bull that Page borrowed and wouldn't lend to us, and that got into our paddock on account of me mending a panel in the party fence, and carelessly leaving the top rail down after sundown while our cows was moving round there in the saplings.

"So there was too much friction for me to go down, but I climbed a tree as near the fence as I could and watched. Bill reckoned he'd found that rooster at last. The white rooster wouldn't come down from the stack, so Bill went up to him, and they fought there till they tumbled down the other side, and I couldn't see any more. Wasn't I wild? I'd have given my dog to have seen the rest of the fight. I went down to the far side of Page's fence and climbed a tree there, but of course I couldn't see anything, so I came home the back way. Just as I got home Page came round to the front and sung out, 'Insoid there!' And me and Jim went under the house like snakes and looked out round a pile. But Page was all right—he had a broad grin on his face, and Bill safe under his arm. He put Bill down on the ground very carefully, and says he to the old folks:

" 'Yer rooster knocked the stuffin' out of my rooster, but I bear no malice. 'Twas a grand foight.'

"And then the old man and Page had a yarn, and got pretty friendly after that. And Bill didn't seem to bother about any more ventriloquism; but the white rooster spent a lot of time looking for that other rooster. Perhaps he thought he'd have better luck with him. But Page was on the look-out all the time to get a rooster that would lick ours. He did nothing else for a month but ride round and inquire about roosters; and at last he borrowed a game-bird in town, left five pounds deposit on him, and brought him home. And Page and the old man agreed to have a match—about the only thing they'd agreed about for five years. And they fixed it up for a Sunday when the old lady and the girls and kids were going on a visit to some relations, about fifteen miles away—to stop all night. The guv'nor made me go with them on horseback; but I knew what was up, and so my pony went lame about a mile along the road, and I had to come back and turn him out in the top paddock, and hide the saddle and bridle in a hollow log, and sneak home and climb up on the roof of the shed. It was an awful hot day, and I had to keep climbing backward and forward over the ridge-pole all the morning to keep out of sight of the old man, for he was moving about a good deal.

"Well, after dinner, the fellows from round about began to ride in and hang up their horses round the place till it looked as if there was going to be a funeral. Some of the chaps saw me, of course, but I tipped them the wink, and they gave me the office whenever the old man happened around.

"Well, Page came along with his game-rooster. Its name was Jim. It wasn't much to look at, and it seemed a good deal smaller and weaker than Bill. Some of the chaps were disgusted, and said it wasn't a game-rooster at all; Bill'd settle it in one lick, and they wouldn't have any fun.

"Well, they brought the game one out and put him down near the woodheap, and routed Bill out from under his cask. He got interested at once. He looked at Jim, and got up on the woodheap and crowed and looked at Jim again. He reckoned *this* at last was the fowl that had been humbugging him all along. Presently his trouble caught him, and then he'd crow and take a squint at the game 'un, and crow again, and have another squint at gamey, and try to crow and keep his eye on the game-rooster at the same time. But Jim never committed himself, until at last he appeared to gape just after Bill's whole crow went wrong, and Bill spotted him. He reckoned he'd caught him this time, and he got down off that woodheap and went for the foe. But Jim ran away—and Bill ran after him.

"Round and round the woodheap they went, and round the shed, and round the house and under it, and back again, and round the woodheap and over it and round the other way, and kept it up for close on an hour. Bill's bill was just within an inch or so of the game-rooster's tail feathers most of the time, but he couldn't get any nearer, do how he liked. And all the time the fellers kept chyackin' Page and singing out, 'What price yer game 'un, Page! Go it, Bill! Go it, old cock!' and all that sort of thing. Well, the game-rooster went as if it was a go-as-you-please, and he didn't care if it lasted a year. He didn't seem to take any interest in the business, but Bill got excited, and by and by he got mad. He held his head lower and lower and his wings further and further out from his sides, and prodded away harder and harder at the ground behind, but it wasn't any use. Jim seemed to keep ahead without trying. They stuck to the woodheap towards the last. They went round first one way for a while, and then the other for a change, and now and then they'd go over the top to break the monotony; and the chaps got more interested in the race than they would have been in the fight—and bet on it, too. But Bill was handicapped with his weight. He was done up at last; he slowed down till he couldn't waddle, and then, when he was thoroughly knocked up, that game-rooster turned on him, and gave him the father of a hiding.

"And my father caught me when I'd got down in the excitement, and wasn't thinking, and *he* gave *me* the stepfather of a hiding. But he had a lively time with the old lady afterwards, over the cock-fight.

"Bill was so disgusted with himself that he went under the cask and died."

A Bush Dance

"TAP, tap, tap, tap."

The little school-house and residence in the scrub was lighted brightly in the midst of the close, solid blackness of that moonless December night, when the sky and stars were smothered and suffocated by drought haze.

It was the evening of the school children's "feast". That is to say that the children had been sent, and "let go", and the younger ones "fetched" through the blazing heat to the school, one day early in the holidays, and raced—sometimes in couples tied together by the legs, and caked, and bunned, and finally improved upon by the local Chadband, and got rid of. The schoolroom had been cleared for dancing, the maps rolled and tied, the desks and blackboards stacked against the wall outside. Tea was over, and the trestles and boards, whereon had been spread better things than had been provided for the unfortunate youngsters, had been taken outside to keep the desks and blackboards company.

On stools running end to end along one side of the room sat about twenty more or less blooming country girls of from fifteen to twenty-odd.

On the rest of the stools, running end to end along the other wall, sat about twenty more or less blooming chaps.

It was evident that something was seriously wrong. None of the girls spoke above a hushed whisper. None of the men spoke above a hushed oath. Now and again two or three sidled out, and if you had followed them you would have found that they went outside to listen hard into the darkness and to swear.

"Tap, tap, tap."

The rows moved uneasily, and some of the girls turned pale faces nervously towards the side door, in the direction of the sound.

"Tap—tap."

The tapping came from the kitchen at the rear of the teacher's residence, and was uncomfortably suggestive of a coffin being made: it was also accompanied by a sickly, indescribable odour—more like that of warm cheap glue than anything else.

In the schoolroom was a painful scene of strained listening. Whenever one of the men returned from outside, or put his head in at the door, all eyes were fastened on him in the flash of a single eye, and then withdrawn hopelessly. At the sound of a horse's step all eyes and ears were on the door, till someone muttered, "It's only the horses in the paddock."

Some of the girls' eyes began to glisten suspiciously, and at last the belle of the party—a great, dark-haired, pink-and-white Blue Mountains girl, who had been sitting for a full minute staring before her, with blue eyes unnaturally bright, suddenly covered her face with her hands, rose and started blindly from the room, from which she was steered in a hurry by two sympathetic and rather upset girl friends, and as she passed out she was heard sobbing hysterically:

"Oh, I can't help it! I did want to dance! It's a sh-shame! I can't help it! I—I want to dance! I rode twenty miles to dance—and—and I want to dance!"

A tall, strapping young bushman rose, without disguise, and followed the girl out. The rest began to talk loudly of stock, dogs, and horses, and other bush things; but above their voices rang out that of the girl from the outside—being man comforted:

"I can't help it, Jack! I did want to dance! I—I had such—such—a job—to get mother—and—father to let me come—and—and now!"

The two girl friends came back. "He sez to leave her to him," they whispered, in reply to an interrogatory glance from the schoolmistress.

"It's—it's no use, Jack!" came the voice of grief. "You don't know what—what father and mother—is. I—I won't—be able to ge-get away—again—for—for—not till I'm married, perhaps."

The schoolmistress glanced uneasily along the row of girls. "I'll take her into my room and make her lie down," she whispered to her sister, who was staying with her. "She'll start some of the other girls presently—it's just the weather for it," and she passed out quietly. That schoolmistress was a woman of penetration.

A final "tap-tap" from the kitchen; then a sound like the squawk of a hurt or frightened child, and the faces in the room turned quickly in that direction and brightened. But there came a bang and a sound like "damn" and hopelessness settled down.

A shout from the outer darkness, and most of the men and some of the girls rose and hurried out. Fragments of conversation heard in the darkness:

"It's two horses, I tell you!"

"It's three, you——!"

"Lay you——!"

"Put the stuff up!"

A clack of gate thrown open.

"Who is it, Tom?"

Voices from gatewards, yelling, "Johnny Mears! They've got Johnny Mears!"

Then rose yells, and a cheer such as is seldom heard in scrublands.

Out in the kitchen long Dave Regan grabbed, from the far side of the table, where he had thrown it, a burst and battered concertina, which he had been for the last hour vainly trying to patch and make airtight; and, holding it out towards the back door, between his palms, as a football is held, he let it drop, and fetched it neatly on the toe of his riding-boot. It was a beautiful kick, the concertina shot out into the blackness, from which was projected, in return, first a short, sudden howl, then a face with one eye glaring and the other covered by an enormous brick-coloured hand, and a voice that wanted to know "Who shot that lurid loaf of bread?"

But from the schoolroom was heard the loud, free voice of Joe Matthews, M.C.:

"Take yer partners! Hurry up! Take yer partners! They've got Johnny Mears with his fiddle!"

Telling Mrs Baker

Most bushmen who hadn't "known Bob Baker to speak to", had "heard tell of him". He'd been a squatter, not many years before, on the Macquarie River in New South Wales, and had made money in the good seasons, and had gone in for horse-racing and racehorse-breeding, and long trips to Sydney, where he put up at swell hotels and went the pace. So after a pretty severe drought, when the sheep died by thousands on his runs, Bob Baker went under, and the bank took over his station and put a manager in charge.

He'd been a jolly, open-handed, popular man, which means that he'd been a selfish man as far as his wife and children were concerned, for they had to suffer for it in the end. Such generosity is often born of vanity, or moral cowardice, or both mixed. It's very nice to hear the chaps sing "For he's a jolly good fellow," but you've mostly got to pay for it twice—first in company, and afterwards alone. I once heard the chaps singing that I was a jolly good fellow, when I was leaving a place and they were giving me a send-off. It thrilled me, and brought a warm gush to my eyes; but, all the same, I wished I had half the money I'd lent them, and spent on 'em, and I wished I'd used the time I'd wasted to be a jolly good fellow.

When I first met Bob Baker he was a boss drover on the great north-western route, and his wife lived at the township of Solong on the Sydney side. He was going north to new country round by the Gulf of Carpentaria with a big mob of cattle, on a two years' trip; and I and my mate, Andy M'Culloch, engaged to go with him. We wanted to have a look at the Gulf Country.

After we had crossed the Queensland border it seemed to me that the boss was too fond of going into wayside shanties and town pubs. Andy had been with him on another trip, and he told me that the boss was only going this way lately. Andy knew Mrs Baker well, and seemed to think a deal of her. "She's a good little woman," said Andy. "One of the right stuff. I worked on their station for a while when I was a nipper, and I know. She was always a damned sight too good for the boss, but she believed in him. When I was coming away this time she says to me, 'Look here, Andy, I am afraid Robert is drinking again. Now I want you to look after him for me, as much as you can—you seem to have as much influence with him as anyone. I want you to promise me that you'll never have a drink with him.'

"And I promised," said Andy, "and I'll keep my word." Andy was a chap who could keep his word, and nothing else. And, no matter how the boss persuaded, or sneered, or swore at him, Andy would never drink with him.

It got worse and worse: the boss would ride on ahead and get drunk at a shanty, and sometimes he'd be days behind us; and when he'd catch up to us his temper would be just about as much as we could stand. At last he went on a howling spree at Mulgatown, about a hundred and fifty miles north of the border, and, what was worse, he got in tow with a flash barmaid there—one of those girls who are engaged, by the publicans up-country, as baits for cheque-men.

He went mad over that girl. He drew an advance cheque from the stock-owner's agent there, and knocked that down; then he raised some more money somehow, and spent that—mostly on the girl.

We did all we could. Andy got him along the track for a couple of stages, and just when we thought he was all right, he slipped us in the night and went back.

We had two other men with us, but had the devil's own bother on account of the cattle. It was a mixed-up job all round. You see, it was all big runs round there, and we had to keep the bullocks moving along the route all the time, or else get into trouble for trespass. The agent wasn't going to go to the expense of putting the cattle in a paddock until the boss sobered up; there was very little grass on the route or the travelling-stock reserves or camps, so we had to keep travelling for grass.

The world might wobble and all the banks go bung, but the cattle have to go through—that's the law of the stock-routes. So the agent wired to the owners, and, when he got their reply, he sacked the boss and sent the cattle on in charge of another man. The new boss was a drover coming south after a trip; he had his two brothers with him, so he didn't want me and Andy; but, anyway, we were full up of this trip, so we arranged, between the agent and the new boss, to get most of the wages due to us—the boss had drawn some of our stuff and spent it.

We could have started on the back track at once, but, drunk or sober, mad or sane, good or bad, it isn't bush religion to desert a mate in a hole; and the boss was a mate of ours; so we stuck to him. We camped on the creek outside the town, and kept him in the camp with us as much as possible, and did all we could for him.

"How could I face his wife if I went home without him?" asked Andy. "Or any of his old mates?"

The boss got himself turned out of the pub where the barmaid was, and then he'd hang round the other pubs, and get drink somehow, and fight, and get knocked about. He was an awful object by this time, wild-eyed and gaunt, and he hadn't washed or shaved for days.

Andy got the constable in charge of the police station to lock him up for a night, but it only made him worse: we took him back to the camp next morning, and while our eyes were off him for a few minutes he slipped away into the scrub, stripped himself naked, and started to hang himself to a leaning tree with a piece of clothes-line rope. We got to him just in time.

Then Andy wired to the boss's brother Ned, who was fighting the drought, the rabbit pest, and the banks, on a small station back on the border. Andy reckoned it was about time to do something.

Perhaps the boss hadn't been quite right in his head before he started drinking—he had acted queer sometimes, now we came to think of it; maybe he'd got a touch of sunstroke or got brooding over his troubles—anyway he died in the horrors within the week.

His brother Ned turned up on the last day, and Bob thought he was the devil, and grappled with him. It took the three of us to hold the boss down sometimes.

Sometimes, towards the end, he'd be sensible for a few minutes and talk about his "poor wife and children"; and immediately afterwards he'd fall a-cursing me, and Andy, and Ned, and calling us devils. He cursed everything; he cursed his wife and children, and yelled that they were dragging him down to hell. He died raving mad. It was the worst case of death in the horrors of drink that I ever saw or heard of in the bush.

Ned saw to the funeral: it was very hot weather, and men have to be buried quick who die out there in the hot weather—especially men who die in the state the boss was in. Then Ned went to the public-house where the barmaid was and called the landlord out. It was a desperate fight: the publican was a big man, and a bit of a fighting man; but Ned was one of those quiet, simple-minded chaps who will carry a thing through to death when they make up their minds. He gave that publican nearly as good a thrashing as he deserved. The constable in charge of the station backed Ned, while another policeman picked up the publican. Sounds queer to you city people, doesn't it?

Next morning we three started south. We stayed a couple of days at Ned Baker's station on the border, and then started on our three-hundred-mile ride down-country. The weather was still very hot, so we decided to travel at night for a while, and left Ned's place at dusk. He parted from us at the homestead gate. He gave Andy a small packet, done up in canvas, for Mrs Baker, which Andy told me contained Bob's pocket-book, letters, and papers. We looked back, after we'd gone a piece along the dusty road, and saw Ned still standing by the gate; and a very lonely figure he looked. Ned was a bachelor. "Poor old Ned," said Andy to me. "He was in love with Mrs Bob Baker before she got married, but she picked the wrong man—girls mostly do. Ned and Bob were together on the Macquarie, but Ned left when his brother married, and he's been up in these God-forsaken scrubs ever since. Look, I want to tell you something, Jack: Ned has written to Mrs Bob to tell her that Bob died of fever, and everything was done for him that could be done, and that he died easy—and all that sort of thing. Ned sent her some money, and she is to think it was the money due to Bob when he died. Now I'll have to go and see her when we get to Solong; there's no getting out of it, I'll have to face her—and you'll have to come with me."

"Damned if I will!" I said.

"But you'll have to," said Andy. "You'll have to stick to me; you're surely not crawler enough to desert a mate in a case like this? I'll have to lie like hell—I'll have to lie as I never lied to a woman before; and you'll have to back me and corroborate every lie."

I'd never seen Andy show so much emotion.

"There's plenty of time to fix up a good yarn," said Andy. He said no more about Mrs Baker, and we only mentioned the boss's name casually, until we were within about a day's ride of Solong; then Andy told me the yarn he'd made up about the boss's death.

"And I want you to listen, Jack," he said, "and remember every word—and if you can fix up a better yarn you can tell me afterwards. Now, it was like this: the boss wasn't too well when he crossed the border. He complained of pains in his back and head and a stinging pain in the back of his neck, and he had dysentery bad—but that doesn't matter; it's lucky I ain't supposed to tell a woman all the symptoms. The boss stuck to the job as long as he could, but we managed the cattle and made it as easy as we could for him. He'd just take it easy, and ride on from camp to camp, and rest. One night I rode to a town off the route (or you did, if you like) and got some medicine for him; that made him better for a while, but at last, a day or two this side of Mulgatown, he had to give up. A squatter there drove him into town in his buggy and put him up at the best hotel. The publican knew the boss and did all he could for him—put him in the best room and wired for another doctor. We wired for Ned as soon as we saw how bad the boss was, and Ned rode night and day and got there three days before the boss died. The boss was a bit off his head some of the time with the fever, but was calm and quiet towards the end and died easy. He talked a lot about his wife and children, and told us to tell the wife not to fret but to cheer up for the children's sake. How does that sound?"

I'd been thinking while I listened, and an idea struck me.

"Why not let her know the truth?" I asked. "She's sure to hear of it sooner or later; and if she knew he was only a selfish, drunken blackguard she might get over it all the sooner."

"You don't know women, Jack," said Andy quietly. "And, anyway, even if she is a sensible woman, we've got a dead mate to consider as well as a living woman."

"But she's sure to hear the truth sooner or later," I said. "The boss was so well known."

"And that's just the reason why the truth might be kept from her," said Andy. "If he wasn't well known—and nobody could help liking him, after all, when he was straight—if he wasn't so well known the truth might leak out unawares. She won't know if I can help it, or at least not yet a while. If I see any chaps that come from the north, I'll put them up to it. I'll tell M'Grath, the publican at Solong, too: he's a straight man—he'll keep his ears open and warn chaps. One of Mrs Baker's sisters is staying with her, and I'll give her a hint so that she can warn off any women that might get hold of a yarn. Besides, Mrs Baker is sure to go and live in Sydney, where all her people are—she was a Sydney girl; and she's not likely to meet anyone there that will tell her the truth. I can tell her that it was the last wish of the boss that she should shift to Sydney."

We smoked and thought a while, and by and by Andy had what he called a "happy thought". He went to his saddle-bags and got out the small canvas packet that Ned had given him: it was sewn up with packing-thread, and Andy ripped it open with his pocket-knife.

"What are you doing, Andy?" I asked.

"Ned's an innocent old fool, as far as sin is concerned," said Andy. "I guess he hasn't looked through the boss's letters, and I'm just going to see that there's nothing here that will make liars of us."

He looked through the letters and papers by the light of the fire. There were some letters from Mrs Baker to her husband, also a portrait of her and the children; these Andy put aside. But there were other letters from barmaids and women who were not fit to be seen in the same street with the boss's wife; and there were portraits—one or two flash ones. There were two letters from other men's wives too.

"And one of those men, at least, was an old mate of his!" said Andy, in a tone of disgust.

He threw the lot into the fire; then he went through the boss's pocket-book and tore out some leaves that had notes and addresses on them, and burnt them too. Then he sewed up the packet again and put it away in his saddle-bag.

"Such is life!" said Andy, with a yawn that might have been half a sigh.

We rode into Solong early in the day, turned our horses out in a paddock, and put up at M'Grath's pub until such time as we made up our minds as to what we'd do or where we'd go. We had an idea of waiting until the shearing-season started and then making outback to the big sheds.

Neither of us was in a hurry to go and face Mrs Baker. "We'll go after dinner," said Andy at first; then after dinner we had a drink, and felt sleepy—we weren't used to big dinners of roast-beef and vegetables and pudding, and, besides, it was drowsy weather—so we decided to have a snooze and then go. When we woke up it was late in the afternoon, so we thought we'd put it off until after tea.

"It wouldn't be manners to walk in while they're at tea," said Andy—"it would look as if we only came for some grub."

But while we were at tea a little girl came with a message that Mrs Baker wanted to see us, and would be very much obliged if we'd call up as soon as possible. You see, in those small towns you can't move without the thing getting round inside of half an hour.

"We'll have to face the music now!" said Andy, "and not get out of it." He seemed to hang back more than I did. There was another pub opposite where Mrs Baker lived, and when we got up the street a bit I said to Andy:

"Suppose we go and have another drink first, Andy? We might be kept in there an hour or two."

"You don't want another drink," said Andy rather short. "Why, you seem to be going the same way as the boss!" But it was Andy who edged off towards the pub when we got near Mrs Baker's place. "All right!" he said. "Come on! We'll have this other drink, since you want it so bad."

We had the drink, then we buttoned up our coats and started across the road—we'd bought new shirts and collars, and spruced up a bit. Half-way across Andy grabbed my arm and asked:

"How do you feel now, Jack?"

"Oh, *I'm* all right," I said.

"For God's sake," said Andy, "don't put your foot in it and make a mess of it."

"I won't, if you don't."

Mrs Baker's cottage was a little weatherboard box affair back in a garden. When we went in through the gate Andy gripped my arm again and whispered:

"For God's sake, stick to me now, Jack!"

"I'll stick all right," I said—"you've been having too much beer, Andy."

I had seen Mrs Baker before, and remembered her as a cheerful, contented sort of woman, bustling about the house and getting the boss's shirts and things ready when we started north. Just the sort of woman that is contented with housework and the children, and with nothing particular about her in the way of brains. But now she sat by the fire looking like the ghost of herself. I wouldn't have recognized her at first. I never saw such a change in a woman, and it came like a shock to me.

Her sister let us in, and after a first glance at Mrs Baker I had eyes for the sister and no one else. She was a Sydney girl, about twenty-four or twenty-five, and fresh and fair—not like the sun-browned women we were used to see. She was a pretty, bright-eyed girl, and seemed quick to understand, and very sympathetic. She had been educated, Andy had told me, and wrote stories for the Sydney *Bulletin* and other Sydney papers. She had her hair done and was dressed in the city style, and that took us back a bit at first.

"It's very good of you to come," said Mrs Baker in a weak, weary voice, when we first went in. "I heard you were in town."

"We were just coming when we got your message," said Andy. "We'd have come before, only we had to see to the horses."

"It's very kind of you, I'm sure," said Mrs Baker.

They wanted us to have tea, but we said we'd just had it. Then Miss Standish (the sister) wanted us to have tea and cake; but we didn't feel as if we could handle cups and saucers and pieces of cake successfully just then.

There was something the matter with one of the children in a back room, and the sister went to see to it. Mrs Baker cried a little quietly.

"You mustn't mind me," she said. "I'll be all right presently, and then I want you to tell me all about poor Bob. It's seeing you, that saw the last of him, that set me off."

Andy and I sat stiff and straight, on two chairs against the wall, and held our hats tight, and stared at a picture of Wellington meeting Blücher on the opposite wall. I thought it was lucky that that picture was there.

The child was calling "Mumma," and Mrs Baker went in to it, and her sister came out. "Best tell her all about it and get it over," she whispered to Andy. "She'll never be content until she hears all about poor Bob from someone who was with him when he died. Let me take your hats. Make yourselves comfortable."

She took the hats and put them on the sewing-machine. I wished she'd let us keep them, for now we had nothing to hold on to, and nothing to do with our hands; and as for being comfortable, we were just about as comfortable as two cats on wet bricks.

When Mrs Baker came into the room she brought little Bobby Baker, about four years old; he wanted to see Andy. He ran to Andy at once, and Andy took him up on his knee. He was a pretty child, but he reminded me too much of his father.

"I'm so glad you've come, Andy!" said Bobby.

"Are you Bobby?"

"Yes. I wants to ask you about daddy. You saw him go away, didn't you?" and he fixed his great wondering eyes on Andy's face.

"Yes," said Andy.

"He went up among the stars, didn't he?"

"Yes," said Andy.

"And he isn't coming back to Bobby any more?"

"No," said Andy. "But Bobby's going to him by and by."

Mrs Baker had been leaning back in her chair, resting her head on her hand, tears glistening in her eyes; now she began to sob, and her sister took her out of the room.

Andy looked miserable. "I wish to God I was off this job!" he whispered to me.

"Is that the girl that writes the stories?" I asked.

"Yes," he said, staring at me in a hopeless sort of way, "and poems too."

"Is Bobby going up among the stars?" asked Bobby.

"Yes," said Andy—"if Bobby's good."

"And auntie?"

"Yes."

"And mumma?"

"Yes."

"Are you going, Andy?"

"Yes," said Andy, hopelessly.

"Did you see daddy go up among the stars, Andy?"

"Yes," said Andy, "I saw him go up."

"And he isn't coming down again any more?"

"No," said Andy.

"Why isn't he?"

"Because he's going to wait up there for you and mumma, Bobby."

There was a long pause, and then Bobby asked:

"Are you going to give me a shilling, Andy?" with the same expression of innocent wonder in his eyes.

Andy slipped half a crown into his hand. "Auntie" came in and told him he'd see Andy in the morning and took him away to bed, after he'd kissed us both solemnly; and presently she and Mrs Baker settled down to hear Andy's story.

"Brace up now, Jack, and keep your wits about you," whispered Andy to me just before they came in.

"Poor Bob's brother Ned wrote to me," said Mrs Baker, "but he scarcely told me anything. Ned's a good fellow, but he's very simple, and never thinks of anything."

Andy told her about the boss not being well after he crossed the border.

"I knew he was not well," said Mrs Baker, "before he left. I didn't want him to go. I tried hard to persuade him not to go this trip. I had a feeling that I oughtn't to let him go. But he'd never think of anything but me and the children. He promised he'd give up droving after this trip, and get something to do near home. The life was too much for him—riding in all weathers and camping out in the rain, and living like a dog. But he was never content at home. It was all for the sake of me and the children. He wanted to make money and start on a station again. I shouldn't have let him go. He only thought of me and the children! Oh! my poor, dear, kind, dead husband!" She broke down again and sobbed, and her sister comforted her, while Andy and I stared at Wellington meeting Blücher on the field at Waterloo. I thought the artist had heaped up the dead a bit extra, and I thought that I wouldn't like to be trod on by horses even if I was dead.

"Don't you mind," said Miss Standish, "she'll be all right presently," and she handed us the *Illustrated Sydney Journal*. This was a great relief—we bumped our heads over the pictures.

Mrs Baker made Andy go on again, and he told her how the boss broke down near Mulgatown. Mrs Baker was opposite him and Miss Standish opposite me. Both of them kept their eyes on Andy's face: he sat, with his hair straight up like a brush as usual, and kept his big innocent grey eyes fixed on Mrs Baker's face all the time he was speaking. I watched Miss Standish. I thought she was the prettiest girl I'd ever seen; it was a bad case of love at first sight; but she was far and away above me, and the case was hopeless. I began to feel pretty miserable, and to think back into the past; I just heard Andy droning away by my side.

"So we fixed him up comfortable in the wagonette with the blankets and coats and things," Andy was saying, "and the squatter started into Mulgatown. . . . It was about thirty miles, Jack, wasn't it?" he asked, turning suddenly to me. He always looked so innocent that there were times when I itched to knock him down.

"More like thirty-five," I said, waking up.

Miss Standish fixed her eyes on me, and I had another look at Wellington and Blücher.

"They were all very good and kind to the boss," said Andy. "They thought a lot of him up there. Everybody was fond of him."

"I know it," said Mrs Baker. "Nobody could help liking him. He was one of the kindest men that ever lived."

"Tanner, the publican, couldn't have been kinder to his own brother," said Andy. "The local doctor was a decent chap, but he was only a young fellow, and Tanner hadn't much faith in him, so he wired for an older doctor at Mackintyre, and he even sent out fresh horses to meet the doctor's buggy. Everything was done that could be done, I assure you, Mrs Baker."

"I believe it," said Mrs Baker. "And you don't know how it relieves me to hear it. And did the publican do all this at his own expense?"

"He wouldn't take a penny, Mrs Baker."

"He must have been a good true man. I wish I could thank him."

"Oh, Ned thanked him for you," said Andy, though without meaning more than he said.

"I wouldn't have fancied that Ned would have thought of that," said Mrs Baker. "When I first heard of my poor husband's death, I thought perhaps he'd been drinking again—that worried me a bit."

"He never touched a drop after he left Solong, I can assure you, Mrs Baker," said Andy quickly.

Now I noticed that Miss Standish seemed surprised or puzzled, once or twice, while Andy was speaking, and leaned forward to listen to him; then she leaned back in her chair and clasped her hands behind her head and looked at him, with half-shut eyes, in a way I didn't like. Once or twice she looked at me as if she was going to ask me a question, but I always looked away quick and stared at Blücher and Wellington, or into the empty fire-place, till I felt her eyes were off me. Then she asked Andy a question or two, in all innocence I believe now, but it scared him, and at last he watched his chance and winked at her sharp. Then she gave a little gasp and shut up like a steel trap.

The sick child in the bedroom coughed and cried again. Mrs Baker went to it. We three sat like a deaf-and-dumb institution, Andy and I staring all over the place: presently Miss Standish excused herself, and went out of the room after her sister. She looked hard at Andy as she left the room, but he kept his eyes away.

"Brace up now, Jack," whispered Andy to me, "the worst is coming."

When they came in again Mrs Baker made Andy go on with his story.

"He—he died very quietly," said Andy, hitching round, and resting his elbows on his knees, and looking into the fire-place so as to have his face away from the light. Miss Standish put her arm round her sister. "He died very easy," said Andy. "He was a bit off his head at times, but that was while the fever was on him. He didn't suffer much towards the end—I don't think he suffered at all. . . . He talked a lot about you and the children." (Andy was speaking very softly now.) "He said that you were not to fret, but to cheer up for the children's sake. . . . It was the biggest funeral ever seen round there."

Mrs Baker was crying softly. Andy got the packet half-out of his pocket, but shoved it back again.

"The only thing that hurts me now," said Mrs Baker presently, "is to think of my poor husband buried out there in the lonely bush, so far from home. It's—cruel!" and she was sobbing again.

"Oh, that's all right, Mrs Baker," said Andy, losing his head a little. "Ned will see to that. Ned is going to arrange to have him brought down and buried in Sydney." Which was about the first thing Andy had told her that evening that wasn't a lie. Ned had said he would do it as soon as he sold his wool.

"It's very kind indeed of Ned," sobbed Mrs Baker. "I'd never have dreamed he was so kind-hearted and thoughtful. I misjudged him all along. And that is all you have to tell me about poor Robert?"

"Yes," said Andy—then one of his "happy thoughts" struck him. "Except that he hoped you'd shift to Sydney, Mrs Baker, where you've got friends and relations. He thought it would be better for you and the children. He told me to tell you that."

"He was thoughtful up to the end," said Mrs Baker. "It was just like poor Robert—always thinking of me and the children. We are going to Sydney next week."

Andy looked relieved. We talked a little more, and Miss Standish wanted to make coffee for us, but we had to go and see to our horses. We got up and bumped against each other, and got each other's hats, and promised Mrs Baker we'd come again.

"Thank you very much for coming," she said, shaking hands with us. "I feel much better now. You don't know how much you have relieved me. Now, mind, you have promised to come and see me again for the last time."

Andy caught her sister's eye and jerked his head towards the door to let her know he wanted to speak to her outside.

"Good-bye, Mrs Baker," he said, holding on to her hand. "And don't you fret. You've—you've got the children yet. It's—it's all for the best; and, besides, the boss said you wasn't to fret." And he blundered out after me and Miss Standish.

She came out to the gate with us, and Andy gave her the packet.

"I want you to give that to her," he said: "it's his letters and papers. I hadn't the heart to give it to her, somehow."

"Tell me, Mr M'Culloch," she said. "You've kept something back—you haven't told her the truth. It would be better and safer for me to know. Was it an accident—or the drink?"

"It was the drink," said Andy. "I was going to tell you—I thought it would be best to tell you. I had made up my mind to do it, but, somehow, I couldn't have done it if you hadn't asked me."

"Tell me all," she said. "It would be better for me to know."

"Come a little farther away from the house," said Andy. She came along the fence a piece with us, and Andy told her as much of the truth as he could.

"I'll hurry her off to Sydney," she said. "We can get away this week as well as next." Then she stood for a minute before us, breathing quickly, her hands behind her back and her eyes shining in the moonlight. She looked splendid.

"I want to thank you for her sake," she said quickly. "You are good men! I like the bushmen! They are grand men—they are noble. I'll probably never see either of you again, so it doesn't matter," and she put her white hand on Andy's shoulder and kissed him fair and square on the mouth. "And you, too!" she said to me. I was taller than Andy, and had to stoop. "Good-bye!" she said, and ran to the gate and in, waving her hands to us. We lifted our hats again and turned down the road.

I don't think it did either of us any harm.

Two Dogs and a Fence

"NOTHING makes a dog madder," said Mitchell, "than to have another dog come outside his fence and sniff and bark at him through cracks when he can't get out. The other dog might be an entire stranger; he might be an old chum, and he mightn't bark—only sniff—but it makes no difference to the inside dog. The inside dog generally starts it, and the outside dog only loses his temper and gets wild because the inside dog has lost *his* and got mad and made such a stinking fuss about nothing at all; and then the outside dog barks back and makes matters a thousand times worse, and the inside dog foams at the mouth and dashes the foam about, and goes at it like a million steel traps.

"I can't tell why the inside dog gets so wild about it in the first place, except, perhaps, because he thinks the outside dog has taken him at a disadvantage and is 'poking it at him'; anyway, he gets madder the longer it lasts, and at last he gets savage enough to snap off his own tail and tear it to bits, because he can't get out and chew up that other dog; and if he did get out he'd kill the other dog, or try to, even if it was his own brother.

"Sometimes the outside dog only smiles and trots off; sometimes he barks back good-naturedly; sometimes he only gives a couple of disinterested barks as if he isn't particular, but is expected, because of his dignity and doghood, to say something under the circumstances; and sometimes, if the outside dog is a little dog, he'll get away from that fence in a hurry on the first surprise, or, if he's a cheeky little dog, he'll first make sure that the inside dog can't get out, and then he'll have some fun.

"It's amusing to see a big dog, of the Newfoundland kind, sniffing along outside a fence with a broad, good-natured grin on his face all the time the inside dog is whooping away at the rate of thirty whoops a second, and choking himself, and covering himself with foam, and dashing the spray through the cracks, and jolting and jerking every joint in his body up to the last joint in his tail.

"Sometimes the inside dog is a little dog, and the smaller he is the more row he makes—but then he knows he's safe. And sometimes, as I said before, the outside dog is a short-tempered dog who hates a row, and never wants to have a disagreement with anybody —like a good many peaceful men, who hate rows, and are always nice and civil and pleasant, in a nasty, unpleasant, surly, sneering sort of civil way that makes you want to knock their heads off; men who never start a row, but keep it going, and make it a thousand times worse when it's once started, just because they didn't start it —and keep on saying so, and that the other party did. The short-tempered outside dog gets wild at the other dog for losing his temper, and says:

" 'What are you making such a fuss about? What's the matter with you, anyway? Hey?'

"And the inside dog says:

" 'Who do you think you're talking to? You——! I'll——' etc., etc., etc.

"Then the outside dog says:

" 'Why, you're worse than a flaming old slut!'

"*Then* they go at it, and you can hear them miles off, like a Chinese war—like a hundred great guns firing eighty blank cartridges a minute, till the outside dog is just as wild to get inside and eat the inside dog as the inside dog is to get out and disembowel *him*. Yet if those same two dogs were to meet casually outside they might get chummy at once, and be the best of friends, and swear everlasting mateship, and take each other home."

A Daughter of Maoriland

A SKETCH OF POOR-CLASS MAORIS

THE new native school-teacher, who was green, soft, and poetical, and had a literary ambition, called her August, and fondly hoped to build a romance on her character. She was down in the school registers as Sarah Moses, Maori, sixteen years and three months. She looked twenty; but this was nothing, insomuch as the mother of the youngest child in the school—a dear little half-caste lady of two or three summers—had not herself the vaguest idea of the child's age, nor anybody else's, nor of ages in the abstract. The church register was lost some six years before, when Granny, who was a hundred, if a day, was supposed to be about twenty-five. The teacher had to guess the ages of all the new pupils.

August was apparently the oldest in the school—a big, ungainly, awkward girl, with a heavy negro type of Maori countenance, and about as much animation, mentally or physically, as a cow. She was given to brooding; in fact, she brooded all the time. She brooded all day over her school work, but did it fairly well. How the previous teachers had taught her all she knew was a mystery to the new one. There had been a tragedy in August's family when she was a child, and the affair seemed to have cast a gloom over the lives of the entire family, for the lowering brooding cloud was on all their faces. August would take to the bush when things went wrong at home, and climb a tree and brood till she was found and coaxed home. Things, according to pah-gossip, had gone wrong with her from the date of the tragedy, when she, a bright little girl, was taken—a homeless orphan—to live with her sister, and, afterwards, with an aunt-by-marriage. They treated her, 'twas said, with a brutality which must have been greatly exaggerated by pah-gossip, seeing that unkindness of this description is, according to all the best authorities, altogether foreign to Maori nature.

Pah-gossip—which is less reliable than the ordinary washer-woman kind, because of a deeper and more vicious ignorance—had it that one time when August was punished by a teacher (or beaten by her sister or aunt-by-marriage) she took to the bush for three days, at the expiration of which time she was found on the ground in an exhausted condition. She was evidently a true Maori or savage, and this was one of the reasons why the teacher with the literary ambition took an interest in her. She had a print of a portrait of a man in soldier's uniform, taken from a copy of the *Illustrated London News*, pasted over the fire-place in the whare where she lived, and neatly bordered by vandyked strips of silvered tea-paper. She had pasted it in the place of honour, or as near as she could get to it. The place of honour was sacred to framed representations of the Nativity and Catholic subjects, half-modelled, half-pictured. The print was a portrait of the last Tsar of Russia, of all the men in the world; and August was reported to have said that she loved that man. His father had been murdered, so had her mother. This was one of the reasons why the teacher with the literary ambition thought he could get a romance out of her.

After the first week she hung round the new schoolmistress, dog-like—with "dog-like affection", thought the teacher. She came down often during the holidays, and hung about the veranda and back door for an hour or so; then, by and by, she'd be gone. Her brooding seemed less aggressive on such occasions. The teacher reckoned that she had something on her mind, and wanted to open her heart to "the wife", but was too ignorant or too shy, poor girl; and he reckoned, from this theory of Maori character, that it might take her weeks, or months, to come to the point. One day, after a great deal of encouragement, she explained that she felt "so awfully lonely, Mrs Lorrens". All the other girls were away, and she wished it was school-time.

She was happy and cheerful again, in her brooding way, in the playground. There was something sadly ludicrous about her great, ungainly figure slopping round above the children at play. The schoolmistress took her into the parlour, gave her tea and cake, and was kind to her; and she took it all with broody cheerfulness.

One Sunday morning she came down to the cottage and sat on the edge of the veranda, looking as wretchedly miserable as a girl could. She was in rags—at least, she had a rag of a dress on—and was barefooted and bareheaded. She said that her aunt had turned her out, and she was going to walk down the coast to Whale Bay to her grandmother—a long day's ride. The teacher was troubled, because he was undecided what to do. He had to be careful to avoid any unpleasantness arising out of Maori cliquism. As the teacher he couldn't let her go in the state she was in; from the depths of his greenness he trusted her, from the depths of his softness he pitied her; his poetic nature was fiercely indignant on account of the poor girl's wrongs, and the wife spoke for her. Then he thought of his unwritten romance, and regarded August in the light of copy, and that settled it. While he talked the matter over with his wife, August "hid in the dark of her hair", awaiting her doom. The teacher put his hat on, walked up to the pah, and saw her aunt. She denied that she had turned August out, but the teacher believed the girl. He explained his position, in words simplified for Maori comprehension, and the aunt and relations said they understood, and that he was "perfectly right, Mr Lorrens". They were very respectful. The teacher said that if August would not return home, he was willing to let her stay at the cottage until such time as her uncle, who was absent, returned, and he (the teacher) could talk the matter over with him. The relations thought that that was the very best thing that could be done, and thanked him. The aunt, two sisters, and as many of the others, including the children, as were within sight or hail at the time—most of them could not by any possible means have had the slightest connection with the business in hand—accompanied the teacher to the cottage. August took to the flax directly she caught sight of her relations, and was with difficulty induced to return. There was a lot of talk in Maori, during which the girl and her aunt shuffled and swung round at the back of each other, and each talked over her shoulder, and laughed foolishly and awkwardly once or twice; but in the end the girl was sullenly determined not to return home, so it was decided that she should stay. The schoolmistress made tea.

August brightened from the first day. She was a different girl altogether. "I never saw such a change in a girl," said the young schoolmistress, and one or two others. "I always thought she was a good girl if taken the right way; all she wanted was a change and kind treatment." But the stolid old Maori chairman of the school committee only shrugged his shoulders and said (when the schoolmistress, woman-like, pressed him for an opinion to agree with her own), "You can look at it two ways, Mrs Lorrens." Which, by the way, was about the only expression of opinion that the teacher was ever able to get out of him on any subject.

August worked and behaved well. She was wonderfully quick in picking up English ways and housework. True, she was awkward and not over cleanly in some things, but her mistress had patience with her. Who wouldn't have? She "couldn't do enough" for her benefactress; she hung on her words and sat at her footstool of evenings in a way that gladdened the teacher's sentimental nature; she couldn't bear to see him help his wife with a hat-pin or button—August must do it. She insisted on doing her mistress's hair every night. In short, she tried in every way to show her gratitude. The teacher and his wife smiled brightly at each other behind her back, and thought how cheerful the house was since she came, and wondered what they'd do without her. It was a settled thing that they should take her back to the city with them, and have a faithful and grateful retainer all their lives, and a sort of Aunt Chloe for their children, when they had any. The teacher got yards of copy out of her for his "Maori Sketches and Characters", worked joyously at his romance, and felt great already, and was happy. She had a bed made up temporarily (until the teacher could get a spring mattress for her from town) on the floor in the dining-room, and when she'd made her bed she'd squat on it in front of the fire and sing Maori songs in a soft voice. She'd sing the teacher and his wife, in the next room, to sleep. Then she'd get up and have a feed, but they never heard her.

Her manners at the table (for she was treated "like one of ourselves" in the broadest sense of the term) were surprisingly good, considering that the adults of her people were decidedly cow-like in white society, and scoffed sea-eggs, shell-fish, and mutton-birds at home with a gallop which was not edifying. Her appetite, it was true, was painful at times to the poetic side of the teacher's nature; but he supposed that she'd been half-starved at home, poor girl, and would get over it. Anyway, the copy he'd get out of her would repay him for this and other expenses a hundredfold. Moreover, begging and borrowing had ceased with her advent, and the teacher set this down to her influence.

The first jar came when she was sent on horseback to the town for groceries, and didn't get back till late the next day. She explained that some of her relations got hold of her and made her stay, and wanted her to go into public-houses with them, but she wouldn't. She said that *she* wanted to come home. But why didn't she? The teacher let it pass, and hoped she'd gain strength of character by and by. He had waited up late the night before with her supper on the hob; and he and his wife had been anxious for fear something had happened to the poor girl who was under their care. He had walked to the treacherous river-ford several times during the evening, and waited there for her. So perhaps he was tired, and that was why he didn't write next night.

The sugar-bag, the onion-basket, the potato-bag and the tea-chest began to go down alarmingly, and an occasional pound of candles, a pigeon, a mutton-bird (plucked and ready for Sunday's cooking), and other little trifles went also. August couldn't understand it, and the teacher believed her, for falsehood and deceit are foreign to the simple natures of the modern Maoris. There were no cats; but no score of ordinary cats could have given colour to the cat theory, had it been raised in this case. The breath of August advertised onions more than once, but no human stomach could have accounted for the quantity. She surely could not have eaten the other things raw —and she had no opportunities for private cooking, as far as the teacher and his wife could see. The other Maoris were out of the question; they were all strictly honest.

Thefts and annoyances of the above description were credited to the swaggies who infested the roads, and had a very bad name down that way; so the teacher loaded his gun, and told August to rouse him at once if she heard a sound in the night. She said she would; but a heavy-weight swaggie could have come in and sat on her and had a smoke without waking her.

She couldn't be trusted to go a message. She'd take from three to six hours, and come back with an excuse that sounded genuine from its very simplicity. Another sister of hers lay ill in an isolated hut, alone and uncared for, except by the teacher's wife, and occasionally by a poor pah outcast, who had negro blood in her veins, and a love for a white loafer. God help her! All of which sounds strange, considering that Maoris are very kind to each other. The schoolmistress sent August one night to stay with the sick Maori woman and help her as she could, and gave her strict instructions to come to the cottage first thing in the morning, and tell her how the sick woman was. August turned up at lunch-time next day. The teacher gave her her first lecture, and said plainly that he wasn't to be taken for a fool; then he stepped aside to get cool, and when he returned the girl was sobbing as if her heart would break, and the wife comforting her. She had been up all night, poor girl, and was thoroughly worn out. Somehow the teacher didn't feel uncomfortable about it. He went down to the whare. August had not touched a dish-cloth or broom. She had slept, as she always did, like a pig, all night, while her sister lay and tossed in agony; in the morning she ate everything there was to eat in the house (which, it seemed, was the Maori way of showing sympathy in sickness and trouble), after which she brooded by the fire till the children, running out of school, announced the teacher's lunch hour.

August braced up again for a little while. The master thought of the trouble they had with Ayacanora in *Westward Ho!*, and was comforted and tackled his romance again. Then the schoolmistress fell sick and things went wrong. The groceries went down faster than ever, and the house got very dirty, and began to have a native smell about it. August grew fat, and lazy, and dirty, and less reliable on washing-days, or when there was anything special to do in the house. "The savage blood is strong," thought the teacher, "and she is beginning to long for her own people and free unconventional life." One morning—on washing-day, too, as it happened—she called out, before the teacher and his wife were up, that the Maoris who supplied them with milk were away, and she had promised to go up and milk the cow and bring the milk down. The teacher gave her permission. One of the scholars usually brought the milk early. Lunch-time came and no August, no milk—strangest of all, only half the school children. The teacher put on his hat, and went up to the pah once more. He found August squatted in the midst of a circle of relations. She was entertaining them with one of a series of idealistic sketches of the teacher's domestic life, in which she showed a very vivid imagination, and exhibited an unaccountable savage sort of pessimism. Her intervals of absence had been occupied in this way from the first. The astounding slanders she had circulated concerning the teacher's private life came back, bit by bit, to his ears for a year afterwards, and her character sketches of previous teachers, and her own relations—for she spared nobody—would have earned a white woman a long and well-merited term of imprisonment for criminal libel. She had cunningly, by straightforward and unscrupulous lying, prejudiced the principal mother and boss woman of the pah against the teacher and his wife; as a natural result of which the old lady, who, like the rest, was very ignorant and ungrateful, turned nasty and kept the children from school. The teacher lost his temper, so the children were rounded up and hurried down to school immediately; with them came August and her aunt, with alleged explanations and excuses, and a shell-fish. The aunt and sisters said they'd have nothing to do with August. They didn't want her and wouldn't have her. The teacher said that, under those circumstances, she'd better go and drown herself; so she went home with them.

The whole business had been a plot by her nearest relations. They got rid of the trouble and expense of keeping her, and the bother of borrowing in person, whenever in need of trifles in the grocery line. Borrowing recommenced with her dismissal; but the teacher put a full stop to it, as far as he was concerned. Then August, egged on by her aunt, sent a blackguardly letter to the teacher's wife; the sick sister, by the way, who had been nursed and supplied with food by her all along, was in it, and said she was glad August sent the letter, and it served the schoolmistress right. The teacher went up to the pah once more; an hour later, August in person, accompanied, as usual, by a relation or two, delivered at the cottage an abject apology in writing, the composition of which would have discouraged the most enthusiastic advocate of higher education for the lower classes.

Then various petty annoyances were tried. The teacher is firmly convinced that certain animal-like sounds round the house at night were due to August's trying to find out whether his wife was as likely to be haunted as the Maoris were. He didn't dream of such a thing at the time, for he did not believe that one of them had the pluck to venture out after dark. But savage superstition must give way to savage hate. The girl's last try-on was to come down to the school fence, and ostentatiously sharpen a table-knife on the wires, while she scowled murderously in the direction of the schoolmistress, who was hanging out her washing. August looked, in her dark, bushy, Maori hair, a thoroughly wild savage. Her father had murdered her mother under particularly brutal circumstances, and the daughter took after her father.

The teacher called to her and said: "Now, look here, my lady, the best thing you can do is to drop that nonsense at once" (she had dropped the knife in the ferns behind her), "for we're the wrong sort of people to try it on with. Now you get out of this and tell your aunt—she's sneaking there in the flax—what I tell you, and that she'd better clear out of this quick, or I'll have a policeman out and take the whole gang into town in an hour. Now be off, and shut that gate behind you, carefully, and fasten it." She did, and went.

The worst of it was that the August romance copy was useless. Her lies were even less reliable and picturesque than the common Jones's Alley hag lie. Then the teacher thought of the soft fool he'd been, and that made him wild. He looked like a fool, and was one to a great extent, but it wasn't good policy to take him for one.

Strange to say, he and others had reason to believe that August respected him, and liked him rather than otherwise; but she hated his wife, who had been kind to her, as only a savage can hate. The younger pupils told the teacher, cheerfully and confidently, that August said she'd cut Mrs Lorrens's throat the first chance she got. Next week the aunt sent down to ask if the teacher could sell her a bar of soap, and sent the same old shilling; he was tired of seeing it stuck out in front of him, so he took it, put it in his pocket, and sent the soap. This must have discouraged them, for the borrowing industry petered out. He saw the aunt later on, and she told him, cheerfully, that August was going to live with a half-caste in a certain house in town.

Poor August! For she was only a tool after all. Her "romance" was briefly as follows: She went, per off-hand Maori arrangement, as "housekeeper" in the hut of a labourer at a neighbouring saw-mill. She stayed three months, for a wonder; at the expiration of which time she put on her hat and explained that she was tired of stopping there, and was going home. He said, "All right, Sarah, wait a while and I'll take you home." At the door of her aunt's house he said, "Well, good-bye, Sarah," and she said, in her brooding way, "Good-bye, Jim." And that was all.

As the last apparent result of August's mischief-making, her brother or someone one evening rode up to the cottage, drunk and inclined to bluster. He was accompanied by a friend, also drunk, who came to see the fun, and was ready to use his influence on the winning side. The teacher went inside, brought out his gun, and slipped two cartridges in. "I've had enough of this," he said. "Now then, be off, you insolent blackguards, or I'll shoot you like rabbits. Go!" and he snapped his jaw and the breech of his gun together. As they rode off, the old local hawk happened to soar close over a dead lamb in the fern at the corner of the garden, and the teacher, who had been "laying" for him a long time, let fly both barrels at him, without thinking. When he turned, there was only a cloud of dust down the track.

The teacher taught that school for three years thereafter, without a hitch. But he went no more on universal brotherhood lines. And, for years after he had gone, his name was spoken of with great respect by the Maoris.

Mitchell: A Character Sketch

It was a very mean station, and Mitchell thought he had better go himself and beard the overseer for tucker. His mates were waiting till the overseer went out on the run, and then trying their luck with the cook; but the self-assertive and diplomatic Mitchell decided to go.

"Good day," said Mitchell.

"Good day," said the manager.

"It's hot," said Mitchell.

"Yes, it's hot."

"I don't suppose," said Mitchell; "I don't suppose it's any use asking you for a job?"

"Naw."

"Well, I won't ask you," said Mitchell, "but I don't suppose you want any fencing done?"

"Naw."

"Nor boundary-riding?"

"Naw."

"You ain't likely to want a man to knock round?"

"Naw."

"I thought not. Things are pretty bad just now."

"Na—yes—they are."

"Ah, well; there's a lot to be said on the squatter's side as well as the men's. I suppose I can get a bit of rations?"

"Ye-yes," (*Shortly*)—"Wot d'yer want?"

"Well, let's see; we want a bit of meat and flour—I think that's all. Got enough tea and sugar to carry us on."

"All right. Cook! have you got any meat?"

"No!"

To Mitchell: "Can you kill a sheep?"

"Rather!"

To the cook: "Give this man a cloth and knife and steel, and let him go up to the yard and kill a sheep." (To Mitchell): "You can take a forequarter and get a bit of flour."

Half an hour later Mitchell came back with the carcass wrapped in the cloth.

"Here yer are; here's your sheep," he said to the cook.

"That's all right; hang it in there. Did you take a forequarter?"

"No."

"Well, why didn't you? The boss told you to."

"I didn't want a forequarter. I don't like it. I took a hindquarter."

So he had.

The cook scratched his head; he seemed to have nothing to say. He thought about trying to think, perhaps, but gave it best. It was too hot and he was out of practice.

"Here, fill these up, will you?" said Mitchell. "That's the tea-bag, and that's the sugar-bag, and that's the flour-bag."

He had taken them from the front of his shirt.

"Don't be frightened to stretch 'em a little, old man. I've got two mates to feed."

The cook took the bags mechanically and filled them well before he knew what he was doing. Mitchell talked all the time.

"Thank you," said he—"got a bit of baking-powder?"

"Ye—yes, here you are."

"Thank you. Find it dull here, don't you?"

"Well, yes, pretty dull. There's a bit of cooked beef and some bread and cake there, if you want it!"

"Thanks," said Mitchell, sweeping the broken victuals into an old pillow-slip which he carried on his person for such an emergency. "I s'pose you find it dull round here."

"Yes, pretty dull."

"No one to talk to much?"

"No, not many."

"Tongue gets rusty?"

"Ye—es, sometimes."

"Well, so long, and thank yer."

"So long," said the cook (he nearly added "thank yer").

"Well, good day; I'll see you again."

"Good day."

Mitchell shouldered his spoil and left.

The cook scratched his head; he had a chat with the overseer afterwards, and they agreed that the traveller was a bit gone.

But Mitchell's head wasn't gone—not much: he had been round a bit—that was all.

A Vision of Sandy-blight

I'D been humping my back, and crouching and groaning for an hour or so in the darkest corner of the travellers' hut, tortured by the demon of sandy-blight. It was too hot to travel, and there was no one there except ourselves and Mitchell's cattle-pup. We were waiting till after sundown, for I couldn't have travelled in the daylight, anyway. Mitchell had tied a wet towel round my eyes, and led me for the last mile or two by another towel—one end fastened to his belt behind, and the other in my hand as I walked in his tracks. And oh! but this was a relief. It was out of the dust and glare, and the flies didn't come into the dark hut, and I could hump and stick my knees in my eyes and groan in comfort. I didn't want a thousand a year, or anything; I only wanted relief for my eyes—that was all I prayed for in this world. When the sun got down a bit, Mitchell started poking round, and presently he found amongst the rubbish a dirty-looking medicine bottle, corked tight; when he rubbed the dirt off a piece of notepaper that was pasted on, he saw "eye-water" written on it. He drew the cork with his teeth, smelt the water, stuck his little finger in, turned the bottle upside down, tasted the top of his finger, and reckoned the stuff was all right.

"Here! Wake up, Joe!" he shouted. "Here's a bottle of tears."

"A bottler wot?" I groaned.

"Eye-water," said Mitchell.

"Are you sure it's all right?" I didn't want to be poisoned or have my eyes burnt out by mistake; perhaps some burning acid had got into that bottle, or the label had been put on, or left on, in mistake or carelessness.

"I dunno," said Mitchell, "but there's no harm in tryin'."

I chanced it. I lay down on my back in a bunk, and Mitchell dragged my lids up and spilt half a bottle of eye-water over my eyeballs.

The relief was almost instantaneous. I never experienced such a quick cure in my life. I carried the bottle in my swag for a long time afterwards, with an idea of getting it analysed, but left it behind at last in a camp.

Mitchell scratched his head thoughtfully, and watched me for a while.

"I think I'll wait a bit longer," he said at last, "and if it doesn't blind you I'll put some in my eyes. I'm getting a touch of blight myself now. That's the fault of travelling with a mate who's always catching something that's no good to him."

As it grew dark outside we talked of sandy-blight and fly-bite, and sandflies up north, and ordinary flies, and branched off to Barcoo rot, and struck the track again at bees and bee stings. When we got to bees, Mitchell sat smoking for a while and looking dreamily backwards along tracks and branch tracks, and round corners and circles he had travelled, right back to the short, narrow, innocent bit of track that ends in a vague, misty point—like the end of a long, straight, cleared road in the moonlight—as far back as we can remember.

"I had about fourteen hives," said Mitchell—"we used to call them 'swarms,' no matter whether they were flying or in the box—when I left home first time. I kept them behind the shed, in the shade, on tables of galvanized-iron cases turned down on stakes; but I had to make legs later on, and stand them in pans of water, on account of the ants. When the bees swarmed—and some hives sent out the Lord knows how many swarms in a year, it seemed to me—we'd tin-kettle 'em, and throw water on 'em, to make 'em believe the biggest thunderstorm was coming to drown the oldest inhabitant; and, if they didn't get the start of us and rise, they'd settle on a branch—generally on one of the scraggy fruit-trees. It was rough on the bees—come to think of it; their instinct told them it was going to be fine, and the noise and water told them it was raining. They must have thought that nature was mad, drunk, or gone ratty, or the end of the world had come. We'd rig up a table, with a box upside down, under the branch, cover our face with a piece of mosquito-net, have rags burning round, and then give the branch a sudden jerk, turn the box down, and run. If we got most of the bees in, the rest that were hanging to the bough or flying round would follow, and then we reckoned we'd shook the queen in. If the bees in the box came out and joined the others, we'd reckon we hadn't shook the queen in, and go for them again. When a hive was full of honey we'd turn the box upside down, turn the empty box mouth down on top of it, and drum and hammer on the lower box with a stick till all the bees went up into the top box. I suppose it made their heads ache, and they went up on that account.

"I suppose things are done differently on proper bee-farms. I've heard that a bee-farmer will part a hanging swarm with his fingers, take out the queen bee and arrange matters with her; but our ways suited us, and there was a lot of expectation and running and excitement in it, especially when a swarm took us by surprise. The yell of 'Bees swarmin'!' was as good to us as the yell of 'Fight!' is now, or 'Bolt!' in town, or 'Fire!' or 'Man overboard!' at sea.

"There was tons of honey. The bees used to go to the vineyards at wine-making and get honey from the heaps of crushed grape-skins thrown out in the sun, and get so drunk sometimes that they wobbled in their bee-lines home. They'd fill all the boxes, and then build in between and under the bark, and board, and tin covers. They never seemed to get the idea out of their heads that this wasn't an evergreen country, and it wasn't going to snow all winter. My younger brother Joe used to put pieces of meat on the tables near the boxes, and in front of the holes where the bees went in and out, for the dogs to grab at. But one old dog, Black Bill, was a match for him; if it was worth Bill's while, he'd camp there, and keep Joe and the other dogs from touching the meat—once it was put down—till the bees turned in for the night. And Joe would get the other kids round there, and when they weren't looking or thinking, he'd brush the bees with a stick and run. I'd lam him when I caught him at it. He was an awful young devil, was Joe, and he grew up steady, and respectable, and respected—and I went to the bad. I never trust a good boy now. . . . Ah, well!

"I remember the first swarm we got. We'd been talking of getting a few swarms for a long time. That was what was the matter with us English and Irish and English-Irish Australian farmers: we used to talk so much about doing things while the Germans and Scotch did them. And we even talked in a lazy, easygoing sort of way.

"Well, one blazing hot day I saw father coming along the road, home to dinner (we had it in the middle of the day), with his axe over his shoulder. I noticed the axe particularly because father was bringing it home to grind, and Joe and I had to turn the stone; but when I noticed Joe dragging along home in the dust about fifty yards behind father I felt easier in my mind. Suddenly father dropped the axe and started to run back along the road towards Joe, who, as soon as he saw father coming, shied for the fence and got through. He thought he was going to catch it for something he'd done—or hadn't done. Joe used to do so many things and leave so many things not done that he could never be sure of father. Besides, father had a way of starting to hammer us unexpectedly—when the idea struck him. But father pulled himself up in about thirty yards and started to grab up handfuls of dust and sand and throw them into the air. My idea, in the first flash, was to get hold of the axe, for I thought it was sunstroke, and father might take it into his head to start chopping up the family before I could persuade him to put it (his head, I mean) in a bucket of water. But Joe came running like mad, yelling:

" 'Swarmer—bees! Swawmmer—bee—ee—es! Bring—a—tin—dish —and—a—dippera—wa-a-ter!'

"I ran with a bucket of water and an old frying-pan, and pretty soon the rest of the family were on the spot, throwing dust and water, and banging everything, tin or iron, they could get hold of. The only bullock-bell in the district (if it was in the district) was an old poley cow, and she'd been lost for a fortnight. Mother brought up the rear—but soon worked to the front—with a baking-dish and a big spoon. The old lady—she wasn't old then—had a deep-rooted prejudice that she could do everything better than anybody else, and that the selection and all on it would go to the dogs if she wasn't there to look after it. There was no jolting that idea out of her. She not only believed that she could do anything better than anybody, and hers was the only right or possible way, and that we'd do everything upside down if she wasn't there to do it or show us how—but she'd try to do things herself or insist on making us do them her way, and that led to messes and rows. She was excited now, and took command at once. She wasn't tongue-tied, and had no impediment in her speech.

" 'Don't throw up dust!—Stop throwing up dust!—Do you want to smother 'em?—Don't throw up so much water!—Only throw up a pannikin at a time!—D'yer want to drown 'em? Bang! Keep on banging, Joe!—Look at that child! Run, someone!—run! you, Jack!—D'yer want the child to be stung to death?—Take her inside . . . D'yer hear me? . . . Stop throwing up dust, Tom!' (to father).

'You're scaring 'em away! Can't you see they want to settle?' (Father was getting mad and yelping: 'For Godsake shettup and go inside.') 'Throw up water, Jack! Throw up—Tom! Take that bucket from him and don't make such a fool of yourself before the children! Throw up water! Throw—keep on banging, children! Keep on banging!' (Mother put her faith in banging.) 'There!—they're off! You've lost 'em! I knew you would! I told yer—keep on bang——!'

"A bee struck her in the eye, and she grabbed at it!

"Mother went home—and inside.

"Father was good at bees—could manage them like sheep when he got to know their ideas. When the swarm settled, he sent us for the old washing stool, boxes, bags, and so on; and the whole time he was fixing the bees I noticed that whenever his back was turned to us his shoulders would jerk up as if he was cold, and he seemed to shudder from inside, and now and then I'd hear a grunting sort of whimper like a boy that was just starting to blubber. But father wasn't weeping, and bees weren't stinging him; it was the bee that stung mother that was tickling father. When he went into the house, mother's other eye had bunged for sympathy. Father was always gentle and kind in sickness, and he bathed mother's eyes and rubbed mud on, but every now and then he'd catch inside, and jerk and shudder, and grunt and cough. Mother got wild, but presently the humour of it struck her, and she had to laugh, and a rum laugh it was, with both eyes bunged up. Then she got hysterical, and started to cry, and father put his arm round her shoulder and ordered us out of the house.

"They were very fond of each other, the old people were, under it all—right up to the end.... Ah, well!"

Mitchell pulled the swags out of a bunk, and started to fasten the nose-bags on.

A Child in the Dark

NEW YEAR'S EVE! A hot night in midsummer in the drought. It was so dark—with a smothering darkness—that even the low loom of the scrub-covered ridges, close at hand across the creek, was not to be seen. The sky was not clouded for rain, but with drought haze and the smoke of distant bushfires.

Down the hard road to the crossing at Pipeclay Creek sounded the footsteps of a man. Not the crunching steps of an English labourer, clodhopping contentedly home; these sounded more like the footsteps of one pacing steadily to and fro, and thinking steadily and hopelessly—sorting out the past. Only the steps went on. A glimmer of white moleskin trousers and a suggestion of light-coloured tweed jacket, now and again, as if in the glimmer of a faint ghost light in the darkness.

The road ran along by the foot of a line of low ridges, or spurs, and as he passed the gullies or gaps he felt a breath of hotter air, like blasts from a furnace in the suffocating atmosphere. He followed a two-railed fence for a short distance, and turned in at a white batten gate. It seemed lighter now. There was a house, or rather a hut, suggested, with whitewashed slab walls and a bark roof. He walked quietly round to the door of a detached kitchen, opened it softly, went in and struck a match. A candle stood, stuck in a blot of its own grease, on one end of the dresser. He lit the candle and looked round.

The walls of the kitchen were of split slabs, the roof box-bark, the floor clay, and there was a large clay-lined fireplace, the sides a dirty brown, and the back black. It had evidently never been white-washed. There was a bed of about a week's ashes, and above it, suspended by a blackened hook and chain from a grimy cross-bar, hung a black bucket full of warm water. The man got a fork, explored the bucket, and found what he expected—a piece of raw corned-beef in water which had gone off the boil before the meat had been heated through.

The kitchen was furnished with a pine table, a well-made flour bin, and a meat safe and sideboard, or dresser—evidently the work of a carpenter. The top of the safe was dirty—covered with crumbs and grease and tea stains. On one corner lay a school exercise book, with a stone ink-bottle and a pen beside it. The book was open at a page written in the form of verse, in a woman's hand, and headed: "Misunderstood". He took the edges of the book between his fingers and thumbs, and made to tear it, but, the cover being tough, and resisting the first savage tug, he altered his mind, and put the book down. Then he turned to the table. There was a jumble of dirty crockery on one end, and on the other, set on a sheet of stained newspaper, the remains of a meal—a junk of badly-hacked bread, a basin of dripping (with the fat over the edges), and a tin of treacle. The treacle had run down the sides of the tin on to the paper. Knives, heavy with treacle, lay glued to the paper. There was a dish with some water, a rag, and a cup or two in it—evidently an attempt to wash-up.

The man took up a cup and pressed it hard between his palms, until it broke. Then he felt relieved. He gathered the fragments in one hand, took the candle, and stumbled out to where there was a dust-heap. Kicking a hole in the ashes, he dropped in the bits of broken crockery, and covered them. Then his anger blazed again. He walked quickly to the back door of the house, thrust the door open, and flung in, but a child's voice said from the dark:

"Is that you, father? Don't tread on me, father."

The room was nearly as bare as the kitchen. There was a table, covered with cheap American oilcloth, and, on the other side, a sofa on which a straw mattress, a cloudy blanket, and a pillow without a slip had been thrown in a heap. On the floor, between the sofa and the table, lay a boy—child almost—on a similar mattress, with a cover of coarse sacking, and a bundle of dirty clothes for a pillow. A pale, thin-faced, dark-eyed boy.

"What are you doing here, sonny?" asked the father.

"Mother's bad again with her head. She says to tell you to come in quiet, and sleep on the sofa tonight. I started to wash up and clean up the kitchen, father, but I got sick."

"Why, what is the matter with you, sonny?" His voice quickened, and he held the candle down to the child's face.

"Oh, nothing much, father. I felt sick, but I feel better now."

"What have you been eating?"

"Nothing that I know of; I think it was the hot weather, father."

The father spread the mattress, blew out the candle, and lay down in his clothes. After a while the boy began to toss restlessly.

"Oh, it's too hot, father," he said. "I'm smothering."

The father got up, lit the candle, took a corner of the newspaper-covered "scrim" lining that screened the cracks of the slab wall, and tore it away; then he propped open the door with a chair.

"Oh, that's better already, father," said the boy.

The hut was three rooms long and one deep, with a veranda in front and a skillion, harness and tool room, about half the length, behind. The father opened the door of the next room softly, and propped that open, too. There was another boy on the sofa, younger than the first, but healthy and sturdy-looking. He had nothing on him but a very dirty shirt, a patchwork quilt was slipping from under him, and most of it was on the floor; the boy and the pillow were nearly off, too.

The father fixed him as comfortably as possible, and put some chairs by the sofa to keep him from rolling off. He noticed that somebody had started to scrub this room, and left it. He listened at the door of the third room for a few moments to the breathing within; then he opened it and gently walked in. There was an old-fashioned four-poster cedar bedstead, a chest of drawers, and a baby's cradle made out of a gin-case. The woman was fast asleep. She was a big, strong and healthy-looking woman, with dark hair and strong, square features. There was a plate, a knife and fork, and egg-shells, and a cup and saucer on the top of the chest of drawers; also two candles, one stuck in a mustard-tin, and one in a pickle-bottle, and a copy of *Ardath*.

He stepped out in the skillion, and lifted some harness on to its pegs from chaff-bags in the corner. Coming in again he nearly stumbled over a bucket half full of dirty water on the floor, with a scrubbing brush, some wet rags, and half a bar of yellow soap beside it. He put these things in the bucket, and carried it out. As he passed through the first room the sick boy said:

"I couldn't lift the saddle of the harness on to the peg, father. I had to leave the scrubbing to make some tea and cook some eggs for mother, and put baby to bed, and then I felt too bad to go on with the scrubbing—and I forgot about the bucket."

"Did the baby have any tea, sonny?"

"Yes. I made her bread and milk, and she ate a big plateful. The calves are in the pen all right, and I fixed the gate. And I brought a load of wood this morning, father, before mother took bad."

"You should not have done that. I told you not to. I could have done that on Sunday. Now, are you sure you didn't lift a log into the cart that was too heavy for you?"

"Quite sure, father. Oh, I'm plenty strong enough to put a load of wood on the cart."

The father lay on his back on the sofa, with his hands behind his head, for a few minutes.

"Aren't you tired, father?" asked the boy.

"No, sonny, not very tired; you must try and go to sleep now," and he reached across the table for the candle and blew it out.

Presently the baby cried, and in a moment the mother's voice was heard.

"Nils! Nils! Are you there, Nils?"

"Yes, Emma."

"Then for God's sake come and take this child away before she drives me mad! My head's splitting."

The father went in to the child and presently returned for a cup of water.

"She only wanted a drink," the boy heard him say to the mother.

"Well, didn't I tell you she wanted a drink? I've been calling for the last half-hour, with that child screaming, and not a soul to come near me, and me lying here helpless all day, and not a wink of sleep for two nights."

"But, Emma, you were asleep when I came in."

"How can you tell such infernal lies? I—. To think I'm chained to a man who can't say a word of truth! God help me! To have to lie night after night in the same bed with a liar!"

The child in the first room lay quaking with terror, dreading one of those cruel and shameful scenes which had made a hell of his childhood.

"Hush, Emma!" the man kept saying. "Do be reasonable. Think of the children. They'll hear us."

"I don't care if they do. They'll know soon enough, God knows! I wish I was under the turf."

"Emma, do be reasonable."

"Reasonable! I—"

The child was crying again. The father came back to the first room, got something from his coat pocket, and took it in.

"Nils, are you quite mad, or do you want to drive me mad? Don't give the child that rattle! You must be either mad or a brute, and my nerves in this state. Haven't you got the slightest consideration for—"

"It's not a rattle, Emma; it's a doll."

"There you go again! Flinging your money away on rubbish that'll be on the dust-heap tomorrow, and your poor wife slaving her fingernails off for you in this wretched hole, and not a decent rag to her back. Me, your clever wife that ought to be—Light those candles and bring me a wet towel for my head. I must read now, and try and compose my nerves, if I can."

When the father returned to the first room, the boy was sitting up in bed, looking deathly white.

"Why, what's the matter, sonny?" said the father, bending over him, and putting a hand to his back.

"Nothing, father. I'll be all right directly. Don't you worry, father."

"Where do you feel bad, sonny?"

"In my head and stomach, father; but I'll be all right, d'rectly. I've often been that way."

In a minute or two he was worse.

"For God's sake, Nils, take that boy into the kitchen, or somewhere," cried the woman, "or I'll go mad. It's enough to kill a horse. Do you want to drive me into a lunatic asylum?"

"Do you feel better now, sonny?" asked the father.

"Yes, ever so much better, father," said the boy, white and weak. "I'll be all right in a minute, father."

"You had best sleep on the sofa tonight, sonny. It's cooler there."

"No, father, I'd rather stay here; it's much cooler now."

The father fixed the bed as comfortably as he could, and, despite the boy's protest, put his own pillow under his head. Then he made a fire in the kitchen, and hung the kettle and a big billy of water over it. He was haunted by recollections of convulsions amongst the children while they were teething. He took off his boots, and was about to lie down again when the mother called:

"Nils, Nils, have you made a fire?"

"Yes, Emma."

"Then for God's sake make me a cup of tea. I must have it after all this."

He hurried up the kettle—she calling every few minutes to know if "that kettle was boiling yet". He took her a cup of tea, and then a second. She said the tea was slush, and as sweet as syrup, and called for more, and hot water.

"How do you feel now, sonny?" he asked as he lay down on the sofa once more.

"Much better, father. You can put out the light now if you like."

The father blew out the candle, and settled back again, still dressed save for his coat, and presently the small, weak hand sought the hard, strong, horny, knotted one; and so they lay, as was customary with them. After a while the father leaned over a little and whispered:

"Asleep, sonny?"

"No, father."

"Feel bad again?"

"No, father."

Pause.

"What are you thinking about, sonny?"

"Nothing, father."

"But what is it? What are you worrying about? Tell me."

"Nothing, father, only—it'll be a good while yet before I grow up to be a man, won't it, father?"

The father lay silent and troubled for a few moments.

"Why do you ask me that question tonight, sonny? I thought you'd done with all that. You were always asking me that question when you were a child. You're getting too old for those foolish fancies now. Why have you always had such a horror of growing up to be a man?"

"I don't know, father. I always had funny thoughts—you know, father. I used to think that I'd been a child once before, and grew up to be a man, and grew old and died."

"You're not well tonight, sonny—that's what's the matter. You're queer, sonny; it's a touch of sun—that's all. Now, try to go to sleep. You'll grow up to be a man, in spite of laying awake worrying about it. If you do, you'll be a man all the sooner."

Suddenly the mother called out:

"Can't you be quiet? What do you mean by talking at this hour of the night? Am I never to get another wink of sleep? Shut those doors, Nils, for God's sake, if you don't want to drive me mad—and make that boy hold his tongue!"

The father closed the doors.

"Better try to go to sleep now, sonny," he whispered, as he lay down again.

The father waited for some time, then, moving very softly he lit the candle at the kitchen fire, put it where it shouldn't light the boy's face, and watched him. And the child knew he was watching him, and pretended to sleep, and, so pretending, he slept. And the old year died as many old years had died.

The father was up about four o'clock—he worked at his trade in a farming town about five miles away, and was struggling to make a farm and a home between jobs. He cooked bacon for breakfast, washed-up the dishes and tidied the kitchen, gave the boys some bread and bacon fat, of which they were very fond, and told the eldest to take a cup of tea and some bread and milk to his mother and the baby when they woke.

The boy milked the three cows, set the milk, and heard his mother calling:

"Nils! Nils!"

"Yes, mother."

"Why didn't you answer when I called you? I've been calling here for the last three hours. Is your father gone out?"

"Yes, mother."

"Thank God! It's a relief to be rid of his everlasting growling. Bring me a cup of tea and the *Australian Journal*, and take this child out and dress her; she should have been up hours ago."

And so the New Year began.

The Darling River

THE Darling—which is either a muddy gutter or a second Mississippi—is about six times as long as the distance, in a straight line, from its head to its mouth. The state of the river is vaguely but generally understood to depend on some distant and foreign phenomena to which bushmen refer in an off-hand tone of voice as the "Queenslan' rains", which seem to be held responsible, in a general way, for most of the outback trouble.

It takes less than a year to go up-stream by boat to Walgett or Bourke in a dry season; but after the first three months the passengers generally go ashore and walk. They get sick of being stuck in the same sort of place, in the same old way; they grow weary of seeing the same old whaler drop his swag on the bank opposite whenever the boat ties up for wood; they get tired of lending him tobacco, and listening to his ideas, which are limited in number and narrow in conception.

It shortens the journey to get out and walk; but then you will have to wait so long for your luggage—unless you hump it with you.

We heard of a man who determined to stick to a Darling boat and travel the whole length of the river. He was a newspaper man. He started on his voyage of discovery one Easter in flood-time, and a month later the captain got bushed between the Darling and South Australian border. The waters went away before he could find the river again, and left his boat in a scrub. They had a cargo of rations, and the crew stuck to the craft while the tucker lasted; when it gave out they rolled up their swags and went to look for a station, but didn't find one. The captain would study his watch and the sun, rig up dials and make out courses, and follow them without success. They ran short of water, and didn't smell any for weeks; they suffered terrible privations, and lost three of their number, *not* including the newspaper liar. There were even dark hints of considering the drawing of lots in connection with something too terrible to mention. They crossed a thirty-mile plain at last, and sighted a black gin. She led them to a boundary-rider's hut, where they were taken in and provided with rations and rum.

Later on a syndicate was formed to explore the country and recover the boat; but they found her thirty miles from the river and about eighteen from the nearest waterhole deep enough to float her, so they left her there. She's there still, or else the man that told us about it is the greatest liar outback.

Imagine the hull of a North Shore ferry-boat, blunted a little at the ends and cut off about a foot below the water-line, and parallel to it, then you will have something shaped somewhat like the hull of a Darling mud-rooter. But the river boat is much stronger. The boat we were on was built and repaired above deck after the different ideas of many bush carpenters, of whom the last seemed by his work to have regarded the original plan with a contempt only equalled by his disgust at the work of the last carpenter but one. The wheel was boxed in, mostly with round sapling-sticks fastened to the frame with bunches of nails and spikes of all shapes and sizes, most of them bent. The general result was decidedly picturesque in its irregularity, but dangerous to the mental welfare of any passenger who was foolish enough to try to comprehend the design; for it seemed as though every carpenter had taken the opportunity to work in a little abstract idea of his own.

The way they dock a Darling River boat is beautiful for its simplicity. They choose a place where there are two stout trees about the boat's length apart, and standing on a line parallel to the river. They fix pulley-blocks to the trees, lay sliding planks down into the water, fasten a rope to one end of the steamer, and take the other end through the block attached to the tree and thence back aboard a second steamer; then they carry a rope similarly from the other end through the block on the second tree, and aboard a third boat. At a given signal one boat leaves for Wentworth, and the other starts for the Queensland border. The consequence is that craft number one climbs the bank amid the cheers of the local loafers, who congregate and watch the proceedings with great interest and approval. The crew pitch tents, and set to work on the hull, which looks like a big, rough shallow box.

We once travelled on the Darling for a hundred miles or so on a boat called the *Mud Turtle*—at least, that's what *we* called her. She might reasonably have haunted the Mississippi fifty years ago. She didn't seem particular where she went, or whether she started again or stopped for good after getting stuck. Her machinery sounded like a chapter of accidents and was always out of order, but she got along all the same, provided the steersman kept her off the bank.

Her skipper was a young man, who looked more like a drover than a sailor, and the crew bore a greater resemblance to the unemployed than to any other body we know of, except that they looked a little more independent. They seemed clannish, too, with an unemployed or free-labour sort of isolation. We have an idea that they regarded our personal appearance with contempt.

Above Louth we picked up a whaler, who came aboard for the sake of society and tobacco. Not that he hoped to shorten his journey. He had no destination. He told us many reckless and unprincipled lies, and gave us a few ornamental facts. One of them took our fancy, and impressed us—with its beautiful simplicity, I suppose. He said: "Some miles above where the Darlin' and the Warrygo runs inter each other there's a billygong runnin' right across between the two rivers and makin' a sort of tryhangular hyland; 'n' I can tel'yer a funny thing about it." Here he paused to light his pipe. "Now," he continued impressively, jerking the match overboard, "when the Darlin's up, and the Warrygo's low, the billygong runs from the Darlin' into the *Warrygo*; and, when the Warrygo's up 'n' the Darlin's down, the waters runs *from* the Warrygo 'n' inter the Darlin'."

What could be more simple?

The steamer was engaged to go up a billabong for a load of shearers from a shed which was cutting out; and first it was necessary to tie up in the river and discharge the greater portion of the cargo in order that the boat might safely negotiate the shallow waters. A local fisherman, who volunteered to act as pilot, was taken aboard, and after he was outside about a pint of whisky he seemed to have the greatest confidence in his ability to take us to hell, or anywhere else—at least, he said so. A man was sent ashore with blankets and tucker, to mind the wool, and we crossed the river, butted into the anabranch, and started outback. Only the Lord and the pilot knew how we got there. We travelled over the bush, through its branches sometimes, and sometimes through grass and mud, and every now and then we struck something that felt and sounded like a collision. The boat slid down one hill, and "fetched" a stump at the bottom with a force that made every mother's son bite his tongue or break a tooth.

The shearers came aboard next morning, with their swags and two cartloads of boiled mutton, bread, brownie, and tea and sugar. They numbered about fifty, including the rouseabouts. This load of sin sank the steamer deeper into the mud; but the passengers crowded over to port, by request of the captain, and the crew poked the bank away with long poles. When we began to move the shearers gave a howl like the yell of a legion of lost souls escaping from down below. They gave three cheers for the rouseabouts' cook, who stayed behind; then they cursed the station with a mighty curse. They cleared a space on deck, had a jig, and afterwards a fight between the shearers' cook and his assistant. They gave a mighty bush whoop for the Darling when the boat swung into that grand old gutter, and in the evening they had a general all-round time. We got back, and the crew had to reload the wool without assistance, for it bore the accursed brand of a freedom-of-contract shed.

We slept, or tried to sleep, that night on the ridge of two wool-bales laid with the narrow sides up, having first been obliged to get ashore and fight six rounds with a shearer for the privilege of roosting there. The live cinders from the fire box went up the chimney all night, and fell in showers on deck. Every now and again a spark would burn through the Wagga rug of a sleeping shearer, and he'd wake suddenly and get up and curse. It was no use shifting round, for the wind was all ways, and the boat steered north, south, east, and west to humour the river. Occasionally a low branch would root three or four passengers off their wool-bales, and they'd get up and curse in chorus. The boat started two snags; and towards daylight struck a stump. The accent was on the stump. A wool-bale went overboard, and took a swag and a dog with it; then the owner of the swag and dog and the crew of the boat had a swearing match between them. The swagman won.

About daylight we stretched our cramped limbs, extricated one leg from between the wool-bales, and found that the steamer was just crayfishing away from a mud island, where she had tied up for more wool. Some of the chaps had been ashore and boiled four or five buckets of tea and coffee. Shortly after the boat had settled down to work again an incident came along. A rouseabout rose late, and, while the others were at breakfast, got an idea into his head that a good "sloosh" would freshen him up; so he mooched round until he found a big wooden bucket with a rope to it. He carried the bucket aft of the wheel. The boat was butting up-stream for all she was worth, and the stream was running the other way, of course, and about a hundred times as fast as a train. The jackeroo gave the line a turn round his wrist; before anyone could see him in time to suppress him, he lifted the bucket, swung it to and fro, and dropped it cleverly into the water.

This delayed us for nearly an hour. A couple of men jumped into the rowboat immediately and cast her adrift. They picked up the jackeroo about a mile down the river, clinging to a snag, and when we hauled him aboard he looked like something the cat had dragged in, only bigger. We revived him with rum and got him on his feet; and then, when the captain and crew had done cursing him, he rubbed his head, went forward, and had a look at the paddle; then he rubbed his head again, thought, and remarked to his mates:

"Wasn't it lucky I didn't dip that bucket *for'ard* the wheel?"

This remark struck us forcibly. We agreed that it was lucky—for him; but the captain remarked that it was damned unlucky for the world, which, he explained, was over-populated with fools already.

Getting on towards afternoon we found a barge loaded with wool and tied up to a tree in the wilderness. There was no sign of a man to be seen, nor any sign, except the barge, that a human being had ever been there. The captain took the craft in tow, towed it about ten miles up the stream, and left it in a less likely place than where it was before.

Floating bottles began to be more frequent, and we knew by that same token that we were nearing "Here's Luck!"—Bourke, we mean. And this reminds us.

When the Brewarrina people observe a more than ordinary number of bottles floating down the river, they guess that Walgett is on the spree; when the Louth chaps see an unbroken procession of dead marines for three or four days they know that Bourke's drunk. The poor, God-abandoned whaler sits in his hungry camp at sunset and watches the empty symbols of hope go by, and feels more God-forgotten than ever—and thirstier, if possible—and gets a great, wide, thirsty, quaking, empty longing to be up where those bottles come from. If the townspeople knew how much misery they caused by their thoughtlessness they would drown their dead marines, or bury them, but on no account allow them to go drifting down the river, and stirring up hells in the bosoms of less fortunate fellow-creatures.

There came a man from Adelaide to Bourke once, and he collected all the empty bottles in town, stacked them by the river, and waited for a boat. What he wanted them for the legend sayeth not, but the people reckoned he had a private still, or something of that sort, somewhere down the river, and were satisfied. What he came from Adelaide for, or whether he really did come from there, we do not know. All the Darling bunyips are supposed to come from Adelaide. Anyway, the man collected all the empty bottles he could lay his hands on, and piled them on the bank, where they made a good show. He waited for a boat to take his cargo, and, while waiting, he got drunk. That excited no comment. He stayed drunk for three weeks, but the townspeople saw nothing unusual in that. In order to become an object of interest in their eyes, and in that line, he would have to stay drunk for a year and fight three times a day—oftener, if possible—and lie in the road in the broiling heat between whiles, and be walked on by camels and Afghans and free-labourers, and be locked up every time he got sober enough to smash a policeman, and try to hang himself naked, and be finally squashed by a loaded wool-team.

But while he drank, the Darling rose, for reasons best known to itself, and floated those bottles off. They strung out and started for the Antarctic Ocean, with a big old wicker-worked demijohn in the lead.

For the first week the down-river men took no notice; but after the bottles had been drifting past with scarcely a break for a fortnight or so, they began to get interested. Several whalers watched the procession until they got the jim-jams by force of imagination, and when their bodies began to float down with the bottles, the down-river people got anxious.

At last the mayor of Wilcannia wired Bourke to know whether Dibbs or Parkes was dead, or democracy triumphant, or if not, wherefore the jubilation? Many telegrams of a like nature were received during that week, and the true explanation was sent in reply to each. But it wasn't believed, and to this day Bourke has the name of being the most drunken town on the river.

After dinner a humorous old hard case mysteriously took us aside and said he had a good yarn which we might be able to work up.

We asked him how, but he winked a mighty cunning wink and said that he knew all about us. Then he asked us to listen. He said:

"There was an old feller down the Murrumbidgee named Kelly. He was a bit gone here. One day Kelly was out lookin' for some sheep, when he got lost. It was gettin' dark. Byemby there came an old crow in a tree overhead.

" 'Kel-ley, you're lo-o-st! Kel-ley, you're lo-o-st!' sez the crow.

" 'I know I am,' sez Kelly.

" 'Fol-ler me, fol-ler me,' sez the crow.

" 'Right y'are,' sez Kelly, with a jerk of his arm. 'Go ahead.'

"So the crow went on, and Kelly follered, an' byemby he found he was on the right track.

"Sometime after Kelly was washin' sheep (this was when we useter wash the sheep instead of the wool). Kelly was standin' on the platform with a crutch in his hand landin' the sheep, when there came a old crow in the tree overhead.

" 'Kelly, I'm hun-gry! Kel-ley, I'm hun-ger-ry!' sez the crow.

" 'All right,' sez Kelly; 'be up at the hut about dinner-time 'n' I'll sling you out something.'

" 'Drown—a—sheep! Drown—a—sheep, Kel-ley,' sez the crow.

" 'Blanked if I do,' sez Kelly. 'If I drown a sheep I'll have to pay for it, be-God!'

" 'Then I won't find yer when yer lost agin,' sez the crow.

" 'I'm damned if yer will,' says Kelly. 'I'll take blanky good care I won't get lost again, to be found by a gory ole crow.' "

There are a good many fishermen on the Darling. They camp along the banks in all sorts of tents, and move about in little box boats that will only float one man. The fisherman is never heavy. He is mostly a withered little old madman, with black claws, dirty rags (which he never changes), unkempt hair and beard, and a "ratty" expression. We cannot say that we ever saw him catch a fish, or even get a bite, and we certainly never saw him offer any for sale.

He gets a dozen or so lines out into the stream, with the shore end fastened to pegs or roots on the bank, and passed over sticks about four feet high, stuck in the mud; on the top of these sticks he hangs bullock-bells, or substitutes—jam-tins with stones fastened inside to bits of string. Then he sits down and waits. If the cod pulls the line the bell rings.

The fisherman is a great authority on the river and fish, but has usually forgotten everything else, including his name. He chops firewood for the boats sometimes, but it isn't his profession—he's a fisherman. He is only sane on points concerning the river, though he has all the fisherman's eccentricities. Of course he is a liar.

When he gets his camp fixed on one bank it strikes him he ought to be over on the other, or at a place up round the bend, so he shifts. Then he reckons he was a fool for not stopping where he was before. He never dies. He never gets older, or drier, or more withered-looking, or dirtier, or loonier—because he can't. We cannot imagine him as ever having been a boy, or even a youth. We cannot even try to imagine him as a baby. He is an animated mummy, who used to fish on the Nile three thousand years ago, and catch nothing.

We forgot to mention that there are wonderfully few wrecks on the Darling. The river boats seldom go down—their hulls are not built that way—and if one did go down it wouldn't sink far. But, once down, a boat is scarcely ever raised again; because, you see, the mud silts up round it and over it, and glues it, as it were, to the bottom of the river. Then the forty-foot alligators—which come down with the "Queenslan' rains", we suppose—root in the mud and fill their bellies with sodden flour and drowned deck-hands.

They tried once to blow up a wreck with dynamite because it (the wreck) obstructed navigation; but they blew the bottom out of the river instead, and all the water went through. The Government have been boring for it ever since. I saw some of the bores myself—there is one at Coonamble.

There is a yarn along the Darling about a cute Yankee who was invited up to Bourke to report on a proposed scheme for locking the river. He arrived towards the end of a long and severe drought, and was met at the railway-station by a deputation of representative bushmen, who invited him, in the first place, to accompany them to the principal pub—which he did. He had been observed to study the scenery a good deal while coming up in the train, but kept his conclusions to himself. On the way to the pub he had a look at the town, and it was noticed that he tilted his hat forward very often, and scratched the back of his head a good deal, and pondered a lot; but he refrained from expressing an opinion—even when invited to do so. He guessed that his opinions wouldn't do much good, anyway, and he calculated that they would keep till he got back "over our way"—by which it was reckoned he meant the States.

When they asked him what he'd have, he said to Watty the publican:

"Wal, I reckon you can build me your national drink. I guess I'll try it."

A long colonial was drawn for him, and he tried it. He seemed rather startled at first, then he looked curiously at the half-empty glass, set it down very softly on the bar, and leaned against the same and fell into reverie; from which he roused himself after a while, with a sorrowful jerk of his head.

"Ah, well," he said. "Show me this river of yourn."

They led him to the Darling, and he had a look at it.

"Is this your river?" he asked.

"Yes," they replied, apprehensively.

He tilted his hat forward till the brim nearly touched his nose, scratched the back of his long neck, shut one eye, and looked at the river with the other. Then, after spitting half a pint of tobacco juice into the stream, he turned sadly on his heel and led the way back to the pub. He invited the boys to "pisen themselves"; after they were served he ordered out the longest tumbler on the premises, poured a drop into it from nearly every bottle on the shelf, added a lump of ice, and drank slowly and steadily.

Then he took pity on the impatient and anxious population, opened his mouth, and spake.

"Look here, fellows," he drawled, jerking his arm in the direction of the river, "I'll tell you what I'll dew. I'll bottle that damned river of yourn in twenty-four hours!"

Later on he mellowed a bit, under the influence of several drinks which were carefully and conscientiously built from plans and specifications supplied by himself, and then, among other things, he said:

"If that there river rises as high as you say it dew—and if this was the States—why, we'd have had the *Great Eastern* up here twenty years ago"—or words to that effect.

Then he added, reflectively:

"When I come over here I calculated that I was going to make things hum, but now I guess I'll have to change my prospectus. There's a lot of loose energy laying round over our way, but I guess that if I wanted to make things move in your country I'd have to bring over the entire American nation—also his wife and dawg. You've got the makings of a glorious nation over here, but you don't get up early enough!"

The only national work performed by the blacks is on the Darling. They threw a dam of rocks across the river—near Brewarrina, we think—to make a fish-trap. It's there yet. But God only knows where they got the stones from, or how they carried them, for there isn't a pebble within forty miles.

Send Round the Hat

Now this is the creed from the Book of the Bush—
Should be simple and plain to a dunce:
"If a man's in a hole you must pass round the hat—
Were he jail-bird or gentleman once."

"Is it any harm to wake yer?"

It was about nine o'clock in the morning, and, though it was Sunday morning, it was no harm to wake me; but the shearer had mistaken me for a deaf jackeroo, who was staying at the shanty and was something like me, and had good-naturedly shouted almost at the top of his voice, and he woke the whole shanty. Anyway he woke three or four others who were sleeping on beds and stretchers, and one on a shake-down on the floor, in the same room. It had been a wet night, and the shanty was full of shearers from Big Billabong Shed which had cut out the day before. My room mates had been drinking and gambling overnight, and they swore luridly at the intruder for disturbing them.

He was six-foot-three or thereabout. He was loosely built, bony, sandy-complexioned and grey-eyed. He wore a good-humoured grin at most times, as I noticed later on; he was of a type of bushman that I always liked—the sort that seem to get more good-natured the longer they grow, yet are hard-knuckled and would accommodate a man who wanted to fight, or thrash a bully in a good-natured way. The sort that like to carry somebody's baby round, and cut wood, carry water and do little things for overworked married bushwomen. He wore a saddle-tweed sac suit two sizes too small for him, and his face, neck, great hands and bony wrists were covered with sun-blotches and freckles.

"I hope I ain't disturbin' yer," he shouted, as he bent over my bunk, "but there's a cove——"

"You needn't shout!" I interrupted, "I'm not deaf."

"Oh—I beg your pardon!" he shouted. "I didn't know I was yellin'. I thought you was the deaf feller."

"Oh, that's all right," I said. "What's the trouble?"

H

"Wait till them other chaps is done swearin' and I'll tell yer," he said. He spoke with a quiet, good-natured drawl, with something of the nasal twang, but tone and drawl distinctly Australian—altogether apart from that of the Americans.

"Oh, spit it out for Christ's sake, Long-'un!" yelled One-eyed Bogan, who had been the worst swearer in a rough shed, and he fell back on his bunk as if his previous remarks had exhausted him.

"It's that there sick jackeroo that was pickin'-up at Big Billabong," said the Giraffe. "He had to knock off the first week, an' he's been here ever since. They're sendin' him away to the hospital in Sydney by the speeshall train. They're just goin' to take him up in the wagonette to the railway-station, an' I thought I might as well go round with the hat an' get him a few bob. He's got a missus and kids in Sydney."

"Yer always goin' round with yer gory hat!" growled Bogan. "Yer'd blanky well take it round in hell!"

"That's what he's doing, Bogan," muttered Gentleman Once, on the shake-down, with his face to the wall.

The hat was a genuine cabbage-tree, one of the sort that "last a lifetime". It was well coloured, almost black in fact with weather and age, and it had a new strap round the base of the crown. I looked into it and saw a dirty pound note and some silver. I dropped in half a crown, which was more than I could spare, for I had only been a green-hand at Big Billabong.

"Thank yer!" he said. "Now then, you fellers!"

"I wish you'd keep your hat on your head, and your money in your pockets and your sympathy somewhere else," growled Jack Moonlight as he raised himself painfully on his elbow and felt under his pillow for two half-crowns. "Here," he said, "here's two half-casers. Chuck 'em in and let me sleep for God's sake!"

Gentleman Once, the gambler, rolled round on his shake-down, bringing his good-looking dissipated face from the wall. He had turned in in his clothes and, with considerable exertion he shoved his hand down into the pocket of his trousers, which were a tight fit. He brought up a roll of pound notes and could find no silver.

"Here," he said to the Giraffe, "I might as well lay a quid. I'll chance it anyhow. Chuck it in."

"You've got rats this mornin', Gentleman Once," growled the Bogan. "It ain't a blanky horse-race."

"P'r'aps I have," said Gentleman Once, and he turned to the wall again with his head on his arm.

"Now, Bogan, yer might as well chuck in somethin'," said the Giraffe.

"What's the matter with the —— jackeroo?" asked the Bogan, tugging his trousers from under the mattress.

Moonlight said something in a low tone.

"The —— he has!" said Bogan. "Well, I pity the ——! Here, I'll chuck in half a —— quid!" and he dropped half a sovereign into the hat.

The fourth man, who was known to his face as "Barcoo-Rot", and behind his back as "The Mean Man", had been drinking all night, and not even Bogan's stump-splitting adjectives could rouse him. So Bogan got out of bed, and calling on us (as blanky female cattle) to witness what he was about to do, he rolled the drunkard over, prospected his pockets till he made up five shillings (or a "caser" in bush language), and "chucked" them into the hat.

And Barcoo-Rot is probably unconscious to this day that he was ever connected with an act of charity.

The Giraffe struck the deaf jackeroo in the next room. I heard the chaps cursing Long-'un for waking them, and Deaf-'un for being, as they thought at first, the indirect cause of the disturbance. I heard the Giraffe and his hat being condemned in other rooms and cursed along the veranda where more shearers were sleeping; and after a while I turned out.

The Giraffe was carefully fixing a mattress and pillows on the floor of a wagonette, and presently a man, who looked like a corpse, was carried out and lifted into the trap.

As the wagonette started, the shanty-keeper—a fat, soulless-looking man—put his hand in his pocket and dropped a quid into the hat which was still going round, in the hands of the Giraffe's mate, little Teddy Thompson, who was as far below medium height as the Giraffe was above it.

The Giraffe took the horse's head and led him along on the most level parts of the road towards the railway-station, and two or three chaps went along to help get the sick man into the train.

The shearing season was over in that district, but I got a job of house-painting, which was my trade, at the Great Western Hotel (a two-storey brick place), and I stayed in Bourke for a couple of months.

The Giraffe was a Victorian native from Bendigo. He was well known in Bourke and to many shearers who came through the great dry scrubs from hundreds of miles round. He was stake-holder, drunkard's banker, peace-maker where possible, referee or second to oblige the chaps when a fight was on, big brother or uncle to most of the children in town, final court of appeal when the youngsters had a dispute over a foot-race at the school picnic, referee at their fights, and he was the stranger's friend.

"The feller as knows can battle around for himself," he'd say. "But I always like to do what I can for a hard-up stranger cove. I was a green-hand jackeroo once meself, and I know what it is."

"You're always bothering about other people, Giraffe," said Tom Hall, the Shearers' Union secretary, who was only a couple of inches shorter than the Giraffe. "There's nothing in it, you can take it from me—I ought to know."

"Well, what's a feller to do?" said the Giraffe. "I'm only hangin' round here till shearin' starts agen, an' a cove might as well be doin' something. Besides, it ain't as if I was like a cove that had old people or a wife an' kids to look after. I ain't got no responsibilities. A feller can't be doin' nothin'. Besides, I like to lend a helpin' hand when I can."

"Well, all I've got to say," said Tom, most of whose screw went in borrowed quids, etc.; "all I've got to say is that you'll get no thanks, and you might blanky well starve in the end."

"There ain't no fear of me starvin' so long as I've got me hands about me; an' I ain't a cove as wants thanks," said the Giraffe.

He was always helping someone or something. Now it was a bit of a "darnce" that we was gettin' up for the girls; again it was Mrs Smith, the woman whose husban' was drowned in the flood in the Bogan River lars' Crismas, or that there poor woman down by the Billabong—her husband cleared out and left her with a lot o' kids. Or Bill Something, the bullocky, who was run over by his own wagon, while he was drunk, and got his leg broke.

Towards the end of his spree One-eyed Bogan broke loose and smashed nearly all the windows of the Carriers' Arms, and next morning he was fined heavily at the police court. About dinner-time I encountered the Giraffe and his hat, with two half-crowns in it for a start.

"I'm sorry to trouble yer," he said, "but One-eyed Bogan carn't pay his fine, an' I thought we might fix it up for him. He ain't half a bad sort of feller when he ain't drinkin'. It's only when he gets too much booze in him."

After shearing, the hat usually started round with the Giraffe's own dirty crumpled pound note in the bottom of it as a send-off, later on it was half a sovereign; till in the end he would borrow a "few bob"—which he always repaid after next shearing—"just to start the thing goin'."

There were several yarns about him and his hat. 'Twas said that the hat had belonged to his father, whom he resembled in every respect, and it had been going round for so many years that the crown was worn as thin as paper by the quids, half-quids, casers, half-casers, bobs and tanners or sprats—to say nothing of the scrums—that had been chucked into it in its time and shaken up.

They say that when a new Governor visited Bourke the Giraffe happened to be standing on the platform close to the exit, grinning good-humouredly, and the local toady nudged him urgently and said in an awful whisper, "Take off your hat! Why don't you take off your hat?"

"Why?" drawled the Giraffe, "he ain't hard up, is he?"

And they fondly cherish an anecdote to the effect that, when the One-Man-One-Vote Bill was passed (or Payment of Members, or when the first Labour Party went in—I forget on which occasion they said it was) the Giraffe was carried away by the general enthusiasm, got a few beers in him, "chucked" a quid into his hat, and sent it round. The boys contributed by force of habit, and contributed largely, because of the victory and the beer. And when the hat came back to the Giraffe, he stood holding it in front of him with both hands and stared blankly into it for a while. Then it dawned on him.

"Blowed if I haven't bin an' gone an' took up a bloomin' collection for meself!" he said.

He was almost a teetotaller, but he stood his shout in reason. He mostly drank ginger-beer.

"I ain't a feller that boozes, but I ain't got nothin' agen chaps enjoyin' themselves, so long as they don't go too far."

It was common for a man on the spree to say to him:

"Here! here's five quid. Look after it for me, Giraffe, will yer, till I get off the booze."

His real name was Bob Brothers, and his bush names, Long-'un, The Giraffe, Send-round-the-hat, Chuck-in-a-bob, and Ginger-ale.

Some years before, camels and Afghan drivers had been imported to the Bourke district; the camels did very well in the dry country, they went right across the country and carried everything from sardines to flooring-boards. And the teamsters loved the Afghans nearly as much as Sydney furniture makers love the cheap Chinese in the same line. They loved 'em even as union shearers on strike love blacklegs brought up-country to take their places.

Now the Giraffe was a good, straight unionist, but in cases of sickness or trouble he was as apt to forget his unionism, as all bushmen are, at all times (and for all time), to forget their creed. So, one evening, the Giraffe blundered into the Carriers' Arms—of all places in the world—when it was full of teamsters; he had his hat in his hand and some small silver and coppers in it.

"I say, you fellers, there's a poor, sick Afghan in the camp down there along the——"

A big, brawny bullock-driver took him firmly by the shoulders, or rather by the elbows, and ran him out before any damage was done. The Giraffe took it as he took most things, good-humouredly; but, about dusk, he was seen slipping down towards the Afghan camp with a billy of soup.

"I believe," remarked Tom Hall, "that when the Giraffe goes to heaven—and he's the only one of us, as far as I can see, that has a ghost of a show—I believe that when he goes to heaven, the first thing he'll do will be to take his infernal hat round amongst the angels—getting up a collection for this damned world that he left behind."

"Well, I don't think there's so much to his credit, after all," said Jack Mitchell, shearer. "You see, the Giraffe is ambitious; he likes public life, and that accounts for him shoving himself forward with his collections. As for bothering about people in trouble, that's only common curiosity; he's one of those chaps that are always shoving their noses into other people's troubles. And as for looking after sick men—why! there's nothing the Giraffe likes better than pottering round a sick man, and watching him and studying him. He's awfully interested in sick men, and they're pretty scarce out here. I tell you there's nothing he likes better—except, maybe, it's pottering round a corpse. I believe he'd ride forty miles to help and sympathize and potter round a funeral. The fact of the matter is that the Giraffe is only enjoying himself with other people's troubles—that's all it is. It's only vulgar curiosity and selfishness. I set it down to his ignorance; the way he was brought up."

A few days after the Afghan incident the Giraffe and his hat had a run of luck. A German, one of a party who were building a new wooden bridge over the Big Billabong, was helping unload some girders from a truck at the railway-station when a big log slipped on the skids and his leg was smashed badly. They carried him to the Carriers' Arms, which was the nearest hotel, and into a bedroom behind the bar, and sent for the doctor. The Giraffe was in evidence as usual.

"It vas not that at all," said German Charlie, when they asked him if he was in much pain. "It vas not that at all. I don't cares a damn for der bain; but dis is der tird year—und I vas going home dis year—after der gontract—und der gontract yoost commence!"

That was the burden of his song all through, between his groans.

There were a good few chaps sitting quietly about the bar and veranda when the doctor arrived. The Giraffe was sitting at the end of the counter, on which he had laid his hat while he wiped his face, neck, and forehead with a big speckled sweat-rag. It was a very hot day.

The doctor, a good-hearted young Australian, was heard saying something. Then German Charlie, in a voice that rung with pain:

"Make that leg right, doctor—quick! Dis is der tird pluddy year—und I must go home!"

The doctor asked him if he was in great pain.

"Neffer mind der pluddy bain, doctor! Neffer mind der pluddy bain! Dot vas nossing. Make dat leg vell quick, doctor. Dis vas der last contract, and I vas going home dis year." Then the words jerked out of him by physical agony: "Der girl vas vaiting dree year, and—by Got! I must go home."

The publican—Watty Braithwaite, known as Watty Broadweight, or, more familiarly, Watty Bothways—turned over the Giraffe's hat in a tired, bored sort of way, dropped a quid into it, and nodded resignedly at the Giraffe.

The Giraffe caught up the hint and the hat with alacrity. The hat went all round town, so to speak; and as soon as his leg was firm enough not to come loose on the road German Charlie went home.

It was well known that I contributed to the Sydney *Bulletin* and several other papers. The Giraffe's bump of reverence was very large, and swelled especially for sick men and poets. He treated me with much more respect than is due from a bushman to a man, and with an odd sort of extra gentleness I sometimes fancied. But one day he rather surprised me.

"I'm sorry to trouble yer," he said in a shamefaced way. "I don't know as you go in for sportin', but One-eyed Bogan an' Barcoo-Rot is goin' to have a bit of a scrap down the Billybong this evenin', an'——"

"A bit of a what?" I asked.

"A bit of a fight to a finish," he said apologetically. "An' the chaps is tryin' to fix up a fiver to put some life into the thing. There's bad blood between One-eyed Bogan and Barcoo-Rot, an' it won't do them any harm to have it out."

It was a great fight, I remember. There must have been a couple of score blood-soaked handkerchiefs (or sweat-rags) buried in a hole on the field of battle, and the Giraffe was busy the rest of the evening helping to patch up the principals. Later on he took up a small collection for the loser, who happened to be Barcoo-Rot in spite of the advantage of an eye.

The Salvation Army lassie, who went round with the *War Cry*, nearly always sold the Giraffe three copies.

A newchum parson, who wanted a subscription to build or enlarge a chapel, or something, sought the assistance of the Giraffe's influence with his mates.

"Well," said the Giraffe, "I ain't a churchgoer meself. I ain't what you might call a religious cove, but I'll be glad to do what I can to help yer. I don't suppose I can do much. I ain't been to church since I was a kiddy."

The parson was shocked, but later on he learned to appreciate the Giraffe and his mates, and to love Australia for the bushman's sake, and it was he who told me the above anecdote.

The Giraffe helped fix some stalls for a Catholic Church bazaar, and some of the chaps chaffed him about it in the union office.

"You'll be taking up a collection for a joss-house down in the Chinamen's camp next," said Tom Hall in conclusion.

"Well, I ain't got nothin' agen the Roming Carflicks," said the Giraffe. "An' Father O'Donovan's a very decent sort of cove. He stuck up for the unions all right in the strike anyway." ("He wouldn't be Irish if he wasn't," someone commented.) "I carried swags once for six months with a feller that was a Carflick, an' he was a very straight feller. And a girl I knowed turned Carflick to marry a chap that had got her into trouble, an' she was always jes' the same to me after as she was before. Besides, I like to help everything that's goin' on."

Tom Hall and one or two others went out hurriedly to have a drink. But we all loved the Giraffe.

He was very innocent and very humorous, especially when he meant to be most serious and philosophical.

"Some of them bush girls is regular tomboys," he said to me solemnly one day. "Some of them is too cheeky altogether. I remember once I was stoppin' at a place—they was sort of relations o' mine—an' they put me to sleep in a room off the verander, where there was a glass door an' no blinds. An' the first mornin' the girls —they was sort o' cousins o' mine—they come gigglin' and foolin' round outside the door on the verander, an' kep' me in bed till nearly ten o'clock. I had to put me trowsis on under the bed-clothes in the end. But I got back on 'em the next night," he reflected.

"How did you do that, Bob?" I asked.

"Why, I went to bed in me trowsis!"

One day I was on a plank, painting the ceiling of the bar of the Great Western Hotel. I was anxious to get the job finished. The work had been kept back most of the day by chaps handing up long beers to me, and drawing my attention to the alleged fact that I was putting on the paint wrong side out. I was slapping it on over the last few boards when:

"I'm very sorry to trouble yer; I always seem to be troublin' yer; but there's that there woman and them girls——"

I looked down—about the first time I had looked down on him—and there was the Giraffe, with his hat brim up on the plank and two half-crowns in it.

"Oh, that's all right, Bob," I said, and I dropped in half a crown.

There were shearers in the bar, and presently there was some barracking. It appeared that that there woman and them girls were strange women, in the local as well as the Biblical sense of the word, who had come from Sydney at the end of the shearing-season, and had taken a cottage on the edge of the scrub on the outskirts of the town. There had been trouble this week in connection with a row at their establishment, and they had been fined, warned off by the police, and turned out by their landlord.

"This is a bit too red-hot, Giraffe," said one of the shearers. "Them ——s has made enough out of us coves. They've got plenty of stuff, don't you fret. Let 'em go to ——! I'm blanked if I give a sprat."

"They ain't got their fares to Sydney," said the Giraffe. "An', what's more, the little 'un is sick, an' two of them has kids in Sydney."

"How the —— do you know?"

"Why, one of 'em come to me an' told me all about it."

There was an involuntary guffaw.

"Look here, Bob," said Billy Woods, the rouseabouts' secretary, kindly. "Don't you make a fool of yourself. You'll have all the chaps laughing at you. Those girls are only working you for all you're worth. I suppose one of 'em came crying and whining to you. Don't you bother about 'em. *You* don't know 'em; they can pump water at a moment's notice. You haven't had any experience with women yet, Bob."

"She didn't come whinin' and cryin' to me," said the Giraffe, dropping his twanging drawl a little. "She looked me straight in the face an' told me all about it."

"I say, Giraffe," said Box-o'-Tricks, "what have you been doin'? You've bin down there on the nod. I'm surprised at yer, Giraffe."

"An' he pretends to be so gory soft an' innocent, too," growled the Bogan. "We know all about you, Giraffe."

"Look here, Giraffe," said Mitchell the shearer. "I'd never have thought it of you. We all thought you were the only virgin youth west the river; I always thought you were a moral young man. You mustn't think that because your conscience is pricking you everyone else's is."

"I ain't had anythin' to do with them," said the Giraffe, drawling again. "I ain't a cove that goes in for that sort of thing. But other chaps has, and I think they might as well help 'em out of their fix."

"They're a rotten crowd," said Billy Woods. "You don't know them, Bob. Don't bother about them—they're not worth it. Put your money in your pocket. You'll find a better use for it before next shearing."

"Better shout, Giraffe," said Box-o'-Tricks.

Now in spite of the Giraffe's softness he was the hardest man in Bourke to move when he'd decided on what he thought was "the fair thing to do". Another peculiarity of his was that on occasion, such for instance as "sayin' a few words" at a strike meeting, he would straighten himself, drop the twang, and rope in his drawl, so to speak.

"Well, look here, you chaps," he said now. "I don't know anything about them women. I s'pose they're bad, but I don't suppose they're worse than men has made them. All I know is that there's four women turned out, without any stuff, and every woman in Bourke, an' the police, an' the law agen 'em. An' the fact that they is women is agenst 'em most of all. You don't expect 'em to hump their swags to Sydney! Why, only I ain't got the stuff I wouldn't trouble yer. I'd pay their fares meself. Look," he said, lowering his voice, "there they are now, an' one of the girls is cryin'. Don't let 'em see yer lookin'."

I dropped softly from the plank and peeped out with the rest.

They stood by the fence on the opposite side of the street, a bit up towards the railway-station, with their portmanteaux and bundles at their feet. One girl leant with her arms on the fence rail and her face buried in them, another was trying to comfort her. The third girl and the woman stood facing our way. The woman was good-looking: she had a hard face, but it might have been made hard. The third girl seemed half defiant, half inclined to cry. Presently she went to the other side of the girl who was crying on the fence and put her arm round her shoulder. The woman suddenly turned her back on us and stood looking away over the paddocks.

The hat went round. Billy Woods was first, then Box-o'-Tricks, and then Mitchell.

Billy contributed with eloquent silence. "I was only jokin', Giraffe," said Box-o'-Tricks, dredging his pockets for a couple of shillings. It was some time after the shearing, and most of the chaps were hard up.

"Ah, well," sighed Mitchell. "There's no help for it. If the Giraffe would take up a collection to import some decent girls to this God-forgotten hole there might be some sense in it. . . . It's bad enough for the Giraffe to undermine our religious prejudices, and tempt us to take a morbid interest in sick Chows and Afghans, and blacklegs and widows; but when he starts mixing us up with strange women it's time to buck." And he prospected his pockets and contributed two shillings, some odd pennies, and a pinch of tobacco dust.

"I don't mind helping the girls, but I'm damned if I'll give a penny to help the old ——," said Tom Hall.

"Well, she was a girl once herself," drawled the Giraffe.

The Giraffe went round to the other pubs and to the union offices, and when he returned he seemed satisfied with the plate, but troubled about something else.

"I don't know what to do for them for tonight," he said. "None of the pubs or boardin'-houses will hear of them, an' there ain't no empty houses, an' the women is all agen 'em."

"Not all," said Alice, the big, handsome barmaid from Sydney. "Come here, Bob." She gave the Giraffe half a sovereign and a look for which some of us would have paid him ten pounds—had we had the money, and had the look been transferable.

"Wait a minute, Bob," she said, and she went in to speak to the landlord.

"There's an empty bedroom at the end of the store in the yard," she said when she came back. "They can camp there for tonight if they behave themselves. You'd better tell 'em, Bob."

"Thank yer, Alice," said the Giraffe.

Next day, after work, the Giraffe and I drifted together and down by the river in the cool of the evening, and sat on the edge of the steep, drought-parched bank.

"I heard you saw your lady friends off this morning, Bob," I said, and was sorry I said it, even before he answered.

"Oh, they ain't no friends of mine," he said. "Only four poor devils of women. I thought they mightn't like to stand waitin' with the crowd on the platform, so I jest offered to get their tickets an' told 'em to wait round at the back of the station till the bell rung. An' what do yer think they did, Harry?" he went on, with an exasperatingly unintelligent grin. "Why, they wanted to kiss me."

"Did they?"

"Yes. An' they would have done it, too, if I hadn't been so long. Why, I'm blessed if they didn't kiss me hands."

"You don't say so."

"God's truth. Somehow I didn't like to go on the platform with them after that; besides, they was cryin', and I can't stand women cryin'. But some of the chaps put them into an empty carriage." He thought a moment. Then:

"There's some terrible good-hearted fellers in the world," he reflected.

I thought so too.

"Bob," I said, "you're a single man. Why don't you get married and settle down?"

"Well," he said, "I ain't got no wife an' kids, that's a fact. But it ain't my fault."

He may have been right about the wife. But I thought of the look that Alice had given him, and——

"Girls seem to like me right enough," he said, "but it don't go no further than that. The trouble is that I'm so long, and I always seem to get shook after little girls. At least there was one little girl in Bendigo that I was properly gone on."

"And wouldn't she have you?"

"Well, it seems not."

"Did you ask her?"

"Oh, yes, I asked her right enough."

"Well, and what did she say?"

"She said it would be redicilus for her to be seen trottin' alongside of a chimbly like me."

"Perhaps she didn't mean that. There are any amount of little women who like tall men."

"I thought of that too—afterwards. P'r'aps she didn't mean it that way. I s'pose the fact of the matter was that she didn't cotton on to me, and wanted to let me down easy. She didn't want to hurt me feelin's, if yer understand—she was a very good-hearted little girl. There's some terrible tall fellers where I come from, and I know two as married little girls."

He seemed a hopeless case.

"Sometimes," he said, "sometimes I wish that I wasn't so blessed long."

"There's that there deaf jackeroo," he reflected presently. "He's something in the same fix about girls as I am. He's too deaf and I'm too long."

"How do you make that out?" I asked. "He's got three girls, to my knowledge, and as for being deaf, why, he gasses more than any man in the town, and knows more of what's going on than old Mother Brindle the washer-woman."

"Well, look at that now!" said the Giraffe, slowly. "Who'd have thought it? He never told me he had three girls, an' as for hearin' news, I always tell him anything that's goin' on that I think he doesn't catch. He told me his trouble was that whenever he went out with a girl people could hear what they was sayin'—at least they could hear what she was sayin' to him, an' draw their own conclusions, he said. He said he went out one night with a girl, and some of the chaps foxed 'em an' heard her sayin' 'don't' to him, an' put it all round town."

"What did she say 'don't' for?" I asked.

"He didn't tell me that, but I s'pose he was kissin' her or huggin' her or something."

"Bob," I said presently, "didn't you try the little girl in Bendigo a second time?"

"No," he said. "What was the use. She was a good little girl, and I wasn't goin' to go botherin' her. I ain't the sort of cove that goes hangin' round where he isn't wanted. But somehow I couldn't stay about Bendigo after she gave me the hint, so I thought I'd come over an' have a knock round on this side for a year or two."

"And you never wrote to her?"

"No. What was the use of goin' pesterin' her with letters? I know what trouble letters give me when I have to answer one. She'd have only had to tell me the straight truth in a letter an' it wouldn't have done me any good. But I've pretty well got over it by this time."

A few days later I went to Sydney. The Giraffe was the last I shook hands with from the carriage window, and he slipped something in a piece of newspaper into my hand.

"I hope yer won't be offended," he drawled, "but some of the chaps thought you mightn't be too flush of stuff—you've been shoutin' a good deal; so they put a quid or two together. They thought it might help yer to have a bit of a fly round in Sydney."

I was back in Bourke before next shearing. On the evening of my arrival I ran against the Giraffe; he seemed strangely shaken over something, but he kept his hat on his head.

"Would yer mind takin' a stroll as fur as the Billerbong?" he said. "I got something I'd like to tell yer."

His big, brown, sunburnt hands trembled and shook as he took a letter from his pocket and opened it.

"I've just got a letter," he said. "A letter from that little girl at Bendigo. It seems it was all a mistake. I'd like yer to read it. Somehow I feel as if I want to talk to a feller, and I'd rather talk to you than any of them other chaps."

It was a good letter, from a big-hearted little girl. She had been breaking her heart for the great ass all these months. It seemed that he had left Bendigo without saying good-bye to her. "Somehow I couldn't bring meself to it," he said, when I taxed him with it. She had never been able to get his address until last week; then she got it from a Bourke man who had gone south. She called him "an awful long fool", which he was, without the slightest doubt, and she implored him to write, and come back to her.

"And will you go back, Bob?" I asked.

"My oath! I'd take the train tomorrow only I ain't got the stuff. But I've got a stand in Big Billerbong Shed an' I'll soon knock a few quid together. I'll go back as soon as ever shearin's over. I'm goin' to write away to her tonight."

The Giraffe was the ringer of Big Billabong Shed that season. His tallies averaged a hundred and twenty a day. He only sent his hat round once during shearing, and it was noticed that he hesitated at first and only contributed half a crown. But then it was a case of a man being taken from the shed by the police for wife desertion.

"It's always that way," commented Mitchell. "Those soft, good-hearted fellows always end by getting hard and selfish. The world makes 'em so. It's the thought of the soft fools they've been that finds out sooner or later and makes 'em repent. Like as not the Giraffe will be the meanest man outback before he's done."

When Big Billabong cut out, and we got back to Bourke with our dusty swags and dirty cheques, I spoke to Tom Hall:

"Look here, Tom," I said. "That long fool, the Giraffe, has been breaking his heart for a little girl in Bendigo ever since he's been outback, and she's been breaking her heart for him, and the ass didn't know it till he got a letter from her just before Big Billabong started. He's going tomorrow morning."

That evening Tom stole the Giraffe's hat. "I s'pose it'll turn up in the mornin'," said the Giraffe. "I don't mind a lark," he added, "but it does seem a bit red-hot for the chaps to collar a cove's hat and a feller goin' away for good, p'r'aps, in the mornin'."

Mitchell started the thing going with a quid.

"It's worth it," he said, "to get rid of him. We'll have some peace now. There won't be so many accidents or women in trouble when the Giraffe and his blessed hat are gone. Anyway, he's an eyesore in the town, and he's getting on my nerves for one. . . . Come on, you sinners! Chuck 'em in; we're only taking quids and half-quids."

About daylight next morning Tom Hall slipped into the Giraffe's room at the Carriers' Arms. The Giraffe was sleeping peacefully. Tom put the hat on a chair by his side. The collection had been a record one, and besides the packet of money in the crown of the hat there was a silver-mounted pipe with case—the best that could be bought in Bourke—a gold brooch, and several trifles, besides an ugly valentine of a long man in his shirt walking the room with a twin on each arm.

Tom was about to shake the Giraffe by the shoulder when he noticed a great foot, with about half a yard of big-boned ankle and shank, sticking out at the bottom of the bed. The temptation was too great. Tom took up the hair-brush, and, with the back of it, he gave a smart rap on the point of an ingrowing toe-nail, and slithered.

We heard the Giraffe swearing good-naturedly for a while, and then there was a pregnant silence. He was staring at the hat we supposed.

We were all up at the station to see him off. It was rather a long wait. The Giraffe edged me up to the other end of the platform.

He seemed overcome.

"There's—there's some terrible good-hearted fellers in this world," he said. "You mustn't forgit 'em, Harry, when you makes a big name writin'. I'm—well, I'm blessed if I don't feel as if I was just goin' to blubber!"

I was glad he didn't. The Giraffe blubberin' would have been a spectacle. I steered him back to his friends.

"Ain't you going to kiss me, Bob?" said the Great Western's big, handsome barmaid, as the bell rang.

"Well, I don't mind kissin' you, Alice," he said, wiping his mouth. "But I'm goin' to be married, yer know." And he kissed her fair on the mouth.

"There's nothin' like gettin' into practice," he said, grinning round.

We thought he was improving wonderfully; but at the last moment something troubled him.

"Look here, you chaps," he said, hesitatingly, with his hand in his pocket, "I don't know what I'm going to do with all this stuff. There's that poor washer-woman that scalded her legs liftin' the boiler of clothes off the fire——"

We shoved him into the carriage. He hung—about half of him—

out the window, wildly waving his hat, till the train disappeared in the scrub.

And, as I sit here writing by lamplight at midday, in the midst of a great city of shallow social sham, of hopeless, squalid poverty, of ignorant selfishness, cultured or brutish, and of noble and heroic endeavour frowned down or callously neglected, I am almost aware of a burst of sunshine in the room, and a long form leaning over my chair, and:

"Excuse me for troublin' yer; I'm always troublin' yer; but there's that there poor woman . . ."

And I wish I could immortalize him!

"Rats"

"WHY, there's two of them, and they're having a fight! Come on!"

It seemed a strange place for a fight—that hot, lonely, cotton-bush plain. And yet not more than half a mile ahead there were apparently two men struggling together on the track.

The three travellers postponed their smoke-oh and hurried on. They were shearers—a little man and a big man, known respectively as Sunlight and Macquarie, and a tall, thin, young jackeroo whom they called Milky.

"I wonder where the other man sprang from? I didn't see him before," said Sunlight.

"He muster bin layin' down in the bushes," said Macquarie. "They're goin' at it proper, too. Come on! Hurry up and see the fun!"

They hurried on.

"It's a funny-lookin' feller, the other feller," panted Milky. "He don't seem to have no head. Look! he's down—they're both down! They must ha' clinched on the ground. No! they're up an' at it again. . . . Why, good Lord! I think the other's a woman!"

"My oath! so it is!" yelled Sunlight. "Look, the brute's got her down again! He's kickin' her. Come on, chaps; come on, or he'll do for her!"

They dropped swags, water-bags and all, and raced forward; but presently Sunlight, who had the best eyes, slackened his pace and dropped behind. His mates glanced back at his face, saw a peculiar expression there, looked again, and then dropped into a walk.

They reached the scene of the trouble, and there stood a little withered old man by the track, with his arms folded close up under his chin; he was dressed mostly in calico patches; and half a dozen corks, suspended on bits of string from the brim of his hat, dangled before his bearded optics to scare away the flies. He was scowling malignantly at a stout, dumpy swag which lay in the middle of the track.

"Well, old Rats, what's the trouble?" asked Sunlight.

"Oh, nothing, nothing," answered the old man, without looking round. "I fell out with my swag, that's all. He knocked me down, but I've settled him."

"But look here," said Sunlight, winking at his mates, "we saw you jump on him when he was down. That ain't fair, you know."

"But you didn't see it all," cried Rats, getting excited. "He hit *me* down first! And look here, I'll fight him again for nothing, and you can see fair play."

They talked a while; then Sunlight proposed to second the swag, while his mate supported the old man, and, after some persuasion, Milky agreed, for the sake of the lark, to act as time-keeper and referee.

Rats entered into the spirit of the thing; he stripped to the waist, and while he was getting ready the travellers pretended to bet on the result.

Macquarie took his place behind the old man, and Sunlight up-ended the swag. Rats shaped and danced around, then he rushed, feinted, ducked, retreated, darted in once more, and suddenly went down like a shot on the broad of his back. No actor could have done it better; he went down from that imaginary blow as if a cannon-ball had struck him on the forehead.

Milky called time, and the old man came up, looking shaky. However, he got in a tremendous blow which knocked the swag into the bushes.

Several rounds followed with varying success.

The men pretended to get more and more excited, and betted freely; and Rats did his best. At last they got tired of the fun, Sunlight let the swag lie after Milky called time, and the jackeroo awarded the fight to Rats. They pretended to hand over the stakes, and then they went back for their swags, while the old man put on his shirt.

Then he calmed down, carried his swag to the side of the track, sat down on it and talked rationally about bush matters for a while; but presently he grew silent and began to feel his muscles and smile idiotically.

"Can you len' us a bit o' meat?" said he suddenly.

They spared him half a pound; but he said he didn't want it all, and cut off about an ounce, which he laid on the end of his swag. Then he took the lid off his billy and produced a fishing-line. He baited the hook, threw the line across the track, and waited for a bite. Soon he got deeply interested in the line, jerked it once or twice, and drew it in rapidly. The bait had been rubbed off in the grass. The old man regarded the hook disgustedly.

"Look at that!" he cried. "I had him, only I was in such a hurry. I should ha' played him a little more."

Next time he was more careful. He drew the line in warily, grabbed an imaginary fish and laid it down on the grass. Sunlight and Co. were greatly interested by this time.

"Wot yer think o' that?" asked Rats. "It weighs thirty pound if it weighs an ounce! Wot yer think o' that for a cod? The hook's half-way down his blessed gullet!"

He caught several cod and a bream while they were there, and invited them to camp and have tea with him. But they wished to reach a certain shed next day, so—after the ancient had borrowed about a pound of meat for baits—they went on, and left him fishing contentedly.

But first Sunlight went down into his pocket and came up with half a crown, which he gave to the old man, along with some tucker. "You'd best push on to the water before dark, old chap," he said kindly.

When they turned their heads again, Rats was still fishing: but when they looked back for the last time before entering the timber, he was having another row with his swag; and Sunlight reckoned that the trouble arose out of some lies which the swag had been telling about the bigger fish it caught.

A Wild Irishman

ABOUT seven years ago I drifted from outback in Australia to Wellington, the capital of New Zealand, and up-country to a little town called Pahiatua, which meaneth the "home of the gods", and is situated in the Wairarappa (rippling or sparkling water) district. They have a pretty little legend to the effect that the name of the district was not originally suggested by its rivers, streams, and lakes, but by the tears alleged to have been noticed, by a dusky squire, in the eyes of a warrior chief who was looking his first, or last—I don't remember which—upon the scene. He was the discoverer, I suppose, now I come to think of it, else the place would have been already named. Maybe the scene reminded the old cannibal of the home of his childhood.

Pahiatua was not the home of my god; and it rained for five weeks. While waiting for a remittance, from an Australian newspaper—which, I anxiously hoped, would arrive in time for enough of it to be left (after paying board) to take me away somewhere—I spent many hours in the little shop of a shoemaker who had been a digger; and he told me yarns of the old days on the West Coast of Middle Island. And, ever and anon, he returned to one, a hard case from the West Coast, called "The Flour of Wheat", and his cousin, and his mate, Dinny Murphy, dead. And ever and again the shoemaker (he was large, humorous, and good-natured) made me promise that, when I dropped across an old West Coast digger—no matter who or what he was, or whether he was drunk or sober—I'd ask him if he knew the Flour of Wheat, and hear what he had to say.

I make no attempt to give any one shade of the Irish brogue—it can't be done in writing.

"There's the little red Irishman," said the shoemaker, who was Irish himself, "who always wants to fight when he has a glass in him; and there's the big sarcastic dark Irishman who makes more trouble and fights at a spree than half a dozen little red ones put together; and there's the cheerful easygoing Irishman. Now the

Flour was a combination of all three and several other sorts. He was known from the first amongst the boys at Th' Canary as the Flour o' Wheat, but no one knew exactly why. Some said that the right name was the F-l-o-w-e-r, not F-l-o-u-r, and that he was called that because there was no flower on wheat. The name might have been a compliment paid to the man's character by someone who understood and appreciated it—or appreciated it without understanding it. Or it might have come of some chance saying of the Flour himself, or his mates—or an accident with bags of flour. He might have worked in a mill. But we've had enough of that. It's the man—not the name. He was just a big, dark, blue-eyed Irish digger. He worked hard, drank hard, fought hard—and didn't swear. No man had ever heard him swear (except once); all things were 'lovely' with him. He was always lucky. He got gold and threw it away.

"The Flour was sent out to Australia (by his friends) in connection with some trouble in Ireland in eighteen-something. The date doesn't matter; there was mostly trouble in Ireland in those days; and nobody that knew the man could have the slightest doubt that he helped the trouble—provided he was there at the time. I heard all this from a man who knew him in Australia. The relatives that he was sent out to were soon very anxious to see the end of him. He was as wild as they made them in Ireland. When he had a few drinks he'd walk restlessly to and fro outside the shanty, swinging his right arm across in front of him with elbow bent and hand closed, as if he had a head in chancery, and muttering, as though in explanation to himself:

" 'Oi must be walkin' or foightin'!—Oi must be walkin' or foightin'!—Oi must be walkin' or foightin'!"

"They say that he wanted to eat his Australian relatives before he was done; and the story goes that one night, while he was on the spree, they put their belongings into a cart and took to the bush.

"There's no Floury record for several years; then the Flour turned up on the West Coast of New Zealand and was never very far from a pub kept by a cousin (that he had tracked, unearthed, or discovered somehow) at a place called Th' Canary. I remember the first time I saw the Flour.

"I was on a bit of a spree myself, at Th' Canary, and one evening I was standing outside Brady's (the Flour's cousin's place) with Tom Lyons and Dinny Murphy, when I saw a big man coming across the flat with a swag on his back.

"'B' God, there's the Flour o' Wheat comin' this minute,' says Dinny Murphy to Tom, 'an' no one else.'

"'B' God, ye're right!' says Tom.

"There were a lot of newchums in the big room at the back, drinking and dancing and singing, and Tom says to Dinny:

"'Dinny, I'll bet you a quid an' the Flour'll run against some of those newchums before he's an hour on the spot.'

"But Dinny wouldn't take him up. He knew the Flour.

"'Good day, Tom! Good day, Dinny!'

"'Good day to you, Flour!'

"I was introduced.

"'Well, boys, come along,' says the Flour.

"And so we went inside with him. The Flour had a few drinks, and then he went into the back room where the newchums were. One of them was dancing a jig, and so the Flour stood up in front of him and commenced to dance too. And presently the newchum made a step that didn't please the Flour, so he hit him between the eyes, and knocked him down—fair an' flat on his back.

"'Take that,' he says. 'Take that, me lovely whipper-snapper, an' lay there! You can't dance. How dare ye stand up in front of me face to dance when ye can't dance?'

"He shouted and drank, and gambled, and danced, and sang, and fought the newchums all night, and in the morning he said:

"'Well, boys, we had a grand time last night. Come and have a drink with me.'

"And of course they went in and had a drink with him.

"Next morning the Flour was walking along the street, when he met a drunken disreputable old hag, known among the boys as the 'Nipper'.

"'Good *morning*, me lovely Flour o' Wheat!' says she.

"'Good *morning*, me lovely Nipper!' says the Flour.

"And with that she outs with a bottle she had in her dress, and smashed him across the face with it. Broke the bottle to smithereens!

"A policeman saw her do it, and took her up; and they had the Flour as a witness, whether he liked it or not. And a lovely sight he looked, with his face all done up in bloody bandages, and only one damaged eye and a corner of his mouth on duty.

"'It's nothing at all, your Honour,' he said to the S.M.; 'only a pin-scratch—it's nothing at all. Let it pass. I had no right to speak to the lovely woman at all.'

"But they didn't let it pass—they fined her a quid.

"And the Flour paid the fine.

"But, alas for human nature! It was pretty much the same even in those days, and amongst those men, as it is now. A man couldn't do a woman a good turn without the dirty-minded blackguards taking it for granted there was something between them. It was a great joke amongst the boys who knew the Flour, and who also knew the Nipper; but as it was carried too far in some quarters, it got to be no joke to the Flour—nor to those who laughed too loud or grinned too long.

"The Flour's cousin thought he was a sharp man. The Flour got 'stiff'. He hadn't any money, and his credit had run out, so he went and got a blank summons from one of the police he knew. He pretended that he wanted to frighten a man who owed him some money. Then he filled it up and took it to his cousin.

" 'What d'ye think of that?' he says, handing the summons across the bar. 'What d'ye think of me lovely Dinny Murphy now?'

" 'Why, what's this all about?'

" 'That's what I want to know. I borrowed a five-pound note off him a fortnight ago when I was drunk, an' now he sends me that.'

" 'Well, I never would have dream'd that of Dinny,' says the cousin, scratching his head and blinking. 'What's come over him at all?"

" 'That's what I want to know.'

" 'What have you been doing to the man?'

" 'Divil a thing that I'm aware of.'

"The cousin rubbed his chin-tuft between his forefinger and thumb.

" 'Well, what am I to do about it?' asked the Flour impatiently.

" 'Do? Pay the man, of course.'

" 'How can I pay the lovely man when I haven't got the price of a drink about me?'

"The cousin scratched his chin.

" 'Well—here, I'll lend you a five-pound note for a month or two. Go and pay the man, and get back to work.'

"And the Flour went and found Dinny Murphy, and the pair of

them had a howling spree together up at the opposition pub. And the cousin said he thought all the time he was being had.

"He was nasty sometimes, when he was about half-drunk. For instance, he'd come on the ground when the Orewell sports were in full swing and walk round, soliloquizing just loud enough for you to hear; and just when a big event was coming off he'd pass within earshot of some committee men—who had been bursting themselves for weeks to work the thing up and make it a success—saying to himself:

"'Where's the Orewell sports that I hear so much about? I don't see them! Can anyone direct me to the Orewell sports?'

"Or he'd pass a raffle, lottery, lucky-bag, or golden-barrel business of some sort——

"'No gamblin' for the Flour. I don't believe in their little shwindles. It ought to be shtopped. Leadin' young people ashtray.'

"Or he'd pass an Englishman he didn't like——

"'Look at Jinneral Roberts! He's a man! He's an Irishman! England has to come to Ireland for its Jinnerals! Look at Jinneral Roberts in the marshes of Candyhar!'

"They always had sports at Orewell Creek on New Year's Day—except once—and old Duncan was always there—never missed it till the day he died. He was a digger, a humorous and good-hearted hard case. They all knew 'old Duncan'.

"But one New Year's Eve he didn't turn up, and was missed at once. 'Where's old Duncan? Anyone seen old Duncan?' 'Oh, he'll turn up all right.' They inquired, and argued, and waited, but Duncan didn't come.

"Duncan was working at Duffers. The boys inquired of fellows who came from Duffers, but they hadn't seen him for two days. They had fully expected to find him at the Creek. He wasn't at Aliaura nor Notown. They inquired of men who came from Nelson Creek, but Duncan wasn't there.

"'There's something happened to the lovely man,' said the Flour of Wheat at last. 'Some of us had better see about it.'

"Pretty soon this was the general opinion, and so a party started out over the hills to Duffers before daylight in the morning, headed by the Flour.

"The door of Duncan's whare was closed--*but not padlocked*. The Flour noticed this, gave his head a jerk, opened the door, and went in. The hut was tidied up and swept out—even the fire-place. Duncan had 'lifted the boxes' and 'cleaned up', and his little bag of gold stood on a shelf by his side—all ready for his spree. On the table lay a clean neckerchief folded ready to tie on. The blankets had been folded neatly and laid on the bunk, and on them was stretched old Duncan, with his arms lying crossed on his chest, and one foot—with a boot on—resting on the ground. He had his 'clean things' on, and was dressed except for one boot, the necktie, and his hat. Heart disease.

" 'Take your hats off and come in quietly, lads,' said the Flour. 'Here's the lovely man lying dead in his bunk.'

"There were no sports at Orewell that New Year. Someone said that the crowd from Nelson Creek might object to the sports being postponed on old Duncan's account, but the Flour said he'd see to that.

"One or two did object, but the Flour reasoned with them and there were no sports.

"And the Flour used to say, afterwards, 'Ah, but it was a grand time we had at the funeral when Duncan died at Duffers.'

"The Flour of Wheat carried his mate, Dinny Murphy all the way in from Th' Canary to the hospital on his back. Dinny was very bad—the man was dying of the dysentery or something. The Flour laid him down on a spare bunk in the reception-room and hailed the staff.

" 'Inside there—come out!'

"The doctor and some of the hospital people came to see what was the matter. The doctor was a heavy swell, with a big cigar held up in front of him between two fat, soft, yellow-white fingers, and a dandy little pair of gold-rimmed eye-glasses nipped on to his nose with a spring.

" 'There's me lovely mate lying there dying of the dysentery,' says the Flour, 'and you've got to fix him up and bring him round.'

"Then he shook his fist in the doctor's face and said:

" 'If you let that lovely man die—look out!'

"The doctor was startled. He backed off at first; then he took a puff at his cigar, stepped forward, had a careless look at Dinny, and gave some order to the attendants. The Flour went to the door, turned half round as he went out, and shook his fist at them again, and said:

" 'If you let that lovely man die—mind!'

"In about twenty minutes he came back, wheeling a case of whisky in a barrow. He carried the case inside, and dumped it down on the floor.

" 'There,' he said, 'pour that into the lovely man.'

"Then he shook his fist at such members of the staff as were visible, and said:

" 'If you let that lovely man die—look out!'

"They were used to hard cases, and didn't take much notice of him, but he had the hospital in an awful mess; he was there all hours of the day and night; he would go down town, have a few drinks and a fight maybe, and then he'd say, 'Ah, well, I'll have to go up and see how me lovely mate's getting on.'

"And every time he'd go up he'd shake his fist at the hospital in general and threaten to murder 'em all if they let Dinny Murphy die.

"Well, Dinny Murphy died one night. The next morning the Flour met the doctor in the street, and hauled off and hit him between the eyes, and knocked him down before he had time to see who it was.

" 'Stay there, ye little whipper-snapper,' said the Flour of Wheat; 'you let that lovely man die!'

"The police happened to be out of town that day, and while they were waiting for them the Flour got a coffin and carried it up to the hospital, and stood it on end by the doorway.

" 'I've come for me lovely mate!' he said to the scared staff—or as much of it as he bailed up and couldn't escape him. 'Hand him over. He's going back to be buried with his friends at Th' Canary. Now, don't be sneaking round and sidling off, you there; you needn't be frightened; I've settled with the doctor.'

"But they called in a man who had some influence with the Flour, and between them—and with the assistance of the prettiest nurse on the premises—they persuaded him to wait. Dinny wasn't ready yet; there were papers to sign; it wouldn't be decent to the dead; he had to be prayed over; he had to be washed and shaved, and fixed up decent and comfortable. Anyway, they'd have him ready in an hour, or take the consequences.

"The Flour objected on the ground that all this could be done equally as well and better by the boys at Th' Canary. 'However,' he said, 'I'll be round in an hour, and if you haven't got me lovely mate ready—look out!' Then he shook his fist sternly at them once more and said:

"'I know yer dirty tricks and dodges, and if there's e'er a pin-scratch on me mate's body—look out! If there's a parin' of Dinny's toe-nail missin'—look out!'

"Then he went out—taking the coffin with him.

"And when the police came to his lodgings to arrest him, they found the coffin on the floor by the side of the bed, and the Flour lying in it on his back, with his arms folded peacefully on his bosom. He was as dead drunk as any man could get to be and still be alive. They knocked air-holes in the coffin lid, screwed it on, and carried the coffin, the Flour, and all to the local lock-up. They laid their burden down on the bare, cold floor of the prison-cell, and then went out, locked the door, and departed several ways to put the 'boys' up to it. And about midnight the 'boys' gathered round with a supply of liquor, and waited, and somewhere along in the small hours there was a howl, as of a strong Irishman in Purgatory, and presently the voice of the Flour was heard to plead in changed and awful tones:

"'Pray for me soul, boys—pray for me soul! Let bygones be bygones between us, boys, and pray for me lovely soul! The lovely Flour's in Purgatory!'

"Then silence for a while; and then a sound like a dray-wheel passing over a packing-case. . . . That was the only time on record that the Flour was heard to swear. And he swore then.

"They didn't pray for him—they gave him a month. And when he came out he went half-way across the road to meet the doctor, and he—to his credit, perhaps—came the other half. They had a drink together, and the Flour presented the doctor with a fine specimen of coarse gold for a pin.

"'It was the will o' God, after all, doctor,' said the Flour. 'It was the will o' God. Let bygones be bygones between us; gimme your hand, doctor. . . . Good-bye.'

"Then he left for Th' Canary."

"Lord Douglas"

They hold him true, who's true to one,
However false he be.

—The Rouseabout of Rouseabouts.

THE Imperial Hotel was rather an unfortunate name for an outback town pub, for outback is the stronghold of Australian democracy; it was the outback vote and influence that brought about One Man One Vote, Payment of Members, and most of the democratic legislation of late years, and from outback came the overwhelming vote in favour of Australian as against Imperial Federation.

The name Royal Hotel is as familiar as that of the Railway Hotel, and passes unnoticed and ungrowled at, even by bush republicans. The Royal Hotel at Bourke was kept by an Irishman, one O'Donohoo, who was union to the backbone, loudly in favour of "Australia for the Australians", and, of course, against even the democratic New South Wales Government of the time. He went round town all one St Patrick's morning with a bunch of green ribbon fastened to his coat-tail with a large fish-hook, and wasn't aware of the fact till he sat down on the point of it. But that's got nothing to do with it.

The Imperial Hotel at Bourke was unpopular from the first. It was said that the very existence of the house was the result of a swindle. It had been built with money borrowed on certain allotments in the centre of the town and on the understanding that it should be built on the mortgaged land, whereas it was erected on a free allotment. Which fact was discovered, greatly to its surprise, by the building society when it came to foreclose on the allotments some years later. While the building was being erected the Bourke people understood, in a vague way, that it was to be a convent (perhaps the building society thought so, too), and when certain ornaments in brick and cement in the shape of a bishop's mitre were placed over the corners of the walls the question seemed decided. But when the place was finished a bar was fitted up, and up went the sign, to the disgust of the other publicans, who didn't know a licence had been taken out—for licensing didn't go by local option in those days. It was rumoured that the place belonged to, and the whole business was engineered by, a priest. And priests are men of the world.

The Imperial Hotel was patronized by the pastoralists, the civil servants, the bank manager and clerks—all the scrub aristocracy; it was the headquarters of the Pastoralists' Union in Bourke; a barracks for blacklegs brought up from Sydney to take the place of union shearers on strike; and the new Governor, on his inevitable visit to Bourke, was banqueted at the Imperial Hotel. The editor of the local "capitalistic rag" stayed there; the pastoralists' member was elected mostly by dark ways and means devised at the Imperial Hotel, and one of its managers had stood as a dummy candidate to split the Labour vote; the management of the hotel was his reward. In short, it was there that most of the plots were hatched to circumvent Freedom, and put away or deliver into the clutches of law and order certain sons of Light and Liberty who believed in converting blacklegs into jellies by force of fists when bribes, gentle persuasion and pure Australian language failed to convert them to clean unionism. The Imperial Hotel was called the "Squatters' Pub", the "Scabbery", and other and more expressive names.

The hotel became still more unpopular after Percy Douglas had managed it for a while. He was an avowed enemy of Labour Unionists. He employed Chinese cooks, and that in the height of the anti-Chinese agitation in Australia, and he was known to have kindly feelings towards the Afghans who, with their camels, were running white carriers off the roads. If an excited unionist called a man a "blackleg" or "scab" in the Imperial bar he was run out—sometimes with great difficulty, and occasionally as far as the lock-up.

Percy Douglas was a fine-looking man, "wid a chest on him an' well hung—a fine fee-*gure* of a man", as O'Donohoo pronounced it. He was tall and erect, he dressed well, wore small side-whiskers, had an eagle nose, and looked like an aristocrat. Like many of his type, who start sometimes as billiard-markers and suddenly become hotel managers in Australia, nothing was known of his past. Jack Mitchell reckoned, by the way he treated his employees and spoke to workmen, that he was the educated son of an English farmer—gone wrong and sent out to Australia. Someone called him "Lord Douglas", and the nickname caught on.

He made himself well hated. He got One-eyed Bogan "three months' hard" for taking a bottle of whisky off the Imperial bar counter because he (Bogan) was drunk and thirsty and had knocked down his cheque, and because there was no one minding the bar at the moment.

Lord Douglas dismissed the barmaid, and, as she was leaving, he had her boxes searched and gave her in charge for stealing certain articles belonging to the hotel. The chaps subscribed to defend the case, and subsequently put a few pounds together for the girl. She proved her gratitude by bringing a charge of a baby against one of the chaps—but that was only one of the little ways of the world, as Mitchell said. She joined a Chinese camp later on.

Lord Douglas employed a carpenter to do some work about the hotel, and because the carpenter left before the job was finished, Lord Douglas locked his tools in an outhouse and refused to give them up; and when the carpenter, with the spirit of an Australian workman, broke the padlock and removed his tool-chest, the landlord gave him in charge for breaking and entering. The chaps defended the case and won it, and hated Lord Douglas as much as if he were their elder brother. Mitchell was the only one to put in a word for him.

"I've been puzzling it out," said Mitchell, as he sat nursing his best leg in the Union Office, "and, as far as I can see, it all amounts to this—we're all mistaken in Lord Douglas. We don't know the man. He's all right. We don't understand him. He's really a sensitive, good-hearted man who's been shoved a bit off the track by the world. It's the world's fault—he's not to blame. You see, when he was a youngster he was the most good-natured kid in the school; he was always soft, and, consequently, he was always being imposed upon, and bullied, and knocked about. Whenever he got a penny to buy lollies he'd count 'em out carefully and divide 'em round amongst his schoolmates and brothers and sisters. He was the only one that worked at home, and consequently they all hated him. His father respected him, but didn't love him, because he wasn't a younger son, and wasn't bringing his father's grey hairs down in sorrow to the grave. If it was in Australia, probably Lord Douglas was an elder son and had to do all the hard graft, and teach himself at night, and sleep in a bark skillion while his younger brothers benefited—they were born in the new brick house and went to boarding-schools. His mother had a contempt for him because he wasn't a black sheep and a prodigal, and when the old man died the rest of the family got all the stuff and Lord Douglas was kicked out because they could do without him now. And the family hated him like poison ever afterwards (especially his mother), and spread lies about him—because they had treated him shamefully and because his mouth was shut—they knew he wouldn't speak. Then probably he went in for Democracy and worked for Freedom, till Freedom trod on him once too often with her hob-nailed boots. Then the chances are, in the end, he was ruined by a girl or woman, and driven, against his will, to take refuge in pure individualism. He's all right, only we don't appreciate him. He's only fighting against his old ideals—his old self that comes up sometimes—and that's what makes him sweat his barmaids and servants, and hate us, and run us in; and perhaps when he cuts up extra rough it's because his conscience kicks him when he thinks of the damned soft fool he used to be. He's all right—take my word for it. It's all a mask. Why, he might be one of the kindest-hearted men in Bourke underneath."

Tom Hall rubbed his head and blinked, as if he was worried by an idea that there might be some facts in Mitchell's theories.

"You're allers findin' excuses for blacklegs an' scabs, Mitchell," said Barcoo-Rot, who took Mitchell seriously (and who would have taken a laughing-jackass seriously). "Why, you'd find a white spot on a squatter. I wouldn't be surprised if you blacklegged yourself in the end."

This was an unpardonable insult, from a union point of view, and the chaps half-unconsciously made room on the floor for Barcoo-Rot to fall after Jack Mitchell hit him. But Mitchell took the insult philosophically.

"Well, Barcoo-Rot," he said, nursing the other leg, "for the matter of that, I did find a white spot on a squatter once. He lent me a quid when I was hard up. There's white spots on the blackest characters if you only drop prejudice and look close enough. I suppose even Jack-the-Ripper's character was speckled. Why, I can even see spots on your character, sometimes, Barcoo-Rot. I've known white spots to spread on chaps' characters until they were little short of saints. Sometimes I even fancy I can feel my own wings sprouting. And as for turning blackleg—well, I suppose I've got a bit of the crawler in my composition (most of us have), and a man never knows what might happen to his principles."

"Well," said Barcoo-Rot, "I beg yer pardon—ain't that enough?"

"No," said Mitchell, "you ought to wear a three-bushel bag and ashes for three months, and drink water; but since the police would send you to an asylum if you did that, I think the best thing we can do is to go out and have a drink."

Lord Douglas married an Australian girl somewhere, somehow, and brought her to Bourke, and there were two little girls—regular little fairies. She was a gentle, kind-hearted little woman, but she didn't seem to improve him much, save that he was very good to her.

"It's mostly that way," commented Mitchell. "When a boss gets married and has children he thinks he's got a greater right to grind his fellowmen and rob their wives and children. I'd never work for a boss with a big family—it's hard enough to keep a single boss nowadays in this country."

After one stormy election, at the end of a long and bitter shearing strike, One-eyed Bogan, his trusty enemy, Barcoo-Rot, and one or two other enthusiastic reformers were charged with rioting, and got from one to three months' hard. And they had only smashed three windows of the Imperial Hotel and chased the Chinese cook into the river.

"I used to have some hopes for Democracy," commented Mitchell, "but I've got none now. How can you expect Liberty, Equality or Fraternity—how can you expect Freedom and Universal Brotherhood and Equal Rights in a country where Sons of Light get three months' hard for breaking windows and bashing a Chinaman? It almost makes me long to sail away in a gallant barque."

There were other cases in connection with the rotten-egging of Capitalistic candidates on the Imperial Hotel balcony, and it was partly on the evidence of Douglas and his friends that certain respectable Labour leaders got heavy terms of imprisonment for rioting and "sedition" and "inciting" in connection with organized attacks on blacklegs and their escorts.

Retribution, if it was retribution, came suddenly and in a most unexpected manner to Lord Douglas.

It seems he employed a second carpenter for six months to repair and make certain additions to the hotel, and put him off under various pretences until he owed him a hundred pounds or thereabout. At last, immediately after an exciting interview with Lord Douglas, the carpenter died suddenly of heart disease. The widow, a strong-minded bushwoman, put a bailiff in the hotel on very short notice—and against the advice of her lawyer, who thought the case hopeless—and the Lord Douglas bubble promptly burst. He had somehow come to be regarded as the proprietor of the hotel, but now the real proprietors or proprietor—he was still said to be a priest—turned Douglas out and put in a new manager. The old servants were paid after some trouble. The local storekeepers and one or two firms in Sydney, who had large accounts against the Imperial Hotel (and had trusted it, mainly because it was patronized by Capitalism and Fat), were never paid.

Lord Douglas cleared out to Sydney, leaving his wife and children, for the present, with her brother, a hay-and-corn storekeeper, who also had a large and hopeless account against the hotel; and when the brother went broke and left the district she rented a two-roomed cottage and took in dressmaking.

Dressmaking didn't pay so well in the bush then as it did in the old digging days when sewing-machines were scarce and the possession of one meant an independent living to any girl—when diggers paid ten shillings for a strip of "flannen" doubled over and sewn together, with holes for arms and head, and called a shirt. Mrs Douglas had a hard time, with her two little girls, who were still better and more prettily dressed than any other children in Bourke. One grocer still called on her for orders and pretended to be satisfied to wait "till Mr Douglas came back", and when she would no longer order what he considered sufficient provisions for her and the children, and commenced buying sugar, etc., by the pound, for cash, he one day sent a box of groceries round to her. He pretended it was a mistake.

"However," he said, "I'd be very much obliged if you could use 'em, Mrs Douglas. I'm overstocked now; haven't got room for another tin of sardines in the shop. Don't you worry about bills, Mrs Douglas; I can wait till Douglas comes home. I did well enough out of the Imperial Hotel when your husband had it, and a pound's worth of groceries won't hurt me now. I'm only too glad to get rid of some of the stock."

She cried a little, thought of the children, and kept the groceries.

"I suppose I'll be sold up soon meself if things don't git brighter," said that grocer to a friend, "so it doesn't matter much."

The same with Foley the butcher, who had a brogue with a sort of drawling groan in it, and was a cynic of the Mitchell school.

"You see," he said, "she's as proud as the devil, but when I send round a bit o' rawst, or porrk, or the undercut o' the blade-bawn, she thinks o' the little gur-r-rls before she thinks o' sendin' it back to me. That's where I've got the pull on her."

The Giraffe borrowed a horse and tip-dray one day at the beginning of winter and cut a load of firewood in the bush, and next morning, at daylight, Mrs Douglas was nearly startled out of her life by a crash at the end of the cottage, which made her think that the chimney had fallen in, or a tree fallen on the house; and when she slipped on a wrapper and looked out, she saw a load of short-cut wood by the chimney, and caught a glimpse of the back view of the Giraffe, who stood in the dray with his legs wide apart and was disappearing into the edge of the scrub; and soon the rapid clock-clock-clock of the wheels died away in the west, as if he were making for West Australia.

The next time we heard of Lord Douglas he had got two years' hard for embezzlement in connection with some canvassing he had taken up. Mrs Douglas fell ill—a touch of brain-fever—and one of the labourers' wives took care of the children while two others took turns in nursing. While she was recovering, Bob Brothers sent round the hat, and, after a conclave in the Union Office—as mysterious as any meeting ever called with the object of downing bloated Capitalism—it was discovered that one of the chaps—who didn't wish his name to be mentioned—had borrowed just twenty-five pounds from Lord Douglas in the old days and now wished to return it to Mrs Douglas. So the thing was managed, and if she had any suspicions she kept them to herself. She started a little fancy-goods shop and got along fairly comfortable.

Douglas, by the way, was publicly supposed, for her sake and because of the little girls, to be away in West Australia on the gold-fields.

Time passes without much notice outback, and one hot day, when the sun hung behind the fierce sandstorms from the north-west as dully lurid as he ever showed in a London fog, Lord Douglas got out of the train that had just finished its five-hundred-miles' run, and not seeing a newchum porter, who started forward by force of habit to take his bag, he walked stiffly off the platform and down the main street towards his wife's cottage.

He was very gaunt, and his eyes, to those who passed him closely, seemed to have a furtive, hunted expression. He had let his beard grow, and it had grown grey.

It was within a few days of Christmas—the same Christmas that we lost the Pretty Girl in the Salvation Army. As a rule the big shearing-sheds within a fortnight of Bourke cut out in time for the shearers to reach the town and have their Christmas dinners and sprees—and for some of them to be locked up over Christmas Day —within sound of a church-going bell. Most of the chaps gathered in the Shearers' Union Office on New Year's Eve and discussed Douglas amongst other things.

"I vote we kick the cow out of the town!" snarled One-eyed Bogan, viciously.

"We can't do that," said Bob Brothers (the Giraffe), speaking more promptly than usual. "There's his wife and youngsters to consider, ye know."

"He something well deserted his wife," snarled Bogan, "an' now he comes crawlin' back to her to keep him."

"Well," said Mitchell, mildly, "but we ain't all got as much against him as you have, Bogan."

"He made a crimson jail-bird of me!" snapped Bogan.

"Well," said Mitchell, "that didn't hurt you much, anyway; it rather improved your character if anything. Besides, he made a jail-bird of himself afterwards, so you ought to have a fellow-feeling—a feathered feeling, so to speak. Now you needn't be offended, Bogan, we're all jail-birds at heart, only we haven't all got the pluck."

"I'm in favour of blanky well tarrin' an' featherin' him an' kickin' him out of the town!" shouted Bogan. "It would be a good turn to his wife, too; she'd be well rid of the ——."

"Perhaps she's fond of him," suggested Mitchell; "I've known such cases before. I saw them sitting together on the veranda last night when they thought no one was looking."

"He deserted her," said One-eyed Bogan, in a climbing-down tone, "and left her to starve."

"Perhaps the police were to blame for that," said Mitchell. "You know you deserted all your old mates once for three months, Bogan, and it wasn't your fault."

"He seems to be a crimson pet of yours, Jack Mitchell," said Bogan, firing up.

"Ah, well, all I know," said Mitchell, standing up and stretching himself wearily, "all I know is that he looked like a gentleman once, and treated us like a gentleman, and cheated us like a gentleman, and ran some of us in like a gentleman, and, as far as I can see, he's served his time like a gentleman and come back to face us and live himself down like a man. I always had a sneaking regard for a gentleman."

"Why, Mitchell, I'm beginning to think you are a gentleman yourself," said Jake Boreham.

"Well," said Mitchell, "I used to have a suspicion once that I had a drop of blue blood in me somewhere, and it worried me a lot; but I asked my old mother about it one day, and she scalded me—God bless her!—and father chased me with a stockwhip, so I gave up making inquiries."

"You'll join the bloomin' Capitalists next," sneered One-eyed Bogan.

"I wish I could, Bogan," said Mitchell. "I'd take a trip to Paris and see for myself whether the Frenchwomen are as bad as they're made out to be, or go to Japan. But what are we going to do about Douglas?"

"Kick the skunk out of town, or boycott him!" said one or two. "He ought to be tarred and feathered and hanged."

"Couldn't do worse than hang him," commented Jake Boreham, cheerfully.

"Oh, yes we could," said Mitchell, sitting down, resting his elbows on his knees, and marking his points with one forefinger on the other. "For instance, we might boil him slow in tar. We might skin him alive. We might put him in a cage and poke him with sticks, with his wife and children in another cage to look on and enjoy the fun."

The chaps, who had been sitting quietly listening to Mitchell, and grinning, suddenly became serious and shifted their positions uneasily.

"But I can tell you what would hurt his feelings more than anything else we could do," said Mitchell.

"Well, what is it, Jack?" said Tom Hall, rather impatiently.

"Send round the hat and take up a collection for him," said Mitchell, "enough to let him get away with his wife and children and start life again in some less respectable town than Bourke. You needn't grin, I'm serious about it."

There was a thoughtful pause, and one or two scratched their heads.

"His wife seems pretty sick," Mitchell went on in a reflective tone. "I passed the place this morning and saw him scrubbing out the floor. He's been doing a bit of house-painting for old Heegard today. I suppose he learnt it in jail. I saw him at work and touched my hat to him."

"What!" cried Tom Hall, affecting to shrink from Mitchell in horror.

"Yes," said Mitchell, "I'm not sure that I didn't take my hat off. Now I know it's not bush religion for a man to touch his hat, except to a funeral, or a strange roof or woman sometimes; but when I meet a braver man than myself I salute him. I've only met two in my life."

"And who were they, Jack?" asked Jake Boreham.

"One," said Mitchell—"one is Douglas, and the other—well, the other was the man I used to be. But that's got nothing to do with it."

"But perhaps Douglas thought you were crowing over him when you took off your hat to him—sneerin' at him, like, Mitchell," reflected Jake Boreham.

"No, Jake," said Mitchell, growing serious suddenly. "There are ways of doing things that another man understands."

They all thought for a while.

"Well," said Tom Hall, "supposing we do take up a collection for him, he'd be too damned proud to take it."

"But that's where we've got the pull on him," said Mitchell, brightening up. "I heard Dr Morgan say that Mrs Douglas wouldn't live if she wasn't sent away to a cooler place, and Douglas knows it; and, besides, one of the little girls is sick. We've got him in a corner and he'll have to take the stuff. Besides, two years in jail takes a lot of the pride out of a man."

"Well, I'm damned if I'll give a sprat to help the man who tried his best to crush the unions!" said One-eyed Bogan.

"Damned if I will either!" said Barcoo-Rot.

"Now, look here, One-eyed Bogan," said Mitchell, "I don't like to harp on old things, for I know they bore you, but when you returned to public life that time no one talked of kicking you out of town. In fact, I heard that the chaps put a few pounds together to help you get away for a while till you got over your modesty."

No one spoke.

"I passed Douglas's place on my way here from my camp to-night," Mitchell went on musingly, "and I saw him walking up and down in the yard with his sick child in his arms. You remember that little girl, Bogan? I saw her run and pick up your hat and give it to you one day when you were trying to put it on with your feet. You remember, Bogan? The shock nearly sobered you."

There was a very awkward pause. The position had become too psychological altogether and had to be ended somehow. The awkward silence had to be broken, and Bogan broke it. He turned up Bob Brothers's hat, which was lying on the table, and chucked in a quid, qualifying the hat and the quid, and disguising his feelings with the national oath of the land.

"We've had enough of this gory, maudlin, sentimental tommy-rot," he said. "Here, Barcoo, stump up or I'll belt it out of your hide! I'll—I'll take yer to pieces!"

But Douglas didn't leave the town. He sent his wife and children to Sydney until the heat-wave was past, built a new room on to the cottage, and started a book and newspaper shop, and a poultry farm in the back paddock, and flourished.

They called him Mr Douglas for a while, then Douglas, then Percy Douglas, and now he is well-known as Old Daddy Douglas, and the Sydney *Worker*, *Truth*, and *Bulletin*, and other democratic rags are on sale at his shop. He is big with schemes for locking the Darling River, and he gets his drink at O'Donohoo's. He is scarcely yet regarded as a straight-out democrat. He was a gentleman once, Mitchell said, and the old blood was not to be trusted. But, last elections, Douglas worked quietly for unionism, and gave the leaders certain hints, and put them up to various electioneering dodges which enabled them to return, in the face of Monopoly, a Labour member who is as likely to go straight as long as any other Labour member.

The Ironbark Chip

DAVE REGAN and party—bush-fencers, tank-sinkers, and rough carpenters—were finishing the third and last culvert of their contract on the last section of the new railway-line, and had already sent in their vouchers for the completed contract, so that there might be no excuse for extra delay in connection with the cheque.

Now it had been expressly stipulated in the plans and specifications that the timber for certain beams and girders was to be ironbark and no other, and government inspectors were authorized to order the removal from the ground of any timber or material they might deem inferior, or not in accordance with the stipulations. The railway contractor's foreman and inspector of sub-contractors was a practical man and a bushman, but he had been a timber-getter himself; his sympathies were bushy, and he was on winking terms with Dave Regan. Besides, extended time was expiring, and the contractors were in a hurry to complete the line. But the government inspector was a reserved man who poked round on his independent own and appeared in lonely spots at unexpected times —with apparently no definite object in life—like a grey kangaroo bothered by a new wire fence, but unsuspicious of the presence of humans. He wore a grey suit, rode, or mostly led, an ashen-grey horse; the grass was long and grey, so he was seldom spotted until he was well within the horizon and bearing leisurely down on a party of sub-contractors, leading his horse.

Now, ironbark was scarce and distant on those ridges, and another timber, similar in appearance, but much inferior in grain and "standing" quality, was plentiful and close at hand. Dave and party were "about full of" the job and place, and wanted to get their cheque and be gone to another "spec" they had in view. So they came to reckon they'd get the last girder from a handy tree, and have it squared, in place, and carefully and conscientiously tarred before the inspector happened along, if he did. But they didn't. They got it squared, and ready to be lifted into its place; the kindly darkness of tar was ready to cover a fraud that took four strong men with crowbars and levers to shift; and now (such is the regular cussedness of things) as the fraudulent piece of timber lay its last hour on the ground, looking and smelling, to their guilty imaginations, like anything but ironbark, they were aware of the government inspector drifting down upon them obliquely, with something of the atmosphere of a casual Bill or Jim who had dropped out of his easygoing track to see how they were getting on, and borrow a match. They had more than half hoped that, as he had visited them pretty frequently during the progress of the work, and knew how near it was to completion, he wouldn't bother coming any more. But it's the way with the government. You might move heaven and earth in vain endeavour to get the "guvermunt" to flutter an eyelash over something of the most momentous importance to yourself and mates and the district—even to the country; but just when you are leaving authority severely alone, and have strong reasons for not wanting to worry or interrupt it, and not desiring it to worry about you, it will take a fancy into its head to come along and bother.

"It's always the way!" muttered Dave to his mates. "I knew the beggar would turn up! . . . And the only cronk log we've had, too!" he added, in an injured tone. "If this had 'a' been the only blessed ironbark in the whole contract, it would have been all right. . . . Good day, sir!" (to the inspector). "It's hot?"

The inspector nodded. He was not of an impulsive nature. He got down from his horse and looked at the girder in an abstracted way; and presently there came into his eyes a dreamy, far-away, sad sort of expression, as if there had been a very sad and painful occurrence in his family, way back in the past, and that piece of timber in some way reminded him of it and brought the old sorrow home to him. He blinked three times, and asked, in a subdued tone:

"Is that ironbark?"

Jack Bentley, the fluent liar of the party, caught his breath with a jerk and coughed, to cover the gasp and gain time. "I—ironbark? Of course it is! I thought you would know ironbark, mister." (Mister was silent.) "What else d'yer think it is?"

The dreamy, abstracted expression was back. The inspector, by the way, didn't know much about timber, but he had a great deal of instinct, and went by it when in doubt.

"L—look here, mister!" put in Dave Regan, in a tone of innocent puzzlement and with a blank bucolic face. "B—but don't the plans and specifications say ironbark? Ours does, anyway. I—I'll git the papers from the tent and show yer, if yer like."

It was not necessary. The inspector admitted the fact slowly. He stooped, and with an absent air picked up a chip. He looked at it abstractedly for a moment, blinked his threefold blink; then, seeming to recollect an appointment, he woke up suddenly and asked briskly:

"Did this chip come off that girder?"

Blank silence. The inspector blinked six times, divided in threes, rapidly, mounted his horse, said "Day," and rode off.

Regan and party stared at each other.

"Wha—what did he do that for?" asked Andy Page, the third in the party.

"Do what for, you fool?" inquired Dave.

"Ta—take that chip for?"

"He's taking it to the office!" snarled Jack Bentley.

"What—what for? What does he want to do that for?"

"To get it blanky well analysed! You ass! Now are yer satisfied?" And Jack sat down hard on the timber, jerked out his pipe, and said to Dave, in a sharp, toothache tone:

"Gimmiamatch!"

"We—well! what are we to do now?" inquired Andy, who was the hardest grafter, but altogether helpless, hopeless, and useless in a crisis like this.

"Grain and varnish the bloomin' culvert!" snapped Bentley.

But Dave's eyes, that had been ruefully following the inspector, suddenly dilated. The inspector had ridden a short distance along the line, dismounted, thrown the bridle over a post, laid the chip (which was too big to go in his pocket) on top of it, got through the fence, and was now walking back at an angle across the line in the direction of the fencing party, who had worked up on the other side, a little more than opposite the culvert.

Dave took in the lay of the country at a glance and thought rapidly.

"Gimme an ironbark chip!" he said suddenly.

Bentley, who was quick-witted when the track was shown him, as is a kangaroo-dog (Jack ran by sight, not scent), glanced in the line of Dave's eyes, jumped up, and got a chip about the same size as that which the inspector had taken.

Now the "lay of the country" sloped generally to the line from both sides, and the angle between the inspector's horse, the fencing party, and the culvert was well within a clear concave space; but a couple of hundred yards back from the line and parallel to it (on the side on which Dave's party worked their timber) a fringe of scrub ran to within a few yards of a point which would be about in line with a single tree on the cleared slope, the horse, and the fencing party.

Dave took the ironbark chip, ran along the bed of the watercourse into the scrub, raced up the sidling behind the bushes, got safely through without breathing, across the exposed space, and brought the tree into line between him and the inspector, who was talking to the fencers. Then he began to work quickly down the slope towards the tree (which was a thin one), keeping it in line, his arms close to his sides, and working, as it were, down the trunk of the tree, as if the fencing party were kangaroos and Dave was trying to get a shot at them. The inspector, by the by, had a habit of glancing now and then in the direction of his horse, as though under the impression that it was flighty and restless and inclined to bolt on opportunity. It was an anxious moment for all parties concerned—except the inspector. They didn't want *him* to be perturbed. And, just as Dave reached the foot of the tree, the inspector finished what he had to say to the fencers, turned, and started to walk briskly back to his horse. There was a thunderstorm coming. Now was the critical moment—there were certain prearranged signals between Dave's party and the fencers which might have interested the inspector, but none to meet a case like this.

Jack Bentley gasped, and started forward with an idea of intercepting the inspector and holding him for a few minutes in bogus conversation. Inspirations come to one at a critical moment, and it flashed on Jack's mind to send Andy instead. Andy looked as innocent and guileless as he was, but was uncomfortable in the vicinity of "funny business", and must have an honest excuse. "Not that that mattered," commented Jack afterwards; "it would have taken the inspector ten minutes to get at what Andy was driving at, whatever it was."

"Run, Andy! Tell him there's a heavy thunderstorm coming and he'd better stay in our humpy till it's over. Run! Don't stand staring like a blanky fool. He'll be gone!"

Andy started. But just then, as luck would have it, one of the fencers started after the inspector, hailing him as "Hi, mister!" He wanted to be set right about the survey or something—or to pretend to want to be set right—from motives of policy which I haven't time to explain here.

That fencer explained afterwards to Dave's party that he "seen what you coves was up to", and that's why he called the inspector back. But he told them that after they had told their yarn—which was a mistake.

"Come back, Andy!" cried Jack Bentley.

Dave Regan slipped round the tree, down on his hands and knees, and made quick time through the grass, which, luckily, grew pretty tall on the thirty or forty yards of slope between the tree and the horse. Close to the horse, a thought struck Dave that pulled him up, and sent a shiver along his spine and a hungry feeling under it. The horse would break away and bolt! But the case was desperate. Dave ventured an interrogatory "Cope, cope, cope?" The horse turned its head wearily and regarded him with a mild eye, as if he'd expected him to come, and come on all fours, and wondered what had kept him so long; then he went on thinking. Dave reached the foot of the post; the horse obligingly leaning over on the other leg. Dave reared head and shoulders cautiously behind the post, like a snake; his hand went up twice, swiftly—the first time he grabbed the inspector's chip, and the second time he put the ironbark one in its place. He drew down and back, and scuttled off for the tree like a gigantic tailless goanna.

A few minutes later he walked up to the culvert from along the creek, smoking hard to settle his nerves.

The sky seemed to darken suddenly; the first great drops of the thunderstorm came pelting down. The inspector hurried to his horse, and cantered off along the line in the direction of the fettlers' camp.

He had forgotten all about the chip, and left it on top of the post!

Dave Regan sat down on the beam in the rain and swore comprehensively.

That Pretty Girl in the Army

Now I often sit at Watty's, when the night is very near,
With a head that's full of jingles—and the fumes of bottled beer;
For I always have a fancy that, if I am over there
When the Army prays for Watty, I'm included in the prayer.
It would take a lot of praying, lots of thumping on the drum,
To prepare our sinful, straying, erring souls for Kingdom Come.
But I love my fellow-sinners! and I hope, upon the whole,
That the Army gets a hearing when it prays for Watty's soul.

—When the World was Wide.

THE Salvation Army does good business in some of the outback towns of the great pastoral wastes of Australia. There's the thoughtless, careless generosity of the bushman, whose pockets don't go far enough down his trousers (that's what's the matter with him), and who contributes to anything that comes along, without troubling to ask questions, like long Bob Brothers of Bourke, who, chancing to be "a Protestant by rights", unwittingly subscribed towards the erection of a new Catholic church, and being chaffed for his mistake, said:

"Ah, well, I don't suppose it'll matter a hang in the end, anyway it goes. I ain't got nothink agenst the Roming Carflicks."

There's the shearer, fresh with his cheque from a cut-out shed, gloriously drunk and happy, in love with all the world, and ready to subscribe towards any creed and shout for all hands—including Old Nick if he happened to come along. There's the shearer, half-drunk and inclined to be nasty, who has got the wrong end of all things with a tight grip, and who flings a shilling in the face of outback conventionality (as he thinks) by chucking a bob into the Salvation Army ring. Then he glares round to see if he can catch anybody winking behind his back. There's the cynical joker, a queer mixture, who contributes generously and tempts the reformed boozer afterwards. There's the severe-faced old station-hand—in clean shirt and neckerchief and white moleskins—in for his annual or semi-annual spree, who contributes on principle, and then drinks religiously until his cheque is gone and the horrors are come. There's the shearer, feeling mighty bad after a spree, and in danger of seeing things when he tries to go to sleep. He has dropped ten or twenty pounds over bar counters and at cards, and he now "chucks" a repentant shilling into the ring, with a very private and rather vague sort of feeling that something might come of it. There's the stout, contented, good-natured publican, who tips the Army as if it were a barrel-organ. And there are others and other reasons—black sheep and ne'er-do-wells—and faint echoes of other times in Salvation Army tunes.

Bourke, the metropolis of the Great Scrubs, on the banks of the Darling River, about five hundred miles from Sydney, was suffering from a long drought when I was there in ninety-two; and the heat may or may not have been another cause contributing to the success, from a business point of view, of the Bourke garrison. There was much beer boozing—and, besides, it was vaguely understood (as most things are vaguely understood out there in the drought-haze) that the place the Army came to save us from was hotter than Bourke. We didn't hanker to go to a hotter place than Bourke. But that year there was an extraordinary reason for the Army's great financial success there.

She was a little girl, nineteen or twenty, I should judge, the prettiest girl I ever saw in the Army, and one of the prettiest I've ever seen out of it. She had the features of an angel, but her expression was wonderfully human, sweet and sympathetic. Her big grey eyes were sad with sympathy for sufferers and sinners, and her poke bonnet was full of bunchy, red-gold hair. Her first appearance was somewhat dramatic—perhaps the Army arranged it so.

The Army used to pray, and thump the drum, and sing, and take up collections every evening outside Watty Bothways's Hotel, the Carriers' Arms. They performed longer and more often outside Watty's than any other pub in town—perhaps because Watty was considered the most hopeless publican and his customers the hardest crowd of boozers in Bourke. The band generally began to play about dusk. Watty would lean back comfortably in a basket easy-chair on his wide veranda, and clasp his hands, in a calm, contented way, while the Army banged the drum and got steam up, and whilst, perhaps, there was a barney going on in the bar, or a bloodthirsty fight in the backyard. On such occasions there was something like an indulgent or fatherly expression on his fat and usually emotionless face. And by and by he'd move his head gently and doze. The banging and the singing seemed to soothe him, and the praying, which was often very personal, never seemed to disturb him in the least.

Well, it was about dusk one day; it had been a terrible day, a hundred and something startling in the shade, but there came a breeze after sunset. There had been several dozen buckets of water thrown on the veranda floor and the ground outside. Watty was seated in his accustomed place when the Army arrived. There was no Barney in the bar because there was a fight in the backyard, and that claimed the attention of all the customers.

The Army prayed for Watty and his clients; then a reformed drunkard started to testify against publicans and all their works. Watty settled himself comfortably, folded his hands, and leaned back and dozed.

The fight was over, and the chaps began to drop round to the bar. The man who was saved waved his arms, and danced round and howled.

"Ye-es!" he shouted hoarsely. "The publicans, and boozers, and gamblers, and sinners may think that Bourke is hot, but hell is a thousand times hotter! I tell you——"

"Oh, Lord!" said Mitchell, the shearer, and he threw a penny into the ring.

"Ye-es! I tell you that hell is a million times hotter than Bourke! I tell you——"

"Oh, look here," said a voice from the background, "that won't wash. Why, don't you know that when the Bourke people die they send back for their blankets?"

The saved brother glared round.

"I hear a freethinker speaking, my friends," he said. Then, with sudden inspiration and renewed energy, "I hear the voice of a freethinker. Show me the face of a freethinker," he yelled, glaring round like a hunted, hungry man. "Show me the face of a freethinker, and I'll tell you what he is."

Watty hitched himself into a more comfortable position and clasped his hands on his knee and closed his eyes again.

"Ya-a-a-s!" shrieked the brand. "I tell you, my friends, I can tell a freethinker by his face. Show me the face of a——"

At this point there was an interruption. One-eyed, or Wall-eyed Bogan, who had a broken nose, and the best side of whose face was reckoned the ugliest and most sinister—One-eyed Bogan thrust his face forward from the ring of darkness into the torchlight of salvation. He had got the worst of a drawn battle; his nose and mouth were bleeding, and his good eye was damaged.

"Look at my face!" he snarled, with dangerous earnestness. "Look at my face! That's the face of a freethinker, and I don't care who knows it. Now! what have you got to say against my face, Man-without-a-shirt?"

The brother drew back. He had been known in the north-west in his sinful days as "Man-without-a-shirt", *alias* "Shirty", or "The Dirty Man", and was flabbergasted at being recognized in speech. Also, he had been in a shearing-shed and in a shanty orgy with One-eyed Bogan, and knew the man.

Now most of the chaps respected the Army, and, indeed, anything that looked like religion, but the Bogan's face, as representing free thought, was a bit too sudden for them. There were sounds on the opposite side of the ring as of men being smitten repeatedly and rapidly below the belt, and long Tom Hall and one or two others got away into the darkness in the background, where Tom rolled helplessly on the grass and sobbed.

It struck me that Bogan's face was more the result of free speech than anything else.

The Army was about to pray when the Pretty Girl stepped forward, her eyes shining with indignation and enthusiasm. She had arrived by the evening train, and had been standing shrinkingly behind an Army lass of fifty Australian summers, who was about six feet high, flat and broad, and had a square face, and a mouth like a joint in boiler plates.

The Pretty Girl stamped her pretty foot on the gravel, and her eyes flashed in the torchlight.

"You ought to be ashamed of yourselves," she said. "Great big men like you to be going on the way you are. If you were ignorant or poor, as I've seen people, there might be some excuse for you. Haven't you got any mothers, or sisters, or wives to think of? What sort of life is this you lead? Drinking, and gambling, and fighting, and swearing your lives away! Do you ever think of God and the time when you were children? Why don't you make homes? Look at that man's face!" (she pointed suddenly at Bogan, who collapsed and sidled behind his mates out of the light). "Look at that man's face! Is it a face for a Christian? And you help and encourage him to fight. You're worse than he is. Oh, it's brutal. It's—it's wicked. Great big men like you, you ought to be ashamed of yourselves."

Long Bob Brothers—about six-foot-four—the longest and most innocent there, shrunk down by the wall and got his inquiring face out of the light. The Pretty Girl fluttered on for a few moments longer, greatly excited, and then stepped back, seemingly much upset, and was taken under the wing of the woman with the boiler-plate mouth.

It was a surprise, and very sudden. Bogan slipped round to the backyard, and was seen bathing his battered features at the pump. The rest wore the expression of men who knew that something unusual has happened, but don't know what, and are waiting vacantly for developments—except Tom Hall, who had recovered and returned. He stood looking over the head of the ring of bushmen, and apparently taking the same critical interest in the girl as he would in a fight—his expression was such as a journalist might wear who is getting exciting copy.

The Army had it all their own way for the rest of the evening, and made a good collection. The Pretty Girl stood smiling round with shining eyes as the bobs and tanners dropped in, and then, being shoved forward by the flat woman, she thanked us sweetly, and said we were good fellows, and that she was sorry for some things she'd said to us. Then she retired, fluttering and very much flushed, and hid herself behind the hard woman—who, by the way, had an excrescence on her upper lip which might have stood for a rivet.

Presently the Pretty Girl came from behind the big woman and stood watching things with glistening eyes. Some of the chaps on the opposite side of the ring moved a little to one side and all were careful not to meet her eye—not to be caught looking at her—lest she should be embarrassed. Watty had roused himself a little at the sound of a strange voice in the Army (and such a clear, sweet voice too!) and had a look; then he settled back peacefully again, but it was noticed that he didn't snore that evening.

And when the Army prayed, the Pretty Girl knelt down with the rest on the gravel. One or two tall bushmen bowed their heads as if they had to, and One-eyed Bogan, with the blood washed from his face, stood with his hat off, glaring round to see if he could catch anyone sniggering.

Mitchell, the shearer, said afterwards that the whole business made him feel for the moment like he felt sometimes in the days when he used to feel things.

The town discussed the Pretty Girl in the Army that night and for many days thereafter, but no one could find out who she was or where she belonged to—except that she came from Sydney last. She kept her secret, if she had one, very close—or else the other S.A. women were not to be pumped. She lived in skillion-rooms at the back of the big weatherboard Salvation Army barracks with two other "lassies", who did washing and sewing and nursing, and went shabby, and half starved themselves, and were baked in the heat, like scores of women in the bush, and even as hundreds of women, suffering from religious mania, slave and stint in city slums, and neglect their homes, husbands and children—for the glory of Booth.

The Pretty Girl was referred to as Sister Hannah by the Army people, and came somehow to be known by sinners as "Miss Captain". I don't know whether that was her real name or what rank she held in the Army, if indeed she held any.

She sold *War Crys*, and the circulation doubled in a day. One-eyed Bogan, being bailed up unexpectedly, gave her "half a caser" for a *Cry*, and ran away without the paper or the change. Jack Mitchell bought a *Cry* for the first time in his life, and read it. He said he found some of the articles intensely realistic, and many of the statements were very interesting. He said he read one or two things in the *Cry* that he didn't know before. Tom Hall, taken unawares, bought three *Crys* from the Pretty Girl, and blushed to find it fame.

Little Billy Woods, the Labourers' Union secretary—who had a poetic temperament and more than the average bushman's reverence for higher things—Little Billy Woods told me in a burst of confidence that he generally had two feelings, one after the other, after encountering that girl. One was that unfathomable far-away feeling of loneliness and longing that comes at odd times to the best of married men, with the best of wives and children—as Billy had. The other feeling, which came later on, and was a reaction in fact, was the feeling of a man who thinks he's been twisted round a woman's little finger for the benefit of somebody else. Billy said that he couldn't help being reminded by the shy, sweet smile and the shy, sweet "Thank you" of the Pretty Girl in the Army, of the shy, sweet smile and the shy, sweet gratitude of a Sydney private barmaid, who had once roped him in, in the days before he was married. Then he'd reckon that the Army lassie had been sent outback to Bourke as a business speculation.

Tom Hall was inclined to reckon so too—but that was after he'd been chaffed for a month about the three *War Crys*.

The Pretty Girl was discussed from psychological points of view; not forgetting the sex problem. Donald Macdonald—shearer, union leader and labour delegate to other colonies on occasion—Donald Macdonald said that whenever he saw a circle of plain or ugly, dried-up women or girls round a shepherd, evangelist or a Salvation Army drum, he'd say "Sexually starved!" They were hungry for love. Religious mania was sexual passion damned out of its course. Therefore he held that morbidly religious girls were the most easily seduced.

But this couldn't apply to the Pretty Girl in the Army. Mitchell reckoned that she'd either had a great sorrow—a lot of trouble, or a disappointment in love (the "or" is Mitchell's); but they couldn't see how a girl like her could possibly be disappointed in love—unless the chap died or got into jail for life. Donald decided that her soul had been starved somehow.

Mitchell suggested that it might be only a craving for notoriety, the same thing that makes women and girls go amongst lepers, and out to the battlefield, and nurse ugly pieces of men back to life again; the same thing that makes some women and girls swear ropes round men's necks. The Pretty Girl might be the daughter of well-to-do people—even aristocrats, said Mitchell—she was pretty enough and spoke well enough. " 'Every woman's a barmaid at heart,' as the *Bulletin* puts it," said Mitchell.

But not even one of the haggard women of Bourke ever breathed a suspicion of scandal against her. They said she was too good and too pretty to be where she was. You see, it was not in an old settled town where hags blacken God's world with their tongues. Bourke was just a little camping town in a big land, where free, good-hearted democratic Australians, and the best of black sheep from the old world were constantly passing through; where husbands were often obliged to be away from home for twelve months, and the storekeepers had to trust the people, and mates trusted each other, and the folks were broad-minded. The mind's eye had a wide range.

After her maiden speech the Pretty Girl seldom spoke, except to return thanks for collections—and she never testified. She had a sweet voice and used to sing.

Now, if I were writing pure fiction, and were not cursed with an obstinate inclination to write the truth, I might say that, after the advent of the Pretty Girl, the morals of Bourke improved suddenly and wonderfully. That One-eyed Bogan left off gambling and drinking and fighting and swearing, and put on a red coat and testified and fought the devil only; that Mitchell dropped his mask of cynicism; that Donald Macdonald ate no longer of the tree of knowledge and ceased to worry himself with psychological problems, and was happy; and that Tom Hall was no longer a scoffer. That no one sneaked round through the scrub after dusk to certain necessary establishments in weatherboard cottages on the outskirts of the town; and that the broadminded and obliging ladies thereof became Salvation Army lassies.

But none of these things happened. Drunks quieted down or got out of the way if they could when the Pretty Girl appeared on the scene, fights and games of "headin' 'em" were adjourned, and weak, ordinary language was used for the time being, and that was about all.

Nevertheless, most of the chaps were in love with that Pretty Girl in the Army—all those who didn't *worship* her privately. Long Bob Brothers hovered round in hopes, they said, that she'd meet with an accident—get run over by a horse or something—and he'd have to carry her in; he scared the women at the barracks by dropping firewood over the fence after dark. Barcoo-Rot, the meanest man in the back country, was seen to drop a threepenny bit into the ring, and a rumour was industriously circulated (by Tom Hall) to the effect that One-eyed Bogan intended to shave and join the Army disguised as a lassie.

Handsome Jake Boreham (*alias* Bore-'em), a sentimental shearer from New Zealand, who had read Bret Harte, made an elaborate attempt for the Pretty Girl, by pretending to be going to the dogs headlong, with an idea of first winning her sorrowful interest and sympathy, and then making an apparently hard struggle to straighten up for her sake. He related his experience with the cheerful and refreshing absence of reserve which was characteristic of him, and is of most bushmen.

"I'd had a few drinks," he said, "and was having a spell under a gum by the river, when I saw the Pretty Girl and another Army woman coming down along the bank. It was a blazing hot day. I thought of Sandy and the schoolmistress in Bret Harte, and I thought it would be a good idea to stretch out in the sun and pretend to be helpless; so I threw my hat on the ground and lay down, with my head in a blazing heat, in the most graceful position I could get at, and I tried to put a look of pained regret on my face, as if I was dreaming of my lost boyhood and me mother. I thought, perhaps, the Girl would pity me, and I felt sure she'd stoop and pick up my hat and put it gently over my poor troubled head. Then I was going to become conscious for a moment, and look hopelessly round, and into her eyes, and then start and look sorrowful and ashamed, and stagger to my feet, taking off my hat like the Silver King does to the audience when he makes his first appearance drunk on the stage; and then I was going to reel off, trying to walk as straight as I could. And next day I was going to clean up my teeth and nails and put on a white shirt, and start to be a new man henceforth.

"Well, as I lay there with my eyes shut, I heard the footsteps come up and stop, and heard 'em whisper, and I thought I heard the Pretty Girl say 'Poor fellow!' or something that sounded like that; and just then I got a God-almighty poke in the ribs with an umbrella—at least I suppose it was aimed for my ribs; but women are bad shots, and the point of the umbrella caught me in the side, just between the bottom rib and the hip-bone, and I sat up with a click, like the blade of a pocket-knife.

"The other lassie was the big square-faced woman. The Pretty Girl looked rather more frightened and disgusted than sentimental, but she had plenty of pluck, and soon pulled herself together. She said I ought to be ashamed of myself, a great big man like me, lying there in the dust like a drunken tramp—an eyesore and a disgrace to all the world. She told me to go to my camp, wherever that was, and sleep myself sober. The square-jawed woman said I looked like a fool sitting there. I did feel ashamed, and I reckon I did look like a fool—a man generally does in a fix like that. I felt like one, anyway. I got up and walked away and it hurt me so much that I went over to West Bourke and went to the dogs properly for a fortnight, and lost twenty quid on a game of draughts against a blindfolded player. Now both those women had umbrellas, but I'm not sure to this day which of 'em it was that gave me that poke. It wouldn't have mattered much, anyway. I haven't borrowed one of Bret Harte's books since."

Jake reflected a while.

"The worst of it was," he said ruefully, "that I wasn't sure that the girl or the woman didn't see through me, and that worried me a bit. You never can tell how much a woman suspects, and that's the worst of 'em. I found that out after I got married."

The Pretty Girl in the Army grew pale and thin and bigger-eyed. The women said it was a shame, and that she ought to be sent home to her friends, wherever they were. She was laid up for two or three days, and some of the women cooked delicacies and handed 'em over the barracks fence, and offered to come in and nurse her; but the square woman took washing home and nursed the girl herself.

The Pretty Girl still sold *War Crys* and took up collections, but in a tired, listless, half shamefaced way. It was plain that she was tired of the Army, and growing ashamed of the Salvationists. Perhaps she had come to see things too plainly.

You see, the Army does no good outback in Australia—except from a business point of view. It is simply there to collect funds for hungry headquarters. The bushmen are much too intelligent for the Army. There was no poverty in Bourke—as it is understood in the city; there was plenty of food; and camping out and roughing it come natural to the bushmen. In cases of sickness, accident, widows or orphans, the chaps sent round the hat, without banging a drum or testifying, and that was all right. If a chap was hard up he borrowed a couple of quid from his mate. If a strange family arrived without a penny, someone had to fix 'em up, and the storekeepers helped them till the man got work. For the rest, we work out our own salvation, or damnation—as the case is—in the bush, with no one to help us, except a mate, perhaps. The Army can't help us, but a fellow-sinner can, sometimes, who has been through it all himself. The Army is only a drag on the progress of democracy, because it attracts many who would otherwise be aggressive democrats—and for other reasons.

Besides, if we all reformed the Army would get deuced little from us for its city mission.

The Pretty Girl went to service for a while with the stock-inspector's wife, who could get nothing out of her concerning herself or her friends. She still slept at the barracks, stuck to the Army, and attended its meetings.

It was Christmas morning, and there was peace in Bourke and

goodwill towards all men. There hadn't been a fight since yesterday evening, and that had only been a friendly one, to settle an argument concerning the past ownership, and, at the same time, to decide as to the future possession of a dog.

It had been a hot, close night, and it ended in a suffocating sunrise. The free portion of the male population were in the habit of taking their blankets and sleeping out in "the Park", or town square, in hot weather; the wives and daughters of the town slept, or tried to sleep with bedroom windows and doors open, while husbands lay outside on the verandas. I camped in a corner of the park that night, and the sun woke me.

As I sat up I caught sight of a swagman coming along the white, dusty road from the direction of the bridge, where the cleared road ran across west and on, a hundred and thirty miles, through the barren, broiling mulga scrubs, to Hungerford, on the border of Sheol. I knew that swagman's walk. It was John Merrick (Jack Moonlight), one-time Shearers' Union secretary at Coonamble, and generally "Rep." (shearers' representative) in any shed where he sheared. He was a "better-class shearer", one of those quiet, thoughtful men of whom there are generally two or three in the roughest of rough sheds, who have great influence, and give the shed a good name from a union point of view. Not quiet with the resentful or snobbish reserve of the educated Englishman, but with a sad or subdued sort of quietness that has force in it—as if they fully realized that their intelligence is much higher than the average, that they have suffered more real trouble and heartbreak than the majority of their mates, and that their mates couldn't possibly understand them if they spoke as they felt and couldn't see things as they do—yet men who understand and are intensely sympathetic in their loneliness and sensitive reserve.

I had worked in a shed with Jack Moonlight, and had met him in Sydney, and to be mates with a bushman for a few weeks is to know him well—anyway, I found it so. He had taken a trip to Sydney the Christmas before last, and when he came back there was something wanting. He became more silent, he drank more, and sometimes alone, and took to smoking heavily. He dropped his mates, took little or no interest in union matters, and travelled alone, and at night.

The Australian bushman is born with a mate who sticks to him through life—like a mole. They may be hundreds of miles apart sometimes, and separated for years, yet they are mates for life. A bushman may have many mates in his roving, but there is always one *his* mate, "my mate"; and it is common to hear a bushman, who is, in every way, a true mate to the man he happens to be travelling with, speak of *his mate's mate*—"Jack's mate"—who might be in Klondyke or South Africa. A bushman has always a mate to comfort him and argue with him, and work and tramp and drink with him, and lend him quids when he's hard up, and call him a b—— fool, and fight him sometimes; to abuse him to his face and defend his name behind his back; to bear false witness and perjure his soul for his sake; to lie to the girl for him if he's single, and to his wife if he's married; to secure a pen for him at a shed where he isn't on the spot, or, if the mate is away in New Zealand or South Africa, to write and tell him if it's any good coming over this way. And each would take the word of the other against all the world, and each believes that the other is the straightest chap that ever lived—"a white man!" And next best to your old mate is the man you're tramping, riding, working, or drinking with.

About the first thing the cook asks you when you come along to a shearers' hut is, "Where's your mate?" I travelled alone for a while one time, and it seemed to me sometimes, by the tone of the inquiry concerning the whereabouts of my mate, that the bush had an idea that I might have done away with him and that the thing ought to be looked into.

When a man drops mateship altogether and takes to "hatting" in the bush it's a step towards a convenient tree and a couple of saddle-straps buckled together.

I had an idea that I, in a measure, took the place of Jack Moonlight's mate about this time.

" 'Ullo, Jack!" I hailed as he reached the corner of the park.

"Good morning, Harry!" said Jack, as if he'd seen me yesterday evening instead of three months ago. "How are you getting on?"

We walked together towards the Union Office, where I had a camp in the skillion-room at the back. Jack was silent. But there's no place in the world where a man's silence is respected so much (within reasonable bounds) as in the Australian bush, where every man has a past more or less sad, and every man a ghost—perhaps from other lands that we know nothing of, and speaking in a foreign tongue. They say in the bush, "Oh, Jack's only thinking!"

And they let him think. Generally you want to think as much as your mate; and when you've been together some time it's quite natural to travel all day without exchanging a word. In the morning Jim says, "Well, I think I made a bargain with that horse, Bill," and some time late in the afternoon, say twenty miles farther on, it occurs to Bill to "rejoin", "Well, I reckon the blank as sold it to you had yer proper!"

I like a good thinking mate, and I believe thinking in company is a lot more healthy and more comfortable, as well as less risky, than thinking alone.

On the way to the Union Office Jack and I passed the Royal Hotel, and caught a glimpse, through the open door of a bedroom off the veranda, of the landlord's fresh, fair, young Sydney girl-wife, sleeping prettily behind the mosquito-net, like a sleeping beauty, while the boss lay on a mattress outside on the veranda, across the open door. (He wasn't necessary for publication, but an evidence of good faith.)

I glanced at Jack for a grin, but didn't get one. He wore the pained expression of a man who is suddenly hit hard with the thought of something that might have been.

I boiled the billy and fried a pound of steak.

"Been travelling all night, Jack?" I asked.

"Yes," said Jack. "I camped at Emus yesterday."

He didn't eat. I began to reckon that he was brooding too much for his health. He was much thinner than when I saw him last, and pretty haggard, and he had something of the hopeless, haggard look that I'd seen in Tom Hall's eyes after the last big shearing strike, when Tom had worked day and night to hold his mates up all through the hard, bitter struggle, and the battle was lost.

"Look here, Jack!" I said at last. "What's up?"

"Nothing's up, Harry," said Jack. "What made you think so?"

"Have you got yourself into any fix?" I asked. "What's the Hungerford track been doing to you?"

"No, Harry," he said, "I'm all right. How are you?" And he pulled some string and papers and a roll of dusty pound notes from his pocket and threw them on the bunk.

I was hard up just then, so I took a note and the billy to go to the Royal and get some beer. I thought the beer might loosen his mind a bit.

"Better take a couple of quid," said Jack. "You look as if you want some new shirts and things." But a pound was enough for me, and I think he had reason to be glad of that later on, as it turned out.

"Anything new in Bourke?" asked Jack as we drank the beer.

"No," I said, "not a thing—except there's a pretty girl in the Salvation Army."

"And it's about time," growled Jack.

"Now, look here, Jack," I said presently, "what's come over you lately at all? I might be able to help you. It's not a bit of use telling me that there's nothing the matter. When a man takes to brooding and travelling alone it's a bad sign, and it will end in a leaning tree and a bit of clothes-line as likely as not. Tell me what the trouble is. Tell us all about it. There's a ghost, isn't there?"

"Well, I suppose so," said Jack. "We've all got our ghosts for that matter. But never you mind, Harry; I'm all right. I don't go interfering with your ghosts, and I don't see what call you've got to come haunting mine. Why, it's as bad as kicking a man's dog." And he gave the ghost of a grin.

"Tell me, Jack," I said, "is it a woman?"

"Yes," said Jack, "it's a woman. Now are you satisfied?"

"Is it a girl?" I asked.

"Yes," he said.

So there was no more to be said. I'd thought it might have been a lot worse than a girl. I'd thought he might have got married somewhere, sometime, and made a mess of it.

We had dinner at Billy Woods's place, and a sensible Christmas dinner it was—everything cold, except the vegetables, with the hose going on the veranda in spite of the by-laws, and Billy's wife and her sister, fresh and cool-looking and jolly, instead of being hot and brown and cross like most Australian women who roast themselves over a blazing fire in a hot kitchen on a broiling day, all the morning, to cook scalding plum pudding and red-hot roasts, for no other reason than that their grandmothers used to cook hot Christmas dinners in England.

And in the afternoon we went for a row on the river, pulling easily up the anabranch and floating down with the stream under the shade of the river timber—instead of going to sleep and waking up helpless and soaked in perspiration, to find the women with headaches, as many do on Christmas Day in Australia.

Mrs Woods tried to draw Jack out, but it was no use, and in the evening he commenced drinking, and that made Billy uneasy. "I'm afraid Jack's on the wrong track," he said.

After tea most of us collected about Watty's veranda. Most things that happened in Bourke happened at Watty's pub, or near it.

If a horse bolted with a buggy or cart he was generally stopped outside Watty's, which seemed to suggest, as Mitchell said, that most of the heroes drank at Watty's—also that the pluckiest men were found amongst the hardest drinkers. (But sometimes the horse fetched up against Watty's sign and lamp-post—which was a stout one of ironbark—and smashed the trap.) Then Watty's was the Carriers' Arms, a union pub; and the Australian teamsters are mostly hard cases: while there was something in Watty's beer which made men argue fluently, and the best fights came off in his back-yard. Watty's dogs were the most quarrelsome in town, and there was a dog-fight there every other evening, followed as often as not by a man-fight. If a bushman's horse ran away with him the chances were than he'd be thrown on to Watty's veranda, if he wasn't pitched into the bar; and victims of accidents, and sick, hard-up shearers, were generally carried to Watty's pub, as being the most convenient and comfortable for them. Mitchell denied that it was generosity or good nature on Watty's part, he said it was all business—advertisement. Watty knew what he was doing. He was very deep, was Watty. Mitchell further hinted that if he was sick *he* wouldn't be carried to Watty's, for Watty knew what a thirsty business a funeral was. Tom Hall reckoned that Watty bribed the Army on the quiet.

I was sitting on a stool along the veranda wall with Donald Macdonald, Bob Brothers (the Giraffe) and Mitchell, and one or two others, and Jack Moonlight sat on the floor with his back to the wall and his hat well down over his eyes. The Army came along at the usual time, but we didn't see the Pretty Girl at first—she was a bit late. Mitchell said he liked to be at Watty's when the Army prayed and the Pretty Girl was there; he had no objection to being prayed for by a girl like that, though he reckoned that nothing short of a real angel could save him now. He said his old grand-mother used to pray for him every night of her life and three times on Sunday, with Christmas Day extra when Christmas Day didn't fall on a Sunday; but Mitchell reckoned that the old lady couldn't have had much influence because he became more sinful every year, and went deeper in ways of darkness, until finally he embarked on a career of crime.

The Army prayed, and then a thin "ratty" little woman bobbed up in the ring; she'd gone mad on religion as women do on woman's rights and hundreds of other things. She was so skinny in the face, her jaws so prominent, and her mouth so wide, that when she opened it to speak it was like a ventriloquist's dummy and you could almost see the cracks open down under her ears.

"They say I'm cracked!" she screamed in a shrill, cracked voice. "But I'm not cracked—I'm only cracked on the Lord Jesus Christ! That's all I'm cracked on——." And just then the Amen man of the Army—the Army groaner we called him, who was always putting both feet in it—just then he blundered forward, rolled up his eyes, threw his hands up and down as if he were bouncing two balls, and said, with deep feeling:

"Thank the Lord she's got a crack in the right place!"

Tom Hall doubled up, and most of the other sinners seemed to think there was something very funny about it. And the Army, too, seemed struck with an idea that there was something wrong somewhere, for they started a hymn.

A big American negro, who'd been a night watchman in Sydney, stepped into the ring and waved his arms and kept time, and as he got excited he moved his hands up and down rapidly, as if he was hauling down a rope in a great hurry through a pulley block above, and he kept saying, "Come down, Lord!" all through the hymn, like a bass accompaniment, "Come down, Lord; come down, Lord; come down, Lord; come down, Lord!" and the quicker he said it the faster he hauled. He was as good as a drum. And when the hymn was over he started to testify.

"My frens!" he said, "I was once black as der coals in der mined! I was once black as der ink in der ocean of sin! But now—thank an' bless the Lord!—I am whiter dan der dribben snow!"

Tom Hall sat down on the edge of the veranda and leaned his head against a post and cried. He had contributed a bob this evening, and he was getting his money's worth.

Then the Pretty Girl arrived and was pushed forward into the ring. She looked thinner and whiter than I'd ever seen her, and there was a feverish brightness in her eyes that I didn't like.

"Men!" she said, "this is Christmas Day——"

I didn't hear any more, for, at the sound of her voice, Jack

Moonlight jumped up as if he'd sat on a baby. He started forward, stared at her for a moment as if he couldn't believe his eyes, and then said, "Hannah!" short and sharp. She started as if she was shot, gave him a wild look, and stumbled forward; the next moment he had her in his arms and was steering for the private parlour.

I heard Mrs Bothways calling for water and smelling-salts; she was as fat as Watty, and very much like him in the face, but she was emotional and sympathetic. Then presently I heard, through the open window, the Pretty Girl say to Jack, "Oh, Jack, Jack! Why did you go away and leave me like that? It was cruel!"

"But you told me to go, Hannah," said Jack.

"That—that didn't make any difference. Why didn't you write?" she sobbed.

"Because you never wrote to me, Hannah," he said.

"That—that was no excuse!" she said. "It was so k-k-k-cruel of you, Jack."

Mrs Bothways pulled down the window. A newcomer asked Watty what the trouble was, and he said that the Army girl had only found her chap, her husband, or long-lost brother or something, but the missus was looking after the business; then he dozed again.

And then we adjourned to the Royal and took the Army with us.

"That's the way of it," said Donald Macdonald. "With a woman it's love or religion; with a man it's love or the devil."

"Or with a man," said Mitchell, presently, "it's love and the devil both, sometimes, Donald."

I looked at Mitchell hard, but for all his face expressed he might only have said, "I think it's going to rain."

The Hairy Man

As far back as I can remember, the yarn of the Hairy Man was told in the Blue Mountains district of New South Wales. It scared children coming home by bush tracks from school and boys out late after lost cows; and even grown bushmen, when going along a lonely track after sunset, would hold their backs hollow and whistle a tune when they suddenly heard a thud, thud of a kangaroo leaping off through the scrub. Other districts also had spooks and bogies—the escaped tiger; the ghost of the convict who had been done to death and buried in his irons; ghosts of men who had hanged themselves; the ghost of the hawker's wife whose husband had murdered her with a tomahawk in the lonely camp by the track; the ghost of the murdered bushman whose mate quietly stepped behind him as he sat reflecting over a pipe and broke in the back of his head with an axe, and afterwards burnt the body between two logs; ghosts of victims whose murders had been avenged and of undiscovered murders that had been done right enough—all sorts and conditions of ghosts, none of them cheerful, most of them grimly original and characteristic of the weirdly melancholy and aggressively lonely Australian bush. But the Hairy Man was permanent, and his country spread from the eastern slopes of the Great Dividing Range right out to the ends of the western spurs. He had been heard of and seen and described so often and by so many reliable liars that most people agreed that there must be something. The most popular and enduring theory was that he was a gorilla, or an orang-outang which had escaped from a menagerie long ago. He was also said to be a new kind of kangaroo, or the last of a species of Australian animals which hadn't been discovered yet. Anyway, in some places, he was regarded as a danger to children coming home from school, as were wild bullocks, snakes, and an occasional bushman in the d.t.'s. So now and then, when the yarn had a revival, search parties were organized, and went out with guns to find the Hairy Man, and to settle him and the question one way or the other. But they never found him.

Dave Regan, Jim Bentley and Andy Page, bush mates, had taken a contract to clear and fence the ground for a new cemetery about three miles out of the thriving township of Mudgee-Budgee. Mudgee-Budgee had risen to the dignity of a three-pub town, and people were beginning to die. Up to now the casual and scarce corpses of Mudgee-Budgee or of Home Rule, a goldfield six miles to the west—the bushman who had been thrown from his horse or smashed against a tree while riding recklessly, as bushmen do, or the boozer who had died during a spree in hot weather—had to be taken to the cemetery belonging to the farming town of Buckaroo, about nine miles east of Mudgee-Budgee. This meant a nine-mile, or, in the case of Home Rule, a fifteen-mile drag, which was a long-drawn-out agony in blazing hot, dusty weather, or even in the rain when the roads were boggy. The Buckaroo undertaker could only be induced to bring his hearse out two miles along the road to meet the corpse, which was carried so far in a drag, spring-cart, or wagonette. This so detracted from the dignity of Mudgee-Budgee and Home Rule that they agreed to get a cemetery between them, and Dave Regan got the contract to prepare the ground for corpse planting.

Dave and his mates camped in an old deserted slab and bark hut which happened to stand on the ground. It was a lonely place, which stood in a dark stringybark bush, the nearest house being the hut of a timber-getter and his family, about two miles along the track on the Home Rule side.

It was the day after Anniversary Day. Dave and Jim were patriots, and therefore were feeling very repentant and shaky. They had spent the day at the Buckaroo races, half the night in Buckaroo, and the other half in Home Rule, where the early-closing law as regarded public-houses was not stringent. They had enjoyed a good time; had betted and shouted away all their cash, as well as an advance drawn on the contract, had run up scores at all the pubs, and had been in several rows, and at least three fights. They weren't sure with whom, that was the trouble, but had a drink-lurid recollection of having got off their horses several times on the way home to fight each other. They were too sick to eat or to smoke yet; so they sat outside the hut with their nerves all unstrung and their imaginations therefore particularly active. Under these conditions they so magnified the awful importance of the unknown and the nightmare portions of the prior night that they felt very dismal and hopeless indeed. Dave had a haunting idea, which grew at last to be a sickening conviction, that he had insulted and had wanted to fight the big squatter of the district, from whom he had the promise of a big fencing contract. Jim had a smothering recollection of a row with the leading Mudgee-Budgee storekeeper, who gave them credit. And so they swore off drink—they were going to chuck it for good. Each was firmly resolved this time. But they said nothing about it to each other. They had sworn off mutually so often that the thing had become boresome. But the worst of it was that they had broken the bottle with the morning reviver, and had nothing to straighten up on, and their nerves were not in a fit state to allow of their going to Mudgee-Budgee at the risk of hearing some new and awful truths of last night's doings, and they hadn't the courage to ask Andy to go. They were very contrite and gentle towards him with their "Yes, Andy," and "No, Andy," and "No thank you, Andy," when he fried chops and made coffee for them. The day before they had both sworn to him—solemnly, affectionately, and at last impatiently, and even angrily—that they wouldn't get drunk, that they wouldn't bet, that they wouldn't draw a penny on the contract, that they'd buy a week's provisions first thing, that they'd bring the things home with them on their horses, and that they'd come home early. And now—they'd spent his money as well as their own! Andy made no remarks and asked no questions when they woke at midday; and they took his silence in a chastened spirit.

Andy Page was a patriot and a democrat, too, the most earnest of the three; but he was as obstinately teetotal as he was honest and truthful. Dave was the head of the party, but Andy was the father. Andy had, on several occasions, gone into town with Dave and Jim on pay nights—to look after them, to fight for them if necessary, and to get them home, if possible, when they'd had enough. It was a thankless job, but Andy was loved by his mates, who nevertheless, when drunk, even wanted to fight him when he stood out against "one more drink for the last". He was as strong physically, as well as morally, as the two put together; and was respected even by the publican whom he abused for serving his mates when they'd had enough. But the last spree but one had disgusted Andy. He swore he'd never go into town with them again, and like most simple-minded, honest, good-natured fellows whose ideas come slowly, who are slow to arriving at decisions (and whose decisions are nearly invariably right), when he'd once made up his mind nothing short of a severe shock of earthquake could move him. So he stayed at home on Anniversary Day, and washed and mended his clothes.

Dave and Jim were still moping wretchedly about the hut when, towards the middle of the afternoon, an angel came along on horseback. It was Jack Jones from Mudgee-Budgee, a drinking mate of theirs, a bush-telegraph joker, and the ne'er-do-well of the district. He hung up his shy, spidery filly under a shed at the back of the hut.

"I thought you chaps would be feeling shaky," he said, "and I've been feeling as lonely and dismal as a bandicoot on a burnt ridge, so I thought I'd come out. I've brought a flask of whisky."

Never were two souls more grateful. Bush mateship is a grand thing, drunk or sober.

Andy promptly took charge of the whisky, and proceeded to dole out judicious doses at decent intervals.

Jack, who was a sandy-complexioned young fellow with the expression of a born humorist, had some news.

"You know Corny George?" They had heard of him. He was an old Cornishman who split shingles and palings in the Black Range, and lived alone in a hut in a dark gully under the shadow of Dead Man's Gap.

"He went in to Buckaroo to the police station yesterday," said Jack Jones, "in a very bad state. He swore he'd seen the Hairy Man."

"The watter?"

"Yes, the Hairy Man. He swore that the Hairy Man had come down to his hut the night before last, just after dark, and tried to break in. The Hairy Man stayed about the hut all night, trying to pull the slabs off the walls, and get the bark off the roof, and didn't go away till daylight. Corny says he fired at him two or three times, through the cracks, with his old shot-gun, but the Hairy Man didn't take any notice. The old chap was pretty shaky on it."

"Drink, I s'pose," grunted Andy contemptuously.

"No, it wasn't drink. They reckoned he'd been 'hatting' it too long. They've got him at the police station."

"What did he say the Hairy Man was like?" asked Jim Bentley.

"Oh, the usual thing," said Jack. " 'Bout as tall as a man and twice as broad, arms nearly as long as himself, big wide mouth with grinning teeth—and covered all over with red hair."

"Why, that's just what my uncle said he was like!" exclaimed Andy Page, suddenly taking great interest in the conversation. He was passing in with some firewood to stick under a pot in which he was boiling a piece of salt-beef; but he stood stock-still and stared at Jim Bentley, with the blank, breathless expression of a man who had just heard astounding news.

"Did your uncle see the Hairy Man, Andy?" inquired Dave Regan feebly. He felt too sick to take much interest.

"Yes," said Andy, staring at Jack with great earnestness. "Didn't I tell you? He was drivin' home up the pass to Dead Man's Gap, where he lived then, and he seen the Hairy Man, bundlin' off among the rocks."

Andy paused impressively, and stared at Jack.

"And what did your uncle do, Andy?" asked Jack, with a jerky little cough.

"He stood up in the cart and hammered into the horse, and galloped it all the way home, full-bat up to the door; then he jumped down, leaving the cart and horse standing there, and went in and lay down on the bed, and wouldn't speak to anybody for two hours."

"How long?" asked Jim, still feebly.

"Two hours," said Andy earnestly, as he went in with the firewood.

Jack Jones proposed "a bit of a stroll"; he said it would do them good. He felt an irresistible inclination to giggle, and wished to get out of the hearing of Andy, whom he respected. As they slouched along the track there was an incident, which proved the state of their nerves. A big brown snake whipped across the dusty path into a heap of dead boughs. They stared at each other for a full minute, then Jack summoned courage to ask:

"Did you chaps see that snake?"

"Yes."

And so it was all right. Then they put a match to the boughs, and stood round with long sticks till the snake came out.

They went back to the hut, and managed a cup of coffee. Presently they got on to ghost and Hairy Man yarns again.

"That was God's truth," said Jack, "that yarn I told you about what happened to me going up Dead Man's Pass. It was just as I told you. I was driving slowly up in that little old spring-cart of mine, when something—I don't know what it was—made me look behind, and there was a woman walking along behind the cart with her hands on the tail-board. It was just above the spot where the hawker's wife was murdered. She was dressed in black, and had black hair, and her face was dead white. At first I thought that it was some woman who wanted a lift, or a chap in woman's clothes playing the ghost, so I pulled up. And when I looked round again she was gone. I thought she'd crouched under the cart, so I whipped up the horse and then looked round again, but there was nothing there. Then I reckon I drove home as fast as Andy's uncle did. You needn't believe me unless you like."

"Thunderstorm coming," said Dave, sniffing and looking round the corner to the east. "I thought this weather would bring something."

"My oath," said Jim, "a regular old-man storm, too."

The big, blue-black bank of storm cloud rose bodily from the east, and was right overhead and sweeping down the sunset in a very few minutes. Then the lightning blazed out, and swallowed up daylight as well as darkness. But it was not a rain storm—it was the biggest hail storm ever experienced in that district. Orchards and vineyards were stripped, and many were ruined. Some said there were stones as big as hen's eggs; some said the storm lasted over an hour, and some said more—but the time was probably half or three-quarters of an hour. Hail lay feet deep in the old diggers' holes for a fortnight after. The mates half expected the hail to come through the roof of the hut.

Just as the storm began to hold up a little, they heard a louder pattering outside, and a bang at the door. The door was of hardwood boards with wide cracks; Andy rose to open it, but squinted through a crack first. Then he snatched the big crowbar from the corner, dug the foot of it into the earth floor, and jammed the pointed head under a cross-piece of the door; he did the same with a smaller crowbar, and looked wildly round for more material for a barricade.

"What are you doing? Who is it, Andy?" wildly cried the others.

"It's the Hairy Man!" gasped Andy.

They quickly got to the door and squinted through the cracks. One squint was sufficient. It was the Hairy Man right enough. He was about as tall as an ordinary man, but seemed twice as broad across the shoulders. He had long arms, and was covered with hair, face and all. He had a big, ugly mouth, and wild, bloodshot eyes. So they helped Andy to barricade the door.

There was another bang at the door. A cart rattled past, a woman screamed, and the cart went on at an increased pace. There was a shot-gun hanging on the wall, loaded—Andy had left it loaded to save ammunition the last time he'd been out kangaroo shooting. Andy, like most slow-thinking men, often did desperate things in a crisis. He snatched down the gun, stepped back a pace or two, aimed at the door low down, and fired. He doesn't know why he aimed low down—except that it "was too much like shooting at a man". They heard a howl, and the thing, whatever it was, running off. Then they barricaded the door some more ere they scanned the door planking and found that about half the charge had gone through.

"The powder must have got damp," said Andy. "I'll put in a double charge to make sure," and re-loaded the gun with trembling hands.

The other three bumped their heads over the whisky. They can't say for certain how they got through that night or what they said or did. The first idea was to get out of there and run to Mudgee-Budgee, but they were reluctant to leave their fort. "Who'd go out and reconnoitre?" "Besides," said Jack Jones, "we're safer here, and the thing's gone, whatever it was. What would they think of us if we went into town with a yarn about a Hairy Man?" He had heard his horse breaking away, and didn't care to take the chance of being chased on foot.

About an hour later they heard a horse galloping past, and, looking through the cracks, saw a boy riding towards Mudgee-Budgee.

"It's young Foley," said Jack, "the son of that old timber-getter that's just taken up a selection along the road near Home Rule."

"I wonder what's up?" said Andy. "Perhaps the Hairy Man's been there. We ought to go along and help."

"They can take care of themselves," said Jack hurriedly. "They're close to Home Rule, and can get plenty of help. The boy wouldn't ride to Mudgee-Budgee if there was anything wrong."

The moon had risen full. Some two or three hours later they saw Mahoney, the mounted constable, and the young doctor from Buckaroo, ride past towards Home Rule.

"There's something up, right enough," said Jim Bentley.

Later on, about daybreak, Andy was sitting obstinately on guard, with the gun across his knees and the others dozing on the bunks (and waking now and then with jerks), when Constable Mahoney rode up to the door and knocked a business knock that brought them all to their feet.

Andy asked him to come in, and placed a stool for him, but he didn't see it. He looked round the hut.

"Whose fowlin' piece is that?" he asked.

"It's—it's mine," said Andy.

Mahoney took the gun up and examined it.

"Is this fowlin' piece loaded?" he asked.

"Yes," said Andy, "it is."

"Now listen to me, boys," said the constable. "Was the fowlin' piece discharged last night?"

"Yes," said Andy, "it was."

"What's up? What have we done?" asked Jim Bentley, desperately.

"Done?" shouted Mahoney. "Done? Why, you've filled old Foley's legs with kangaroo-shot. That's what you've done! Do you know what that is?"

"No," said Jack Jones. He was thinking hard.

"It's manslaughter!" roared Mahoney. "That's the meanin' of it!"

They explained what had happened as far as they were able. Now, Mahoney had a weakness for the boys, and a keen sense of humour—outside himself.

"Best come along with me," he said.

Andy had a stiff Sunday sac suit, of chocolate colour, and a starched white shirt and collar, which he kept in a gin case. He always put them all on when anything happened. On this occasion he fastened his braces over his waistcoat, and didn't notice it until he had gone some distance along the road.

There was great excitement at Foley's shanty—women and children crying, and neighbours hanging round.

Foley was lying on his face on a stretcher, while the young doctor was taking shot from the hairiest leg that Regan and Co. had ever seen on man or beast. The doctor said afterwards that some of the shot had only flattened inside the outer skin, and that others had a covering of hair twisted round them. When Foley was turned round to give his "dispositions", as Mahoney called them, they saw that he had enough hair on his chest to stuff a set of buggy cushions. He had red whiskers all over his face, rusty-red, spiky hair all over his head, and a big mouth and bloodshot eyes. He was the hairiest and ugliest man in the district.

His language was hardly understandable, partly because of the excitement he was still labouring under, and partly because of his peculiar shade of brogue. Where Mahoney said "shtone" Foley would say "stawn"—a brogue with a drawl which sounded ridiculous in an angry man. He drawled most over his oaths.

It seems that he was splitting fencing timber down "beyant the new cimitry", when the storm came on. He thought it would be the usual warm thunderstorm, and it was too far to run home. He didn't want to get wet, so he took his clothes off, and put them in a hollow log till the storm should be past. Then the lightning played round his tools—the cross-cut saw, axe, wedges, etc.—and he had to get away from there. He didn't bargain for "thim blanky hail-sta-w-ns". "It's a wonder I wasn't scalped and drilled full of hawls." He thought of the hut, and made for it, but they wouldn't let him in. Then he suddenly saw some women in a tilt cart comin' round a bend in the road, and saw no chance of getting out of sight—there was a clearing round the hut, and so he banged at the door again. "I thawt the wimmin would stop."

"Whoy did ye think that?" asked Mahoney. "What would they shtop for?"

"How th' hell was I to know?—curiosity, I suppose. They welted into their old hawse, an', as I turned to look after thim, the murderin' villains inside shot a gun at me. I got back to me clawthes, an' dressed somehow. Someone will have to pay for it. I'll be laid up on me back for six weeks."

The young doctor excused himself, and went out for a few minutes. Mahoney winked at Regan and party—a wink you could hear—and it comforted them mightily. When they went out they saw the doctor hanging to a sapling, some distance from the hut. He swung with his back to the sapling, and slid to the ground, his legs stretched out in front of him. He said he would be all right presently.

The thing was fixed up, but the young doctor wanted badly to have the case brought into court. He said it would cheer up the district for years, and add ten years to the life of the oldest inhabitant.

The Hypnotized Township

THEY said that Harry Chatswood, the mail contractor, would do anything for Cobb & Co., even to stretching fencing-wire across the road in a likely place: but I don't believe that—Harry was too good-hearted to risk injuring innocent passengers, and he had a fellow feeling for drivers, being an old coach-driver on rough outback tracks himself. But he did rig up fencing-wire for old Mac, the carrier, one night, though not across the road. Harry, by the way, was a city-born bushman, who had been everything for some years. Anything from six-foot-six to six-foot-nine, fourteen stone, and a hard case. He is a very successful coach-builder now, for he knows the wood, the roads, and the weak parts in a coach.

It was in the good seasons when competition was keen and men's hearts were hard—not as it is in times of drought, when there is no competition, and men's hearts are soft, and there is all kindness and goodwill between them. He had had much opposition in fighting Cobb & Co., and his coaches had won through on the outer tracks. There was little malice in his composition, but when old Mac, the teamster, turned his teams over to his sons and started a light van for parcels and passengers out from Cunnamulla (that place which always sounds to me suggestive of pumpkin pies), in seeming opposition to Harry Chatswood, Harry was annoyed.

Perhaps Mac only wished to end his days on the road with parcels that were light and easy to handle (not like loads of fencing-wire) and passengers that were sociable; but he had been doing well with his teams, and, besides, Harry thought he was after the mail contract: so Harry was annoyed more than he was injured. Mac was mean with the money he had—not because of the money he had a chance of getting; and he mostly slept in his van, in all weathers, when away from home, which was kept by his wife about half-way between the half-way house and the next "township".

One dark, gusty evening, Harry Chatswood's coach dragged, heavily though passengerless, into Cunnamulla, and as he turned into the yard of the local Royal, he saw Mac's tilted four-wheeler (which he called his "van") drawn up opposite by the kerbing round the post office. Mac always chose a central position—with a vague idea of advertisement perhaps. But the nearness to the P.O. reminded Harry of the mail contracts, and he knew that Mac had taken up a passenger or two and some parcels in front of him (Harry) on the trip in. And something told Harry that Mac was asleep inside his van. It was a windy night, with signs of rain, and the curtains were drawn close.

Old Mac was there all right, and sleeping the sleep of a tired driver after a long drowsy day on a hard box-seat, with little or no back railing to it. But there was a lecture on, or an exhibition of hypnotism or mesmerism—"a blanky spirit rappin' fake", they called it, run by "some blanker" in "the hall"; and when old Mac had seen to his horses, he thought he might as well drop in for half an hour and see what was going on. Being a Mac, he was, of course, theological, scientific, and argumentative. He saw some things which woke him up, challenged the performer to hypnotize him, was "operated" on or "fooled with" a bit, had a "numb sorter light-headed feelin' ", and was told by a voice from the back of the hall that his "leg was being pulled, Mac", and by another buzzin' far-away kind of "ventrillick" voice that he would make a good subject, and that, if he only had the will power and knew how (which he would learn from a book the professor had to sell for five shillings) he would be able to drive his van without horses or anything, save the pole sticking straight out in front. These weren't the professor's exact words—— But, anyway, Mac came to himself with a sudden jerk, left with a great Scottish snort of disgust and the sound of heavy boots along the floor; and after a resentful whisky at the Royal, where they laughed at his scrooging bushy eyebrows, fierce black eyes and his deadly-in-earnest denunciation of all humbugs and impostors, he returned to the aforesaid van, let down the flaps, buttoned the daft and "feekle" world out, and himself in, and then retired some more and slept, as I have said, rolled in his blankets and overcoats on a bed of cushions and chaff-bags.

Harry Chatswood got down from his empty coach, and was helping the yard-boy take out the horses, when his eye fell on the remnant of a roll of fencing-wire standing by the stable wall in the light of the lantern. Then an idea struck him unexpectedly, and his mind became luminous. He unhooked the swingle-bar, swung it up over his leader's rump (he was driving only three horses that trip), and hooked it on to the horns of the hames. Then he went inside (there was another light there) and brought out a bridle and an old pair of spurs that were hanging on the wall. He buckled on the spurs at the chopping-block, slipped the winkers off the leader and the bridle on, and took up the fencing-wire, and started out the gate with the horse. The boy gaped after him once, and then hurried to put up the other two horses. He knew Harry Chatswood, and was in a hurry to see what he would be up to.

There was a good crowd in town for the show, or the races, or a stock sale, or land ballot, or something; but most of them were tired, or at tea—or in the pubs—and the corners were deserted. Observe how fate makes time and things fit when she wants to do a good turn—or play a practical joke. Harry Chatswood, for instance, didn't know anything about the hypnotic business.

It was the corners of the main street or road and the principal short cross street, and the van was opposite the pub stables in the main street. Harry crossed the streets diagonally to the opposite corner, in a line with the van. There he slipped the bar down over the horse's rump, and fastened one end of the wire on to the ring of it. Then he walked back to the van, carrying the wire and letting the coils go wide, and, as noiselessly as possible, made a loop in the loose end and slipped it over the hooks on the end of the pole. ("Unnecessary detail!" my contemporaries will moan, "Overloaded with uninteresting details!" But that's because they haven't got the details—and it's the details that go.) Then Harry skipped back to his horse, jumped on, gathered up the bridle reins, and used his spurs. There was a swish and a clang, a scrunch and a clock-clock and rattle of wheels, and a surprised human sound; then a bump and a shout—for there was no underground drainage, and the gutters belonged to the Stone Age. There was a swift clocking and rattle, more shouts, another bump, and a yell. And so on down the longish main street. The stable-boy, who had left the horses in his excitement, burst into the bar, shouting, "The Hypnertism's on, the Mesmerism's on! Ole Mac's van's runnin' away with him without no horses all right!" The crowd scuffled out into the street; there were some unfortunate horses hanging up of course at the panel by the pub trough, and the first to get to them jumped on and rode; the rest ran. The hall—where they were clearing the willing professor out in favour of a "darnce"—and the other pubs decanted their contents, and chance souls skipped for the verandas of weather-board shanties out of which other souls popped to see the runaway.

They saw a weird horseman, or rather, something like a camel (for Harry rode low, like Tod Sloan with his long back humped—for effect)—apparently fleeing for its life in a veil of dust, along the long white road, and some forty rods behind, an unaccountable tilted coach careered in its own separate cloud of dust. And from it came the shouts and yells. Men shouted and swore, women screamed for their children, and kids whimpered. Some of the men turned with an oath and stayed the panic with:

"It's only one of them flamin' motor-cars, you fools."

It might have been, and the yells the warning howls of a motorist who had burst or lost his honk-konk and his head.

"It's runnin' away!" or "The toff's mad or drunk!" shouted others. "It'll break its crimson back over the bridge."

"Let it!" was the verdict of some. "It's all the crimson carnal things are good for."

But the riders still rode and the footmen ran. There was a clatter of hoofs on the short white bridge looming ghostly ahead, and then, at a weird interval, the rattle and rumble of wheels, with no hoof-beats accompanying. The yells grew fainter. Harry's leader was a good horse, of the rather heavy coach-horse breed, with a little of the racing blood in her, but she was tired to start with, and only excitement and fright at the feel of the "pull" of the twisting wire kept her up to that speed; and now she was getting winded, so half a mile or so beyond the bridge Harry thought it had gone far enough, and he stopped and got down. The van ran on a bit, of course, and the loop of the wire slipped off the hooks of the pole. The wire recoiled itself roughly along the dust nearly to the heels of Harry's horse. Harry grabbed up as much of the wire as he could claw for, took the mare by the neck with the other hand, and vanished through the dense fringe of the scrub off the road, till the wire caught and pulled him up; he stood still for a moment, in the black shadow on the edge of a little clearing to listen. Then he fumbled with the wire until he got it untwisted, cast it off, and moved off silently with the mare across the soft rotten ground, and left her in a handy bush stockyard, to be brought back to the stables at a late hour that night—or rather an early hour next morning—by a jackeroo stable-boy who would have two half-crowns in his pocket and afterthought instructions to look out for that wire and hide it if possible.

Then Harry Chatswood got back quickly, by a roundabout way,

and walked into the bar of the Royal, through the back entrance from the stables, and stared, and wanted to know where all the chaps had gone to, and what the noise was about, and whose trap had run away, and if anybody was hurt.

The growing crowd gathered round the van, silent and awe-struck, and some of them threw off their hats, and lost them, in their anxiety to show respect for the dead, or render assistance to the hurt, as men do, round a bad accident in the bush. They got the old man out, and two of them helped him back along the road, with great solicitude, while some walked round the van, and swore beneath their breaths, or stared at it with open mouths, or examined it curiously, with their eyes only, and in breathless silence. They muttered, and agreed, in the pale moonlight now showing, that the sounds of the horses' hoofs had only been "spirit-rappin' sounds"; and after some more muttering, two of the stoutest, with subdued oaths, laid hold of the pole and drew the van to the side of the road, where it would be out of the way of chance night traffic. But they stretched and rubbed their arms afterwards, and then, and on the way back, they swore to admiring acquaintances that they felt the "blanky 'lectricity" runnin' all up their arms and "elbers" while they were holding the pole, which, doubtless, they did—in imagination.

They got old Mac back to the Royal, with sundry hasty whiskies on the way. He was badly shaken, both physically, mentally, and in his convictions, and, when he'd pulled himself together, he had little to add to what they already knew. But he confessed that, when he got under his possum rug in the van, he couldn't help thinking of the professor and his creepy (it was "creepy", or "uncanny", or "awful", or "rum" with 'em now)—his blanky creepy hypnotism: and he (old Mac) had just laid on his back comfortable, and stretched his legs out straight, and his arms down straight by his sides, and drew long, slow breaths, and tried to fix his mind on nothing—as the professor had told him when he was "operatin' on him" in the hall. Then he began to feel a strange sort of numbness coming over him, and his limbs went heavy as lead, and he seemed to be gettin' lightheaded. Then, all on a sudden, his arms seemed to begin to lift, and just when he was goin' to pull 'em down the van started as they had heard and seen it. After a while he got on to his knees and managed to wrench a corner of the front curtain clear of the button and get his head out. And there was the van going helter-skelter, and feeling like Tam o'Shanter's mare (the old man said), and he on her bare-backed. And there was no horses, but a cloud of dust—or a spook—on ahead, and the bare pole steering straight for it, just as the professor had said it would be. The old man thought he was going to be taken clear across the Never-Never country and left to roast on a sandhill, hundreds of miles from anywhere, for his sins, and he said he was trying to think of a prayer or two all the time he was yelling. They handed him more whisky from the publican's own bottle. Hushed and cautious inquiries for the Professor (with a big P now) elicited the hushed and cautious fact that he had gone to bed. But old Mac caught the awesome name and glared round, so they hurriedly filled out another for him, from the boss's bottle. Then there was a slight commotion. The housemaid hurried scaredly into the bar behind and whispered to the boss. She had been startled nearly out of her wits by the Professor suddenly appearing at his bedroom door and calling upon her to have a stiff nobbler of whisky hot sent up to his room. The jackeroo yard-boy, aforesaid, volunteered to take it up, and while he was gone there were hints of hysterics from the kitchen, and the boss whispered in his turn to the crowd over the bar. The jackeroo just handed the tray and glass in through the partly opened door, had a glimpse of pyjamas, and after what seemed an interminable wait, he came tiptoeing into the bar amongst its awe-struck haunters with an air of great mystery, and no news whatever.

They fixed old Mac on a shake-down in the Commercial Room, where he'd have light and some overflow guests on the sofas for company. With a last whisky in the bar, and a stiff whisky by his side on the floor, he was understood to chuckle to the effect that he knew he was all right when he'd won "the keystone o' the brig". Though how a wooden bridge with a level plank floor could have a keystone I don't know—and they were too much impressed by the event of the evening to inquire. And so, with a few cases of hysterics to occupy the attention of the younger women, some whimpering of frightened children and comforting or chastened nagging by mothers, some unwonted prayers muttered secretly and forgettingly, and a good deal of subdued blasphemy, Cunnamulla sank to its troubled slumbers—some of the sleepers in the commercial and billiard-rooms and parlours at the Royal to start up in a cold sweat, out of their beery and hypnotic nightmares, to find

Harry Chatswood making elaborate and fearsome passes over them with his long, gaunt arms and hands, and a flaming red table-cloth tied round his neck.

To be done with old Mac, for the present. He made one or two more trips, but always by daylight, taking care to pick up a swagman or a tramp when he had no passenger; but his "conveections" had had too much of a shaking, so he sold his turn-out (privately and at a distance, for it was beginning to be called "the haunted van") and returned to his teams—always keeping one of the lads with him for company. He reckoned it would take the devil's own hypnotism to move a load of fencing-wire, or pull a wool-team of bullocks out of a bog; and before he invoked the ungodly power—which he let them believe he could—he'd stick there and starve till he and his bullocks died a "natural" death. (He was a bit Irish—as all Scots are—back on one side.)

But the strangest is to come. The Professor, next morning, proved uncomfortably unsociable, and though he could have done a roaring business that night—and for a week of nights after, for that matter—and though he was approached several times, he, for some mysterious reason known only to himself, flatly refused to give one more performance, and said he was leaving the town that day. He couldn't get a vehicle of any kind, for fear, love, or money, until Harry Chatswood, who took a day off, volunteered, for a stiff consideration, to borrow a buggy and drive him (the Professor) to the next town towards the then railway terminus, in which town the Professor's fame was not so awesome, and where he might get a lift to the railway. Harry ventured to remark to the Professor once or twice during the drive that "there was a rum business with old Mac's van last night", but he could get nothing out of him, so gave it best, and finished the journey in contemplative silence.

Now, the fact was that the Professor had been the most surprised and startled man in Cunnamulla that night; and he brooded over the thing till he came to the conclusion that hypnotism was a dangerous power to meddle with unless a man was physically and financially strong and carefree—which he wasn't. So he threw it up.

He learnt the truth, some years later, from a brother of Harry Chatswood, in a Home or Retreat for Geniuses, where "friends were paying", and his recovery was so sudden that it surprised and disappointed the doctor and his friend, the manager of the home. As it was, the Professor had some difficulty in getting out of it.

The Golden Graveyard

MOTHER MIDDLETON was an awful woman, an "old hand" (transported convict) some said. The prefix "mother" in Australia mostly means "old hag", and is applied in that sense. In early boyhood we understood, from old diggers, that Mother Middleton—in common with most other "old hands"—had been sent out for "knocking a donkey off a hen-roost". We had never seen a donkey. She drank like a fish and swore like a trooper when the spirit moved her; she went on periodical sprees, and swore on most occasions. There was a fearsome yarn, which impressed us greatly as boys, to the effect that once, in her best (or worst) days, she had pulled a mounted policeman off his horse, and half-killed him with a heavy pick-handle, which she used for poking down clothes in her boiler. She said that he had insulted her.

She could still knock down a tree and cut a load of firewood with any bushman; she was square and muscular, with arms like a navvy's; she had often worked shifts, below and on top, with her husband, when he'd be putting down a prospecting shaft without a mate, as he often had to do—because of her, mainly. Old diggers said that it was lovely to see how she'd spin up a heavy greenhide bucket full of clay and tailings, and land and empty it with a twist of her wrist. Most men were afraid of her, and few diggers' wives were strong-minded enough to seek a second row with Mother Middleton. Her voice could be heard right across Golden Gully and Specimen Flat, whether raised in argument or in friendly greeting. She came to the old Pipeclay diggings with the "rough crowd" (mostly Irish), and when the old and new Pipeclays were worked out, she went with the rush to Gulgong (about the last of the great alluvial or "poor-man's" goldfields) and came back to Pipeclay when the Log Paddock goldfield "broke out", adjacent to the old fields, and so helped prove the truth of the old diggers' saying, that no matter how thoroughly ground has been worked, there is always room for a new Ballarat.

Jimmy Middleton died at Log Paddock, and was buried, about the last, in the little old cemetery—appertaining to the old farming town on the river, about four miles away—which adjoined the district racecourse, in the bush, on the far edge of Specimen Flat. She conducted the funeral. Some said she made the coffin, and there were alleged jokes to the effect that her tongue had provided the corpse; but this, I think, was unfair and cruel, for she loved Jimmy Middleton in her awful way, and was, for all I ever heard to the contrary, a good wife to him. She then lived in a hut in Log Paddock, on a little money in the bank, and did sewing and washing for single diggers.

I remember hearing her one morning in neighbourly conversation, carried on across the gully, with a selector, Peter Olsen, who was hopelessly slaving to farm a dusty patch in the scrub.

"Why don't you chuck up that dust-hole and go up-country and settle on good land, Peter Olsen? You're only slaving your stomach out here." (She didn't say stomach.)

Peter Olsen (mild-whiskered little man, afraid of his wife): "But then you know my wife is so delicate, Mrs Middleton. I wouldn't like to take her out in the bush."

Mrs Middleton: "Delicate be damned! She's only shamming!" (At her loudest.) "Why don't you kick her off the bed and the book out of her hand, and make her go to work? She's as delicate as I am. Are you a man, Peter Olsen, or a——?"

This for the edification of the wife and of all within half a mile.

Log Paddock was "petering". There were a few claims still being worked down at the lowest end, where big red-and-white waste-heaps of clay and gravel, rising above the blue-grey gum-bushes, advertised deep sinking; and little, yellow, clay-stained streams, running towards the creek over the drought-parched surface, told of trouble with the water below—time lost in bailing and extra expense in timbering. And diggers came up with their flannels and moleskins yellow and heavy, and dripping with wet mullock.

Most of the diggers had gone to other fields, but there were a few prospecting, in parties and singly, out on the flats and amongst the ridges round Pipeclay. Sinking holes in search of a new Ballarat.

Dave Regan—lanky, easy-going bush native; Jim Bently—a bit of a "Flash Jack"; and Andy Page—a character like what Kit (in *The Old Curiosity Shop*) might have been after a voyage to Australia and some colonial experience. These three were mates from habit and not necessity, for it was all shallow sinking where they worked. They were poking down pot-holes in the scrub in the vicinity of the racecourse, where the sinking was from ten to fifteen feet.

Dave had theories—"ideers" or "notions" he called them; Jim Bently laid claim to none—he ran by sight, not scent, like a kangaroo-dog. Andy Page—by the way, great admirer and faithful retainer of Dave Regan—was simple and trusting but, on critical occasions, he was apt to be obstinately, uncomfortably, exasperatingly truthful, honest, and he had reverence for higher things.

Dave thought hard all one quiet drowsy Sunday afternoon, and next morning he, as head of the party, started to sink a hole as close to the cemetery fence as he dared. It was a nice quiet spot in the thick scrub, about three panels along the fence from the farthest corner post from the road. They bottomed here at nine feet, and found encouraging indications. They drove inwards at right angles to the fence, and at a point immediately beneath it they were "making tucker"; a few feet farther and they were making wages. The old alluvial bottom sloped gently that way. The bottom here, by the way, was shelving, brownish, rotten rock.

Just inside the cemetery fence, and at right angles to Dave's drive, lay the shell containing all that was left of the late fiercely lamented James Middleton, with older graves close at each end. A grave was supposed to be six feet deep, and local grave-diggers had been conscientious. The old alluvial bottom sloped from nine to fifteen feet here.

Dave worked the ground all round from the bottom of his shaft, timbering—i.e., putting in a sapling prop—here and there where he worked wide; but the "payable dirt" ran in under the cemetery, and in no other direction.

Dave, Jim, and Andy held a consultation in camp over their pipes after tea, as a result of which Andy next morning rolled up his swag, sorrowfully but firmly shook hands with Dave and Jim, and started to tramp outback to look for work on a sheep-station.

This was Dave's theory—drawn from a little experience and many long yarns with old diggers:—

He had bottomed on a slope to an old original watercourse, covered with clay and gravel from the hills by centuries of rains to the depth of from nine or ten to twenty feet; he had bottomed on a gutter running into the bed of the old buried creek, and carrying patches and streaks of wash (or gold-bearing dirt). If he went on he might strike it rich at any stroke of his pick; he might strike the rich lead which was supposed to exist round there. (There was always supposed to be a rich lead round there somewhere. "There's gold in them ridges yet—if a man can only git at it," says the toothless old relic of the Roaring Days.)

Dave might strike a ledge, pocket, or pot-hole holding wash rich with gold. He had prospected on the opposite side of the cemetery, found no gold, and the bottom sloping upwards towards the graveyard. He had prospected at the back of the cemetery, found a few colours, and the bottom sloping downwards towards the point under the cemetery towards which all indications were now leading him. He had sunk shafts across the road opposite the cemetery frontage and found the sinking twenty feet and not a colour of gold. Probably the whole of the ground under the cemetery was rich—maybe the richest in the district. The old grave-diggers had not been gold-diggers—besides, the graves, being six feet, would, none of them, have touched the alluvial bottom. There was nothing strange in the fact that none of the crowd of experienced diggers who rushed the district had thought of the cemetery and racecourse. Old brick chimneys and houses, the clay for the bricks of which had been taken from sites of subsequent goldfields, had been put through the crushing-mill in subsequent years and had yielded payable gold. Fossicking Chinamen were said to have been the first to detect a case of this kind.

Dave reckoned to strike the lead (or a shelf or ledge with a good streak of wash lying along it) at a point about forty feet within the cemetery. But a theory in alluvial gold-mining was much like a theory in gambling, in some respects. The theory might be right enough, but old volcanic disturbances—"the shrinkage of the earth's surface", and that sort of old thing—upset everything. You might follow good gold along a ledge, just under the grass, till it suddenly broke off and the continuation might be a hundred feet or so under your nose.

Had the ground in the cemetery been "open" Dave would have gone to the point under which he expected the gold to lie, sunk a shaft there, and worked the ground. It would have been the quickest and easiest way—it would have saved the labour and the time lost in dragging heavy buckets of dirt along a low lengthy drive to the shaft outside the fence. But it was very doubtful if the Government could have been moved to open the cemetery even on the strongest evidence of the existence of a rich goldfield under it, and backed by the influence of a number of diggers and their backers—which last was what Dave wished for least of all. He wanted, above all things, to keep the thing shady. Then, again, the old clannish local spirit of the old farming town, rooted in years way back of the goldfields, would have been too strong for the Government, or even a rush of wild diggers.

"We'll work this thing on the strict Q.T.," said Dave.

He and Jim had a consultation by the camp-fire outside their tent. Jim grumbled, in conclusion:

"Well, then best go under Jimmy Middleton. It's the shortest and straightest, and Jimmy's the freshest, anyway."

Then there was another trouble. How were they to account for the size of the waste-heap of clay on the surface which would be the result of such an extraordinary length of drive or tunnel for shallow sinkings? Dave had an idea of carrying some of the dirt away by night and putting it down a deserted shaft close by; but that would double the labour, and might lead to detection sooner than anything else. There were boys possum-hunting on those flats every night. Then Dave got an idea.

There was supposed to exist—and it has since been proved—another, a second gold-bearing alluvial bottom on that field, and several had tried for it. One, the town watchmaker, had sunk all his money in duffers, trying for the second bottom. It was supposed to exist at a depth of from eighty to a hundred feet—on solid rock, I suppose. This watchmaker, an Italian, would put men on to sink, and superintend in person, and whenever he came to a little colour-showing shelf, or false bottom, thirty or forty feet down—he'd go rooting round and spoil the shaft, and then start to sink another. It was extraordinary that he hadn't the sense to sink straight down, thoroughly test the second bottom, and if he found no gold there, to fill the shaft up to the other bottoms, or build platforms at the proper level and then explore them. He was living in a lunatic asylum the last time I heard of him. And the last time I heard from that field they were boring the ground like a sieve, with the latest machinery, to find the best place to put down a deep shaft, and finding gold from the second bottom on the bore. But I'm right off the line again.

"Old Pinter", Ballarat digger—his theory on second and other bottoms ran as follows:—

"Ye see *this* here grass surface—this here surface with trees an' grass on it, that we're livin' on, has got nothin' to do with us. This here bottom in the shaller sinkin's that we're workin' on is the slope to the bed of the *new* crick that was on the surface about the time that men was missin'-links. The false bottoms, thirty or forty feet down, kin be said to have been on the surface about the time that men was monkeys. The *secon'* bottom—eighty or a hundred feet down—was on the surface about the time when men was frogs. Now——"

But it's with the missing-link surface we have to do, and had the friends of the local departed known what Dave and Jim were up to they would have regarded them as something lower than missing-links.

"We'll give out we're tryin' for the second bottom," said Dave Regan. "We'll have to rig a fan for air, anyhow, and you don't want air in shallow sinkings."

"And someone will come poking round, and look down the hole and see the bottom," said Jim Bently.

"We must keep 'em away," said Dave. "Tar the bottom, or cover it with tarred canvas, to make it black. Then they won't see it. There's not many diggers left, and the rest are going; they're chucking up the claims in Log Paddock. Besides, I could get drunk and pick rows with the rest and they wouldn't come near me. The farmers ain't in love with us diggers, so they won't bother us. No man has a right to come poking round another man's claim: it ain't ettykit—I'll root up that old ettykit and stand to it—it's rather worn out now, but that's no matter. We'll shift the tent down near the claim and see that no one comes nosing round on Sunday. They'll think we're only some more second-bottom lunatics, like Francea [the mining watchmaker]. We're going to get our fortune out from under that old graveyard, Jim. You leave it all to me till you're born again with brains."

Dave's schemes were always elaborate, and that was why they so often came to the ground. He logged up his windlass platform a little higher, bent about eighty feet of rope to the bole of the windlass, which was a new one, and thereafter, whenever a suspicious-looking party (that is to say, a digger) hove in sight, Dave would let down about forty feet of rope and then wind, with simulated exertion, until the slack was taken up and the rope lifted the bucket from the shallow bottom.

"It would look better to have a whip-pole and a horse, but we can't afford them just yet," said Dave.

But I'm a little behind. They drove straight in under the cemetery, finding good wash all the way. The edge of Jimmy Middleton's box appeared in the top corner of the face (the working end) of the drive. They went under the butt-end of the grave. They shoved up the end of the shell with a prop, to prevent the possibility of an accident which might disturb the mound above; they puddled—i.e., rammed—stiff clay up round the edges to keep the loose earth from dribbling down; and having given the bottom of the coffin a good coat of tar, they got over, or rather under, an unpleasant matter.

Jim Bently smoked and burnt paper during his shift below, and grumbled a good deal. "Blowed if I ever thought I'd be rooting for gold down among the blanky dead men," he said. But the dirt panned out better every dish they washed, and Dave worked the wash out right and left as they drove.

But, one fine morning, who should come along but the very last man whom Dave wished to see round there—Old Pinter (James Poynton), Californian and Victorian digger of the old school. He'd been prospecting down the creek, carried his pick over his shoulder—threaded through the eye in the heft of his big-bladed, short-handled shovel that hung behind—and his gold-dish under his arm.

" 'Ello, Dave!" said Pinter, after looking with mild surprise at the size of Dave's waste-heap. "Tryin' for the second bottom?"

"Yes," said Dave, guttural.

Pinter dropped his tools with a clatter at the foot of the waste-heap and scratched under his ear like an old cockatoo, which bird he resembled. Then he went to the windlass, and resting his hands on his knees, he peered down, while Dave stood by helpless and hopeless.

Pinter straightened himself, blinking like an owl, and looked carelessly over the graveyard.

"Tryin' for a secon' bottom," he reflected absently. "Eh, Dave?"

Dave only stood and looked black.

Pinter tilted his head and scratched the roots of his chin-feathers, which stuck out all round like a dirty, ragged fan held horizontally.

"Kullers is safe," reflected Pinter.

"All right," snapped Dave. "I suppose we must let him into it."

"Kullers" was a big American buck nigger, and had been Pinter's mate for some time—Pinter was a man of odd mates; and what Pinter meant was that Kullers was safe to hold his tongue.

Next morning Pinter and his coloured mate appeared on the ground early, Pinter with some tools and the nigger with a windlass-bole on his shoulders. Pinter chose a spot about three panels or thirty feet along the other fence, the back fence of the cemetery, and started his hole. He lost no time for the sake of appearances; he sank his shaft and started to drive straight for the point under the cemetery for which Dave was making; he gave out that he had bottomed on good "indications" running in the other direction, and would work the ground outside the fence. Meanwhile Dave rigged a fan—partly for the sake of appearances, but mainly because his and Jim's lively imaginations made the air in the drive worse than it really was.

Dave was working the ground on each side as he went, when one morning a thought struck him that should have struck him the day Pinter went to work. He felt mad that it hadn't struck him sooner.

Pinter and Kullers had also shifted their tent down into a nice quiet place in the bush close handy; so, early next Sunday morning, while Pinter and Kullers were asleep, Dave posted Jim Bently to watch their tent, and whistle an alarm if they stirred, and then dropped down into Pinter's hole and saw at a glance what he was up to.

After that Dave lost no time: he drove straight on, encouraged by the thuds of Pinter's and Kuller's picks drawing nearer. They would strike his tunnel at right angles. Both parties worked long hours, only knocking off to fry a bit of steak in the pan, boil the billy, and throw themselves dressed on their bunks to get a few hours' sleep. Pinter had practical experience and a line clear of graves, and he made good time. The two parties now found it more comfortable to be not on speaking terms. Individually they grew furtive, and began to feel criminal like—at least Dave and Jim did. They'd start if a horse stumbled through the bush, and expected to see a mounted policeman ride up at any moment and hear him ask questions. They had driven about thirty-five feet when, one Saturday afternoon, the strain became too great, and Dave and Jim got drunk. The spree lasted over Sunday, and Monday morning they felt too shaky to come to work, and had more drink. On Monday afternoon, Kullers, whose shift it was below, stuck his pick through the face of his drive into the wall of Dave's, about four feet from the end of it: the clay flaked away, leaving a hole as big as a wash-hand basin. They knocked off for the day and decided to let the other party take the offensive.

Tuesday morning Dave and Jim came to work, still feeling shaky. Jim went below, crawled along the drive, lit his candle, and stuck it in the spiked iron socket and the spike in the wall of the drive, quite close to the hole, without noticing either the hole or the increased freshness of the air. He started picking away at the face, and scraping the clay back from under his feet, and didn't hear Kullers come to work. Kullers came in softly and decided to try a bit of cheerful bluff. He stuck his great round black face through the hole, the whites of his eyes rolling horribly in the candle-light, and said, with a deep guffaw:

"'Ullo! you dar'?"

No bandicoot ever went into his hole with the dogs after him quicker than Jim came out of his. He scrambled up the shaft by the foot-holes, and sat on the edge of the waste-heap, looking very pale.

"What's the matter?" asked Dave. "Have you seen a ghost?"

"I've seen the—the devil!" gasped Jim. "I'm—I'm done with this here ghoul business."

The parties got on speaking terms again. Dave was very warm, but Jim's language was worse. Pinter scratched his chin-feathers reflectively till the other party cooled. There was no appealing to the commissioner for goldfields; they were outside all law, whether of the goldfields or otherwise—so they did the only thing possible and sensible, they joined forces and became Poynton, Regan & Party. They agreed to work the ground from the separate shafts, and decided to go ahead, irrespective of appearances, and get as much dirt out and cradled as possible before the inevitable exposure came along. They found plenty of payable dirt, and soon the drive ended in a cluster of roomy chambers. They timbered up many coffins of various ages, burnt tarred canvas and brown paper, and kept the fan going. Outside they paid the storekeeper with difficulty and talked of hard times.

But one fine sunny morning, after about a week of partnership, they got a bad scare. Jim and Kullers were below, getting out dirt for all they were worth, and Pinter and Dave at their windlasses, when who should march down from the cemetery gate but Mother Middleton herself. She was a hard woman to look at. She still wore the old-fashioned crinoline and her hair in a greasy net; and on this as on most other sober occasions, she wore the expression of a rough Irish navvy who had just enough drink to make him nasty, and is looking out for an excuse for a row. She had a stride like a grenadier. A digger had once measured her step by her footprints in the mud where she had stepped across a gutter; it measured three feet from toe to heel.

She marched to the grave of Jimmy Middleton, laid a dingy bunch of flowers thereon, with the gesture of an angry man banging his fist down on the table, turned on her heel, and marched out. The diggers were dirt beneath her feet. Presently they heard her drive on in her spring-cart on her way into town, and they drew breaths of relief.

It was afternoon. Dave and Pinter were feeling tired, and were just deciding to knock off work for that day when they heard a scuffling in the direction of the different shafts, and both Jim and Kullers dropped down and bundled in in a great hurry. Jim chuckled in a silly way, as if there was something funny, and Kullers guffawed in sympathy.

"What's up now?" demanded Dave apprehensively.

"Mother Middleton," said Jim; "she's blind mad drunk, and she's got a bottle in one hand and a new pitchfork in the other, that she's bringing out for someone."

"How the hell did she drop to it?" exclaimed Pinter.

"Dunno," said Jim. "Anyway, she's coming for us. Listen to her!"

They didn't have to listen hard. The language which came down the shaft—they weren't sure which one—and along the drive was enough to scare up the dead and make them take to the bush.

"Why didn't you fools make off into the bush and give us a chance, instead of giving her a lead here?" asked Dave.

Jim and Kullers began to wish they had done so.

Mrs Middleton began to throw stones down the shaft—it was Pinter's—and they, even the oldest and most anxious, began to grin in spite of themselves, for they knew she couldn't hurt them from the surface, and that, though she had been a working digger herself, she couldn't fill both shafts before the fumes of liquor overtook her.

"I wonder which shaf' she'll come down?" asked Kullers in a tone befitting the place and occasion.

"You'd better go and watch your shaft, Pinter," said Dave, "and Jim and I'll watch mine."

"I—I won't," said Pinter hurriedly, "I'm—I'm a modest man."

Then they heard a clang in the direction of Pinter's shaft.

"She's thrown her bottle down," said Dave.

Jim crawled along the drive a piece, urged by curiosity, and returned hurriedly.

"She's broken the pitchfork off short, to use in the drive, and I believe she's coming down."

"Her crinoline'll handicap her," said Pinter vacantly, "that's a comfort."

"She's took it off!" said Dave excitedly; and peering along Pinter's drive, they saw first an elastic-sided boot, then a red-striped stocking, then a section of scarlet petticoat.

"Lemme out!" roared Pinter, lurching forward and making a swimming motion with his hands in the direction of Dave's drive. Kullers was already gone and Jim well on the way. Dave, lanky and awkward, scrambled up the shaft last. Mrs Middleton made good time, considering she had the darkness to face and didn't know the workings, and when Dave reached the top he had a tear in the leg of his moleskins, and the blood ran from a nasty scratch. But he didn't wait to argue over the price of a new pair of trousers. He made off through the bush in the direction of an encouraging whistle thrown back by Jim.

"She's too drunk to get her story listened to tonight," said Dave. "But tomorrow she'll bring the neighbourhood down on us."

"And she's enough, without the neighbourhood," reflected Pinter.

Some time after dark they returned cautiously, reconnoitred their camp, and after hiding in a hollow log such things as they couldn't carry, they rolled up their tents like the Arabs, and silently stole away.

Mr Smellingscheck

I MET him in a sixpenny restaurant—"All meals, 6d.—Good beds, 1s." That was before sixpenny restaurants rose to a third-class position, and became possibly respectable places to live in, through the establishment, beneath them, of fourpenny hash-houses (good beds, 6d.), and beneath *them* again, of *three*-penny "dining-rooms—*clean* beds, 4d.".

There were five beds in our apartment, the head of one against the foot of the next, and so on round the room, with a space where the door and wash-stand were. I chose the bed the head of which was near the foot of his, because he looked like a man who took his bath regularly. I should like, in the interests of sentiment, to describe the place as a miserable, filthy, evil-smelling garret; but I can't—because it wasn't. The room was large and airy; the floor was scrubbed and the windows cleaned at least once a week, and the beds kept fresh and neat, which is more—a good deal more—than can be said of many genteel private boarding-houses. The lodgers were mostly respectable unemployed, and one or two—fortunate men!—in work; it was the casual boozer, the professional loafer, and the occasional spieler—the one-shilling-bed men—who made the place objectionable, not the hard-working people who paid ten pounds a week for the house; and, but for the one-night lodgers and the big gilt black-and-red bordered and "shaded" "6d." in the window—which made me glance guiltily up and down the street, like a burglar about to do a job, before I went in—I was pretty comfortable there.

They called him "Mr Smellingscheck", and treated him with a peculiar kind of deference, the reason for which they themselves were doubtless unable to explain or even understand. The haggard woman who made the beds called him "Mr Smell-'is-check". Poor fellow! I don't think, by the look of him, that he'd smelt his cheque, or anyone else's, or that anyone else had smelt his, for many a long day. He was a fat man, slow and placid. He looked like a typical monopolist who had unaccountably got into a suit of clothes belonging to a Domain unemployed, and hadn't noticed, or had entirely forgotten, the circumstances in his business cares—if such a word as care could be connected with such a calm, self-contained nature. He wore a suit of cheap slops of some kind of shoddy tweed. The coat was too small and the trousers too short, and they were drawn up to meet the waistcoat—which they did with painful difficulty, now and then showing, by way of protest, two pairs of brass buttons and the ends of the brace-straps; and they seemed to blame the irresponsive waistcoat or the wearer for it all. Yet he never gave way to assist them. A pair of burst elastic-sides were in full evidence, and a rim of cloudy sock, with a hole in it, showed at every step.

But he put on his clothes and wore them like—like a gentleman. He had two white shirts, and they were both dirty. He'd lay them out on the bed, turn them over, regard them thoughtfully, choose that which appeared to his calm understanding to be the cleaner, and put it on, and wear it until it was unmistakably dirtier than the other; then he'd wear the other till it was dirtier than the first. He managed his three collars the same way. His handkerchiefs were washed in the bathroom, and dried, without the slightest disguise, in the bedroom. He never hurried in anything. The way he cleaned his teeth, shaved, and made his toilet almost transformed the place, in my imaginatioin, into a gentleman's dressing-room.

He talked politics and such things in the abstract—always in the abstract—calmly in the abstract. He was an old-fashioned Conservative of the Sir Leicester Dedlock style. When he was moved by an extra shower of aggressive democratic cant—which was seldom—he defended Capital, but only as if it needed no defence, and as if its opponents were merely thoughtless, ignorant children whom he condescended to set right because of their inexperience and for their own good. He stuck calmly to his own order—the order which had dropped him like a foul thing when the bottom dropped out of his boom, whatever that was. He never talked of his misfortunes.

He took his meals at the little greasy table in the dark corner downstairs, just as if he were dining at the Exchange. He had a chop—rather well-done—and a sheet of the *Herald* for breakfast. He carried two handkerchiefs; he used one for a handkerchief and the other for a table-napkin, and sometimes folded it absently and laid it on the table. He rose slowly, putting his chair back, took down his battered old green hat, and regarded it thoughtfully—as though it had just occurred to him in a calm, casual way that he'd drop into his hatter's, if he had time, on his way down town, and get it blocked, or else send the messenger round with it during business hours. He'd draw his stick out from behind the next chair, plant it, and, if you hadn't quite finished your side of the conversation, stand politely waiting until you were done. Then he'd look for a suitable reply into his hat, put it on, give it a twitch to settle it on his head—as gentlemen do a "chimney-pot"—step out into the gangway, turn his face to the door, and walk slowly out on to the middle of the pavement—looking more placidly well-to-do than ever. The saying is that clothes make a man, but *he* made his almost respectable just by wearing them. Then he'd consult his watch—(he stuck to the watch all through, and it seemed a good one—I often wondered why he didn't pawn it); then he'd turn slowly, right turn, and look down the street. Then slowly back, left-about turn, and take a cool survey in that direction, as if calmly undecided whether to take a cab and drive to the Exchange, or (as it was a very fine morning, and he had half an hour to spare) walk there and drop in at his club on the way. He'd conclude to walk. I never saw him go anywhere in particular, but he walked and stood as if he could.

Coming quietly into the room one day, I surprised him sitting at the table and his arms lying on it and his face resting on them. I heard something like a sob. He rose hastily, and gathered up some papers which were on the table; then he turned round, rubbing his forehead and eyes with his forefinger and thumb, and told me that he suffered from—something, I forget the name of it, but it was a well-to-do ailment. His manner seemed a bit jolted and hurried for a minute or so, and then he was himself again. He told me he was leaving for Melbourne next day. He left while I was out, and left an envelope downstairs for me. There was nothing in it except a pound note.

I saw him in Brisbane afterwards, well-dressed, getting out of a cab at the entrance of one of the leading hotels. But his manner was no more self-contained and well-to-do than it had been in the old sixpenny days—because it couldn't be. We had a well-to-do whisky together, and he talked of things in the abstract. He seemed just as if he'd met me in the Australia.

Johnson's Jag

THE lane runs from George Street North to nowhere in particular. You can climb out of it by a green hill if you think you're wanted at the other end (there's an old pub on the top of that hill, and many ways of escape); but if you stick to it, it will lead you to a dingy North Shore horse-ferry, and so may be said to lead to all the Northern Suburbs. For the matter of that, it might even be said to lead to Europe, Asia, Africa and America, and a good many of the South Sea Islands; for there's a short side-branch, or bottomless pocket, a step down to the wharves where the principal liners lie. A good deal of our raw material goes out of the country that way, so "bottomless pocket" fits the case. The lane itself is boomerang-shaped, so you can't see what's at the end of it till you get there. It's like Middle Age Lane in this respect. I know of no other lane less frequented by ordinary folk, or the aristocracy, or the *demi-monde*; but the dead pass through it often. Also the deadbeat, and those who wish they were dead or drunk.

Occasionally, about nine o'clock on a fine morning you'll see a fairly well-dressed and apparently respectable citizen and businessman coming over on the horse-ferry, or perhaps he has left the ferry and got into Elder Man's Lane. On the ferry he holds himself aloof, paces up and down slowly, even nervously, or resolutely surveys the beautiful harbour with his back to the world and all its paltriness; yet he seems to have a definite immediate object in view. And you may be almost sure (1) that the man has been in very recent trouble, extending over breakfast this morning; (2) that he has eaten little or no breakfast; and (3) that the definite object is to get a good whisky and soda just as soon as he reaches a bar he knows. I'll tell you how it was.

There's my friend Johnson—or, rather there was. Better put it all in the past tense. Johnson lived on the Shore, and was employed in a government office where he was indispensable. Say, draughtsman or something. He was exceedingly clever in his profession, and so, of course, he drank too much. When his "week" came to him—generally at the end of the month—he'd leave the office with his screw, and have a few drinks with the fellows at the Exchange or Empire; then, as repeatedly instructed right out to the gate that morning, he'd conscientiously take a tram back and down to Anthony Hordern's, with a finger and thumb constantly and anxiously feeling a half-sheet of cheap, closely-folded notepaper in his upper left-hand waistcoat pocket—a scrap of paper he had been constantly losing, and hunting for, and finding again all day, and which contained something as follows, written in a feminine hand that was characteristic:

1 yard Black Satin for Piping.
¾ yard Fancy Cream Lace for Yoke.
2 doz. Black Satin Buttons.
1 yard cream gipuirieging (it looks like that).
2 reels of silk to match material.
2 doz. Pat Fasteners.
2 cards hooks and eyes.
1 set collar supports.

Be sure you go to Hordern's, and don't forget what I told you. *And don't lose this.*

Then Johnson would have another drink to clear his brain and brace him up; and then a hurried, blurred recollection of carved lifts, and vistas of varnish and everything a woman knows, and lovely, graceful, saint-like shop girls (or sales ladies) and a smiling, sympathetic shop-walker taken into his (Johnson's) confidence, and asked if he was a married man, and informed in return that he (Johnson) was a married man, too, and shaken hands with, with the exaggerated warmth of affected sympathy—and shown that list. The various stairs and different departments. The shop-walkers and salesmen on different floors and behind different counters would stick to Johnson like a brother and see him through. Perhaps they were mostly married men, too. Then, after a friendly and jocular (on Johnson's part) interval, he'd be conducted gently to the right lift and bowed in, after the last shop-walker had smilingly declined an invitation to come out and have a drink. And Johnson would find himself on the level again, with his bag half full of very soft and perishable feminine rubbish in brown tissue paper parcels—and in urgent need of another whisky.

Then Johnson would charge two Circular Quay trams, catch a third, and cling to it tooth and nail, possibly with an instinctive idea of putting as much of the jumbled city behind him as he could in the shortest possible time and regaining the beloved vicinity of

Circular Quay, where he would feel safe. He'd drop off short of the Quay, have another drink, and then go into Jack Sotero's, the Greek hairdresser's, to have a shave and a shampoo, maybe, to freshen him up, and to collect his thoughts. (It's all right! We'll get back to the horse-ferry and Elder Man's Lane soon enough.) And he'd get talking with Sotero about the Eastern Question, and maybe argue, and they'd both get excited. Sotero would, sure.

Then Johnson, partly sober, would retire to a private place and take stock of his finances. He'd abstract a few more shillings, for current expenses, from that portion of his monthly "screw" set apart earlier in the afternoon for the use of his wife, wrap the remainder up tight in another half-sheet of newspaper, and button it up in his hip pocket. Then he'd make for the Quay, and get another drink and more inspiration on the way. After which the world would begin to move.

Fate would have one (or, more likely, two; they mostly go by twos) of Johnson's deplorable acquaintances loitering on the footpath, opposite the Quay; and Johnson would stumble into their arms; and they'd go into one of the first-and-last hotels to see if they could keep another down. And, as likely as not, they'd find others of the Johnsonian school there.

The vicinity would remind Johnson of fish and another thing; so they'd adjourn, and maybe there'd be stewed oysters; and Johnson would make one or two purchases on his own account. But the fat, futile, vacuously smiling, oily faces of degenerate Italy would exasperate Johnson by and by, and the trouble in Southern Europe would come to the surface again, and Johnson would hold forth to the edification of the cropped and grinning Dagoes. He'd be all Turk now (he was always for the weaker side, was Johnson). But his friends would steer him out before Tripoli had a chance of being avenged.

Then they'd adjourn to keep another one down, and Johnson would buy a "parrot" (i.e., flask of whisky for the morning), with the fixed intention of going right across and straight home now. His friends would see him to the turnstiles, and he'd go through, informing an unresponsive public, in a loud voice and with curious inconsistency (considering the fish-shop), that Her Naid grace had brought him home. To the grandeur which was Greece. And the glory which was Rome. He had the choice of two ferry-boats—Milson's Point and Lavender Bay—and he was known equally well on either; but his Fate would put him on the most crowded one of the evening, and the one with the greatest number of his acquaintances, friends, enemies, neighbours, and those who knew him by sight. And, of course, he'd make a prize ass of himself. He'd surpass all previous efforts. He'd hold forth on politics, and he'd sing and recite revolutionary verses. He'd be "Wae's me for Prince Chairlie" till his friends were heart-broken, and he'd bellow while his enemies applauded. He was pro-Russ, pro-Boer, pro-Australia, pro-husband, pro-man, pro-beer—all pro at this stage; and he'd arise on the upper deck and denounce the Antis with indignation and enthusiasm that brought him to the verge of tears. And he'd continue on the tram, only interrupted when he refused to pay a degenerate Government a fare, and one of his friends, the tram-guard, took his name and address for appearances' sake. They used to have their books full of Johnson's name and address. He wrote it himself sometimes.

At the last pub on the Heights, near his home, Johnson would pull himself together a bit and seek a private parlour (or still more private place) and once more review his finances. (Elder Man's Lane is very near now.) He'd carefully distribute threepences and sixpences through his pockets for his wife to find when he'd be asleep. Then, if short, he'd borrow another half-crown or five shillings from her share to finish up the night with, and have something in hand for the morning; then he'd carefully wrap up the share again and button it down in his hip pocket; then he'd put one half-crown in one of the other pockets, take off his boot, put the other half-crown in his sock under the instep, put on his boot again, and seek the bar. Where, as likely as not, he'd meet yet another of the Johnsonian Brotherhood and they'd finish the night—unless his Fate led him home through the main street, singing, just as the majority of his fellow-suburbanites were pouring out of the picture-shows and down to the tramline. Anyway, he'd go his way, singing in the moonlight, with two bottles on top of his wife's forgotten vanities (all is vanity), and he'd arrive at his own gate, still singing and still flourishing the Crayfish of Confidence or the Lobster of Faith. (Those vain peace offerings!)

He knew, or thought he knew, his wife's tastes on all occasions. He'd tell her to put her hand in his coat pocket, and see what she'd find, and as like as not she'd find nothing there but dampness. Also, as like as not, she'd find it afterwards, under the bottles, and on top of her precious dress trimmings—a squashed and busted newspaper parcel of very damp and stringy prawns. But he's utterly hopeless now, lying on his back on the bed, and singing, or rather roaring, at the top of his voice, that he'll vote for Andy Fisher, no matter what he said! So she undresses him hastily, gives him a stiff nip, and puts him under cover. And silence reigneth.

Now you've already forgotten the fairly well-dressed and apparently respectable citizen and man of business (or professional man, or artist) seen occasionally on the horse-ferry, or in Elder Man's Lane, on a fine morning about nine. I said I'd tell you how it was. It was Johnson the Morning after the Night Before. Clean-shirted, clean-collared, and clean-socked; also cleaned out and trey-bitless. Remember the Sock of Precaution? The "half-caser" was in *her* stocking now, along with the rest.

His wife knew Johnson's ways. He would humbly accept the copper she spared (at great personal inconvenience, according to herself) from that voracious little instrument of unblushing capitalism (though it *is* painted red) and demoralizer of good housewives, the accursed gas-meter. Johnson had a season ticket on the passenger-ferry; but he'd be far too shaky and ashamed to face it, so he'd slip unobtrusively down by-streets and lanes, and along Blue's Point Road, and into the horse-ferry. Then he'd get a couple of good whiskies in the Bar that Knew Him; and feel his manhood returning, and go to work.

He'd slip out and have another during the forenoon and one or two during the lunch hour, and maybe one in mid-afternoon, to keep his deft right hand steady. Then, between four and five, several with bachelor mates or unprincipled husbands who still held a fair share of their salaries. The previous night would then be repeated, but on a grander scale and with trimmings. Johnson, with no shopping or shampooing to cut into his time, would make a more glorious ass of himself than ever. A patriot, an orator, a fine singer and reciter, and the only possible saviour of his country; and with loftier contempt for the alleged spirit of Sydney (and more especially that of North Sydney) he'd time himself to catch the most crowded ferry-boat across.

Sometimes he'd insist on taking a stray mongrel home with him, in premeditated defiance of the Company and Government, even if he had to fight for it all the way. And rather earlier that night he'd be steered lovingly to his own gate by one or more of the brethren. And they'd utter words of caution in whispers that could be heard at the end of the street, and part with affection and difficulty. Then Johnson would pull himself together, creep in, shut the gate softly, and go down on his knees and hide two half-crowns in the dirt under a geranium bush, fixing the spot in his memory as only a drunk can, while his careful little wife watched him thoughtfully from the front-room window.

Then, next morning, the Blast of Repentance on awakening, the horse-ferry and Elder Man's Lane. And so the thing would be repeated to the end of Johnson's jag, with perhaps an interval of a day or two at home to recuperate. It was bad judgment; for, whereas the people of North Sydney might have seen him sober once a day during his week or fortnight, they never did. He should have gone *home* by the horse-ferry.

But, there! What's the use of arguing with a drunk? They don't see things as you do.

We Called Him "Ally" for Short

I DON'T believe in ghosts; I never did have any sympathy with them, being inclined to regard them as a nuisance and a bore. A ghost generally comes fooling around when you want to go to sleep, and his conversation, if he speaks at all, invariably turns on murders and suicides and other unpleasant things in which you are not interested, and which only disturb your rest. It is no use locking the door against a ghost, for, as is well known, he can come in through the keyhole, and there are cases on record when a ghost has been known to penetrate a solid wall. You cannot kick a ghost out; he is impervious to abuse; and if you throw a boot at him, likely as not it will go right through a new looking-glass worth eighteen shillings.

I remember, about five years ago, I was greatly annoyed by a ghost, while doing a job of fencing in the bush between here and Perth. I was camping in an old house which had been used as a barrack for the convicts or their keepers (I'm not sure which) in the lively old days of the broad arrow. He was a common-looking ghost of a skeleton kind, and was arrayed in what appeared to be the tattered remnants of an old-time convict uniform. He still wore a pair of shadowy manacles, but, being very elastic and unsubstantial and stretching the full length of his stride, he did not seem to notice them at all. He had a kind of Artful Dodger expression about his bare jaw-bones, and in place of the ordinary halo of the ring variety he wore a shining representation of a broad arrow which shed a radiance over his skull. He used to come round and wake me about midnight with a confounded rigmarole about a convict who was buried alive in his irons, and whose representative my unwelcome visitor claimed to be. I tried all I knew to discourage him. I told him I wasn't interested and wanted to go to sleep; but his perseverance wore me out at last, and I tried another tack. I listened to his confounded yarn from beginning to end, and sympathized with him, and told him that he, or the individual he represented, had been treated confoundedly badly; and I promised to make a poem about it.

But even then he wasn't satisfied. Nothing would suit him but he must spin his old yarn, and be sympathized with about seven times a week, always choosing the most unbusinesslike hours (between one and three in the morning) for his disclosures. At last I could stand it no longer. I was getting thin and exhausted from want of sleep, so I determined on a course of action. I had a dog at home, a big black dog with unpleasant eyes, and a chewing-up apparatus that an alligator might have envied. He had a most enterprizing appetite, and wasn't afraid of anything on the surface of this earth—or under it, as far as he could burrow. He would gnaw a log to pieces rather than let the possum it contained escape him. He was not the sort of dog to stand any nonsense even from a ghost. His full name was Alligator-Desolation (we called him Ally for short): and, as I considered that if any person on earth could lay the ghost that annoyed me that person was Alligator-Desolation, I declared to bring him.

The next time I journeyed home for rations I brought Alligator-Desolation back with me. On the trip back he killed 5 kangaroos, 16 possums, 4 native rats, 2 native bears, 3 sheep, a cow and a calf, and another dog that happened by; and before he had been two hours at the hut he had collected enough carcasses of indigenous animals to stink a troop out in a week, or to feed all the dogs in Constantinople.

I had tea and a smoke while Ally was resting, and about 11 o'clock I lay down in my bunk, dressed as I was, and waited. At about one I heard the usual unearthly noises which accompanied the arrival of my friend the ghost, and Ally went out to investigate. While the dog was gone, the ghost strolled in through the door of the end room, apparently unconscious of his danger. He glided straight up to the side of my bunk, took his accustomed seat on a gin-case, and commenced in a doleful voice to pitch his confounded old yarn again; but he hadn't uttered half a dozen ghostly words when Alligator-Desolation came in through the side door.

The ghost caught sight of Ally before the latter saw him, and made for the window. Ally wasn't far behind; he made a grab at the ghost's nether garments, but they gave way easily, being of a ghostly material. Then Ally leapt out through the window and chased the ghost three times round the house, and then the latter came in through an opening in the wall where a slab had fallen out. Being of an easily compressible constitution he came through, of course, with the facility peculiar to his kind, but the crack was narrow and the dog stuck fast. His ghostship made the best of his opportunity, and, approaching my bed, hurriedly endeavoured to continue his story, as though his ghostly existence depended on it. But his utterances were drowned by the language of Alligator, whose canine oaths were simply terrific. At last, collecting all his energy for one mighty effort, Alligator came through, bringing down the slabs on each side of him.

He made for the ghost at once, and the ghost made for the window. This time Alligator made a grab for the spectre's ankle, and his teeth came together with a crash that threatened their destruction. Ally must have been greatly astonished and disgusted, because he so seldom missed anything he reached for. But he wasn't the kind of dog to give up. He leapt through the window, and, after a race round the hut, lasting some minutes, the ghost gave it up, and made for the scrub. Seeing the retreat through a crack in the slabs, I immediately rose, went outside and mounted my horse, which I had kept ready saddled in case of emergency. I followed the chase for about five miles, and at last reached a mound under some trees, which looked like an old grave. Down through this mound the ghost dived.

Alligator-Desolation immediately commenced to dig, and made two feet in no time. It appeared that a wombat had selected the grave as a suitable site for the opening of his burrow and, after having sunk about three feet, was resting from his labours. There was a short and angry interview between Alligator and the wombat, during which the latter expired, and then Ally continued his work of excavation. After sinking two feet deeper he dragged out what appeared to be the leg-bone of a human being, attached to which was a pair of heavy leg-irons, such as were used in the old convict days. Ally went down the hole again, but presently he paused in his digging operations, and I heard a noise like a row in the infernal regions. Then a thin, shadowy form issued from the grave and made off through the scrub with the dog in pursuit.

My horse was knocked up, so I left the chase to Alligator and returned home to await developments. Ally came back about three days later with his hair badly singed and smelling strongly of brimstone. I have no doubt that he chased the ghost to the infernal regions and perhaps had an interview with Cerberus at the gate, or the boss himself; but the dog's tail was well up and a satisfied grin oozed from the roots of every fang, and by the same tokens I concluded that the other party, whoever he was, had got left.

I haven't seen the ghost since.

"Buckolts' Gate"

PROLOGUE

OLD Abel Albury had a genius for getting the bull by the tail with a tight grip and holding on with both hands, and an obstinacy born of ignorance—and not necessarily for the sake of self-preservation or selfishness—while all the time the bull might be, so to speak, rooting up lifelong friendships and neighbourly relations, and upsetting domestic customs and traditions with his horns.

Yes, Uncle Abel was always grasping the wrong end of things, and sticking to it with that human mulishness which is often stronger, and more often wearies and breaks down the opposition than an intelligent man's arguments. He was—or professed to be, the family said—unable for a long time to distinguish between his two grand-nephews, one of whom was short and fat, while the other was tall and thin, the only points of resemblance between them being that each possessed the old family nose and eyes. When they were boys he used to lay the strap about one in mistake for the other. They had a saying that Uncle Abel saw with ten squinting eyes.

Also, he could never—or would not, as the family said—remember names. He referred to Mrs Porter, a thin, haggard selector's wife, as "Mrs Stout" and he balanced matters by calling Mrs Southwick "Mrs Porterwicket"—when he didn't address her as "Mrs What's-the-woman's-name"—and he succeeded in deeply offending both ladies.

Uncle Abel was Mrs Carey's uncle. Down at the lower end of Carey's selection at Rocky Rises, in the extreme corner of the lower or outer paddock, were sliprails opening into the main road, which ran down along the sidling, round the foot of the spur from the ridge, and out west. These sliprails were called "The Lower Sliprails" by the family, and it occurred to Uncle Abel to refer to them as "Buckolts' Gate", for no other reason apparently than that Buckolts' farm lay in that direction. The farm was about a mile farther on, on the other side of the creek, and the gate leading to it from the main road was round the spur, out of sight of Carey's selection. It is quite possible that Uncle Abel reasoned the thing out for days, for of such material are some human brains. Sliprails, or a slip-panel, is a panel of fencing of which the rails are made to be slipped out of the mortise holes in the posts so as to give passage to horses, vehicles and cattle. I suppose Abel called it a gate because he was always going to hang a proper gate there some day. The family were unaware of his new name for the Lower Sliprails, and after he had, on one or two occasions, informed the boys that they would find a missing cow or horse at the Buckolts' Gate, and they had found it calmly camped at the Lower Sliprails, and after he had made several appointments to meet parties at Buckolts' Gate, and had been found leaning obstinately on the fence by the Lower Sliprails with no explanation to offer other than that he *was* waiting at Buckolts' Gate, they began to fear that he was becoming weak in his mind.

ACT I

It was New Year's Eve at Rocky Rises. There was no need for fireworks nor bonfires, for the bushfires were out all along the ranges to the east, and, as night came on, lines and curves of lights—clear lights, white lights, and, in the near distance, red lights and smoky lights—marked the sidlings and ridges of a western spur of the Blue Mountains range, and seemed suspended against a dark sky, for the stars and the loom of the hills were hidden by smoke and drought haze.

There was a dance at Careys'. Old Carey was a cheerful, broad-minded bushman, haunted at times by the memories of old days, when he was the beau of the bush balls, and so when he built his new slab-and-bark barn he had it properly floored with hardwood, and the floor well-faced "to give the young people a show when they wanted a dance", he said. The floor had a spring in it, and bush boys and girls often rode twenty miles and more to dance on that floor. The girls said it was a lovely floor.

On this occasion Carey had stacked his wheat outside until after the New Year. Spring-carts, and men and girls on horseback came in from miles round. "Sperm" candles had been cut up and thrown on the floor during the afternoon, and rubbed over by feet cased tightly in 'lastic-sides; and hoops were hung horizontally from the tie-beams, with candles stuck round them. There were fresh-faced girls, and sweet, freckled-faced girls, and jolly girls, and shy girls—all sorts of girls except sulky, "toney" girls—and lanky chaps, most of them sawney, and weird, whiskered agriculturalists, who watched the dancers with old, old time-worn smiles, or stood, or sat on their heels yarning, with their pipes, outside, where two boilers were slung over a log-fire to boil water for tea; and there were leathery women, with complexions like dried apples, who gossiped—for the first time in months perhaps—and watched the young people, and thought at times, no doubt, of other days—of other days when they were girls. (And not so far distant either, in some cases, for women dry quickly in the bush.)

And there were one or two old soldiers and their wives, whose eyes glistened when Jim Bullock played "The Girl I Left Behind Me".

Jim Bullock was there with his concertina. He sat on a stool in front of a bench, on which was a beer-keg, piles of teacups and saucers, several big tin teapots, and plates of sandwiches, sponge-cakes, and tarts. Jim sat in his shirt-sleeves, with his flat-brimmed, wire-bound, "hard-hitter" hat on, slanting over his weaker eye. He held one leg loosely and the other rigid, with the concertina on his knee, and swanked away at the instrument by the hour, staring straight in front of him with the expression of a cod-fish, and never moving a muscle except the muscles of his great hairy arms and big chapped and sun-blotched hands; while chaps in tight "larstins", slop suits of black, bound with braid, and with coats too short in the neck and arms, and trousers bell-mouthed at the bottoms, and some with paper collars, narrow red ribbon ties, or scarfs through walnut shells, held their partners rigidly, and went round the room with their eyes—most of them—cocked at the rafters in semi-idiotic ecstasy.

But there was tall, graceful, pink-and-white Bertha Buckolt, blue-eyed and blue-and-black haired, and little Mary Carey with the kind, grey eyes and red-gold hair; there was Mary's wild brother Jim, with curly black hair and blue eyes and dimples of innocence; and there was Harry Dale, the drover, Jim's shearing and droving mate, a tall, good-looking, brown-eyed and brown-haired young fellow, a "better-class" bushman and the best dancer in the district.

Uncle Abel usurped the position of M.C., and roared "Now then! take yer partners!" and bawled instructions and interrupted and tangled up the dancers, until they got used to taking no notice of his bull voice. Mary Carey was too shy—because she loved him, and secretly and fondly hoped and doubted that he cared for her—to be seen dancing more than once with Harry Dale, so he shared Bertha Buckolt, the best girl dancer there, with Jim Carey, who danced with his sister when Harry was dancing with Bertha Buckolt, and who seemed, for some reason best known to himself, to be perfectly satisfied with the arrangement. Poor little Mary began to fret presently, and feel a little jealous of Bertha, her old schoolmate. She was little and couldn't dance like Bertha, and she couldn't help noticing how well Bertha looked tonight, and what a well-matched pair she and Harry made; and so, when twelve o'clock came and they all went outside to watch the Old Year out and the New Year in—with a big bonfire on the distant ridge where the grass fires had reached a stretch of dry scrub—and to join hands all round and sing "Auld Lang Syne", little Mary was not to be found, for she was sitting on a log round behind the cow-yard, crying softly to herself.

And when about three o'clock they all started home, Mary gave Bertha her cheek to kiss instead of her mouth, and that hurt Bertha, who had *her* cry riding home, to the astonishment and irritation of her brother Jack, who rode home with her.

But when they were all gone Mary was missing again and when her mother called her, and, after a pause, the voice of Harry Dale said, respectfully, in the darkness, "She's here, Mrs Carey, she's all right," the two were discovered sitting on a convenient log of the wood-heap, with an awkward and overacted interval of log between them.

Old Carey liked Harry Dale, and seemed very well satisfied with the way things appeared to be going. He pressed Harry to stay at the selection overnight. "The missus will make you a shake-down on the floor," he said. Harry had no appointments, and stayed cheerfully, and old Carey, having had a whisky or two, insisted on Mary making the shake-down, and the old folks winked at each other behind the young folks' backs to see how poor little Mary spread a spare mattress, with red-hot, averted face, and found an extra pillow and a spare pair of ironed sheets for the shake-down.

At sunrise she stole out to milk the cows, which was her regular duty; there was no other way out from her room than through the dining-room, where Harry lay on his back, with his arms folded, resting peacefully. He seemed sound asleep and safe for a good two hours, so she ventured. As she passed out she paused a moment looking down on him with all the lovelight in her eyes, and, obeying a sudden impulse, she stooped softly and touched his forehead with her lips, then she slipped out. Harry stretched, opened his eyes, winked solemnly at the ceiling, and then, after a decent interval, he got up, dressed, and went out to help her to milk.

Harry Dale and Jim Carey were going out to take charge of a mob of bullocks going north-west, away up in Queensland, and as they had lost a day and night to be at the dance, they decided to start in the cool of the evening and travel all night. Mary walked from the homestead to the Lower Sliprails between her brother, who rode—because he was her brother—and led a packhorse on the other side, and Harry, who walked and led his horse—because he was her sweetheart, avowed only since last night.

There were thunderstorms about, and Mary had repented sufficiently with regard to Bertha Buckolt to wear on her shoulders a cape which Bertha had left behind her last night.

When they reached the Lower Sliprails Jim said he'd go on and that Harry needn't hurry: he stooped over his horse's neck, kissed his sister, promised to keep away from the drink, not to touch a card, and to leave off fighting, and rode on. And when he rounded the Spur he saw a tall, graceful figure slipping through the trees from the creek towards Buckolts' Gate.

Then came the critical time at the Lower Sliprails. The shadows from the setting sun lengthened quickly on the sidling, and then the sun slipped out of sight over a saddle in the ridges, and all was soon dusk save the sunlit peaks of the Blue Mountains away to the east over the sweeps of blue-grey bush.

"Ah, well! Mary," said Harry, "I must make a start now."

"You'll—you'll look after Jim, won't you, Harry?" said Mary.

"I will, Mary, for your sake."

Her mouth began to twitch, her chin to tremble, and her eyes brimmed suddenly.

"You must cheer up, Mary," he said with her in his arms. "I'll be back before you know where you are, and then we'll be married right off at once and settle down for life."

She smiled bravely.

"Good-bye, Mary!"

"Good-bye, Harry!"

He led his horse through the rails and lifted them, with trembling hands, and shot them home. Another kiss across the top rail and he got on his horse. She mounted the lower rail, and he brought his horse close alongside the fence and stooped to kiss her again.

"Cheer up, Mary!" he said. "I'll tell you what I'll do—when I come back I'll whistle when I reach the Spur and you be here to let the sliprails down for me. I'll time myself to get here about sundown. I'll whistle 'Willie Riley', so you'll know it's me. Good-bye, little girl! I must go now. Don't fret—the time will soon go by."

He turned, swung his horse, and rode slowly down the track, turning now and again to wave his hand to her, with a farewell flourish of his hat as he rounded the Spur. His track, five hundred miles, or perhaps, a thousand, into the great north-west; his time, six months, or perhaps a year. Hers a hundred yards or so back to the dusty, dreary drudgery of selection life.

The daylight faded into starlight, the sidlings grew very dim, and a faint white figure blurred against the bars of the slip-panel.

ACT II

It was the last day of the threshing—shortly after New Year—at Rocky Rises. The green boughs, which had been lashed to the veranda-posts on Christmas Eve, had withered and been used for firewood. The travelling steamer had gone with its gang of men, and the family sat down to tea, the men tired with hard work and heat, and with prickly heat and irritating wheaten chaff and dust under their clothes—and with smut (for the crop had been a smutty one) "up their brains" as Uncle Abel said—the women worn out with cooking for a big gang of shearers.

Good-humoured Aunt Emma—who was Uncle Abel's niece—recovered first, and started the conversation. There were one or two neighbours' wives who had lent crockery and had come over to help with the cooking in their turns. Jim Carey's name came up incidentally, but was quickly dropped, for ill reports of Jim had come home. Then Aunt Emma mentioned Harry Dale, and glanced meaningly at Mary, whose face flamed as she bent over her plate.

"Never mind, Mary," said Aunt Emma, "it's nothing to be

ashamed of. We were all girls once. There's many a girl would jump at Harry."

"Who says I'm ashamed?" said Mary, straightening up indignantly.

"Don't tease her, Emma," said Mrs Carey, mildly.

"I'll tell yer what," said young Tom Carey, frankly, "Mary got a letter from him today. I seen her reading it behind the house."

Mary's face flamed again and went down over her plate.

"Mary," said her mother, with sudden interest, "did Harry say anything of Jim?"

"No, mother," said Mary. "And that's why I didn't tell you about the letter."

There was a pause. Then Tommy said, with that delightful tact which usually characterizes young Tommies:

"Well, Mary needn't be so cocky about Harry Dale, anyhow. I seen him New Year's Eve when we had the dance. I seen him after the dance liftin' Bertha Buckolt onter her horse in the dark—as if she couldn't get on herself—she's big enough. I seen him lift her on, an' he took her right up an' lifted her right inter the saddle, 'stead of holdin' his hand for her to tread on like that newchum jackeroo we had. An', what's more, I seen him hug her an' give her a kiss before he lifted her on. He told her he was as good as her brother."

"What did he mean by that, Tommy?" asked Mrs Porter, to break an awkward pause.

"How'm I ter know what he means?" said Tommy, politely.

"And, Tommy, I seen Harry Dale giving young Tommy Carey a lick with a strap the day before New Year's Eve for throwing his sister's cat into the dam," said Aunt Emma, coming to poor Mary's rescue. "Never mind, Mary, my dear, he said good-bye to you last."

"No, *he didn't*!" roared Uncle Abel.

They were used to Uncle Abel's sudden bellowing, but it startled them this time.

"Why, Uncle Abel," cried both Aunt Emma and Mrs Carey, "whatever do you mean?"

"What I means is that I ain't a-goin' to have the feelin's of a niece of mine trifled with. What I means is that I seen Harry Dale with Bertha Buckolt New Year's night after he left here. That's what I means——"

"Don't speak so loud, Abel, we're not deaf," interrupted Carey, as Mary started up white-faced. "What do you always shout for?"

"I speak loud because I want people to hear me!" roared Uncle Abel, turning on him.

"Go on, Uncle Abel," said Mary, "tell me what you mean."

"I mean," said Uncle Abel, lowering his voice a little, "that I seen Harry Dale and Bertha Buckolt at Buckolts' Gate that night—I seen it all——"

"*At Buckolts' Gate*!" cried Mary.

"*Yes*! at Buckolts' Gate! Ain't I speakin' loud enough?"

"And where were you?"

"Never mind wheers I was. I was comin' home along the ridges, and I seen them. I seen them say good-bye; I seen them hug an' kiss——"

"Uncle Abel!" exclaimed Aunt Emma.

"It's no use Uncle Abelin' me. What I sez I sez. I ain't a-goin' to have a niece of mine bungfoodled——"

"Uncle Abel," cried Mary, staring at him wild-eyed, "do be careful what you say. You must have made a mistake. Are you sure it was Bertha and Harry?"

"Am I sure my head's on me neck?" roared Uncle Abel. "Would I see 'em if I didn't see 'em? I tell you——"

"Now wait a moment, Uncle Abel," interrupted Mary, with dangerous calmness. "Listen to me. Harry Dale and I are engaged to be married, and——"

"Have you got the writin's!" shouted Uncle Abel.

"The what?" said Mary.

"The writin's."

"No, of course not."

"Then that's where you are," said Uncle Abel, triumphantly. "If you had the writin's you could sue him for breach of contract."

Uncle Abel, who couldn't read, had no faith whatever in verbal agreements (he wouldn't sign one, he said), all others he referred to as "writings".

"Now, listen to me, Uncle Abel," said Mary, trembling now. "Are you sure you saw Harry Dale and Bertha Buckolt at Buckolts' Gate after he left here that night?"

"Yes. An' what's more, I seen young Tommy there ridin' on his pony along by the Spur a little while after, an' he muster seen them too, if he's got a tongue."

Mary turned quickly to her brother.

"Well, all I can say," said Tommy, quietened now, "is that I seen *her* at Buckolts' Gate that night. I was comin' home from Two-Mile Flat, and I met Jim with his packhorse about a mile the other side of Buckolts', and while we was talkin' Harry Dale caught up, so I jist said 'So-long' an' left 'em. And when I got to Buckolts' Gate I seen Bertha Buckolt. She was standin' under a tree, and she looked as if she was cryin'——"

But Mary got her bonnet and started out.

"Where are you going to, Mary?" asked her mother, starting up nervously.

"I'm going across to Buckolts to find out the truth," said Mary, and she went out.

"Better let her go, Lizzie," said Aunt Emma, detaining her sister. "You've done it now, Uncle Abel."

"Well, why didn't she get the writin's?" retorted Uncle Abel.

Half-way to Buckolts' Mary met Bertha Buckolt herself, coming over to the selection for the first time since the night of the party. Bertha started forward to kiss Mary, but stopped short as Mary stood stock-still and faced her, with her hands behind her back.

"Why! whatever is the matter, Mary?" exclaimed Bertha.

"You know very well, Bertha."

"Why! Whatever do you mean? What have I done?"

"What haven't you done? You've—you've broken my heart."

"Good gracious me! Whatever are you talking about? Tell me what it is, Mary?"

"You met him at your gate that night?"

"I know I did."

"Oh, Bertha! How could you be so mean and deceitful?"

"Mean and deceitful! What do you mean by that? Whatever are you talking about? I suppose I've got as good a right to meet him as anyone else."

"No, you haven't," retorted Mary, "you're only stringing him on. You only did it to spite me. You helped him to deceive me. You ought to be ashamed to look me in the face."

"Good gracious! Whatever are you talking about? Ain't I good enough for him? I ought to be, God knows! I suppose he can marry who he likes, and if I'm poor fool enough to love him and marry him, what then? Mary, you ought to be the last to speak—speak to—to me like that."

"Yes. He can marry all the girls in the country for all I care. I never want to see either him or you any more. You're a cruel, deceitful, brazen-faced hussy, and he's a heartless, deceiving blackguard."

"Mary! I believe you're mad," said Bertha, firmly. "How dare you speak to me like that! And as for him being a blackguard. Why, you ought to be the last in the world to say such a thing; you ought to be the last to say a word against him. Why, I don't believe you ever cared a rap for him in spite of all your pretence. He could go to the devil for all you cared."

"That's enough, Bertha Buckolt!" cried Mary. "*You*—you! Why, you're a barefaced girl, that's what you are! I don't want to see your brazen face again." With that she turned and stumbled blindly in the direction of home.

"Send back my cape," cried Bertha as she, too, turned away.

Mary walked wildly home and fled to her room and locked the door. Bertha did likewise.

Mary let Aunt Emma in after a while, ceased sobbing and allowed herself to be comforted a little. Next morning she was out milking at the usual time, but there were dark hollows under her eyes, and her little face was white and set. After breakfast she rolled the cape up very tight in a brown-paper parcel, addressed it severely to—

MISS BERTHA BUCKOLT,
Eurunderee Creek

and sent it home by one of the school children.

She wrote to Harry Dale and told him that she knew all about it (not stating what), but she forgave him and hoped he'd be happy. She never wanted to see his face again, and enclosed his portrait.

Harry, who was as true and straight as a bushman could be, puzzled it out and decided that some one of his old love affairs must have come to Mary's ears, and wrote demanding an explanation.

She never answered that letter.

ACT III

It was Christmas Day at Rocky Rises. The plum puddings had been made, as usual, weeks beforehand, and hung in rags to the tie-beams and taken down and boiled again. Poultry had been killed and plucked and cooked, and all the toil had been gone through, and every preparation made for a red-hot dinner on a blazing hot day—and for no other reason than that our great-grandmothers used to do it in a cold climate at Christmas-times that came in mid-winter. Merry men hadn't gone forth to the wood to gather in the mistletoe (if they ever did in England, in the olden days, instead of sending shivering, wretched vassals in rags to do it); but Uncle Abel had gone gloomily up the ridge on Christmas Eve, with an axe on his shoulder (and Tommy unwillingly in tow, scowling and making faces behind his back), and had cut young pines and dragged them home and lashed them firmly to the veranda-posts, which was the custom out there.

There was little goodwill or peace between the three or four farms round Rocky Rises that Christmas Day, and Uncle Abel had been the cause of most of the ill-feeling, though they didn't know, and he was least aware of it of any.

It all came about in this way.

Shortly after last New Year Ryan's bull had broken loose and gone astray for two days and nights, breaking into neighbours' paddocks and filling himself with hay and damaging other bulls, and making love by night and hiding in the scrub all day. On the second night he broke through and jumped over Reid's fences, and destroyed about an acre of grape-vines and adulterated Reid's stock, besides interfering with certain heifers which were not of a marriageable age. There was a £5 penalty on a stray bull. Reid impounded the bull and claimed heavy damages. Ryan, a small selector of little account, was always pulling some neighbour to court when he wasn't being "pulled" himself, so he went to court over this case.

Now, it appears that the bull, on his holiday, had spent a part of the first night in Carey's lower paddock, and Uncle Abel (who was out mooching about the bush at all hours, "havin' a look at some timber" or some "indercations" [of gold], or on some mysterious business or fad, the mystery of which was of his own making) —Uncle Abel saw the bull in the paddock at daylight and turned it out the sliprails, and talked about it afterwards, referring to the sliprails as "Buckolts' Gate", of course, and spoke mysteriously of the case, and put on an appearance of great importance, and allowed people to get an idea that he knew a lot if he only liked to speak; and finally he got himself "brought up" as a witness for Ryan.

He had a lot of beer in town before he went to the court-house.

All he knew would have been of no use to either party, but he swore that he had seen Ryan's bull inside Buckolts' Gate at daylight (on the day which wasn't in question) and had turned him out. Uncle Abel mixed up the court a good deal, and roared like the bull, and became more obstinate the more he was cross-examined, and narrowly escaped being committed for contempt of court.

Ryan, who had a high opinion of the breed of his bull, got an idea that the Buckolts had enticed or driven the bull into their paddock for stock-raising purposes, instead of borrowing it honestly or offering to pay for the use of it. Then Ryan wanted to know why Abel had driven his bull out of Buckolts' Gate, and the Buckolts wanted to know what business Abel Albury had to drive Ryan's bull out of their paddock, if the bull had really ever been there. And so it went on till Rocky Rises was ripe for a tragedy.

The breach between the Careys and the Buckolts was widened, the quarrel between Ryan and Reid intensified. Ryan got a down on the Careys because he reckoned that Uncle Abel had deliberately spoilt his case with his evidence; and the Reids and Careys were no longer on speaking terms, because nothing would convince old Reid that Abel hadn't tried to prove that Ryan's bull had never been in Reid's paddock at all.

Well, it was Christmas Day, and the Carey family and Aunt Emma sat down to dinner. Jim was present, having arrived overnight, with no money, as usual, and suffering a recovery. The elder brother, Bob (who had a selection up-country), and his wife were there. Mrs Carey moved round with watchful eyes and jealous ears, lest there should be a word or a look which might hurt the feelings of her wild son—for of such are mothers.

Dinner went on very moodily, in spite of Aunt Emma, until at last Jim spoke—almost for the first time, save for a long-whispered and, on his part, repentant conversation with his mother.

"Look here, Mary!" said Jim. "What did you throw Harry Dale over for?"

"Don't ask me, Jim."

"Rot! What did he do to you? I'm your brother" (with a glance at Bob), "and I ought to know."

"Well, then, ask Bertha Buckolt. She saw him last."

"What!" cried Jim.

"Hold your tongue, Jim! You'll make her cry," said Aunt Emma.

"Well, what's it all about, anyway?" demanded Jim. "All I know is that Mary wrote to Harry and threw him over, and he ain't been the same man since. He swears he'll never come near the district again."

"Tell Jim, Aunt Emma," said Mary. And Aunt Emma started to tell the story as far as she knew.

"Saw her at Buckolts' sliprails!" cried Jim, starting up. "Well, he couldn't have had time to more than say good-bye to her, for I was with her there myself, and Harry caught up to me within a mile of the gate—and I rode pretty fast."

"He had a jolly long good-bye with her," shouted Uncle Abel. "Look here, Jim! I ain't goin' to stand by and see a nephew of mine bungfoodled by no girl; an' I tell you I seen 'em huggin' and kissin' and canoodlin' for half an hour at Buckolts' Gate!"

"It's a—a—— Look here, Uncle Abel, be careful what you say. You've got the bull by the tail again, that's what it is!" Jim's face grew whiter—and it had been white enough on account of the drink. "How did you know it was them? You're always mistaking people. It might have been someone else."

"I know Harry Dale on horseback two miles off!" roared Uncle Abel. "And I knowed her by her cape."

It was Mary's turn to gasp and stare at Uncle Abel.

"Uncle Abel," she managed to say, "Uncle Abel! Wasn't it at our Lower Sliprails you saw them and not Buckolts' Gate?"

"Well!" bellowed Uncle Abel. "You might call 'em the Lower Sliprails, but I calls 'em Buckolts' Gate! They lead to'r'ds Buckolts', don't they? Hey? Them other sliprails"—jerking his arms in the direction of the upper paddock—"them theer other sliprails that leads outer Reid's lane I calls Reid's Sliprails. I don't know nothing about no upper or lower, or easter or wester, or any other la-di-dah names you like to call 'em."

"Oh, uncle," cried Mary, trembling like a leaf, "why didn't you explain this before? Why didn't you tell us?"

"What cause have I got to tell any of you everything I sez or does or thinks? It 'ud take me all me time. Ain't you got any more brains than Ryan's bull, any of you? Hey!—You've got heads, but so has cabbages. Explain! Why, if the world wasn't stuffed so full of jumped-up fools there'd be never no need for explainin'."

Mary left the table.

"What is it, Mary?" cried Aunt Emma.

"I'm going across to Bertha," said Mary, putting on her hat with trembling hands. "It was me Uncle Abel saw. I had Bertha's cape on that night."

"Oh, Uncle Abel," cried Aunt Emma, "whatever have you done?"

"Well," said Uncle Abel, "why didn't she get the writin's as I told her? It's to be hoped she won't make such a fool of herself next time."

Half an hour later, or thereabouts, Mary sat on Bertha Buckolt's bed, with Bertha beside her and Bertha's arm round her, and they were crying and laughing by turns.

"But—but—why didn't you *tell* me it was Jim?" said Mary.

"Why didn't you tell me it was Harry, Mary?" asked Bertha. "It would have saved all this year of misery."

"I didn't see Harry Dale at all that night," said Bertha. "I was—I was crying when Jim left me, and when Harry came along I slipped behind a tree until he was past. And now, look here, Mary, I can't marry Jim until he steadies down, but I'll give him another chance. But, Mary, I'd sooner lose him than you."

Bertha walked home with Mary, and during the afternoon she took Jim aside and said:

"Look here, Jim, I'll give you another chance—for a year. Now I want you to ride into town and send a telegram to Harry Dale. How long would it take him to get here?"

"He couldn't get here before New Year," said Jim.

"That will do," said Bertha, and Jim went to catch his horse.

Next day Harry's reply came: "Coming."

ACT IV

New Year's Eve. The dance was at Buckolts' this year, but Bertha didn't dance much; she was down by the gate most of the time with little Mary Carey, waiting, and watching the long, white road, and listening for horses' feet, and disappointed often as other horsemen rode by or turned up to the farm.

And in the hot sunrise that morning, within a hundred miles of Rocky Rises, a tired, dusty drover camped in the edge of a scrub, boiled his quart-pot, broiled a piece of mutton on the coals, and lay down on the sand to rest an hour or so before pushing on to a cattle-station he knew to try and borrow fresh horses. He had ridden all night.

Old Buckolt and Carey and Reid smoked socially under the grape-vines, with bottles of whisky and glasses, and nudged each other and coughed when they wanted to laugh at Old Abel Albury, who was, for about the first time in his life, condescending to explain. He was explaining to them what thund'rin' fools they had been.

Later on they sent a boy on horseback with a bottle of whisky and a message to Ryan, who turned up in time to see the New Year in with them and contradict certain slanders concerning the breed of his bull.

Meanwhile Bertha comforted Mary, and at last persuaded her to go home. "He's sure to be here tomorrow, Mary," she said, "and you need to look fresh and happy."

But Mary didn't sleep that night; she was up before daylight, had the kettle on and some chops ready to fry, and at daybreak she was down by the sliprails again. She was turning away for the second time when she heard a clear whistle round the Spur—then the tune of "Willie Riley", and the hobble-chains and camp-ware on the packhorse jingling to the tune.

She pulled out the rails with eager, trembling hands and leaned against the tree.

An hour later a tired drover lay on his back, in his ragged, track-worn clothes and dusty leggings, on Mary's own little bed in the skillion off the living-room, and rested. Mary bustled round getting breakfast ready, and singing softly to herself; once she slipped in, bent over Harry and kissed him gently on the lips, and ran out as he stirred.

"Why, who's that?" exclaimed Uncle Abel, poking round early and catching a glimpse of Harry through the open door.

"It's only Harry, Uncle Abel," said Mary.

Uncle Abel peered in again to make sure.

"Well, be sure you git the writin's this time," he said.

Jones's Alley

SHE lived in Jones's Alley. She cleaned offices, washed, and nursed from daylight until any time after dark, and filled in her spare time cleaning her own place (which she always found dirty—in a "beastly filthy state", she called it—on account of the children being left in possession all day), cooking, and nursing her own sick—for her family, though small, was so in the two senses of the word, and sickly; one or another of the children was always sick, but not through her fault. She did her own, or rather the family, washing, at home too, when she couldn't do it by kind permission, or surreptitiously in connection with that of her employers. She was a haggard woman. Her second husband was supposed to be dead, and she lived in dread of his daily resurrection. Her eldest son was at large, but, not being yet sufficiently hardened in misery, she dreaded his getting into trouble even more than his frequent and interested appearances at home. She could buy off the son for a shilling or two and a clean shirt and collar, but she couldn't purchase the absence of the father at any price—*he* claimed what he called his "conzugal rights" as well as his board, lodging, washing and beer. She slaved for her children, and nag-nag-nagged them everlastingly, whether they were in the right or in the wrong, but they were hardened to it and took small notice. She had the spirit of a bullock. Her whole nature was soured. She had those "worse troubles" which she couldn't tell to anybody, but had to suffer in silence.

She also, in what she called her "spare time", put new cuffs and collar-bands on gentlemen's shirts. The gentlemen didn't live in Jones's Alley—they boarded with a patroness of the haggard woman; they didn't know their shirts were done there—had they known it, and known Jones's Alley, one or two of them, who were medical students, might probably have objected. The landlady charged them just twice as much for repairing their shirts as she paid the haggard woman, who, therefore, being unable to buy the cuffs and collar-bands ready-made for sewing on, had no lack of employment with which to fill in her spare time.

Therefore, she was a "respectable woman", and was known in

Jones's Alley as "Missus" Aspinall, and called so generally, and even by Mother Brock, who kept "that place" opposite. There is implied a world of difference between the "Mother" and the "Missus", as applied to matrons in Jones's Alley; and this distinction was about the only thing—always excepting the everlasting "children"—that the haggard woman had left to care about, to take a selfish, narrow-minded sort of pleasure in—if, indeed, she could yet take pleasure, grim or otherwise, in anything except, perhaps, a good cup of tea and time to drink it in.

Times were hard with Mrs Aspinall. Two coppers and two half-pence in her purse were threepence to *her* now, and the absence of one of the half-pence made a difference to her, especially in Paddy's Market—that eloquent advertisement of a young city's sin and poverty and rotten wealth—on Saturday night. She counted the coppers as anxiously and nervously as a thirsty dead-beat does. And her house was "falling down on her" and her troubles, and she couldn't get the landlord to do a "han'stern" to it.

At last, after persistent agitation on her part (but not before a portion of the plastered ceiling had fallen and severely injured one of her children) the landlord caused two men to be sent to "effect necessary repairs" to the three square, dingy, plastered holes—called "three rooms and a kitchen"—for the privilege of living in which, and calling it "my place", she paid ten shillings a week.

Previously the agent, as soon as he had received the rent and signed the receipt, would cut short her reiterated complaints—which he privately called her "clack"—by saying that he'd see to it, he'd speak to the landlord; and, later on, that he *had* spoken to him, or could do nothing more in the matter—that wasn't his business. Neither it was, to do the agent justice. It was his business to collect the rent, and thereby earn the means of paying his own. He had to keep a family on his own account, by assisting the Fat Man to keep his at the expense of people—especially widows with large families, or women, in the case of Jones's Alley—who couldn't afford it without being half-starved, or running greater and unspeakable risks which "society" is not supposed to know anything about.

So the agent was right, according to his lights. The landlord had recently turned out a family who had occupied one of his houses for fifteen years, because they were six weeks in arrears. He let them take their furniture, and explained: "I wouldn't have been so lenient with them only they were such old tenants of mine." So the landlord was always in the right according to *his* lights.

But the agent naturally wished to earn his living as peacefully and as comfortably as possible, so, when the accident occurred, he put the matter so persistently and strongly before the landlord that he said at last: "Well, tell her to go to White, the contractor, and he'll send a man to do what's to be done; and don't bother me any more."

White had a look at the place, and sent a plasterer, a carpenter, and a plumber. The plasterer knocked a bigger hole in the ceiling and filled it with mud; the carpenter nailed a board over the hole in the floor; the plumber stopped the leak in the kitchen, and made three new ones in worse places; and their boss sent the bill to Mrs Aspinall.

She went to the contractor's yard, and explained that the landlord was responsible for the debt, not she. The contractor explained that he had seen the landlord, who referred him to her. She called at the landlord's private house, and was referred through a servant to the agent. The agent was sympathetic, but could do nothing in the matter—it wasn't his business; he also asked her to put herself in his place, which she couldn't, not being any more reasonable than such women are in such cases. She let things drift, being powerless to prevent them from doing so; and the contractor sent another bill, then a debt collector and then another bill, then the collector again, and threatened to take proceedings, and finally took them. To make matters worse, she was two weeks in arrears with the rent, and the wood-and-coal man (she had dealt with them for ten years) was pushing her, as also were her grocers, with whom she had dealt for fifteen years and never owed a penny before.

She waylaid the landlord, and he told her shortly that he couldn't build houses and give them away, and keep them in repair afterwards.

She sought for sympathy and found it, but mostly in the wrong places. It was comforting, but unprofitable. Mrs Next-door sympathized warmly, and offered to go up as a witness—she had another landlord. The agent sympathized wearily, but not in the presence of witnesses—he wanted her to put herself in his place. Mother Brock, indeed, offered practical assistance, which offer was received in breathlessly indignant silence. It was Mother Brock who first came to the assistance of Mrs Aspinall's child when the plaster accident took place (the mother being absent at the time), and when Mrs Aspinall heard of it her indignation cured her of her fright, and she declared to Mrs Next-door that she would give "that woman"—meaning Mother Brock—"in char-rge the instant she ever *dared* put her foot inside her (Mrs A.'s) respectable door-step again. She was a respectable, honest, hard-working woman, and" ——etc.

Whereat Mother Brock laughed good-naturedly. She was a broad-minded bad woman, and was right according to *her* lights. Poor Mrs A. was a respectable, haggard woman, and was right according to *her* lights and to Mrs Next-door's, perfectly so—they being friends—and vice versa. None of them knew, or would have taken into consideration, the fact that the landlord had lost all his money in a burst financial institution, and half his houses in the general depression, and depended for food for his family on the somewhat doubtful rents of the remainder. So they were all right according to their different lights.

Mrs Aspinall even sought sympathy of "John", the Chinaman (with whom she had dealt for four months only), and got it. He also, in all simplicity, took a hint that wasn't intended. He said: "Al li'. Pay bimeby. Nexy time Flyday. Me tlust." Then he departed with his immortalized smile. It would almost appear that he was wrong—according to our idea of Chinese lights.

Mrs Aspinall went to the court—it was a small local court. Mrs Next-door was awfully sorry, but she couldn't possibly get out that morning. The contractor had the landlord up as a witness. The landlord and the P.M. nodded pleasantly to each other, and wished each other good morning. . . . Verdict for plaintiff with costs. . . . "Next case!" . . . "You mustn't take up the time of the court, my good woman." . . . "Now, constable!" . . . "Arder in the court!" . . . "Now, my good woman," said the policeman in an undertone, "you must go out; there's another case on—come now." And he steered her—but not unkindly—through the door.

"My good woman" stood in the crowd outside, and looked wildly round for a sympathetic face that advertised sympathetic ears. But others had their own troubles, and avoided her. She wanted someone to relieve her bursting heart to; she couldn't wait till she got home.

Even "John's" attentive ear and mildly idiotic expression would have been welcome, but he was gone. He *had* been in court that morning, and had won a small debt case, and had departed cheerfully, under the impression that he lost it.

"Y'aw Mrs Aspinall, ain't you?"

She started, and looked round. He was one of those sharp, blue or grey-eyed, sandy or freckled complexion boys-of-the-world whom we meet everywhere and at all times, who are always going on towards twenty, yet never seem to get clear out of their teens, who know more than most of us have forgotten, who understand human nature instinctively—perhaps unconsciously—and are instinctively sympathetic and diplomatic; whose satire is quick, keen, and dangerous, and whose tact is often superior to that of many educated men-of-the-world. Trained from childhood in the great school of poverty, they are full of the pathos and humour of it.

"Don't you remember me?"

"No; can't say I do. I fancy I've seen your face before somewhere."

"I was at your place when little Arvie died. I used to work with him at Grinder Brothers', you know."

"Oh, of course I remember you! What was I thinking about? I've had such a lot of worry lately that I don't know whether I'm on my head or my heels. Besides, you've grown since then, and changed a lot. You're Billy—Billy——"

"Billy Anderson's my name."

"Of course! To be sure! I remember you quite well."

"How've you been gettin' on, Mrs Aspinall?"

"Ah! Don't mention it—nothing but worry and trouble—nothing but worry and trouble. This grinding poverty! I'll never have anything else but worry and trouble and misery so long as I live."

"Do you live in Jones's Alley yet?"

"Yes."

"Not been there ever since, have you?"

"No; I shifted away once, but I went back again. I was away nearly two years."

"I thought so, because I called in to see you there once. Well, I'm goin' that way now. You goin' home, Mrs Aspinall?"

"Yes."

"Well, I'll go along with you, if you don't mind."

"Thanks. I'd be only too glad of company."

"Goin' to walk, Mrs Aspinall?" asked Bill, as the tram stopped in their way.

"Yes. I can't afford trams now—times are too hard."

"Sorry I don't happen to have no tickets on me!"

"Oh, don't mention it. I'm well used to walking. I'd rather walk than ride."

They waited till the tram passed.

"Some people"—said Bill, reflectively, but with a tinge of indignation in his tone, as they crossed the street—"some people can afford to ride in trams."

"What's your trouble, Mrs Aspinall—if it's a fair thing to ask?" said Bill, as they turned the corner.

This was all she wanted, and more; and when, about a mile later, she paused for breath, he drew a long one, gave a short whistle, and said:

"Well, it's red-hot!"

Thus encouraged, she told her story again, and some parts of it for the third and fourth and even fifth time—and it grew longer, as our stories have a painful tendency to do when we re-write them with a view to condensation.

But Bill heroically repeated that it was "red-hot".

"And I dealt off the grocer for fifteen years, and the wood-and-coal man for ten, and I lived in that house nine years last Easter Monday and never owed a penny before," she repeated for the tenth time.

"Well, that's a mistake," reflected Bill. "I never dealt off nobody more'n twice in my life. . . . I heerd you was married again, Mrs Aspinall—if it's a right thing to ask?"

"Wherever did you hear that? I did get married again—to my sorrow."

"Then you ain't Mrs Aspinall—if it's a fair thing to ask?"

"Oh, yes! I'm known as Mrs Aspinall. They all call me Mrs Aspinall."

"I understand. He cleared, didn't he? Run away?"

"Well, yes—no—he——"

"I understand. He's s'posed to be dead?"

"Yes."

"Well, that's red-hot! So's my old man, and I hope he don't resurrect again."

"You see, I married my second for the sake of my children."

"That's a great mistake," reflected Bill. "My mother married my stepfather for the sake of me, and she's never been done telling me about it."

"Indeed! Did *your* mother get married again?"

"Yes. And he left me with a batch of stepsisters and stepbrothers to look after, as well as mother; as if things wasn't bad enough before. We didn't want no help to be pinched, and poor, and half-starved. I don't see where my sake comes in at all."

"And how's your mother now?"

"Oh, she's all right, thank you. She's got a hard time of it, but she's pretty well used to it."

"And are you still working at Grinder Brothers'?"

"No. I got tired of slavin' there for next to nothing. I got sick of my stepfather waitin' outside for me on pay-day, with a dirty, drunken, spieler pal of his waitin' round the corner for him. There wasn't nothin' in it. It got to be too rough altogether. . . . Blast Grinders!"

"And what are you doing now?"

"Sellin' papers. I'm always tryin' to get a start in somethin' else, but I ain't got no luck. I always come back to sellin' papers."

Then, after a thought, he added reflectively: "Blast papers!"

His present ambition was to drive a cart.

"I drove a cart twice, and once I rode a butcher's horse. A bloke worked me out of one billet, and I worked myself out of the other. I didn't know when I was well off. Then the banks went bust, and my last boss went insolvent, and one of his partners went into Darlinghurst for suicide, and the other went into Gladesville for being mad; and one day the bailiff seized the cart and horse with me in it and a load of timber. So I went home and helped mother and the kids live on one meal a day for six months, and keep the bum-bailiff out. Another cove had my news-stand."

Then, after a thought:

"Blast reconstriction!"

"But you surely can't make a living selling newspapers?"

"No, there's nothin' in it. There's too many at it. The blessed women spoil it. There's one got a good stand down in George Street, and she's got a dozen kids sellin'—they can't all be hers—and then she's got the hide to come up to my stand and sell in front of me. . . . What are you thinkin' about doin', Mrs Aspinall?"

"I don't know," she wailed. "I really don't know what to do."

And there still being some distance to go, she plunged into her tale of misery once more, not forgetting the length of time she had dealt with her creditors.

Bill pushed his hat forward and walked along on the edge of the kerb.

"Can't you shift? Ain't you got no people or friends that you can go to for a while?"

"Oh, yes; there's my sister-in-law; she's asked me times without number to come and stay with her till things get better, and she's got a hard enough struggle herself, Lord knows. She asked me again only yesterday."

"Well, that ain't too bad," reflected Bill. "Why don't you go?"

"Well, you see, if I did they wouldn't let me take my furniture, and she's got next to none."

"Won't the landlord let you take your furniture?"

"No, not him! He's one of the hardest landlords in Sydney—the worst I ever had."

"That's red-hot! . . . I'd take it in spite of him. He can't do nothin'."

"But I daren't; and even if I did I haven't got a penny to pay for a van."

They neared the alley. Bill counted the flagstones, stepping from one to another over the joints. "Eighteen—nineteen—twenty—twenty-one!" he counted mentally, and came to the corner kerbing. Then he turned suddenly and faced her.

"I'll tell you what to do," he said decidedly. "Can you get your things ready by tonight? I know a cove that's got a cart."

"But I daren't. I'm afraid of the landlord."

"The more fool you," said Bill. "Well, I'm not afraid of him. He can't do nothin'. I'm not afraid of a landlady, and that's worse. I know the law. He can't do nothin'. You just do as I tell you."

"I'd want to think over it first, and see my sister-in-law."

"Where does your sister-in-law live?"

"Not far."

"Well, see her, and think over it—you've got plenty of time to do it in—and get your things ready by dark. Don't be frightened. I've shifted mother and an aunt and two married sisters out of worse fixes than yours. I'll be round after dark, and bring a push to lend a hand. They're decent coves."

"But I can't expect your friend to shift me for nothing. I told you I haven't got a——"

"Mrs Aspinall, I ain't that sort of a bloke, neither is my chum, and neither is the other fellows—'relse they wouldn't be friends of mine. Will you promise, Mrs Aspinall?"

"I'm afraid—I—I'd like to keep my few things now. I've kept them so long. It's hard to lose my few bits of things—I wouldn't care so much if I could keep the ironin' table."

"So you could, by law—it's necessary to your living, but it would cost more'n the table. Now, don't be soft, Mrs Aspinall. You'll have the bailiff in any day, and be turned out in the end without a rag. The law knows no 'necessary'. You want your furniture more'n the landlord does. He can't do nothin'. You can trust it all to me. . . . I knowed Arvie. . . . Will you do it?"

"Yes, I will."

At about eight o'clock that evening there came a mysterious knock at Mrs Aspinall's door. She opened, and there stood Bill. His attitude was business-like, and his manner very impressive. Three other boys stood along by the window, with their backs to the wall, deeply interested in the emptying of burnt cigarette-ends into a piece of newspaper laid in the crown of one of their hats, and a fourth stood a little way along the kerb casually rolling a cigarette, and keeping a quiet eye out for suspicious appearances. They were of different makes and sizes, but there seemed an undefined similarity between them.

"This is my push, Mrs Aspinall," said Bill; "at least," he added apologetically, "it's part of 'em. Here, you chaps, this is Mrs Aspinall, what I told you about."

They elbowed the wall back, rubbed their heads with their hats, shuffled round, and seemed to take a vacant sort of interest in abstract objects, such as the pavement, the gas-lamp, and neighbouring doors and windows.

"Got the things ready?" asked Bill.

"Oh, yes."

"Got 'em downstairs?"

"There's no upstairs. The rooms above belong to the next house."

"And a nice house it is," said Bill, "for rooms to belong to. I wonder," he reflected, cocking his eye at the window above; "I wonder how the police manage to keep an eye on the next house without keepin' an eye on yours—but they know."

He turned towards the street end of the alley and gave a low whistle. Out under the lamp from behind the corner came a long, thin, shambling, hump-backed youth, with his hat down over his head like an extinguisher, dragging a small bony horse, which, in its turn, dragged a rickety cart of the tray variety, such as is used in the dead-marine trade. Behind the cart was tied a mangy retriever. This affair was drawn up opposite the door.

"The cove with a cart" was introduced as "Chinny". He had no chin whatever, not even a receding chin. It seemed as though his chin had been cut clean off horizontally. When he took off his hat he showed to the mild surprise of strangers a pair of shrewd grey eyes and a broad high forehead. Chinny was in the empty-bottle line.

"Now, then, hold up that horse of yours for a minute, Chinny," said Bill briskly, " 'relse he'll fall down and break the shaft again." (It had already been broken in several places and spliced with strips of deal, clothes-line, and wire.) "Now, you chaps, fling yourselves about and get the furniture out."

This was a great relief to the push. They ran against each other and the door-post in the eagerness to be at work. The furniture—what Mrs A. called her "few bits of things"—was carried out with elaborate care. The ironing table was the main item. It was placed top down in the cart, and the rest of the things went between the legs without bulging sufficiently to cause Chinny any anxiety.

Just then the picket gave a low, earnest whistle, and they were aware of a policeman standing statue-like under the lamp on the opposite corner, and apparently unaware of their existence. He was looking, sphinx-like, past them towards the city.

"It can't be helped; we must put on front an' go on with it now," said Bill.

"He's all right, I think," said Chinny. "He knows me."

"He can't do nothin'," said Bill; "don't mind him, Mrs Aspinall. Now, then" (to the push), "tie up. Don't be frightened of the dorg—what are you frightened of? Why he'd only apologize if you trod on his tail."

The dog went under the cart, and kept his tail carefully behind him.

The policeman—he was an elderly man—stood still, looking towards the city, and over it, perhaps, and over the sea, to long years agone in Ireland when he and the boys ducked bailiffs, and resisted evictions with "shticks", and "riz" sometimes, and gathered together at the rising of the moon, and did many things contrary to the peace of Gracious Majesty, its laws and constitutions, crown and dignity; as a reward for which he had helped to preserve the said peace for the best years of his life, without promotion; for he had a great aversion to running in "the boys"—which included nearly all mankind—and preferred to keep, and was most successful in keeping, the peace with no other assistance than that of his own rich fatherly brogue.

Bill took charge of two of the children; Mrs Aspinall carried the youngest.

"Go ahead, Chinny," said Bill.

Chinny shambled forward, sideways, dragging the horse, with one long, bony, short-sleeved arm stretched out behind holding the rope reins; the horse stumbled out of the gutter, and the cart seemed to pause a moment, as if undecided whether to follow or not, and then, with many rickety complaints, moved slowly and painfully up on to the level out of the gutter. The dog rose with a long, weary, mangy sigh, but with a lazy sort of calculation, before his rope (which was short) grew taut—which was good judgment on his part, for his neck was sore; and his feet being tender, he felt his way carefully and painfully over the metal, as if he feared that at any step he might spring some treacherous, air-trigger trapdoor which would drop and hang him.

"Nit, you chaps," said Bill, "and wait for me." The push rubbed its head with its hat, said "Good night, Mrs Ashpennel," and was absent, spook-like.

When the funeral reached the street, the lonely "trap" was, somehow, two blocks away in the opposite direction, moving very slowly, and very upright, and very straight, like an automaton.

The Rising of the Court

Oh, then tell us, Kings and Judges, where our meeting is to be,
When the laws of men are nothing, and our spirits all are free—
When the laws of men are nothing, and no wealth can hold the fort,
There'll be thirst for mighty brewers at the Rising of the Court.

THE same dingy court-room, deep and dim, like a well, with the clock high up on the wall, and the doors low down in it; with the bench, which, with some gilding, might be likened to a ginger-bread imitation of a throne; the royal arms above it and the little witness-box to one side, where so many honest poor people are bullied, insulted and laughed at by third-rate blackguardly little lawyers, and so many pitiful, pathetic and noble lies are told by pitiful sinners and disreputable heroes for a little liberty for a lost self, or the sake of a friend—of a pal or a cobber. The same overworked and underpaid magistrate trying to keep his attention fixed on the same old miserable scene before him; as a weary, overworked and underpaid journalist or author strives to keep his attention fixed on his proofs. The same row of big, strong, healthy, good-natured policemen trying not to grin at times; and the police-court solicitors ("The place stinks with 'em," a sergeant told me) wrangling over some miserable case for a crust, and the reporters, shabby some of them, eager to get a brutal joke for their papers out of the accumulated mass of misery before them, whether it be at the expense of the deaf, blind, or crippled man, or the alien.

And opposite the bench, the dock, divided by a partition, with the women to the left and the men to the right, as it is on the stairs or the block in polite society. They bring children here no longer. The same shaking, wild-eyed, bloodshot-eyed and blear-eyed drunks and disorderlies, though some of the women have nerves yet; and the same decently dressed, but trembling and conscience-stricken little wretch up for petty larceny or something, whose motor-car bosses of a big firm have sent a solicitor, "manager", or some understrapper here to prosecute and give evidence.

But, over there, on a form to one side of the bench—opposite the witness-box—and as the one bright spot in this dark, and shameful, and useless scene—and in a patch of sunlight from the skylight as it happens—sit representatives of the Prisoners' Aid Society, Prison Gate and Rescue Brigades, etc. (one or two of the ladies in nurses' uniforms), who are come to help us and to fight for us against the Law of their Land and of ours, God help us!

Mrs Johnson, of Red Rock Lane, is here, and her rival in revolution, One-Eyed Kate, and Cock-Eyed Sal, and one or two of the other aristocrats of the alley. And the weeping bedraggled remains of what was once, and not so long ago, a pretty, slight, fair-haired and blue-eyed Australian girl. She is up for inciting One-Eyed Kate to resist the police. Also, Three-Pea Ginger, Stousher, and Wingy, for some participation in the row amongst the aforementioned ladies. (Wingy, by the way, is a ratty little one-armed man, whose case is usually described in the head-line as "A 'Armless Case" by one of our great dailies.) And their pals are waiting outside in the vestibule—Frowsy Kate (The Red Streak), Boko Bill, Pincher and his "piece", etc., getting together the stuff for the possible fines, and the ten-bob fee for the lawyer, in one case, and ready to swear to anything, if called upon. And I myself—though I have not yet entered Red Rock Lane Society—on bail, on a charge of "plain drunk". It was "drunk and disorderly", by the way, but a kindly sergeant changed it to plain drunk—(though I always thought my drunk was ornamental).

Yet I am not ashamed—only comfortably dulled and a little tired—dully interested and observant, and hopeful for the sunlight presently. We low persons get too great a contempt for things to feel much ashamed at any time; and this very contempt keeps many of us from "reforming". We hear too many lies sworn that we *know* to be lies, and see too many unjust and brutal things done that we know to be brutal and unjust.

But let us go back a bit, and suppose we are still waiting for the magistrate, and think of Last Night. "Silence!"—but from no human voice this time. The whispering, shuffling, and clicking of the court typewriter ceases, the scene darkens, and the court is blotted out as a scene is blotted out from the sight of a man who has thrown himself into a mesmeric trance. And:

Drink—lurid recollection of being "searched"—clang of iron cell door, and I grope for and crawl on to the slanting plank. Period of oblivion—or the soul is away in some other world. Clang of cell door again, and soul returns in a hurry to take heed of another soul, belonging to a belated drunk on the plank by my side. Other soul says:

"Gotta match?"

So we're not in hell yet.

We fumble and light up. They leave us our pipes, tobacco and matches; presently, one knocks with his pipe on the iron trap of the door and asks for water, which is brought in a tin-pot. Then follow intervals of smoking, incoherent mutterings that pass for conversation, borrowings of matches, knockings with the pannikin on the cell door wicket or trap for more water, matches, and bail; false and fitful starts into slumber perhaps—or wild attempts at flight on the part of our souls into that other world that the sober and sane know nothing of; and, gradually, suddenly it seems, reason (if this world is reasonable) comes back.

"What's your trouble?"

"Don't know. Bomb outrage, perhaps."

"Drunk?"

"Yes."

"What's yours?"

"Same boat."

But presently he is plainly uneasy (and I am getting that way, too, to tell the truth), and, after moving about, and walking up and down in the narrow space as well as we can, he "rings up" another policeman, who happens to be the fat one who is to be in charge all night.

"Wot's up here?"

"What have I been up to?"

"Killin' a Chinaman. Go to sleep."

Policemen peers in at me inquiringly, but I forbear to ask questions.

Blankets are thrown in by a friend of mine in the force, though we are not entitled to them until we are bailed or removed to the "Paddock" (the big drunks' dormitory and dining cell at the Central), and we proceed to make ourselves comfortable. My mate wonders whether he asked them to send to his wife to get bail, and hopes he didn't.

They have left our wicket open, seeing, or rather hearing, that we are quiet. But they have seemingly left some other wickets open also, for from a neighbouring cell comes the voice of Mrs Johnson holding forth. The locomotive has apparently just been run into the cleaning sheds, and her fires have not had time to cool. They say that Mrs Johnson was a "lady once", like many of her kind; that she is not a "bad woman"—that is, not a woman of loose character—but gets money sent to her from somewhere—from her "family", or her husband, perhaps. But when she lets herself loose—or rather, when the beer lets her loose—she is a tornado and a terror in Red Rock Lane, and it is only her fierce, practical kindness to her unfortunate or poverty-stricken sisters in her sober moments that keeps her forgiven in that classic thoroughfare. She can certainly speak "like a lady" when she likes, and like an intelligent, even a clever, woman—not like a "woman of the world", but as a woman who knew and knows the world, and is in hell. But now her language is the language of a rough shearer in a rough shed on a blazing hot day.

After a while my mate calls out to her:

"Oh! for God's sake give it a rest!"

Whereupon Mrs Johnson straightaway opens on him and his ancestry, and his mental, moral, and physical condition—especially the latter. She accuses him of every crime known to Christian countries and some Asiatic and ancient ones. She wants to know how long he has been out of jail for kicking his wife to pieces that time when she was up as a witness against him, and whether he is in for the same thing again? (She has never set eyes on him, by the way, nor he on her.)

He calls back that she is not a respectable woman, and he knows all about her.

Thereupon she shrieks at him and bangs and kicks at her door, and demands his name and address. It would appear that she *is* a respectable woman, and hundreds can prove it, and she is going to make him prove it in open court.

He calls back that his name is Percy Reginald Grainger, and his town residence is The Mansions, Macleay Street, next to Mr Isaacs, the magistrate, and he also gives her the address of his solicitor.

She bangs and shrieks again, and states that she will get his name from the charge-sheet in the morning and have him up for criminal libel, and have his cell mate up as a witness—and hers, too. But just here a policeman comes along and closes her wicket with a bang and cuts her off, so that her statements becomes indistinct, or come only as shrieks from a lost soul in an underground dungeon. He also threatens to cut us off and smother us if we don't shut up. I wonder whether they've got her in the padded cell.

We settle down again, but presently my fellow-captive nudges me and says: "Listen!" From another cell comes the voice of a woman singing—the girl who is in for "inciting to resist, your worship", in fact. "Listen!" he says, "that woman could sing once." Her voice is low and sweet and plaintive, as of a woman who had been a singer but had lost her voice. And what do you think it is?

The crowd in accents hushed reply—
"Jesus of Nazareth passeth by."

Mrs Johnson's cell is suddenly silent. Then, not mimickingly, mockingly, or scornfully, but as if the girl is a champion of Jesus of Nazareth, and is hurt at the ignorance of the multitude, and pities *Him*;

Now who is this Jesus of Nazareth, say?

The policeman, coming along the passage, closes the wicket in her door, but softly this time, and not before we catch the plaintive words again.

The crowd in accents hushed reply—
"Jesus of Nazareth passeth by."

My fellow-felon throws the blanket off him impatiently, sits up with a jerk, and gropes for his pipe.

"God!" he says. "But this is red hot! Have you got another match?"

I wonder what the Nazarene would have to say about it.

Sleep for a while. I wonder whether they'll give us time, or we'll be able to sleep some of our sins off in the end, as we sleep our drink off here? Then the "Paddock" and daylight; but there's little time for the Paddock here, for we must soon be back in court. The men borrow and lend and divide tobacco, lend even pipes, while some break up hard tobacco and roll cigarettes with bits of newspaper. If it is Sunday morning, even those who have no hope for bail, and have a long horrible day and night before them, will sometimes join in a cheer as the more fortunate are bailed. But the others have tea and bread and butter brought to them by one of the Prisoners' Aid Societies, who ask for no religion in return. They come to save bodies, and not to fish for souls. The men walk up and down and to and fro, and cross and recross incessantly, as caged men and animals always do—and as some uncaged men do too.

"Any of you gentlemen want breakfast?" Those who have money and appetites order; some order for the sake of the tea alone; and some shout two or three extra breakfasts for those who had nothing on them when they were run in. We low people can be very kind to each other in trouble. But now it's time to call us out by the lists, marshal us up in the passage, and draft us into court. Ladies first. But I forgot that I am out on bail, and that the foregoing belongs to another occasion. Or was it only imagination, or hearsay? Journalists have got themselves run in before now, in order to see and hear and feel and smell for themselves—and write.

"Silence! Order in the Court." I come like a shot out of my nightmare, or trance, or what you will, and we all rise as the magistrate takes his seat. None of us noticed him come in, but he's there, and I've a quaint idea that he bowed to his audience. Kindly, humorous Mr Isaacs, whom we have lost, always gave me that idea. And, while he looks over his papers, the women seem to group themselves, unconsciously as it were, with Mrs Johnson as front centre, as though they depended on her in some vague way. She has slept it off and tidied, or been tidied, up, and is as clear-headed as she ever will be. Crouching directly behind her, supported and comforted on one side by One-Eyed Kate, and on the other by Cock-Eyed Sal, is the poor bedraggled little resister of the Law, sobbing convulsively, her breasts and thin shoulders heaving and shaking under her openwork blouse—the girl who seemed to pity Jesus of Nazareth last night in her cell. There's very little inciting to resist about her now. Most women can cry when they like, I know, and many have cried men to jail and the gallows; but *here* in *this place*, if a woman's tears can avail her anything, who, save perhaps a police-court solicitor and gentleman-by-Act-of-Parliament, would, or dare, raise a sneer.

I wonder what the Nazarene would have to say about it if He came in to speak for her. But probably they'd send Him to the receiving house as a person of unsound mind, or give Him worse punishment for drunkenness and contempt of court.

His Worship looks up.

Mrs Johnson (from the dock): "Good morning, Mr Isaacs. How do you do? You're looking very well this morning, Mr Isaacs."

His Worship (from the Bench): "Thank you, Mrs Johnson. I'm feeling very well this morning."

There's a pause, but there is no "laughter". The would-be satellites don't know whom the laugh might be against. His Worship bends over the papers again, and I can see that he is having trouble with that quaintly humorous and kindly smile, or grin, of his. He has as hard a job to control his smile and get it off his face as some magistrates have to get a smile on to theirs. And there's a case coming by and by that he'll have to look a bit serious over. However——

"Jane Johnson!"

Mrs Johnson is here present, and reminds the Sergeant that she is.

Then begins, or does begin in most courts, the same dreary old drone, like the giving out of a hymn, of the same dreary old charge: "You — Are — Charged — With — Being — Drunk — And — Disorderly — In — Such — And — Such — A — Street — How — Do — You — Plead — Guilty — Or — Not — Guilty?" But they are less orthodox here. The "disorderly" has dropped out of Mrs Johnson's charge somehow, on the way from the charge-room. I don't know what has been going on behind the scenes, but, anyway, it is Christmas-time, and the Sergeant seems anxious to let Mrs Johnson off lightly. It means anything from twenty-four hours or five shillings to three months on the Island for her. The lawyers and the police—especially the lawyers—are secretly afraid of Mrs Johnson.

However, again——

The Sergeant: "This woman has not been here for six weeks, your Worship."

Mrs Johnson (who has him set and has been waiting for him for a year or so): "It's a damned lie, Mr Isaacs. I was here last Wednesday!" Then, after a horrified pause in the Court: "But I beg *your* pardon, Mr Isaacs."

His Worship's head goes down again. The "laughter" doesn't come here, either. There is a whispered consultation, and (it being Christmas-time) they compromise with Mrs Johnson for "five shillings or the risin'", and she thanks his Worship and is escorted out, rather more hurriedly than is comportable with her dignity, for she remarks about it.

The members of the Johnsonian sisterhood have reason to be thankful for the lift she has given them, for they all get off lightly, and even the awful resister of Law-an'-order is forgiven. Mrs Johnson has money and is waiting outside to stand beers for them; she always shouts for the boys when she has it. And—what good does it all do?

It is very hard to touch the heart of a woman who is down, though they are intensely sympathetic amongst themselves. It is nearly as hard as it is to combat the pride of a hard-working woman in poverty. It was such women as Mrs Johnson, One-Eyed Kate, and their sisters who led Paris to Versailles, and a King and a Queen died for it. It is such women as Mrs Johnson and One-Eyed Kate and their sisters who will lead a greater Paris to a greater Versailles some day, and many "Trust" kings and queens, and their princes and princesses shall die for it. And that reminds me of two reports in a recent great daily:

Miss Angelina De Tapps, the youngest daughter of the well-known great family of brewers, was united in the holy bonds of matrimony to Mr Reginald Wells—(here follows a long account of the smart society wedding). The happy pair leave *en route* for Europe per the ——— next Friday.

Jane Johnson, an old offender, again faced the music before Mr Isaacs, S.M., at the Central yesterday morning—(here follows a "humorous" report of the case).

Next time poor Mrs Johnson will leave *en route* for "Th' Island" and stay there three months.

The sisters join Mrs Johnson, who has some money and takes them to a favourite haunt and shouts for them—as she does for the boys sometimes. Their opinions on civilization are not to be printed.

Ginger and Wingy get off with the option, and, though the fine is heavy, it is paid. They adjourn with Boko Bill, and their politics are lurid.

Squinny Peters (plain drunk—five bob or the risin'), who is peculiar for always paying his fine, elects to take it out this time. It appears that the last time Squinny got five bob or the risin' he ante'd up the splosh like a man, and the Court rose immediately, to Squinny's intense disgust. He isn't taking any chances this time.

Wild-Flowers-Charley, who recently did a fortnight, and has been out on bail, has had a few this morning, and, in spite of warnings from and promises to friends, insists on making a statement, though by simply pleading guilty he might get off easily. The statement lasts some ten minutes. Mr Isaacs listens patiently and politely and remarks:

"Fourteen days."

Charley saw the humour of it afterwards, he says.

But what good does it all do?"

I had no wish to treat drunkenness frivolously in beginning this sketch; I have seen women in the horrors—that ought to be enough.

The Green Lady

PREVIOUS CONVICTIONS' little, dumpy, sawn-off swag was standing on end right in the middle of the garden path opposite my front veranda steps, like the daylight ghost of a little, furred, grey-white stump; but Previous himself was nowhere to be detected. However, he faded in presently, round the big grey front gate-post and on to the lower step; and glancing along the bank of the irrigation channel, in the direction from which he had come, I was aware of a turned-down brim of a hat and a pair of drawn-up knees just showing behind a tree.

After a while the voice of Previous was vague in the hot, heavy air.

"I left Dotty along there behind the ornamental tree," he said, "but I lost sight of his hat for a minute when I got here, so I went back to see if he was goin' in for a swim—or tryin' to thieve the canal. But he was only down in the reeds fishing for yabbies with a bit of meat on a string."

(I might mention that yabbies are little things of the crayfish kind that undermine the banks of the irrigation channels and help let the water soak on and waste, while the reeds do their best to choke the channels, and have to be cut every year.)

"I promised once to tell you why I brought Dotty from the river," Previous went on, "after old S'Sam gave us permission to camp an' fish an' shoot there, and after he'd thieved the cow that chased me into the water—I mean Dotty did, not old S'Sam. The fish leave off biting after Easter, and it was the last of the soft nights. You know the rain that come last week? Well, it started next night and we was out in it all. We was miserable—drenched an' wet an' cold, in spite of a fire we had under the lee of the log. Dotty rigged a sort of a fly between the log and two saplings that stood near it—did it with one of his blankets and pieces of clothes-line he'd thieved from somewhere. Thieved 'em for me to hang meself with, I suppose, if I felt that way. But the blanket sagged and leaked worse than the sky did, so I had to take it down to keep us from bein' drowned as well as froze.

"The weather held up a bit to let in the daybreak, and Dotty built the fire and I had a sleep, crouched up against the log. When I woke, Dotty was gone and the rain coming on again, and I didn't know how long I'd been unconscious. I sploshed through it all to the station, but Dotty wasn't there, and they didn't seem like as if old S'Sam or anything else was missin'. They wanted me to stay and have breakfast and dry meself at the big old fireplace; but I told 'em I had to go and look after my mate, and they understood that. One of the stationhands looked up the best part of an old oilcoat that had belonged to him, and an old canvas raincoat that had belonged to a horse, and made me take them. When I got back to the camp Dotty wasn't there again, and just when I was going to give it up I seen him comin' across a creek from the old Hay road. He had a real waterproof tent-fly that he'd borrowed from some civilized blacks—the last of the Hay tribe, that lived in a corrugated-iron camp across the road, towards Yanco railway station. He said they'd lent it to him, and I believed him. You see, Dotty doesn't lie; he either tells the truth or smiles that vacant, idiot smile of his, and says nothing. I wondered what the blacks thought of Dotty; and, to have done with that, when we returned the fly on our way here Dotty and the old king and queen grinned at each other a treat. Perhaps he could talk some of their lingo and sing the songs of their childhood—songs he'd learnt in his first childhood.

"Well, Dotty fixed the fly and cooked breakfast between showers. He built up a roaring fire that held its own in spite of the rain that got at it, and what with the wind and the fire he got the blankets dry. Next he kept throwing hot coals and ashes under the fly, and sweeping 'em off. Then he pulled down a lot of boughs, when it held up a bit, and beat the wet out of 'em against a tree, and dried 'em out against the fire; and we spread the old horse-rug and oilcoat on them and made a good camp-bed. We'd kept the bread and flour and things dry in the burnt-out hollow at the bottom of an old tree, an' we drank hot tea and lay on our backs on a dry bed and under dry blankets, and didn't care for nothing nor nobody—at least, I didn't; I had a book to read. And, if he didn't feel it, Dotty looked as happy as if he'd thieved Heaven.

"Dotty had got some wire-fence posts from a pile up the river-bank and stacked them to the side of me, away from the fire, to make it warmer and keep the wind off. And to make us feel more happy and comfortable the rain and the wind came on like they did the night before. But we were all right so long as the wind stayed in that quarter. A stationhand rode up, between the rainstorms, in a big oilskin overcoat, with the tail of it spread out on his horse's rump, and bent down on his horse's neck and said, 'Day, mates. It's a wet day.' Dotty pointed to the billy of tea on the coals and jerked his thumb up to where there was a pint-pot upside-down on the log. The stationhand said 'Thank yer,' and got down from his horse, and Dotty reached him the sugar-bag and he had some tea. The stationhand's wet sheep-dog came up, too, and shook himself on the other side of the fire; then he dodged round closer to us, and laughed at us in a friendly way. The stationhand stood by the fire for a while; then he scratched the back of his head with his little finger, and said 'So-long,' and got on his horse and rode off, and his dog went after him.

"Nobody else come to see us except an old magpie. Dotty threw it a bit of meat and so startled it that it jumped away—it'd thought Dotty was asleep. It swore at Dotty; and then it snatched up the meat and flew off with it. By and by it come back and cursed Dotty some more an' woke me; so Dotty threw it another bit of meat, and it swore its thanks and flew away with that, too. I suppose it wanted that bit for its wife and kids. Anyway, it come back again and had a last piece comfortably by itself on the dry ground by the fire after cursing Dotty and all his family, good and hard, for about two minutes. It said Dotty was a foundling, or something such—like any other real bushman does when he meets an old mate unexpected after some years.

"I heard that all the wild magpies were half tame round Leeton until young civil-servant gawps came round bangin' off guns at 'em. I've seen one of them fancy fishermen la-di-dahs down there by the river shoot a bird like a curlew and break its leg. There was a strong barb-wire and netted fence between 'em, so he couldn't get at what he'd shot. But the bird kept hopping round on one leg, with his face towards us all the time, screamin' out, for all the world, 'Now-see-what-yer-done!' 'Now-see-what-yer-done!' 'Now-see-what-yer-done!' till his mates come an' got him away.

"Well, to get on with it. The rain and wind come on with the night, worse 'n' the first night; but the wind still held in the right quarter for us—as if all the winds in the Southern World lived there an' was goin' up to blow all the Japs outer the North o' Queensland. But we was as snug as two rugs in a bug—what yer grinnin' at?—an' I slept well. Till something woke me. Yer know how something wakes yer—anywhere in Australia; whether in the bosom of your family, when a child gets sick at night, or in the bush, or in quod. The rain had cleared at midnight, as it does at midday in Sydney mostly, and it was broad moonlight, and all was still. But Dotty was gone agen. I reckoned maybe he mighter gone with that old magpie of his, to look after his red cow an' calf, 'n' inquire how they was gettin' on, an' whether they'd found a warm gully outer the wind to sleep in. So I give it best, an' stood up an' stretched meself, an' put some more limbs on the fire, an' turned round an' took in the scenery.

"The tourists never see the Murrumbidgee as it is; they never see it even in the mountains above Burrinjuck, nor below it, either—except perhaps at Gundagai or Narrandera or Hay. Where they do see it it's like pictures of the Upper Darling at Bourke, except for the river timber, and that grows tall and straight and sound mostly. But down here it's the oldest river in the world, in the oldest bush. Them knotted an' gnarled an' stunted an' twisted old trees have been burnt out in a hundred bushfires, an' rotted in a hundred floods: but they won't die—except where the fire has burnt 'em down, or the floods have undermined 'em an' the river drowned 'em an' poisoned 'em with slime an' mud. But you've been there, an' you know.

"Well, right opposite to that camp we had there on the Murrumbidgee, but a bit lower down," said Previous, "there's a sort of island with a tree right in the middle of the river. It's greener than anything anywhere around. It doesn't seem to belong to Australia at all. The tree and the little island seem all one; the island must be matted roots an' moss mostly, and it's bin through an' under God knows how many floods. The whole thing looks like a lady, dressed just as yer mother used to dress in the seventies or the eighties—bonnet and bustle, full-back skirt an' all, just leanin' forward an' glidin' up the river. They call her the Green Lady, and she's always glidin' up the stream. The faster the current runs the faster the Green Lady seems to glide. While all other trees are dark, with black shadders, there she is green in the moonlight, gliding up the river, and seeming more anxious than ever to get there, as if she had a son in trouble up somewhere at the head of it.

"I'd turned in agen, but just as it seemed I was droppin' off there was sounds—or, rather, one great sound. It seemed to me at first as if it was the Sydney Town Hall organ playin' an' all the kids round Darling Harbour singin'. I thought, for the moment, that my mate Dotty had thieved the Heavenly Choir, or the other one, or both, an' brought 'em to entertain me. I sat up quick, and the sound went. I crawled from under the tent-fly and knelt up and looked over the log that was protectin' us from the weather, but there was nothing there, except the everlasting old haunting of the bush in the moonlight. So I stood up. The wind had changed to another quarter, an' it was blowin' quite warm. The moon went under some of the bluey-white clouds that was flyin' home—like kids that had frightened 'emselves tellin' ghost yarns. An' I heard a man's voice—it seemed like a mad preacher's voice. I jumped round like a party politician that smells dissolution. The moon popped out from behind the flying kiddy-clouds, an' I looked along the steep clay bank. There was Dotty, standin' half-way down near the water, on the steep clay bank, on a sort of ledge we'd dug to fish from, clear in ther moonlight."

Previous Convictions paused a while, and seemed to think of it as if in a vague way he didn't approve of it.

"It was Dotty, all right," he continued—"Dotty standing there on that clay ledge above the river that was full of black snags in the moonlight. But the voice wasn't Dotty's, an' the man, to look at him, wasn't Dotty. Either he was—well, he was another man and was raving; an' the worst of it was it was sane ravin'. He was standin' up straight, facing across the river to the Green Lady, and wavin' his arms and ravin' to her. He was ravin' about his ruined life and his wrongs and woman's devilment and lies—most of the things I knew about him and a good many I didn't. He raved about his life before he was married, and his family, and his wife, and the other man. He raved about relations who spread lies, and he cursed all neighbours who listen to them, and all smug, comfortable magistrates who listen to them, and who send innocent men to jail and starvation and disgrace, and drive them to drink and madness. And he cursed all soft, good-natured fools of husbands; though I don't know what he did that for.

"And the Green Lady didn't say anything, but kept gliding up the river as if she was in a hurry to get past; but all the other crooked old witch trees up on the level seemed to wave their broken, blackened arms and ragged fingers an' sing an' curse an' rave too.

"I sat down on a broken limb of the log, about knocked up, an' took me head in me hands. If that was Dotty sane, I'd rather have him dotty. It was a lot worse than the nights when he pinched the garden-chair and the mat and the stained-glass angel for me to furnish a stable with.

"What with worry and want of rest and sleep, with sheer funk, there were so many sounds and voices in my head that I didn't notice, for a minute or two, that Dotty's new mad voice had stopped. As soon as I noticed it I jumped up, and couldn't see Dotty anywhere. I thought he'd gone into the river and down with it. And then there came to me a new, cold, sudden terror—swift as they say things come to a drownin' man. You know what it would look like to come away from a place like that in the bush without yer mate!

"Perhaps it was the worry an' want of rest, and the guilty knowledge of me old criminal tendencies; but it was worse than all me old previous conwictions put together, with a charge of house-breakin' an' manslaughter thrown in, and detectives standin' across the street lookin' as innercent as fourteen Chinamen outside a fan-tan an' opium joint. An' here, of all times, them lines of 'Gilrooney', the outback poet, come ringin' in me ears:

'Twas Murderin' Mick who killed his mate between the dawn an' day;
He cut his throat from ear to ear, and left him where he lay.
'Twas Murderin' Mick that came to wear a queer white cap at morn,
An' ne'er before in Goulburn Gaol was cap so lightly worn.

"I had a mad thought that I saw the cap, an' wondered how it would fit me. I even felt it over me ears, with an elastic-band under 'em—an' the band seemed to hurt more than the rope did. No, I don't want to wear a queer white cap at morn, or any other time, for that matter; and I don't think I'd wear it lightly, neither, for Dotty nor no one else—no matter how much he deserves it.

"But just as I was sliding down the steep bank to the river—whether with an idea of savin' Dotty from drownin' an' me from ther gallows, or, failin' that, drownin' meself for the same reason, I don't know—but just then I seen a bunyip or something heave itself onter the mud, an' Dotty comes climbin' up the bank on three legs, with a fish in the other. He'd been down attending to the lines, and got a fish off one of 'em. Either his mad-sane fit had passed or it was all a dream.

"Dotty put the fish in an old kerosene-tin half-full of water that he kept for the purpose. He reckoned it was cruel to string 'em through the gills and mouth on a reed or string or piece of wire, and hang 'em from a branch or let 'em die slow in the dust and dirt. No—he kept 'em alive an' as happy as they could be till he was ready to clean 'em. Poor Dotty never knew how he got me in the gills sometimes.

"I turned in an' slept till the sun was up amongst the tree-trunks, bright an' white an' hot; but Dotty had rigged boughs to keep it off my face. He was cookin' breakfast when I woke; it was the smell of it that woke me. (Did yer ever smell bacon or chops cookin' at the camp-fire in the mornin' when you was hungry?) Dotty had fish and ham, and last night's bread from the stationhand cook. Mine was fried ham, and Dotty brought breakfast to me in bed in an old tin-plate that he'd found and straightened and polished with ashes. He was just his same old good-natured idiotic self again. His old red cow and calf came to the edge of the bank and looked down at us—looked at Dotty in a mild, anxious, motherly sort of way, as if she thought he might have been a twin-calf that she'd forgot. Me she gave a last look of disgust and went away."

Previous Convictions thought a while. Then he said: "That last night on the river was enough for me, and I'd made up my mind to bring Dotty away from it, whether he was a stained angel or a stained devil or a moon-struck lunatic—whatever he was. We went to the station to say good-bye to the ratty cook and the good-natured stationhand, and take back the old raincoats they'd lent us; but they wouldn't have 'em, and I'm glad they wouldn't, though they're a bit more load; for we'll want 'em on the Hay track this winter.

"I forgot to tell yer that the men's quarters at Yanco are in the old homestead, behind the Mansion, an' the pint-pots and bread and meat and sugar are slid out fer 'travellers' in the same old hospitable way on the big old cedar dinin'-room table, in the long old dinin'-room with its high panelled ceilin' an' wall and deep panelled doorways and winders, an' the cook standin' with his legs wide apart, an' his back to the big old-fashioned fireplace, presidin' an' beamin' like a prodigal father. He was short and stout, with a big apron, an' looked like a sea-cook, an' he was ratty—like all station and shearers' cooks I'd ever seen. He gave me some poetry he'd wrote about old S'Sam and got printed, and some he'd made up about himself; and as much tucker as we'd like to carry; and so we went back to camp to roll up our swags.

"A lot of magpies come round and cursed us till Dotty threw out the rest of the meat for 'em, and they sung 'For He's a Jolly Good Feller' as we took the track.

"Before we struck the road Dotty called at a little old slab-and-iron cottage standin' by itself in a garden 'longside McCaughey's old main irrigation canal—all full of tall reeds now except for a narrow channel of clear water, and looking wonderfully fresh and green. An old Irish couple lived there, private and independent. They were old retainers, I suppose. They seemed to have seen Dotty before this trip—perhaps in one of his private peregrinations—and knew he was afflicted, for the old woman crossed herself, and the old man took off his hat. It looked as if he only took it off at other times when he went to bed, 'n' perhaps not then. And they told us of a short cut across the paddocks, an' pointed where to strike it. After we left them Dotty's old magpie caught us and come with us, and nagged at us from the top of every wire-fence post for about a mile; but he took us the short cut all right, and gave us a good, hearty, affectionate cursing at the end."

Ah Soon

I don't know whether a story about a Chinaman would be popular or acceptable here and now; and, for the matter of that, I don't care. I am anti-Chinese as far as Australia is concerned; in fact, I am all for a White Australia. But one may dislike, or even hate, a nation without hating or disliking an individual of that nation. One may be on friendly terms; even pals in a way. I had a good deal of experience with the Chinese in the old years; and I never knew or heard of a Chinaman who neglected to pay his debts, who did a dishonest action, or who forgot a kindness to him or his, or was not charitable when he had the opportunity.

I want to tell the story of one Chinaman I knew; a vegetable John who had a white heart. He was an old and extremely plain Chinaman, with a very fat and flabby face; or rather, withered, lined and wrinkled like one of his own turnips that had lain out on the roof during a drought—and about the same colour. If he had any expression at all it was one of agonized anxiety—perhaps for fear his old horse should fall down. He and his countrymen had gardens on Lawson's Creek (not named after the writer), near Mudgee, N.S.W. He drove a long, bony horse, in a long, rickety cart, with a slip of tin on the side of it, whereon was written in white letters on a black ground, the name AH SOON. It looked like a sigh.

Looking out of the front door of a house, or rather hut—say, on a blazing Monday or Friday that made the shadow of the house nearly black—you'd see the hammer-head of Ah Soon's old horse slowly come into focus; then the shoulders, the reins above jerk, jerk, jerking incessantly; then the rest of him up to the step-board of the cart; then the tin plate with its sad "Ah Soon", and above it, well in front, old Ah Soon himself, a withered, drooping image of the Patience of the Ages, jogging the reins unceasingly. I never saw him hit that horse—never saw a whip or stick. How he "got there" the Lord only knows; but he did, for he always turned up to time on his next round—and his was a long weary round through the dusty hot scrubs, too, and back to the Creek. He bought another cart from my father, when his own went to pieces; but he never bought another horse. I remember that he, a younger partner, and a son, or nephew, or something (lately from China), had dinner with us on the conclusion of the bargain, and very decent and unembarrassed Chinamen they proved themselves to be. Let it be understood that this was in the Dry Districts many years ago, when saints and sinners, Christian and heathen, European and Asiatic were fighting a long and cruel drought side by side; through blazing days that seemed black to their blighted eyes. If men couldn't be brothers, or at least charitable and kind and courteous to each other and forgetful of nationality and creed under such conditions—when could they?

Ah Soon used to assure his clients that all his melons were "wi' 'art" (white heart), which, of course, none of them should have been. He knew that that was a good thing about a cabbage, and he applied the phrase to all his goods to indicate their perfect condition. His melons were red-hearted enough, so long as the drought left enough liquid in Lawson's Creek to feed his water-wheel (of a fashion some ten thousand years old), working day and night to water his garden.

His days were Mondays and Fridays, and we called him "Next-time-Friday"; because if he didn't have a vegetable wanted when he came on Monday he'd always say "All li'! Nexy-time-Fliday."

We got to like the old man, and when the Great Drought was coming to a climax he told us that we could come and cart off his hopeless crop of young pumpkins to feed our starving and pleuro-stricken milkers.

At the garden, with the cart, I made the acquaintance of a young Chinaman named Ah See, or something like that. He was a very bright, good-natured, good-humoured, half-childishly shy young fellow—they generally are. He was a son, or nephew, of Ah Soon. He could both speak and write a little English, and was learning something about weights and measures and figures, for business purposes, and I, being a bush schoolboy, used to help him a bit with lbs., cwts., and other things that I've forgotten now; also with his writing—he called it "delightum".

Well, to make a short story shorter, they were one day passing near our place with a cartload of stringybark poles (not the old vegetable horse this time) when the cart went over on a steep siding—this main road hadn't been graded or "made" then. The two other Chinamen on the cart were thrown clear, but poor Ah

Soon got the most of the load on top of him. My father was on hand—he generally was in times of sickness, trouble or danger—and, with the help of the other two Chinamen, he got Ah Soon clear. He seemed hurt about the ribs or chest. Mother came running from the house, dragging the best mattress, and carrying a dipper of water. (She was a strong bushwoman in those days.) We fixed up Ah Soon as well as we could, got the cart righted, and the mattress in it, with the addition of some pillows, and got Ah Soon on to them; and father started off with them for the hospital and the doctor at Mudgee. Ah Soon was conscious all the time, and very "thank you". He said that he was "All li'." Ah See told us "All li'—lospital", when he came out next day for the poles; but Ah Soon never came back "Nexy-time-Fliday", nor the Friday after. He never came back any more, and I have no doubt, from what I saw of Ah See, that Ah Soon's old bones have been peacefully mouldering in China this many a long year.

We left the district shortly after the accident, and drifted to the city, as many a bush family did. And the years went past. And my father went from his earthly toil to his fathers—the same way as Ah Soon went to his. And I went up in the world, and round the world, as the years rolled on, and came down in the world, and at length anchored for a while in a little cottage in a dirty little street in a mean Sydney suburb. And there the bailiff visited me. Or, rather, the landlady put him in. We got friendly, the bailiff and I; but when I sent him out for beer one night while I was trying to write him out in verses he got drunk and was run in; so I had to bail him out and bring him home—but that has got nothing to do with the yarn.

A Chinaman used to come round there with vegetables. There was no white greengrocer handy, and, anyhow, the white fruit and vegetable hawkers in those days were spiteful weeds of the larrikin variety, with the cigarette dribbling out of the corner of their mouths. They'd stick a foot in the doorway and insult the wife, likely as not, if they thought there was no man about. A Chinaman would never do that. This John was flat-faced and deeply wrinkled and anxious-looking. Perhaps he'd gone up in the world, and come down in the world, and had had a bailiff amongst his cabbages, so to speak. He'd come to the front garden gate and call out "Veger-buls!" before setting down his baskets, only stooping so that they just rested on the ground—the stick still heavy on the shoulders. Then, if no one appeared within a reasonable time, he'd call out "Vegerbuls!" again, louder and more gruffly, and with more than a touch of impatience, gripping his stick firmer fore and aft, and stiffening his knees, preparatory to straightening up, after giving his pants a hitch with one hand. Then, if no one came, he'd bark out "Vegerbuls!" like a very gruff watchdog, in one short bark, straighten up, give his baskets a hoist, and depart.

One morning I got into conversation with "Vegerbuls" when he happened to be at the gate. I asked him how he was getting on (I always called him "Asia" to his face), and he said "All li'," with that rare smile of his that redeemed his ugliness and made it pleasing. And then, a tantalizing half-memory recurring to me, I asked him, involuntarily as it were, if he'd ever been up the country. And he said: "Long time ago."

And then it came out that he knew "Log Pladdock", and had worked in a Chinese garden at Lawson's Creek. But even then, of course, I didn't connect him with old Ah Soon.

When, at our next meeting, "Vegerbuls" addressed me by name, I wasn't surprised. I suppose he'd ascertained it from one of the neighbours. But when he asked me if my "sissister" was alive I was rather puzzled and indignant. I suppose now he meant my mother, whose kindness he remembered as a young man. She was only between eighteen and nineteen years older than I. But how he knew later on that I had the bailiff in, the Lord only knows, unless some unknown spiteful neighbour had told him. He brought us the usual jar of preserved ginger a few days earlier this year; also a box of delicious preserved turnip.

A few days before the bailiff was due to sell, "Vegerbuls" told me that he had sold out his garden to a cousin of his, and he was going to China, but he didn't know whether he was coming back. He said his cousin would "come lound". "Never mind vegerbuls," he said; meaning that the "cledit" would go on as usual.

The last day he came was the last day but one of the bailiff—the day before the sale, when the few poor sticks, so hardly got together, would go for half their value—perhaps less. And I felt pretty miserable about it, I can tell you.

We owed "Vegerbuls" money. He said nothing; he lifted out a clean new basket that fitted into the top of one of his big ones.

They were nearly empty, and he was on his way home. It was piled with assorted vegetables, and he placed it inside the gate-post.

"Me go 'way next week," he said.

"I can't pay you, Asia," I said, hopelessly.

"Never mind. Pay my cousin. He send it." He took a long clean deal box from under where the basket had been, and handed it to me.

"Chillun," he said simply.

I supposed it was a box of Chinese sweets or toys for the children. Then he shot this at me: "Bellailiff man here yet?"

I was too dull to be surprised or indignant; but I roused myself just a little bit.

"What do you mean, Asia?" I said.

"Log Pladdock," said Asia, with that innocent centuries-old smile that baffles and disarms one. "My fader."

"Yes, he's here yet," I said, weary of it all—referring to the "bellailiff" man. I couldn't see the connection between Log Pladdock and his "fader" (presumably in China with a long white horse-tail beard and in an outlandish dress) and a miserable, sordid little "selling-up" in a mean, miserable suburb of Sydney. "Sell off tomorrow," I said. "But I'll see your cousin paid. Thank you very much for the things, Asia. Good luck, a pleasant voyage!"

He felt in the pocket of his shabby coat and handed me a flaming red envelope.

"You take that. Open by and by. Give bellailiff man," he said, speaking with fearful rapidity, and fixing his tackle and hoisting his baskets with a lightning dexterity that I'd never seen equalled by a Chinaman. "You teach me delightum!—Ah See! Good-bye!" And with an outward throw of his free arm and hand he trotted round the corner towards the market gardens and departed—for Asia, I suppose, as I never saw or heard of him again.

I had a vague notion that the red envelope contained lottery tickets for the bailiff, and that "Vegerbuls" had thought it fitting and proper to make presents to my entire household. I couldn't make out what he meant by my teaching him "delightum"—unless I had taught him the "luxury of doing good"—and "Ah See?" seemed strange in the mouth of a Chinaman, as I took him to mean "D' yer see?"

When I opened the red envelope I found that it contained a half-sheet of common ruled writing paper, folded over a five-pound note

and a one-pound note; and five pounds was just within a shilling or so of the amount my bailiff was in for! And on both sides of the half-sheet of notepaper was written, or rather printed, the words—
AH SOON.

Then it slowly dawned on me—and I saw: "Vegerbuls" was Ah See, the son of the old Ah Soon, and I was the son of my father and mother; and my father and my mother had been good to Ah Soon, the father of Ah See; and Ah See had remembered. Besides, I used to teach him "delightum" in those dim, half-forgotten days. "You cannot fathom the Oriental mind," they say. It seems very simple to me.

Ah See's cousin came next week, as bland and childlike a young Chinaman as you'd wish to meet. He cheerfully accepted the overdue vegetable money later on, to send to Ah See; but when I wanted him to take and send the six pounds he didn't "savvy", and he went on "no savvying".

A Double Buggy at Lahey's Creek

I

SPUDS, AND A WOMAN'S OBSTINACY

EVER since we were married it had been Mary's great ambition to have a buggy. The house or furniture didn't matter so much—out there in the bush where we were—but, where there were no railways or coaches, and the roads were long and mostly hot and dusty, a buggy was the great thing. I had a few pounds when we were married, and was going to get one then; but new buggies went high, and another party got hold of a second-hand one that I'd had my eye on, so Mary thought it over and at last she said, "Never mind the buggy, Joe; get a sewing-machine and I'll be satisfied. I'll want the machine more than the buggy, for a while. Wait till we're better off."

After that, whenever I took a contract—to put up a fence or woolshed, or sink a dam or something—Mary would say, "You ought to knock a buggy out of this job, Joe;" but something always turned up—bad weather or sickness. Once I cut my foot with the adze and was laid up; and, another time, a dam I was making was washed away by a flood before I finished it. Then Mary would say, "Ah, well—never mind, Joe. Wait till we are better off." But she felt it hard the time I built a woolshed and didn't get paid for it, for we'd as good as settled about another second-hand buggy then.

I always had a fancy for carpentering, and was handy with tools. I made a spring-cart—body and wheels—in spare time, out of colonial hardwood, and got Little the blacksmith to do the ironwork: I painted the cart myself. It wasn't much lighter than one of the tip-drays I had, but it *was* a spring-cart, and Mary pretended to be satisfied with it: anyway, I didn't hear any more of the buggy for a while.

I sold that cart for fourteen pounds, to a Chinese gardener who wanted a strong cart to carry his vegetables round through the bush. It was just before our first youngster came: I told Mary that I wanted the money in case of extra expense—and she didn't fret much at losing the cart. But the fact was that I was going to make another try for a buggy, as a present for Mary when the child was born. I thought of getting the turn-out while she was laid up, keeping it dark from her till she was on her feet again, and then showing her the buggy standing in the shed. But she had a bad time, and I had to have the doctor regularly, and get a proper nurse, and a lot of things extra; so the buggy idea was knocked on the head. I was set on it, too; I'd thought of how, when Mary was up and getting strong, I'd say one morning, "Go round and have a look in the shed, Mary; I've got a few fowls for you," or something like that—and follow her round to watch her eyes when she saw the buggy. I never told Mary about that—it wouldn't have done any good.

Later on I got some good timber—mostly scraps that were given to me—and made a light body for a spring-cart. Galletly, the coach-builder at Cudgegong, had got a dozen pairs of American hickory wheels up from Sydney, for light spring-carts, and he let me have a pair for cost price and carriage. I got him to iron the cart, and he put it through the paint-shop for nothing. He sent it out, too, at the tail of Tom Tarrant's big van—to increase the surprise. We were swells then for a while; I heard no more of a buggy until after we'd been settled at Lahey's Creek for a couple of years.

I told you how I went into the carrying line, and took up a selection at Lahey's Creek—for a run for the horses and to grow a bit of feed—and shifted Mary and little Jim out there from Gulgong, with Mary's young scamp of a brother James to keep them company while I was on the road. The first year I did well enough carrying, but I never cared for it—it was too slow; and, besides, I was always anxious when I was away from home. The game was right enough for a single man—or a married one whose wife had got the nagging habit (as many bushwomen have—God help 'em), and who wanted peace and quietness sometimes. Besides, other small carriers started (seeing me getting on); Tom Tarrant, the coach-builder at Cudgegong, had another heavy spring-van built, and put it on the road, and he took a lot of the light stuff.

The second year I made a rise—out of "spuds", of all the things in the world. It was Mary's idea. Down at the lower end of our selection—Mary called it "the run"—was a shallow watercourse called Snake's Creek, dry most of the year, except for a muddy waterhole or two; and just above the junction, where it ran into

Lahey's Creek, was a low piece of good black-soil flat, on our side—about three acres. The flat was fairly clear when I came to the selection—save a few logs that had been washed up there in some big old-man flood, way back in blackfellows' times: and one day when I had a spell at home I got the horses and trace-chains and dragged the logs together—those that wouldn't split for fencing-timber—and burnt them off. I had a notion to get the flat ploughed and make a lucerne-paddock of it. There was a good waterhole, under a clump of she-oak in the bend, and Mary used to take her stools and tubs and boiler down there in the spring-cart in hot weather, and wash the clothes under the shade of the trees—it was cooler, and saved carrying water to the house. And one evening after she'd done the washing she said to me:

"Look here, Joe; the farmers out here never seem to get a new idea: they don't seem to me ever to try and find out beforehand what the market is going to be like—they just go on farming the same old way, and putting in the same old crops year after year. They sow wheat, and if it comes on anything like the thing, they reap and thresh it; if it doesn't they mow it for hay—and some of 'em don't have the brains to do that in time. Now I was looking at that bit of flat you cleared, and it struck me that it wouldn't be a half-bad idea to get a bag of seed potatoes, and have the land ploughed—old Corny George would do it cheap—and get them put in at once. Potatoes have been dear all round for the last couple of years."

I told her she was talking nonsense, that the ground was no good for potatoes, and the whole district was too dry. "Everybody I know has tried it, one time or another, and made nothing of it," I said.

"All the more reason why you should try it, Joe," said Mary. "Just try one crop. It might rain for weeks, and then you'll be sorry you didn't take my advice."

"But I tell you the ground is not potato-ground," I said.

"How do you know? You haven't sown any there yet."

"But I've turned up the surface and looked at it. It's not rich enough, and too dry, I tell you. You need swampy, boggy ground for potatoes. Do you think I don't know land when I see it?"

"But you haven't tried to grow potatoes there yet, Joe. How do you know——"

I didn't listen to any more. Mary was obstinate when she got an idea into her head. It was no use arguing with her. All the time I'd been talking she'd just knit her forehead and go on thinking straight ahead, on the track she'd started—just as if I wasn't there—and it used to make me mad. She'd keep driving at me till I took her advice or lost my temper—I did both at the same time, mostly.

I took my pipe and went out to smoke and cool down.

A couple of days after the potato breeze I started with the team down to Cudgegong for a load of fencing-wire I had to bring out; and after I'd kissed Mary good-bye, she said:

"Look here, Joe, if you bring out a bag of seed potatoes, James and I will slice them, and old Corny George down the creek would bring his plough up in the dray, and plough the ground for very little. We could put the potatoes in ourselves if the ground were only ploughed."

I thought she'd forgotten all about it. There was no time to argue—I'd be sure to lose my temper, and then I'd either have to waste an hour comforting Mary, or go off in a "huff", as the women call it, and be miserable for the trip. So I said I'd see about it. She gave me another hug and a kiss. "Don't forget, Joe," she said as I started. "Think it over on the road." I reckon she had the best of it that time.

About five miles along, just as I turned into the main road, I heard someone galloping after me, and I saw young James on his hack. I got a start, for I thought that something had gone wrong at home. I remember the first day I left Mary on the creek, for the first five or six miles I was half a dozen times on the point of turning back—only I thought she'd laugh at me.

"What is it, James?" I shouted, before he came up—but I saw he was grinning.

"Mary says to tell you not to forget to bring a hoe out with you."

"You clear off home!" I said, "or I'll lay the whip about your young hide; and don't come riding after me again as if the run was on fire."

"Well, you needn't get shirty with me!" he said. "*I* don't want to have anything to do with a hoe." And he rode off.

I *did* get thinking about those potatoes, though I hadn't meant to. I knew of an independent man in that district who'd made his money out of a crop of potatoes; but that was away back in the roaring fifties—fifty-four—when spuds went up to twenty-eight shillings a hundredweight (in Sydney), on account of the gold-rush. We might get good rain now, and, anyway, it wouldn't cost much to put the potatoes in. If they came on well, it would be a few pounds in my pocket; if the crop was a failure, I'd have a better show with Mary next time she was struck by an idea outside housekeeping, and have something to grumble about when I felt grumpy.

I got a couple of bags of potatoes—we could use those that were left over; and I got a small iron plough and harrow that Little the blacksmith had lying in his yard and let me have cheap—only about a pound more than I told Mary I gave for them. When I took advice I generally made the mistake of taking more than was offered, or adding notions of my own. It was vanity, I suppose. If the crop came on well I could claim the plough-and-harrow part of the idea, anyway. (It didn't strike me that if the crop failed Mary would have the plough and harrow against me, for old Corny would plough the ground for ten or fifteen shillings.) Anyway, I'd want a plough and harrow later on, and I might as well get it now; it would give James something to do.

I came out by the western road, by Guntawang, and up the creek home; and the first thing I saw was old Corny George ploughing the flat. And Mary was down on the bank superintending. She'd got James with the trace-chains and the spare horses, and had made him clear off every stick and bush where another furrow might be squeezed in. Old Corny looked pretty grumpy on it—he'd broken all his ploughshares but one, in the roots; and James didn't look much brighter. Mary had an old felt hat and a new pair of 'lastic-side boots of mine on, and the boots were covered with clay, for she'd been down hustling James to get a rotten old stump out of the way by the time old Corny came round with his next furrow.

"I thought I'd make the boots easy for you, Joe," said Mary.

"It's all right, Mary," I said, "I'm not going to growl." Those boots were a bone of contention between us; but she generally got them off before I got home.

Her face fell when she saw the plough and harrow in the wagon, but I said that would be all right—we'd want a plough anyway.

"I thought you wanted old Corny to plough the ground," she said.

"I never said so."

"But when I sent Jim after you about the hoe to put the spuds in, you didn't say you wouldn't bring it," she said.

I had a few days at home, and entered into the spirit of the thing. When Corny was done, James and I cross-ploughed the land, and got a stump or two, a big log, and some scrub out of the way at the upper end and added nearly an acre, and ploughed that. James was all right at most bushwork: he'd bullock so long as the novelty lasted; he liked ploughing or fencing, or any graft he could make a show at. He didn't care for grubbing out stumps, or splitting posts and rails. We sliced the potatoes of an evening—and there was trouble between Mary and James over cutting through the "eyes". There was no time for the hoe—and besides it wasn't a novelty to James—so I just ran furrows and they dropped the spuds in behind me, and I turned another furrow over them, and ran the harrow over the ground. I think I hilled those spuds, too, with furrows—or a crop of Indian corn I put in later on.

It rained heavens-hard for over a week: we had regular showers all through, and it was the finest crop of potatoes ever seen in the district. I believe at first Mary used to slip down at daybreak to see if the potatoes were up; and she'd write to me about them, on the road. I forget how many bags I got, but the few who had grown potatoes in the district sent theirs to Sydney, and spuds went up to twelve and fifteen shillings a hundredweight in that district. I made a few quid out of mine—and saved carriage, too, for I could take them out on the wagon. Then Mary began to hear (through James) of a buggy that someone had for sale cheap, or a dogcart that somebody else wanted to get rid of—and let me know about it, in an off-hand way.

II

JOE WILSON'S LUCK

THERE was good grass on the selection all the year. I'd picked up a small lot—about twenty head—of half-starved steers for next to nothing, and turned them on the run; they came on wonderfully, and my brother-in-law (Mary's sister's husband), who was running a butchery at Gulgong, gave me a good price for them. His carts ran out twenty or thirty miles, to little bits of goldrushes that were going on at th' Home Rule, Happy Valley, Guntawang, Tallawang, and Cooyal, and those places round there, and he was doing well.

Mary had heard of a light American wagonette, when the steers went—a tray-body arrangement, and she thought she'd do with that. "It would be better than the buggy, Joe," she said. "There'd be more room for the children, and, besides, I could take butter and eggs to Gulgong, or Cobborah, when we get a few more cows." Then James heard of a small flock of sheep that a selector—who was about starved off his selection out Talbragar way—wanted to get rid of. James reckoned he could get them for less than half a crown a head. We'd had a heavy shower of rain, that came over the ranges and didn't seem to go beyond our boundaries. Mary said, "It's a pity to see all that grass going to waste, Joe. Better get those sheep and try your luck with them. Leave some money with me, and I'll send James over for them. Never mind about the buggy—we'll get that when we're on our feet."

So James rode across to Talbragar and drove a hard bargain with that unfortunate selector, and brought the sheep home. There were about two hundred, wethers and ewes, and they were young and looked a good breed too, but so poor they could scarcely travel; they soon picked up, though. The drought was blazing all round and outback, and I think that my corner of the ridges was the only place where there was any grass to speak of. We had another shower or two, and the grass held out. Chaps began to talk of "Joe Wilson's luck".

I would have liked to shear those sheep; but I hadn't time to get a shed or anything ready—along towards Christmas there was a bit of a boom in the carrying line. Wethers in wool were going as high as thirteen to fifteen shillings at the Homebush yards at Sydney, so I arranged to truck the sheep down from the river by rail, with another small lot that was going, and I started James off with them. He took the west road, and down Guntawang way a big farmer who saw James with the sheep (and who was speculating, or adding to his stock, or took a fancy to the wool) offered James as much for them as he reckoned I'd get in Sydney, after paying the carriage and the agents and the auctioneer. James put the sheep in a paddock and rode back to me. He was all there where riding was concerned. I told him to let the sheep go. James made a Greener shot-gun, and got his saddle done up, out of that job.

I took up a couple more forty-acre blocks—one in James's name, to encourage him with the fencing. There was a good slice of land in an angle between the range and the creek, farther down, which everybody thought belonged to Wall, the squatter, but Mary got an idea, and went to the local land office, and found out that it was unoccupied Crown land, and so I took it up on pastoral lease, and got a few more sheep—I'd saved some of the best-looking ewes from the last lot.

One evening—I was going down next day for a load of fencing-wire for myself—Mary said:

"Joe! do you know that the Matthews have got a new double buggy?"

The Matthews were a big family of cockatoos, along up the main road, and I didn't think much of them. The sons were all "bad-eggs", though the old woman and girls were right enough.

"Well, what of that?" I said. "They're up to their neck in debt, and camping like blackfellows in a big bark humpy. They do well to go flashing round in a double buggy."

"But that isn't what I was going to say," said Mary. "They want to sell their old single buggy, James says. I'm sure you could get it for six or seven pounds; and you could have it done up."

"I wish James to the devil!" I said. "Can't he find anything better to do than ride around after cock-and-bull yarns about buggies?"

"Well," said Mary, "it was James who got the steers and the sheep."

Well, one word led to another, and we said things we didn't mean—but couldn't forget in a hurry. I remember I said something about Mary always dragging me back just when I was getting my head above water and struggling to make a home for her and the children; and that hurt her, and she spoke of the "homes" she'd had since she was married. And that cut me deep.

It was about the worst quarrel we had. When she began to cry I got my hat and went out and walked up and down by the creek. I hated anything that looked like injustice—I was so sensitive about it that it made me unjust sometimes. I tried to think I was right, but I couldn't—it wouldn't have made me feel any better if I could have thought so. I got thinking of Mary's first year on the selection and the life she'd had since we were married.

When I went in she'd cried herself to sleep. I bent over and, "Mary," I whispered.

She seemed to wake up.

"Joe—Joe!" she said.

"What is it, Mary?" I said.

"I'm pretty sure that old Spot's calf isn't in the pen. Make James go at once!"

Old Spot's last calf was two years old now; so Mary was talking in her sleep, and dreaming she was back in her first year.

We both laughed when I told her about it afterwards; but I didn't feel like laughing just then.

Later on in the night she called out in her sleep:

"Joe—Joe! Put that buggy in the shed, or the sun will blister the varnish!"

I wish I could say that that was the last time I ever spoke unkindly to Mary.

Next morning I got up early and fried the bacon and made the tea, and took Mary's breakfast in to her—like I used to do, sometimes, when we were first married. She didn't say anything—just pulled my head down and kissed me.

When I was ready to start, Mary said:

"You'd better take the spring-cart in behind the dray, and get the tyres cut and set. They're ready to drop off, and James has been wedging them up till he's tired of it. The last time I was out with the children I had to knock one of them back with a stone: there'll be an accident yet."

So I lashed the shafts of the cart under the tail of the wagon, and mean and ridiculous enough the cart looked, going along that way. It suggested a man stooping along handcuffed, with his arms held out and down in front of him.

It was dull weather, and the scrubs looked extra dreary and endless—and I got thinking of old things. Everything was going all right with me, but that didn't keep me from brooding sometimes—trying to hatch out stones, like an old hen we had at home. I think, taking it all round, I used to be happier when I was mostly hard up—and more generous. When I had ten pounds I was more likely to listen to a chap who said, "Lend me a pound note, Joe," than when I had fifty; *then* I fought shy of careless chaps—and lost mates that I wanted afterwards—and got the name of being mean. When I got a good cheque I'd be as miserable as a miser over the first ten pounds I spent; but when I got down to the last I'd buy things for the house. And now that I was getting on, I hated to spend a pound on anything. But then, the farther I got away from poverty the greater the fear I had of it—and, besides, there was always before us all the thought of the terrible drought, with blazing runs as bare and dusty as the road, and dead stock rotting every yard, all along the barren creeks.

I had a long yarn with Mary's sister and her husband that night in Gulgong, and it brightened me up. I had a fancy that that sort of a brother-in-law made a better mate than a nearer one; Tom Tarrant had one, and he said it was sympathy. But while we were yarning I couldn't help thinking of Mary, out there in the hut on the creek, with no one to talk to but the children, or James, who was sulky at home, or Black Mary or Black Jimmy (our black boy's father and mother), who weren't over-sentimental. Or, maybe, a selector's wife (the nearest was five miles away) who could talk only of two or three things—"lambin'" and "shearin'" and "cookin' for the men", and what she said to her old man, and what he said to her—and her own ailments over and over again.

It's a wonder it didn't drive Mary mad!—I know I could never listen to that woman more than an hour. Mary's sister said:

"Now if Mary had a comfortable buggy, she could drive in with the children oftener. Then she wouldn't feel the loneliness so much."

I said "Good night" then and turned in. There was no getting away from that buggy. Whenever Mary's sister started hinting about a buggy, I reckoned it was a put-up job between them.

III

THE GHOST OF MARY'S SACRIFICE

When I got to Cudgegong I stopped at Galletly's coach-shop to leave the cart. The Galletlys were good fellows: there were two brothers—one was a saddler and harness-maker. Big brown-bearded men—the biggest men in the district, 'twas said.

Their old man had died lately and left them some money; they had men, and only worked in their shops when they felt inclined, or there was a special work to do; they were both first-class tradesmen. I went into the painter's shop to have a look at a double buggy that Galletly had built for a man who couldn't pay cash for it when it was finished—and Galletly wouldn't trust him.

There it stood, behind a calico screen that the coach-painters used to keep out the dust when they were varnishing. It was a first-class piece of work—pole, shafts, cushions, whip, lamps, and all complete. If you only wanted to drive one horse you could take out the pole and put in the shafts, and there you were. There was a tilt over the front seat; if you only wanted the buggy to carry two, you could fold down the back seat, and there you had a handsome, roomy, single buggy. It would go near fifty pounds.

While I was looking at it, Bill Galletly came in and slapped me on the back.

"Now, there's a chance for you, Joe!" he said. "I saw you rubbing your head round that buggy the last time you were in. You wouldn't get a better one in the colonies, and you won't see another like it in the district again in a hurry—for it doesn't pay to build 'em. Now you're a full-blown squatter, and it's time you took little Mary for a fly round in her own buggy now and then, instead of having her stuck out there in the scrub, or jolting through the dust in a cart like some old Mother Flourbag."

He called her "little Mary" because the Galletly family had known her when she was a girl.

I rubbed my head and looked at the buggy again. It was a great temptation.

"Look here, Joe," said Bill Galletly in a quieter tone. "I'll tell you what I'll do. I'll let *you* have the buggy. You can take it out and send along a bit of a cheque when you feel you can manage it, and the rest later on—a year will do, or even two years. You've had a hard pull, and I'm not likely to be hard up for money in a hurry."

They were good fellows the Galletlys, but they knew their men. I happened to know that Bill Galletly wouldn't let the man he built the buggy for take it out of the shop without cash down, though he was a big-bug round there. But that didn't make it easier for me.

Just then Robert Galletly came into the shop. He was rather quieter than his brother, but the two were very much alike.

"Look here, Bob," said Bill; "here's a chance for you to get rid of your harness. Joe Wilson's going to take that buggy off my hands."

Bob Galletly put his foot up on a saw-stool, took one hand out of his pocket, rested his elbow on his knee and his chin on the palm of his hand, and bunched up his big beard with his fingers, as he always did when he was thinking. Presently he took his foot down, put his hand back in his pocket, and said to me, "Well, Joe, I've got a double set of harness made for the man who ordered that damned buggy, and if you like I'll let you have it. I suppose when Bill there has squeezed all he can out of you I'll stand a show of getting something. He's a regular Shylock, he is."

I pushed my hat forward and rubbed the back of my head and stared at the buggy.

"Come across to the Royal, Joe," said Bob.

But I knew that a beer would settle the business, so I said I'd get the wool up to the station first and think it over, and have a drink when I came back.

I thought it over on the way to the station, but it didn't seem good enough. I wanted to get some more sheep, and there was the new run to be fenced in, and the instalments on the selections. I wanted lots of things that I couldn't well do without. Then, again, the farther I got away from debt and hardupedness the greater the horror I had of it. I had two horses that would do; but I'd have to get another later on, and altogether the buggy would run me nearer a hundred than fifty pounds. Supposing a dry season threw me back with that buggy on my hands. Besides, I wanted a spell. If I got the buggy it would only mean an extra turn of hard graft for me. No, I'd take Mary for a trip to Sydney, and she'd have to be satisfied with that.

I'd got it settled, and was just turning in through the big white gates to the goods-shed when young Black, the squatter, dashed past to the station in his big new wagonette, with his wife and a driver and a lot of portmanteaux and rugs and things. They were going to do the grand in Sydney over Christmas. Now it was young Black who was so shook after Mary when she was in service with the Blacks before the old man died, and if I hadn't come along—and if girls never cared for vagabonds—Mary would have been mistress of Haviland homestead, with servants to wait on her; and she was far better fitted for it than the one that was there. She would have been going to Sydney every holiday and putting up at the old Royal, with every comfort that a woman could ask for, and seeing a play every night. And I'd have been knocking around amongst the big stations outback, or maybe drinking myself to death at the shanties.

The Blacks didn't see me as I went by, ragged and dusty, and with an old, nearly black, cabbage-tree hat drawn over my eyes. I didn't care a damn for them, or anyone else, at most times, but I had moods when I felt things.

One of Black's big wool-teams was just coming away from the shed, and the driver, a big, dark, rough fellow, with some foreign blood in him, didn't seem inclined to wheel his team an inch out of the middle of the road. I stopped my horse and waited. He looked at me and I looked at him—hard. Then he wheeled off, scowling, and swearing at his horses. I'd given him a hiding, six or seven years before, and he hadn't forgotten it. And I felt then as if I wouldn't mind trying to give someone a hiding.

The goods-clerk must have thought that Joe Wilson was pretty grumpy that day. I was thinking of Mary, out there in the lonely hut on a barren creek in the bush—for it was little better—with no one to speak to except a haggard, worn-out bushwoman or two, that came to see her on Sunday. I thought of the hardships she went through in the first year—that I haven't told you about yet; of the time she was ill, and I away, and no one to understand; of the time she was alone with James and Jim sick; and of the loneliness she fought through out there. I thought of Mary, outside in the blazing heat, with an old print dress and a felt hat, and a pair of 'lastic-siders of mine, doing the work of a station manager as well as that of a housewife and mother. And her cheeks were getting thin, and the colour was going: I thought of the gaunt, brick-brown saw-file voiced, hopeless and spiritless bushwomen I knew—and some of them not much older than Mary.

When I went back into the town I had a drink with Bill Galletly at the Royal, and that settled the buggy; then Bob shouted, and I took the harness. Then I shouted, to wet the bargain. When I was going, Bob said, "Send in that young scamp of a brother of Mary's with the horses: if the collars don't fit I'll fix up a pair of makeshift, and alter the others." I thought they both gripped my hand harder than usual, but that might have been the beer.

IV

THE BUGGY COMES HOME

I WHIPPED THE CAT a bit, the first twenty miles or so, but then, I thought, what did it matter? What was the use of grinding to save money until we were too old to enjoy it. If we had to go down in the world again, we might as well fall out of a buggy as out of a dray—there'd be some talk about it, anyway, and perhaps a little sympathy. When Mary had the buggy she wouldn't be tied down so much to that wretched hole in the bush; and the Sydney trips needn't be off, either. I could drive down to Wallerawang on the main line, where Mary had some people, and leave her buggy and horses there, and take the train to Sydney, or go right on, by the old coach road, over the Blue Mountains: it would be a grand drive. I thought best to tell Mary's sister at Gulgong about the buggy; I told her to keep it dark from Mary till the buggy came home. She entered into the spirit of the thing, and said she'd give the world to be able to go out with the buggy, if only to see Mary open her eyes when she saw it; but she couldn't go, on account of a new baby she had. I was rather glad she couldn't, for it would spoil the surprise a little, I thought. I wanted that all to myself.

I got home about sunset next day, and, after tea, when I'd finished telling Mary all the news, and a few lies as to why I didn't bring the cart back, and one or two other things, I sat with James, out on a log of the woodheap, where we generally had our smokes and interviews, and told him all about the buggy. He whistled, then he said:

"But what do you want to make it such a bushranging business for? Why can't you tell Mary now? It will cheer her up. She's been pretty miserable since you've been away this trip."

"I want it to be a surprise," I said.

"Well, I've got nothing to say against a surprise, out in a hole like this; but it 'ud take a lot to surprise me. What am I to say to Mary about taking the two horses in? I'll only want one to bring the cart out, and she's sure to ask."

"Tell her you're going to get yours shod."

"But he had a set of slippers only the other day. She knows as much about horses as we do. I don't mind telling a lie so long as a chap has only got to tell a straight lie and be done with it. But Mary asks so many questions."

"Well, drive the other horse up the creek early, and pick him up as you go."

"Yes. And she'll want to know what I want with two bridles. But I'll fix her—*you* needn't worry."

"And, James," I said, "get a chamois leather and sponge—we'll want 'em anyway—and you might give the buggy a wash down in the creek, coming home. It's sure to be covered with dust."

"Oh!—orlright."

"And if you can, time yourself to get here in the cool of the evening, or just about sunset."

"What for?"

I'd thought it would be better to have the buggy there in the cool of the evening, when Mary would have time to get excited and get over it—better than in the blazing hot morning, when the sun rose as hot as at noon, and we'd have the long broiling day before us.

"What do you want me to come at sunset for?" asked James. "Do you want me to camp out in the scrub and turn up like a blooming sundowner?"

"Oh well," I said, "get here at midnight if you like."

We didn't say anything for a while—just sat and puffed at our pipes. Then I said:

"Well, what are you thinking about?"

"I'm thinking it's time you got a new hat, the sun seems to get in through your old one too much," and he got out of my reach and went to see about penning the calves. Before we turned in he said:

"Well, what am I to get out of the job, Joe?"

He had his eye on a double-barrel gun that Franca the gunsmith in Cudgegong had—one barrel shot, and the other rifle; so I said:

"How much does Franca want for that gun?"

"Five-ten; but I think he'd take my single barrel off it. Anyway, I can squeeze a couple of quid out of Phil Lambert for the single barrel." (Phil was his bosom chum.)

"All right," I said. "Make the best bargain you can."

He got his own breakfast and made an early start next morning, to get clear of any instructions or messages that Mary might have forgotten to give him overnight. He took his gun with him.

I'd always thought that a man was a fool who couldn't keep a secret from his wife—that there was something womanish about him. I found out. Those three days waiting for the buggy were about the longest I ever spent in my life. It made me scotty with everyone and everything; and poor Mary had to suffer it. I put in the time patching up the harness and mending the stockyard and roof, and, the third morning, I rode up the ridges to look for trees for fencing-timber. I remember I hurried home that afternoon because I thought the buggy might get there before me.

At tea-time I got Mary on to the buggy business.

"What's the good of a single buggy to you, Mary?" I asked. "There's only room for two, and what are you going to do with the children when we go out together?"

"We can put them on the floor at our feet, like other people do. I can always fold up a blanket or possum rug for them to sit on."

But she didn't take half so much interest in buggy talk as she would have taken at any other time, when I didn't want her to. Women are aggravating that way. But the poor girl was tired and not very well, and both the children were cross. She did look knocked up.

"We'll give the buggy a rest, Joe," she said. (I thought I heard it coming then.) "It seems as far off as ever. I don't know why you want to harp on it today. Now, don't look so cross, Joe—I didn't mean to hurt you. We'll wait until we can get a double buggy, since you're so set on it. There'll be plenty of time when we're better off."

After tea, when the youngsters were in bed, and she'd washed up, we sat on the edge of the veranda floor, Mary sewing, and I smoking and watching the track up the creek.

"Why don't you talk, Joe?" asked Mary. "You scarcely ever speak to me now; it's like drawing blood out of a stone to get a word from you. What makes you so cross, Joe?"

"Well, I've got nothing to say."

"But you should find something. Think of me—it's very miserable for me. Have you anything on your mind? Is there any new trouble? Better tell me, no matter what it is, and not go worrying and brooding and making both our lives miserable. If you never tell me anything, how can you expect me to understand?"

I said there was nothing the matter.

"But there must be, to make you so unbearable. Have you been drinking, Joe—or gambling?"

I asked her what she'd accuse me of next.

"And another thing I want to speak to you about," she went on. "Now, don't knit up your forehead like that, Joe, and get impatient——"

"Well, what is it?"

"I wish you wouldn't swear in the hearing of the children. Now, little Jim today, he was trying to fix his little go-cart, and it wouldn't run right, and—and——"

"Well, what did he say?"

"He—he" (she seemed a little hysterical, trying not to laugh)—"he said, 'Damn it!' "

I had to laugh. Mary tried to keep serious, but it was no use.

"Never mind, old woman," I said, putting an arm round her, for her mouth was trembling, and she was crying more than laughing. "It won't be always like this. Just wait till we're a bit better off."

Just then a black boy we had (I must tell you about him some other time) came sidling along by the wall, as if he were afraid somebody was going to hit him—poor little devil! I never did.

"What is it, Harry?" said Mary.

"Buggy comin', I bin thinkit."

"Where?"

He pointed up the creek.

"Sure it's a buggy?"

"Yes, missus."

"How many horses?"

"One—two."

We knew that he could hear and see things long before we could. Mary went and perched on the woodheap, and shaded her eyes—though the sun had gone—and peered through between the eternal grey trunks of the stunted trees on the flat across the creek. Presently she jumped down and came running in.

"There's someone coming in a buggy, Joe!" she cried, excitedly. "And both my white table-cloths are rough dry. Hurry! put two flat-irons down to the fire, quick, and put on some more wood. It's lucky I kept those new sheets packed away. Get up out of that, Joe! What are you sitting grinning like that for? Go and get on another shirt. Hurry . . . Why, it's only James—by himself."

She stared at me, and I sat there, grinning like a fool.

"Joe!" she said. "Whose buggy is that?"

"Well, I suppose it's yours," I said.

She caught her breath, and stared at the buggy, and then at me again. James drove down out of sight into the crossing, and came up close to the house.

"Oh, Joe! what have you done?" cried Mary. "Why, it's a new double buggy." Then she rushed at me and hugged my head. "Why didn't you tell me, Joe? You poor old boy!—and I've been nagging at you all day!" And she hugged me again.

James got down and started taking the horses out—as if it was an everyday occurrence. I saw the double-barrel gun sticking out from under the seat. He'd stopped to wash the buggy, and I suppose that's what made him grumpy. Mary stood on the veranda, with her eyes twice as big as usual, and breathing hard—taking the buggy in.

James skimmed the harness off, and the horses shook themselves and went down to the dam for a drink. "You'd better look under the seats," growled James, as he took his gun out with great care.

Mary dived for the buggy. There was a dozen of lemonade and ginger-beer in a candle-box from Galletly—James said that Galletly's men had a gallon of beer, and they cheered him, James (I suppose he meant they cheered the buggy), as he drove off; there was a "little bit of a ham" from Pat Murphy, the storekeeper at Home Rule, that he'd "cured himself"—it was the biggest I ever saw; there were three loaves of baker's bread, a cake, and a dozen yards of something "to make up for the children", from Aunt Gertrude at Gulgong; there was a fresh-water cod, that long Dave Regan had caught the night before in the Macquarie River, and sent out packed in salt in a box; there was a holland suit for the black boy, with red braid to trim it; and there was a jar of preserved ginger, and some lollies, "for the lil' boy", and a rum-looking Chinese doll and a rattle, "for lil' girl", from Sun Tong Lee, our storekeeper at Gulgong—James was chummy with Sun Tong Lee, and got his powder and shot and caps there on tick when he was short of money. And James said that the people would have loaded the buggy with "rubbish" if he'd waited. They all seemed glad to see Joe Wilson getting on—and these things did me good.

We got the things inside, and I don't think either of us knew what we were saying or doing for the next half-hour. Then James put his head in and said, in a very injured tone:

"What about my tea? I ain't had anything to speak of since I left Cudgegong. I want some grub."

Then Mary pulled herself together.

"You'll have your tea directly," she said. "Pick up that harness at once, and hang it on the pegs in the skillion; and you, Joe, back that buggy under the end of the veranda, the dew will be on it presently—and we'll put wet bags up in front of it tomorrow, to keep the sun off. And James will have to go back to Cudgegong for the cart—we can't have that buggy to knock about in."

"All right," said James—"anything! Only get me some grub."

Mary fried the fish, in case it wouldn't keep till the morning, and rubbed over the table-cloths, now the irons were hot—James growling all the time—and got out some crockery she had packed away that had belonged to her mother, and set the table in a style that made James uncomfortable.

"I want some grub—not a blooming banquet!" he said. And he growled a lot because Mary wanted him to eat his fish without a knife, "and that sort of tommy-rot". When he'd finished he took his gun, and the black boy, and the dogs, and went out possum-shooting.

When we were alone Mary climbed into the buggy to try the seat, and made me get up alongside her. We hadn't had such a comfortable seat for years; but we soon got down, in case anyone came by, for we began to feel like a pair of fools up there.

Then we sat, side by side, on the edge of the veranda, and talked more than we'd done for years—and there was a good deal of "Do you remember?" in it—and I think we got to understand each other better that night.

And at last Mary said, "Do you know, Joe, why, I feel tonight just —just like I did the day we were married."

And somehow I had that strange, shy sort of feeling too.